MASS

Also by the same author:

**CONVERGENCE
FRAGMENTS**

Jack Fuller

WILLIAM MORROW AND COMPANY, INC.
NEW YORK

Library of Congress Catalog Card Number: 85-61488

ISBN: 0-688-04685-1

Printed in the United States of America

First U.S. Edition

1 2 3 4 5 6 7 8 9 10

For Timothy and Katherine

Note

The epigraphs in this novel follow the sequence of Benjamin Britten's "War Requiem." They are taken from the Latin Requiem Mass and from the poetry of Wilfred Owen.

ONE

Requiem aeternam dona eis, Domine . . .
Kyrie eleison, Christe eleison.

Rest eternal grant unto them, O Lord .
Lord have mercy. Christ have mercy.

The computer screens flashed on and off. Then they froze. Men and women looked nervously about. The green glow from the terminals shone on their faces, as if a wave of sinking nausea had suddenly swept the room. No one spoke. The event was beyond human control now as looming master units, line upon line, searched their memory and logic for any way out.

Then all the screens began to pulse again, and a stir swept through the silence.

Majewski bent over his keyboard, tapping out short commands to retrieve the systems before the critical point was passed.

"Here we go," he whispered as he tried the last, desperate maneuver.

For an instant the thing seemed to respond. His hands were tense on the keys as he searched for the coding that would call everything back from the edge. But nothing could stop it now. The event was absolute. The characters on the screen flickered, then vanished. In their place the words "FATAL TRAP" flashed on and off, and the screen lit up with a chaos of figures and numbers swirling in absurd, unthinkable patterns.

"The balloon is up," he said, slumping back in his chair.

"They're saying ten minutes," said Ruffalino.

"This never happened in the old days, Tony," said Majewski. "We knew what we were dealing with then."

"Take it easy, Stan."

"You know me," said Majewski, and he hit the balky terminal with his open palm, as if he could jolt it back to life like a temperamental old radio. "The soul of patience."

When Ruffalino went back to the city desk, Majewski picked up the sports section. He folded and unfolded it, putting in creases as sharp as a tailor's. Sometimes when the *Herald*'s computer crashed, just the feel of newsprint gave him some comfort, reminding him that no matter how fancy the publisher got with electronics, the end product was still ink on paper, same as always. But today it was no use. He tossed the newspaper aside and wiped his black-smudged hands on a sheet of bond.

"Boy!" he hollered.

Across the room a kewpie doll's head turned his way.

"Boy, bring me the mail."

The doll had a short conversation with her superior, a callow fellow all in black. He held up his arm, fingers stretched in Majewski's direction, and firmly cast her out. The doll slid off the edge of the desk and grudgingly made her way past the switch-board to the corner Majewski called his office. She paused at the bank of cubbyholes, pulled out a stack of envelopes, and slowly leafed through them.

"I didn't ask you to read them for me," Majewski grumbled.

He swung his feet up and crossed them on a stack of papers on the corner of his gray metal desk, pushing the phone to within reach with the rounded heel of his shoe just in case one of the bastards deigned to return his call. The doll deliberately idled at the water fountain, turning her denimed rear to him as she bent for a drink. The fabric stretched. The reinforced stitches pulled. Then she stood up and stuck her hand in her back pocket, pink kewpie flesh against the blue.

"Get a move on, boy," Majewski shouted, hands behind his head. "I'm a very busy man."

The screen of his terminal, alive with winking garble, flashed and went blank. Then some words poked up from the bottom like a shy, peeking innocent.

"We're on line again," somebody said.

"Hear that, boy?" said Majewski. "Back in business."

"You shouldn't call us boys, Mr. Majors," said the girl, her porcelain face all aflush. "We're news clerks. That's what we're called."

Majewski held out his hand and the girl slapped the letters into it.

"The blacks resent it," she said. "They wouldn't tell you, but they really do."

Majewski eased his feet off the desk, taking some of the papers along with them.

10

"The word," he said, "is indiscriminate. They're boys. You're a boy. It's not a matter of gender or race or age. I was a boy myself once. Also a gofer. I used to come when they called copy, but that hardly seems the word anymore, what with these machines." He pulled his finger across the keyboard, and a row of symbols—!@#$%¼&*—lighted up green on the screen, an electronic obscenity. "I would come when they yelled 'son' or 'kid' or 'hey you.' I would come when they were too drunk to let out anything more articulate than a belch. One reporter used to summon me with a duck call. It honked like a rutting fowl. Don't you like your work?"

She stared at him with an expression that seemed harder than her years would justify, even if every one of them had been spent in a newspaper office. Then her face softened.

"You're too much, Mr. Majors," she said. "Like, where have you been?"

"Me?" he said, allowing himself the slightest of smiles. "I've been right here. I haven't moved an inch."

She shook her head and moved off toward the city desk.

"Boy!" Majewski shouted. She stopped but did not turn. "I'll take a black with sugar when you get a chance."

She came back, patience stretched tight as the denim, and took the dollar bill he dangled.

"A large one," he said.

"Brother," she replied.

And as he watched the doll bounce away from him, he *was* a brother, a big brother looking out for all the young Polish girls, the sisters he never had. Quite a few of them had come through the office over the years, each a little more Americanized than the one before. How quickly they lost the old-country looks, except for the full cheeks and ample shoulders, the stoutish arms that no longer had to lift. Most of them **did** not even wear medals or scapulars around their pale necks for providence anymore. They were on their own. And so Majewski took it upon himself to look out for their interests, to kid them the way he had been kidded, to slow them down just a little in their dumb rush to throw off everything that made them special. They all struggled so hard to break away. He knew better: The real challenge was to hold on.

He riffled quickly through the envelopes, pitching out the press releases and dunning letters from all the fringe groups that bought his false name from magazine subscription lists. Only one piece of mail was addressed to Stanislaw Majewski, and that one was from his most dutiful crank.

How John Devine had gotten his real name, Majewski did not know. Even at the paper, where his given name appeared correctly on the payroll, everyone called him by his taken name, Stan Majors. And outside the *Herald*, well, you could sign yourself J. P. Sartre or Herman Melville and not get a single call.

He had become Majors in the first place because his editor did not want to crowd the narrow column with too many letters. More important, he wanted his paper to be true-blue American, one hundred percent, especially since the city it served was still clotted with so many Old World loyalties and grudges. Wave after wave of immigrants had come up the coast to New Haven—Irish, Italians, even a few daring Poles—looking for work and a neighborhood they could claim. And once they had established themselves, they became as jealous as nations. The Irish were lace-and-crystal phonies to the Italians, the Italians lubricious idol-worshippers to the Irish. The Poles were primitive to everybody, especially once they began to succeed. Each group had its own churches and schools, kept in unholy alliance by the supreme authority of the diocese. Each had its restaurants, tailors, and groceries, its youth gangs to keep the borders secure. And until the Italians got control of everything that the law did not force them to cede to the blacks and Hispanics, each had its own little fiefdom in City Hall.

Majewski had never objected to the *Herald* hiding his nationality. He believed that the least significant thing about the most trivial item he had ever read or written was the by-line at the top. But there were some in his family who did not see it that way. First the fancy degree from the university, they said, and the next thing you know he's throwing away his own good name. But that was all right. His family was just not happy unless it had some internecine complaint in play, like a gathering of rival barons. And as insistent as it was upon its national heritage and all the diluted rituals, nobody was quicker than this proud Polish clan, upon spotting a new arrival—Eastern European consonants still thickening his tongue and thin white socks peeking out above his cardboard Sunday shoes—to spit out the derisive letters of superiority: DP.

Displaced person. Of all the family, the words had fit Majewski and his mother best. But nobody had ever used the epithet against them, at least within his hearing. The war, it seemed, had displaced everything, even the sovereign instinct to exclude.

The phone at Majewski's heel began to ring. He dropped the mail on the clutter and picked up the receiver.

"Yeah," he said.

"There was a note here that you called," said the voice on the other end. It was Henry Moll from the FBI.

"I've got a problem with this Tornelli thing, Hank," Majewski said.

"I'll let you in on something, very confidentially," said Moll, and Majewski was ready with his pencil. "It isn't nearly as big a problem as the late Mr. Tornelli's got."

They had found the body in the trunk of a car somebody had been thoughtful enough to run into the deep water of Long Island Sound. Even duly pickled, the corpse was not a pleasant sight. Multiple shotgun wounds. Cause of death: obvious. Tornelli had been talking to somebody.

"I understand the guy'd been spilling his guts to your buddies in New York," said Majewski.

"Write what you know," said Moll. "What are they gonna do, sue you?"

"Let 'em," said Majewski. "Hell, I'd love to have a chance to take Monkey Latto's deposition. Get the bastard under oath."

"Take it from me," said Moll. "It's never quite the thrill you think it's gonna be."

"I just want to be right, that's all."

"You can't go too wrong doubting the loyalty of Angelo Tornelli," said Moll.

That was all the confirmation Majewski needed. He scribbled the words in his notebook, then put down the pencil and took hold of the phone with his right hand, massaging it like a muscle.

"I haven't seen you around, Hank," he said.

"You haven't been to the right places, I guess."

"How's your son?"

This was one thing they had in common. There were times when they could talk about it for hours, weary old veterans, and if they were alone and had enough beer, they sometimes could even laugh. But this time Moll backed away.

"Haven't heard a thing," he said. "How about your boy?"

"He found a place of his own. I don't even like to think about what he's doing there."

"He'll straighten out," said Moll. "He's basically a good kid. A little strung-out. Not quite as hard a case as he thinks he is. But he'll be all right."

"It's so damned easy to lose them."

"Let's get together again soon, huh?" said Moll.

Majewski rang off and then tugged his tie down another half inch to allow himself more breath. Somewhere along the line something had gone terribly wrong with the young. It was as if a deep ravine separated you from them, and all you could do was to shout across it, pleading with them to watch their step as they staggered along the edge. He did not know what it was that kept them apart. But they were different, so completely different, and when you begged them to be careful, they looked at you as if you were the one who was about to fall.

His telephone rang again, and he snatched the receiver to his ear.

"Yeah," he said.

"Stan, look, I got you at a bad time."

"I'm not on edition," Majewski said. "Not for hours. What do you need, Danny?"

"Hey, do I always have to have an angle when I call an old pal on the phone?"

It was a funny question. Since they'd been kids, Danny Cousins had always needed something.

"What's up, Danny?"

"I was just thinking that you must be getting tired of your own cooking by now. Why don't you come over and let Susan whip you up something. She's into Mideast gourmet, taking a class in it. You like lamb?"

"I can take it or leave it," Majewski said. He knew all about Susan Cousins, how Danny treated her. It was not something he liked to get close to.

"Whatever," said Cousins. "Hey, as long as I've got you on the phone, I might as well give you a tip. The Peace Brigade is going to demonstrate outside the federal courthouse next Thursday. Reverend Dugan is coming back to speak. We got music lined up. Guerrilla theater. The works. We're expecting maybe five thousand in the square."

"You'll be lucky if you get two dozen," said Majewski. "The kids don't give a damn anymore. They think the war is over."

The fact was, Danny Cousins had gotten himself in a crack. Up until now, he had always been able to ride with the times. During the dull days of Eisenhower, he was into corporate communications, representing everyone from the small-arms manufacturers to the local Legion post. Then came the Great Society, and Danny found a way to take a skim of the funds pouring into community development. When the Vietnam War went sour, he discovered a new opportunity. While others might have seen a ragtag rabble marching in the streets, not enough change in their pockets to get a decent haircut, Danny saw that there was money behind it. Guilt money, the best kind. Money somebody wanted to get rid of.

He became an impresario of the teach-in. He brokered all the guitar-strumming talent for the rallies. Balding, he let the hair ringing his skull grow long and wispy. His beard was shot through with gray, and he set it off with brightly colored beads around his neck like a man who thinks the key to perpetual youth is folly.

But then the draft ended. The movement split. The guilt money went to election campaigns again, and the factions started to toy with violence. Danny was in a jam.

"Maybe you're going to have to find a new hustle," said Majewski. "Clean air. Clean water. Stop nuclear power. That's where the action is now."

"Sand between the toes?" said Cousins. "Rocky Mountain high? I mean, come on. They're acting like a bunch of kids."

"I thought you were big on youth."

"My guys are realists, Stan. They know they have a problem."

"Who exactly are your guys, Danny?"

"I represent a variety of interests."

"Bomb throwers."

"Come on, Stan. You know me."

"Be careful, Danny. That's all I'm saying. I think I know your guys. And they aren't like you. They really believe in this shit."

"They're committed," said Cousins.

"They're crazy people."

"No crazier than anybody else," said Cousins. "I mean, look at the ink you're giving to this shitty little speech tonight. You know who I mean. What's his name? The Russian."

"He's for peace, too," said Majewski.

15

"Just have somebody at the demonstration at the courthouse, and I personally guarantee it'll be worth your while."

"It's a story," said Majewski. "But not as big a story as you want it to be."

"Every little contribution is gratefully accepted."

"It isn't a favor, Danny. It's news."

Majewski passed the information on to Ruffalino, then he asked the switchboard to take his calls for a while. He picked up the rest of his mail, flipped half of it unopened into the trash and slitted the top of each remaining envelope in turn, leaving the old man Devine's for last. They were mostly junk, wasted words purchased from men like Cousins who were paid handsomely to get somebody's name in the paper when there wasn't much to say about him and to keep it out when there was. Finally, he opened Devine's letter. He did it carefully so as not to damage the onionskin inside. As always, the message was typed letter-perfect. Whoever he was, Devine was not your common crank who underlines in three colors for emphasis or puts every third word in CAPS like some eighteenth-century scribe. Even though Devine's ideas rambled all over the place, his sentences always parsed. The man, of course, was nuts, but at least he was nuts in an engaging way.

Dear Stash,

Anybody with half a brain would have given up trying to straighten out the distinguished writers and editors of your fishwrapper long ago. It is discouraging work, let me tell you. The *Herald* is strong proof against the idea that literacy is its own reward. You don't even know you have a problem, which is the first symptom, my friend.

But nobody ever accused me of having half a brain. So I'm back to pick a nit with you, a nit as big as a fist. Are you still listening, or have you lost the train of thought already? Sometimes I think you aren't even bright enough to get your own name right. How do you plead, Stash? Psst, be careful. We know who you are.

What I'm getting at is this story about the impending visit of one Viktor Shevtsov, who you say is coming to town to remind all the great unweaned multitudes at the university that there are people in this world even more repressive than the Dean of

Students. Do you really think it was enough to identify this man as a Soviet dissident and the winner of the Prize? I mean, this is the very same fella who made the Rooskies the Bomb.

To say that he is an exiled Russian dove is like announcing that the pale horse and pale rider have just cantered into town and then putting the apocalyptic old nag into the morning scratch sheet. Let me give you the line on that, the straight book. When the Bomb comes into it, Stash, you've got yourself a case of Pascal's Wager. Maybe the odds are long, but if you make the wrong bet, you burn.

Stash, remember your name. Try to get it right for once. A good Polack ought to know from bad experience that the only good Rooskie is a dead Rooskie. And that is the moderate Polish view . . .

Majewski put the letter aside when the kewpie finally brought him his coffee. The change from his dollar was painfully hot as he picked the coins from the hollows of the white plastic lid. Before he could squeak off the cover and have his first sip, he heard Ruffalino calling from across the room.

"Stan! Front and center."

Majewski stuffed the letter back into its envelope and put it away in the drawer. He liked to have time to savor all the Devine obsessions: Russia ("she captures nations as some men capture doves, for the sheer sport of caging something beautiful and free"), the ugly state of race relations ("behind every jive-ass, rabble-rousing black telling his brothers that Charlie would kill them all if he had a chance, there's a pale multitude that could not agree more"), and sweet Emily Dickinson, about whom Devine rhapsodized like a lover ("within her ivory, inviolate loins there stretched an unbroken membrane that vibrated to all the sad, whispered voices of loneliness and doom"). Strange, harmless old man.

"Stan!" Ruffalino shouted. "Get over here!"

But Majewski did not hurry. After all the years, he could tell when Ruffalino's shout was urgent and when it was just a case of nerves. He sipped the steamy coffee a half inch down from the rim so he could carry it without spilling. Then he rooted around in his drawer for a fresh notebook.

"You're handling Shitso tonight, right?" said Ruffalino. He sat surrounded by cluttered wire baskets, stacks of clippings pasted on half-sheets, banks of phones, police scanners, and bottles of aspirin, Maalox, and other balms.

"The Shevtsov speech? Why? You have something better?"

"Shitso's not up until when?"

"Seven o'clock."

"What else is on the itinerary?"

"In and out," said Majewski. "No parties. No receptions."

"No free whiskey. No admiring coeds who want to work in the mee-dee-ah," said the deskman, drawing out the hated word.

"They expect a pretty good crowd," said Majewski.

"Demonstrations?" Ruffalino asked. The question had become a matter of habit over the long, troubled years.

"Only the captive nations crew. Free Soviet Jewry. That sort of thing. Tony, Shevtsov is a man of peace."

Ruffalino grunted. It was a city editor's conditioned response to bullshit.

"I'm thinking maybe we should have a profile of this guy as a sidebar," he said, "just in case he says something. Anybody at the university know anything about him?"

"They know everything, Tony."

"Look," said Ruffalino, "get it written this afternoon. We can always cannibalize it for the main story if the speech is a bomb." He lifted a handful of stuff from his desk and let it drop. The papers fluttered down. The police scanners were silent. "I don't see anything else today. You?"

"I've got that Sunday piece working on the Tornelli hit. It'll hold a day."

"Good."

"Did you know that it was Shevtsov who built the Russians their first nuclear device?"

"Was it in your piece the other day?"

"Copydesk trimmed it out. But it's an angle. The physicists have known sin."

"Huh?"

"Somebody said that after Hiroshima," said Majewski. " 'The physicists have known sin.' "

"What the hell did people expect? A bunch of choirboys? Don't get in too deep," said Ruffalino, but he had already turned back to the scatter of clips and notes and quite obviously was thinking of something else.

The professor Majewski arranged to meet wasn't one of the *Herald*'s trained seals. His field did not lend itself to sweeping pronouncements on the great public issues of the day. He was not like the self-promoters on the law and economics faculties who sat by their phones, like schoolgirls before the prom, whenever the Supreme Court handed down a big opinion or the unemployment rate tightened its belt another notch.

He had his office in one of the residential colleges, and Majewski scuffed his way through the wet, matted leaves in the courtyard looking for the right entryway. When he found the door and opened it, loud rock music poured down the stairs from the student digs, the kind of dazed, doomed thing his son always played. The office was down a corridor on the first floor. He knocked.

"It is open," said a small voice. Majewski turned the wobbly knob and stepped inside.

A fire burning in the fireplace took all the dampness out of the air. The office smelled yellow with old books. The walls were lined with them, strange works in many languages, angled this way and that against one another like tired old immigrants leaning in doorways. The professor was sitting in an armchair facing the fire. All that showed were his legs resting on a hassock and a fragile hand clasped on a small, leatherbound volume.

"Do take off your coat." His tiny head peeked around the heavy wing of the chair. "I'm afraid I had dozed off just now."

Professor Alexander Steinman was known, in the small circle in which he was known at all, for his work on the literature of the Holocaust. It was remarkable to Majewski that a man so frail should have taken for his subject the extremities of power and suffering. He would not have survived a week in the camps himself, but his mind had been able to embrace the experience whole when others had fallen into silence. Majewski stripped off his trench coat and hung it on an old wooden tree. Steinman shifted slightly on the cushions and smiled.

"How is your mother?" he asked.

It surprised Majewski that the professor remembered her. On the phone arranging the meeting, neither of them had mentioned the occasion years before when they had first met. Steinman had been in a different office then, a cramped little cubbyhole in one of the towers. That had been before he began publishing his searing, uncompromising books. The results of the meeting with Majewski and his mother had probably been, from the professor's point of view, inconsequential. Majewski realized later that what they had to offer had been of no special value to Steinman. The history was so vast, and theirs was such a small part of it. His father's diary chronicled only the earliest stages. And though he had been quite prominent as a student of history at the time, Majewski's father had never fulfilled his early promise. His name did not endow this record with significance. He had died too soon.

"She's having a hard time of it right now," said Majewski. "Her mind is slipping."

"She is at home?"

"She needs medical attention around the clock. We found a good place. There was no other way."

"It is always hard for a son," said the professor. "And the mind, how could it fail finally to give way under a burden such as the one your mother has carried?"

"I think it is a physiological condition," said Majewski, because that always made it seem easier somehow.

"Memories have a physical component," said Steinman, "a weight. This is something one learns when the body becomes weak. The doctors tell me that I must conserve my strength. I must sit quietly before the fire and draw its heat like a lizard warming in the sun." He was smiling. "So you are going to write of my friend, Viktor."

"An interesting man," said Majewski.

"Every man who wins the Prize is interesting. That is certified, as it were, by the Committee. Viktor can actually be quite tedious. Whenever he happens upon an idea he can lay claim to as his own, he bangs away on it like a little boy with a drum."

"Maybe that was how he built the Bomb."

"To Viktor, all his ideas are the same. The important thing is that they are his. He had the insight into how the weapons technology could come together, and he vindicated it with the explosions. Then he had the idea that the weapons threatened the very existence of life on the planet, and he pushed it with the same determination."

"Without much success."

"Success?" said Steinman, shrugging. Then he brightened. "Viktor did not win the Prize for his physics, you know."

Majewski made a note and caught Steinman peeking at it.

"I hope you don't mind my putting some of this down on paper," he said.

"Please feel free," said Steinman. "I am just curious about what you think is important, the principle of selection."

"Whatever is out of the ordinary," said Majewski. "That's the usual definition of news."

"Is there anything less extraordinary than envy? What could be more predictable than for a man who has not won a prize to say an unkind word about a man who has?"

"You were not so unkind," said Majewski.

"Actually," said the professor, "I do not put much stock in prizes; I suppose I have known too many winners. And anyway, no committee, no matter how distinguished, can confer value on a man's work. That is for history."

"How will history judge Viktor Shevtsov?"

"It would take the apocalypse to disprove his dire warning," Steinman said, as sly as the very gnome of death. "And if he is wrong and men somehow persist, I do not think that under the circumstances they will be very harsh with him for raising the cry. He has positioned himself quite nicely, don't you think?"

Majewski wanted the quote whole, but he went right on with another question in order to hide the principle of selection.

"I'm curious how you got to know him."

"He had read some of my early works and, I take it, found them interesting." Steinman wore his pride tastefully, like the bright handkerchief in his breast pocket, bold in color but folded so that only the smallest corner showed. "When I was in Moscow doing some research, he learned about my visit and sent an emissary to bring me to him. Viktor was quite a figure in the scientific hierarchy then, and his superiors let him indulge himself in meetings with Westerners. At the time I knew his work only vaguely; physics was utterly obscure to me. But I was amused at the prospect of meeting the creator of an instrument of ubiquitous destruction."

"And was it amusing?"

"You must not be shocked at my way of speaking of these things," said Steinman. "When one has lived his life with the voices of the dead, he learns to appreciate their little jokes as well as to share their sorrow."

Majewski nodded. He enjoyed a good laugh, too.

"The first time we met," Steinman went on, "Shevtsov was living quite well. He had won prizes even then—the Stalin Prize, twice named Hero of Socialist Labor, member of the Academy of Sciences. They say that his dacha was as fine as the head of the KGB's.

"He had a driver pick me up in a new Volga. Viktor's office was quite impressive, with high, leaded windows that looked out over a park. He had an enormous leather-covered desk, and the only things on it were a brass lamp, a finely inlaid ink blotter, and a slide rule. He greeted me warmly, and we ate a lavish lunch doused in vodka.

"Later, of course, he sacrificed all of this. The last time I visited him in Moscow he was living in a two-room flat in a drab, gray apartment. We talked in the bedroom. The bed was stripped when visitors came, and some cushions were arranged to make it pass for a couch. He padded around in frayed carpet slippers. His wife served tea, enormous quantities of tea. There was no meal, no vodka. The disaffected do not, I suppose, want to addle their message with drink."

"And what was his message?"

"Shevtsov did not leave off his scientific inquiries with the detonation of the devices. He had seen into the heart of matter, the transmutation of mass. And it destroyed all his faith in continuity. Queer how well the theories of physics reflected the ideological orthodoxy of the state. For the Soviet biologists, of course, ideology had been a great impediment. The Marxists insisted that, despite all evidence, genetic inheritance was unstable. They claimed that it could be altered by the environment; this was the mechanism by which the state could nurture a new Soviet Man. Biological science foundered on this rock of received truth. But in physics, the faith in radical transformation made a perfect fit. Lead into gold."

"Did he talk to you about politics?"

"Once Shevtsov had worked out all the technological problems of weapons design, his mind turned to consequences. And he pursued them with extraordinary vigor. One might almost say remorse. He recognized very early how radiation sickness did its damage. As he carried the analysis forward, he discovered the whole variety of plagues that could descend upon us—darkness, blight, and ice. And from this it was a very short step to the moral point that has marked his latest work, the utter condemnation of the instruments he helped to create. . . . Would you mind putting another log on the fire? My assistant seems to have made himself scarce this afternoon."

Majewski hauled himself out of the deep chair and pulled the screen away from the hearth. The embers glowed hot near his hands as he lifted a large piece of wood onto the broken remnants in the grate.

"The gods punished the man who brought us fire," said Steinman. "Today it seems such a relatively small offense. Now the gods bring prizes."

"I imagine the Soviets were glad to be rid of him."

"I am sure they did not agree to his exile," said Steinman, "let alone drive him away. The circumstances of his flight must, I am afraid, remain somewhat obscure, for the protection of those still behind the Wall. But you have to remember that up until the very end he remained a member of the Academy of Sciences. Though he had been stripped of all connection with nuclear research for some years, he still knew many things the Soviets would have preferred to keep confidential. One hears that there is still a great deal of concern that others will be encouraged to try to follow him."

Steinman raised his hand to hide a yawn.

"What do you suppose he'll speak about tonight?" Majewski asked.

"I have not talked with him about it, but I assume he will make the usual plea for forgiveness."

"Forgiveness?"

"Mercy for his sins. Mercy that redeems the world through his witness. The forgiveness that survivors always seek." Steinman was approaching very close to the center of his own work now. The smile was gone. There was no humor in the voices he spoke for. "It's what drives all visionaries, isn't it? The hope of touching chords of transcendence. But we are poor instruments for them. We are only victims." The professor paused, removed his glasses, rubbed at the shadowed eyes. "Do remember me to your mother, won't you?"

Majewski lifted another log onto the fire before leaving. The flames licked up at his pale hands, and he dropped the wood into a burst of sparks. But the flesh was not burned. The bitter smell was only from the singed hair on his wrists.

"She remembers so little now," he said.

"That," Steinman said as Majewski reached the door, "is a solace."

The vending machines huddled in a corner off the pressroom along with a few wobbly little tables and some ink-stained plastic chairs. Majewski sometimes wondered how long a human body could survive on food from the machines, how long before the skin turned the pasty white of denatured bread, the veins froze up with crystals of artificial sweetener. Since his wife died he had been testing this limit of human endurance, so far with results no more conclusive than a chronic feeling of emptiness that was hard to blame on the food.

He leaned over to see what was available today behind the finger-smudged plastic doors: the usual thin sandwiches, candies, sweet sticky buns. He chose ham and processed American cheese on colorless bread. The little door balked, then yielded. The cellophane wrapper was icy in his fingers. He moved to the soda machine where he made his usual selection. The works heaved and grated before spitting out a can. It was a diet drink. He was always careful about sugar because there was diabetes in his family. They said that his father had suffered from it and that it had killed him—or, more precisely, that it had marked him out as unworthy to survive. The principle of selection in those days had been ruthlessly administered by men.

Majewski was ready to go back upstairs, but he was in no hurry. The Shevtsov profile had been resisting him for hours, and he did not look forward to renewing the struggle. The turns of this strange man's career did not sing under Majewski's fingers. He had gone through draft after draft, and there was nothing to show for it. In the old days he would at least have had piles of wasted paper as evidence of his work. But on the machines, the discarded sentences were dispatched at the touch of a key, ephemeral electronic pulses cast off into the void.

Every writer had days like this when the words just would not come. But he was confident that he could finish the profile on time. And it would be a solid piece of work. Nothing spectacular. No poetry. Just one sentence following another. The measure of a true professional was whether he could work despite the blockages, like a diva singing over laryngitis. And Majewski was in every way a pro.

He had won all the awards worth winning. There had been plenty of acclaim, and with it had come offers to move up to the big papers in New York or Chicago or LA. When he was younger, everybody had been after him, promising national reporting assignments, postings overseas. He had done a fair amount of free-lancing for the national magazines and had been a stringer for all the prestige outfits at one time or another. There had been talk of doing a book, syndicating a column. He had been hot, very hot, when he was younger.

Majewski trudged through the pressroom, nodding now and then to the pressmen in their proud, silly newsprint hats. He moved quickly but carefully among the silent, hunched machines, dodging obstacles, avoiding all contact because every surface was slick with ink. Up the metal backstairs, his footsteps pealed slowly, echoing in the well.

In the old days the city room would have been engulfed by now in a Bolero of rising noise. Typewriters hammering, copyboys hustling paper in intricate patterns of distribution, deskmen shouting headline orders over the din. There would have been boisterous laughter. Hands would have been slamming paper onto spikes, fingers jabbing insistently into chests. The copyboys would have been playing grab-ass and chasing one another like children. And it would have all come together in one great symphony of the news.

But now everything was subdued. Nobody flung handfuls of paper clips across the room to get attention. Nobody raised his voice. The computer keyboards ticked as softly as watches. Majewski moved quietly across the antistatic carpet to his banged-up metal desk in the corner.

At least it was the same old desk. They hadn't replaced that. And he had never even considered leaving it. He had always been very frank about his intentions. Still, the editors had felt they had to offer him management jobs, a place on the organization chart, a ticket to a spot on the masthead, hoping that he might be persuaded to aim for the top of a shorter ladder. He had turned them down, and some of the editors were noticeably relieved, because there wasn't all that much room on the ladder, and Majewski was so damned good. But he only wanted to write and to stay where he was. He aimed at what he had, to keep it. Nothing more.

His family had never done anything to hold him back. Rose would have gone wherever he wanted. She might even secretly have wanted the excitement of distant postings herself, a little romance in a life that all too soon showed the seven signs of being brief. And his son, well, he was a plant that never put down roots. But Majewski wanted to hold everything steady and secure for them. He wanted to stay close to the sustaining network of blood. He had known what it was to cast off from all that abides. He had seen what his mother had gone through, adrift and alone. He had vowed never to allow anything to dislocate them again, but instead to remain true to his idea of the Old World virtues of stability and place. It was for this that he had sacrificed some measure of personal success. And now—wife dead, son wandering in a daze, mother dying alone in a home where the state purchased care by the day—the question whether it was all worth it was not one he cared to entertain from anyone—anyone, that is, except the pitiless interlocutor who spoke in his own cold, newspaperman's voice.

The sandwich took its taste from the wrapper. The diet soda was a parody of sweetness. He put the half-finished can on his desk along with the unread press releases, notebooks, pencil ends, eraser grit, crumpled peanut bags, and spread-eagled books. He finished his meal and tossed the cellophane toward the trash.

"Boy!" he yelled. "Boy, get over here!"

The kewpie was flirting with one of the younger copyreaders, the one with keyhole eyes. Majewski could see that it was time for him to take her aside some morning and warn her about the follies of lonely men who work at night.

It was Joe Stawarz who answered the call. Majewski had noticed the way Joe was quick on his feet, always ready to work. When the others lazed in conversation, Joe was alert, watching. And when you needed something fast, Joe was always there. He was a big, beefy kid only a little younger than Majewski's son. But you could tell from his clothes and the tiny knots in his words that he had not had the same advantages. He was first-generation, and the old language was still in him. Maybe the old strengths were, too.

"Does it bother the black kids when I call for a boy?"

"Huh?"

26

"Boy. When I call for a boy, do they take offense?"

"Beats me."

"I mean," said Majewski, "they don't take it personally, do they? You don't hear them complaining about it."

"Everybody calls you something, I guess."

"There you go," said Majewski, warming to him. "You know, I was a copyboy once myself."

"No lie?"

"When I was a kid, they did all the writing on paper. You had to move it around by hand. I remember one day the managing editor dropped his cigar butt in a GI can full of carbons and it went up like a tinderbox. He sat there at the newsdesk as everyone rushed around for fire extinguishers, and he never even moved. The smoke billowed up to the ceiling. The flames leaped into the air. And he just watched all the activity and whistled through his teeth like an alarm going off. That's what you learn in this business. You have to be ready for anything. It's damned good work."

"Could pay better," said Joe. "Did you have something for me?"

"Come and sit down a minute," he said.

Joe looked nervously around the room for some other assignment to rescue him. But nobody beckoned. Majewski rolled up a chair next to his desk, and Joe eased down onto the edge of it.

"You've been working here, what, about a year?"

"Year and a half," said Joe. "Seems like longer."

"It always does at your age," said Majewski. "You don't want to be a copyboy the rest of your life, do you?"

"Can't say I ever thought about it much, Mr. Majors. You get a job. Then maybe you get another. It's just something that happens. Or else it don't."

"Doesn't," said Majewski.

"Sometimes it does."

Majewski smiled, and a crazy impulse came over him.

"Look," he said, "what do you think about taking a shot at becoming a reporter?"

He was ready for Joe to show surprise or disbelief. But what Majewski saw was quite different. Joe's face hardened into a look Majewski had seen too often on the street when a man thought somebody was getting wise at his expense.

"You've got the drive, the hustle," Majewski said. "You're able

27

to listen. I think you've got the makings of one hell of a fine reporter if you try."

"You got to get through high school first before you can get that kind of work," said Joe.

"Have you dropped out already, Joe?"

The young man stood up and started to walk away.

"No, wait," said Majewski. "There's nothing fatal about that. It can be made up. There are tests you can take. I could help you get ready for them."

"I don't got the time, Mr. Majors," Joe said, from a distance.

"Of course not, Joe. You've got a family to worry about, don't you?"

"My old man's dead, if that's what you mean."

"School can wait," said Majewski. "I'm talking about something else here. I'd like you to work for me. Be my legman. My assistant. What do you say?"

"Don't say nothing," said Joe. "Sounds nuts to me."

"I think I can swing it with Tony Ruffalino. He came up that way, too, you know. A lot of us did."

Joe came back, but he did not sit down.

"It's different now," he said.

"I'm just trying to give you a break, Joe."

Majewski heard the pleading tone come into his voice, and he knew the thing was hopeless. But you had to try to reach them somehow. You had to make the effort, even knowing all their resistances. And you did it again and again—with the young Polish girls, with your son—if only to silence the interlocutor's voice and say that, yes, it could be all right between you again. Yes, goddamnit. Just say yes.

"Don't do me no favors, Mr. Majors."

"You've got to think of your future," said Majewski.

"Future, hell," said Joe, all the unfathomable resentments of his age flaring in his hard, proud face. "It might as well be the end of the world. I got all I can do just getting through today."

Majewski drove alone to the university to cover the speech, rebuking himself. He had pushed Joe too hard. He should never have shown how much it meant to him. That always put them off, the thought that you might really want to help them. They did not believe you had it in you to deliver; they feared a trick. It was almost as if you had already failed them so thoroughly that they could never trust you again. Majewski did not know how he had let them down. All he knew was that when you tried to reach them, they backed away. And when you were careful, you did not even get close.

He found a place to park alongside the cemetery behind the law school. As he got out of his car, the wind lashed tears into his eyes. An early cold snap had already lit up all the trees. The leaves glowed bright red and yellow under the streetlights, like fire.

He walked past a car parked illegally, a big Chrysler with diplomatic plates sitting in front of a hydrant. He crossed the street and moved close to the heavy stone wall of the quadrangle. The building that held the law library loomed up ahead like a great Gothic cathedral. But what at first glance looked reverential, on closer inspection turned out to be an elaborate joke. The gargoyles standing their stone vigils were leering images of constables and convicts. And the figures in the grand stained-glass windows were a Dickensian array of process-servers, bloated barristers, and sneering, wigged judges.

Inside, a crowd had already gathered in the medieval corridor. Students lined up for admission, unshaven and disheveled, dressed in everything from limp, leather-patched sports coats to bib overalls. They looked like characters in a Depression mural celebrating the diversity and disparity of American life. When Majewski was in school, the students had not worn such costumes. There had been no rule requiring uniformity, but the unwritten code was strict, right down to the width of the lapels and the proper roll of the collar. If you were a first-generation immigrant with a name that made professors falter when they called on you in class, you did not even think of going around in peasant garb or workclothes that expressed solidarity with the maintenance staff. You conformed, as best you could on whatever funds you had, and you hoped nobody would notice that you had cut the label out of your coat.

Majewski queued up as the auditorium doors opened and the crowd began to file inside. Behind him some kids were showing off by holding a conversation in Russian. He only recognized a few words they used. In his family a young person studied Latin, if he studied any language at all, and the only Russian anybody used was to curse.

Once inside the auditorium, he made his way to the far side by

29

an exit where he could make a quick dash to a telephone to dictate his story if the speech dragged on late. Up front a bright, blue cloth with the university seal draped the podium. He turned in his seat and saw the TV crews setting up in the balcony. He nodded politely to one of the men he knew. The electronic equipment seemed out of place under the high, arched ceilings, as if it had been transported back in time to record the inscrutable rituals of some ancient parliament.

A nervous, balding man walked briskly up to the low stage and began tapping on the mike and squeaking its long, movable neck.

"Is this on?" he asked. "Is it? Yes. Can you hear me?" There was a rustle in the crowd that could have been either yes or no. The man cleared his throat and went on. "I am informed," he said, "that our distinguished speaker, Viktor Shevtsov, is on his way and will be here momentarily."

He was just turning away from the microphone when something lifted him up and threw him to the floor.

Thunder ripped through the hall. It shattered the high windows and shook the floor. Glass from burst light bulbs rained down as the room went black and the panicked audience surged toward the rear exits away from the windows.

Majewski's instincts drove him against the crowd. Glass cracked underfoot in the darkness as he groped his way to the stage. When he got there, his toe touched something alive.

"Careful," said a voice. "That's my leg."

"Are you hurt?"

"Hard to tell," said the voice. "I think I only twisted my ankle. I may be cut."

"Is there a back way out of here?"

"Door at the side of the stage. There's a corridor that leads outside."

"I'll give you a hand," said Majewski. The sirens were already on the way. Dome lights slashed through the broken windows and flashed on and off against the ceiling. "Can you make it?"

"I might have to lean a little."

With the extra weight, Majewski moved slowly. He found the door, and a few steps later they were out on the street midway down the quad. In the light he saw that the person he was supporting was the balding man who had made the announcement. He did not appear to be badly injured.

"Do you know where I can find a phone?"

"Across the street there," said the man.

"Think you can make it alone?"

"I'm just a little lame. Nothing seems to be broken. You go ahead."

Majewski left him braced against the stone wall. All the action seemed to be around the corner, but the first thing was to get the city desk moving. The cold air cut his lungs, and he was heaving when he reached the booth.

"Give me the desk," he said. "Quick."

Ruffalino picked up.

"We got a big bang here, Tony. I don't know what the hell it was yet. You hear anything?"

"Cops and fire are on the scene. They're saying something about a car."

"Car fleeing or car blowing up?"

"You're the one who's there."

"It's always a pleasure, Tony."

"You have anything to dump now?"

"Not yet. You'd better get somebody to the hospital."

"On their way," said Ruffalino. "Stanford and a photog will meet you at the scene. Get me something, will you, Stan?"

"We have time?"

"Hell yes," said Ruffalino. "And we have money, too. But never enough."

Majewski extricated himself from the booth and jogged toward the corner, notebook slapping against his leg with every second step. A crowd had gathered at the corner where the police had set up sawhorses. He pushed his way through it and saw the mangled wreck of the car. The hood was twisted upward. The tires were smoldering, sending out billows of acrid smoke. The ruined grillwork cried a long, silent scream. Windows were out on both sides of the street, and a fleet of ambulances was already loading up litters. A bloody shoe lay on its side in the middle of the street, a trickle of shiny liquid draining into a pool at the heel.

"You sure got here fast enough," said the sergeant at the barricade.

"What's up, Marco?" asked Majewski, climbing over.

"Somebody didn't like somebody else very much."

"Car bomb?"

"Looks like it, don't it?"

"Injuries?"

"Two dead in the car. Lots of kids cut up by the glass."

Majewski opened his notebook.

"Got any names for me?"

"You better find the lieutenant."

Firemen were hosing down the gasoline. A fine spray hung in the cold air. Down the way the paramedics were putting a body bag into an ambulance. It looked as if a second body was already inside. Radios crackled their emergency orders, the flat, impersonal voices echoing against stone. Technicians were flashing photographs and laying out a grid on the street so they could map where all the pieces of wreckage had fallen. Majewski could not see any sign of a lieutenant. But he did see somebody else he recognized. The small figure huddled alone in a doorway.

"Professor Steinman," he shouted as he moved toward the frail old man. "Are you all right?"

Steinman looked up at him, but the eyes registered nothing. Then the voice spoke and told Majewski the thing he had suspected from the moment of the explosion.

"They've killed Shevtsov," said the professor.

And despite the strongest instincts in his gut, Majewski paused and took the old man's hand to comfort him before bolting back to the phone.

TWO

What candles may be held to speed them all?
Not in the hands of boys, but in their eyes
Shall shine the holy glimmers of good-byes.

The first signal interrupted a strained silence. On Moll's end it came as two high-pitched beeps. On the other, he knew, it was just a momentary deadness on the line.

"Are you still there, Henry?"

"Somebody trying to get through to me, Father," said Moll. "Don't worry. My office likes to check up on its children, too."

Brother James Toolan laughed easily. The awkwardness was all on Moll's side.

"You needn't call me Father."

"I know," said Moll.

"It's harder to be a father than a brother. People expect more of you . . ." Brother James said before the line closed off behind him. "Perhaps you ought to take that other call. There really isn't much more that I can tell you about Thomas."

"I worry about him."

"Of course you do. And I don't want to deceive you. We don't pretend to do miracles." The signal blanked out a word this time, and Moll cursed the intrusion. ". . . just practice some time-tested disciplines and ask the Lord to inspire us in the commitment that redeems."

"He's a hard case," said Moll. "I don't know why, but he is."

"We've had . . . before."

Moll held the phone out in front of his face, gripping it like a club. Damn them. They just never let up on a man. When he put it back to his ear, the connection was clear again.

"Tom ran with a bad crowd," he said. "Drugs. Crazy ideas. I don't know what all."

"I've been through everything with him," said Brother James.

"And I would have to say that I found Thomas to be genuinely contrite."

"Don't let him trick you," said Moll. He hated the bitter, faithless sound of it. But he was speaking from experience. He had let Tom lie to him so many times.

"I think I have developed a pretty good ear for contrition," said Brother James. His voice was gentle, calm, as if the world Moll knew had never touched him.

"I used to think I had a pretty good instinct, too," said Moll.

"It's different in the brotherhood. The men who come here have nothing to gain by dissembling. And as for your own ear, how could you hope to hear him truly? If you forgave too much, it was only because you wanted him to be all right."

"Has he spoken about us at all, his mother and me?"

"I'm afraid I could not tell you if he had," said Brother James. Moll's ear was not so deaf that he did not hear the answer to his question in this evasion; Tom had said nothing.

"I understand . . ." Moll said. The signal interrupted him again.

"They seem very persistent," said Brother James.

Moll was not ready to yield.

"I wonder if Tom might have wanted to call us," he said.

"He very well might have. But he knows that he is not ready. We no longer insist upon absolute silence, but in the first stages we do not permit communication outside the community. It is important that a troubled individual be isolated from all the corrupting influences."

Such as the love of parents, Moll thought, the fool eagerness to forgive.

"Is he happy?"

"That is a troublesome word," said Brother James, for once his voice dark with experience. "He leads an elemental life here. He rises early. He eats our simple fare. He confesses. He prays. He spends his days working with the animals in the stable. No one inquires his pleasure."

Fathers and brothers, they were different that way. Fathers never gave up on happiness for their sons.

Brother James went on: "I think it is important for a young man of Thomas's age to realize that satisfaction is not to be found in pursuit but rather in acceptance of that which is given."

"They want so much and settle for so little," said Moll.

36

"You should try to worry less about him, Henry. He is safe here."

"Yes," said Moll. "Thank you. Thank you for that." The signal came again. And when it passed, Brother James was gone.

Moll laid the phone in its cradle but did not take his hand away. His fingers tightened on the plastic. The ring was like an electric jolt up his spine.

"I hate to keep you waiting," he said into the receiver.

"Jesus, Hank, didn't you hear me trying to break into the line?" It was Sam Parks, the nightside man. "I was signaling the piss out of you. What the hell were you doing? Talking to your bookie?"

"I was talking to a priest, Sam," he said. Brothers and fathers, the difference didn't matter outside of the faith.

"Well, say a little prayer as you grab your hat," said Parks. "There's been a bombing."

Moll pulled himself up in his chair.

"Outfit?"

"One of the dead ones was Russian. Name of Shestov or Shevzot or some damned thing. He was on his way to give a speech at the university."

"You never worked Division Five, did you?"

"Intelligence? No way."

"You say the names better when they're Italian."

"I kind of enjoy it," Parks said, "keeping score."

"Well, you'd better give me all the details, Sam. What have we got?"

"Happened about twenty minutes ago. Car bomb. Over on Wall Street. By the law school. Gave the smart little bastards a taste of life."

"Who was the Russian?"

"Somebody the Russians didn't like," said Parks. "The boss said it would be right up your alley."

"I don't do intelligence work anymore."

"And my old lady won't do windows. Until they get shitty enough. Then she does. Haul ass, will you, Hank?"

Moll hung up the phone and rubbed at his palm. He smelled the roast cooking in the kitchen and heard Sally pinging the silverware. Heaving his raincoat onto his big, bent shoulders, he went in to break the news.

"Oh, Hank," she said when she saw him dressed to leave. "Is Tom in trouble again?"

"No, not that," he said. "It was the office. There's been a bombing downtown."

"Didn't you get to call about Tom at all?"

"I got through to Brother James." He had a hard time looking at her when the subject was their son. "Everything seems fine."

"Did you speak with Tom?"

"It isn't allowed," he said. Even for mercy's sake he could not carry the truth alone. "They don't think it would be good for him."

"Hank," she said as he turned to go. He stopped but did not face her. "Don't let it upset you so."

"I'm all business," he said. Then he caught himself. It was so easy to let this thing they carried divide them. He touched her face as gently as he could. She was about to weep—because he had been too hard, because he had not been hard enough, because there didn't seem to be a damned thing either of them could do about it, and because neither of them could leave it alone. He took a step back.

"The victim was a Russian," he said. "It looks like one of those. They want me on the case anyway. They must think Tom is OK again."

"What do they know?" she said.

Outside, the cold, wet air off the Sound chilled him. He drew his hand over his face and rubbed his eyes. He hated soggy weather, had hated it ever since the tropics. The heavy, mildewed air took everything out of you. Sometimes he felt as if he could barely draw breath. Saipan, Tinian, and Okinawa.

He took the shore road toward the city, catching sight of the distant lights of Long Island whenever the trees gave way to an open stretch of beach. It crouched there in shadows, like some great sea beast ready to defend itself. Moll had an aversion to islands. He had never been able to overcome the feeling that no matter how large and connected they were, once you got on one you might never get off.

He turned inland at the shopping center and sped toward the Interstate. In Bureau terms, this assignment was something of a backwater, overshadowed by the big offices in Boston and New York. But he didn't mind that anymore. There were nice old neighborhoods here with houses you could afford, and the city did not bear down on you. When they had first arrived, Tom was getting bigger by the day. They shopped for good schools and looked around for a place where a kid could stretch and feel safe. The boy needed room, needed beaches to walk alone at night; he had to be able to gaze off into the distance and dream of islands where he would become a man. The spot they found was perfect for raising a strong young son. No, he could not blame the place.

The Interstate cut through the odd outcroppings of stone that verged New Haven. They reared up from the rolling, coastal meadows, some shaped to human forms like ancient, epic statues of deities and reclining giants, others squat pairs of dice on the green-felt grasslands. This part of Connecticut was the strangest place Moll had ever known: mountains, plains, islands, and sea. In the quaint Yankee villages on the outskirts people hung brass eagles over the doors to scare time away. The city itself had more than its share of ugly new buildings, somebody's grim vision of the future, and all around them the ethnic neighborhoods were as unsocialized as immigrants fresh off the boat. Many of the arms factories stood abandoned since the last big military buildup, their high, cracked windows gray with years, their rusting overhead cranes bare to the elements, wasting arches of triumph.

And the university stood in the midst of it all—a walled, medieval city under attack. During the period the provost liked to call the Dark Ages, Moll had been the Bureau's main link to what went on at the school. He had covered the strikes and marches, kept track of antiwar leaders, recruited a platoon of snitches to act as his secret eyes and ears. At Bureau Headquarters they believed that the real war was being fought for the minds of the young. It was different from the battles on the islands, where men faced the simple choice of killing or being killed. Now everyone was hostage within fragile citadels, and the walls were no protection. Weapons were aimed at weapons in a long, numbing standoff, and nobody dared to make a move. No wonder so many of the young ones were troubled. This war did not spare the children.

To reach the bomb site, Moll chose the back way onto campus, through the white-slat neighborhoods. He drove past George and Harry's, where a middle-aged man without love beads could have a shot and a beer without seeming out of place. He had sometimes signaled his young informants there, following an elaborate system of sign and countersign he had once used against the KGB. He drove past Woolsey Hall, where the radicals had held their ardent celebrity rallies. Then he made a turn into Wall Street. The fire department's beacons lighted up the scene ahead. Moll pulled his car over the curb onto the sidewalk and walked the rest of the way. Knots of students huddled against the chill at the edge of the police lines.

Moving toward the tangled steel wreckage, its red finish sparkling in the lights, he dragged the wet air deep into his lungs against the nausea. It was not the sight that sickened him so much as the smell, burnt flesh and hair, the memories it touched off. Sure, you got used to it over the years, but sometimes the effect was cumulative, like certain poisons that do not metabolize, and it all came gagging to your throat.

Bob Raskin, a young assistant United States attorney, huddled with the police near the wreckage. Moll went past them silently and took a look inside what was left of the car. They had taken away the bodies, but the carpet and dash were spattered with gore.

Moll would never offer a formal opinion before he saw all the data from the lab techs and the morgue, but he had handled enough bombings to have a pretty good idea how this one had gone down. It looked as though the device had been placed under the passenger side floorboard, a shaped charge aimed upward into the rider's face. He looked up from the wreckage. The many entryways and grottoes offered plenty of places for the killer to have hidden as he detonated the bomb. Or else he might have been following the victims in another car. He could have let them turn into the one-way street, then thrown the switch and driven calmly away.

Moll noticed some odd pieces of fabric scattered on the ground and stuck to jagged bits of the car's broken frame. He made a note to have the lab check them out.

"You sure took long enough getting here," said Raskin, appearing suddenly at his side. "What do you make of it?"

"Could be anything."

"I guess that gives us probable federal jurisdiction."

"If you want it."

"One of the dead ones was a Russian defector."

"It could have been somebody's jealous husband," said Moll.

"Come on, Hank. Can't you just smell it?"

Smells affected different people in different ways. It all depended on where you had smelled them before.

"You've never worked a security case, have you?" Moll asked.

"I don't know why, Hank, but you don't seem enthusiastic."

"Looks to me like everybody from the Soviet Committee on State Security to Amnesty International is going to try to poke a nose into this one. What's not to be enthusiastic about?"

"I asked your boss to send you," said Raskin.

"Well, that's real kind, Bob."

"I wanted the best."

"Didn't he tell you?" said Moll. "They don't trust me anymore."

Then he stopped himself. He wasn't going to go into all that again. The tight smiles on their faces when they asked him about his son. Nothing personal, of course. Ties of blood, that's all. No question about your own loyalty, Hank. But appearances. Appearances.

"When you guys get through there," said one of the locals as he approached them, "I think you might be interested in what we found in the bushes."

They followed him to a spot where the cops had lowered a ladder into an empty moat that surrounded the quadrangle. Moll was the last to descend into the wet leaves, broken glass, and other rubbish at the bottom. They joined a knot of uniforms and detectives crowding around a spot between blown-out windows. The yellow beams of flashlights played upon the littered ground and then converged on one piece of fire-blackened metal poking out of the mess. It was bent and broken by the blast. It might have been anything, a piece of carburetor or chrome trim, anything. Except that at one end, where the flame had spared it, Moll could make out a symbol etched into the metal, an abstract, stylized phone company bell.

"There's our detonator," said one of the locals.

"What do you mean?" asked Raskin. He was cocky enough that when he did not know something, he felt free to ask.

"My bet is that it's a piece of a paging device," said the local. "A radio receiver. You can use it to get a message. You can use it to set a bomb."

"Who knows?" said Moll. "Maybe Shevtsov was expecting a call."

The police tow hoisted the mangled front end of the car up high in the air and began to inch forward. A piece of tailpipe dragged on the pavement, sparking like a sputtering fuse. The evidence crews finished filtering the water they had pumped from the sewers for anything useful that might have been flushed away when the fire trucks hosed down the gasoline. Police hauled their barricades to the side and loaded them into a pickup. A slow rain began to fall as the big lights snapped off, one by one.

Moll was finished at the scene, but he still had messages to send to get the investigation designated as a special and initiate a review of the central files to pull together the information on Shevtsov and the other man. You had to start by identifying the dead. Not just name, age, address; that was the simple part. You had to find out to whom the dead belonged. Were they theirs or ours? And the question of ownership could get pretty tricky. It wasn't like doing a title search to find the creep who stood to gain on insurance when a torch job was set. The most important liens on a man were too secret to be recorded. Shevtsov had defected shortly after winning the Prize. He had done it without help from the Western intelligence agencies, and there was always the possibility that the Soviets had sponsored the whole thing for reasons of their own. The variations were endless.

Moll offered Raskin a lift back to the courthouse, and the two of them bundled into Moll's old car.

"Can I give you a little advice?" said Raskin as they rolled down the deserted street.

"If you think you have to," said Moll.

"I'm worried about your attitude, Hank. You ought to try to be more communicative."

"Reporters love it when you sneer at them."

"Suit yourself," said Raskin. "But this could be your ticket back, you know."

Moll waited for a light to change, then waited some more.

"It's going to be a very dirty little business," he finally said. "I guarantee it."

"It's a murder," said Raskin, yawning and stretching against the seat belt. "They're always a mess."

"The CIA will meddle. The State Department will, too. You watch."

Moll could tell from the way Raskin shook his head that even these troublesome attentions were only musk to him. It all depended on where you had smelled the smell before.

From here on, the lights all blinked a warning amber. Moll touched the accelerator and eased past the wide, empty green.

"Don't count on me," he said. "Tomorrow I'm gone."

Raskin opened his coat to absorb some of the heat pouring from the defroster.

"I think you might be surprised about that," he said. "I talked to the Special Agent in Charge. I told him about your . . . your reservations. I think I might have been just a little bit testy with him. Changing teams on me, getting off to a rocky start. I may have raised my voice." The younger man looked over at Moll and smiled. "Well, the SAC was very, very reassuring, to say the least. He said he'd cleared your assignment through Headquarters. And he told me not to pay any attention to your complaining. He said you were just clearing your throat. You ready to talk now, Hank?"

Moll did not even look at him as they eased to the curb in front of the courthouse.

"What's to talk about?" he said. "You've got it all figured out."

They went inside, signed in with the guard, then waited in silence for the elevator.

In a way, Moll envied Raskin's confidence. He had lost his own on the islands, long ago. He had left his home in Indiana at the age of seventeen to join the Marines because he was worried that if he waited any longer he would miss out on the great upheaval that from a distance seemed a vision of glory. Before it was over, Moll had learned everything he needed to know about glory—a boy's dream was a man's nightmare.

He had come home from the islands a hero, with medals and a wound. He told the men in the bars tales of the tropics, tall stories of war. He gladly marched in the parades; on parade you did not have to look anyone in the eye. You just marched down the street, and you did not need to explain about Saipan or Okinawa. You did not have to tell the real tale, how it had been on those wracked moonscapes, the way you had hid in open tombs to get cover from the artillery. You did not need to make anyone understand what it had meant to live in a blasted community with the dead. You just came marching home, putting one foot in front of the other, keeping your eyes straight ahead.

He had taken the GI Bill at Notre Dame, studied history, watched the younger men play ball. He would have liked to play a little himself, but he had lost the margin of youth. Still, he yearned for some surrogate for battle. And so when he graduated, he got in line for a place in Mr. Hoover's army.

In those days every candidate had to be presented to Mr. Hoover personally before he became a full-fledged special agent, and woe unto anyone who had a sweaty handshake or a whisker still showing on his throat. When Moll's training class had completed the course, qualified on the weapons, and passed all the exams, the candidates were led in little groups into the huge corner office in the Justice Department building. Moll had never seen anything quite so grand: high ceilings, tall windows looking up Pennsylvania Avenue toward the Capitol. When the Director finally buzzed them into the inner office, Moll was shocked to see how small the great man was—short and grim and dressed like some hoodlum dandy in a movie. He trooped the line, inspecting each candidate, pumping each arid palm. The story had gone around that if Mr. Hoover did not like the looks of one of the candidates, the cut of his hair, the cant of his brow, that man was out. They said that one time, after just such an inspection, the Director had scribbled at the top of the memo listing the candidates' names, "Watch the height." Mr. Hoover's assistants received the message, lined the men up, and washed out the tallest and shortest among them. Only much later did they realize that the Director's note wasn't complaining about the candidates' size at all. It had merely disturbed him that the text of the memo crowded too close to the top of the page. He had been criticizing the typist's margins.

"Mr. Moll," Mr. Hoover said, standing only inches away as Moll braced to a stiff, garrison attention. "Why do you desire to be a special agent of the FBI?"

Moll had practiced a little speech about law and order, the Bureau's reputation for honor, the protection of innocents. But now that the time had come, the text failed him. The real reason spilled out.

"I was in the war," he said. "I don't believe in peace."

Mr. Hoover held Moll's eye for a moment, then moved on. Moll punished himself as the Director went on down the line. He had said it all wrong, made himself seem bloodthirsty when all he really meant was that he could not believe that war had ended with the dropping of the Bomb. A new and more dangerous war had begun. But he had been wrong to talk about battle. He had violated the rules of parade, and he was sure that his career at the Bureau was destroyed. Later that day he learned that the Director had asked for his file when the group left the office, remarked to his aides on the decorations and the wound, and personally assigned him to the intelligence division.

In the early years, Moll's career had seemed to be blessed. He had duty in Washington and New York, Chicago and San Francisco, everywhere the malign Soviet presence showed itself. After a mercifully short apprenticeship on stakeouts of Russian functionaries, he moved off the babysitting details. But it was clear to him early on that the Bureau did not see him as a candidate for administrative responsibilities. "The man's a soldier," Mr. Hoover had once said of him. "He should not be drawn back from the fields of honor." It had been reported to Moll as a supreme compliment. But Moll knew that only a man who had never been mired up to his knees in them could refer to those blasted acres in such a way.

Moll gained a reputation as a streetwise case agent with an instinct for the human flaw. On the street he was courageous without being reckless; this was only natural for one who had survived. But his greatest asset was something deeper, something pounded into him by the mortars and artillery. To find the flaw, he always began by examining the fault lines he had already discovered within himself.

"You getting off here?" Raskin asked as the elevator door bucked against his hand.

"Sorry," said Moll. "I was kind of drifting."

A telephone rang somewhere deep in the empty offices.

"That's got to be for me," said Raskin. "You coming or not?"

Moll pushed off the back wall and into the corridor, letting the car door close behind him as Raskin raced away. He lagged back, stopping at the men's room to splash his face with cold water. He had to try to get the stink off him, the smell of fire and flesh, the smell of the islands.

At first intelligence work had been just what he had wanted. There were secrets to protect, secrets that could start or end a war in one fiery stroke. And even if defending them was not a perfect way of keeping faith with the community of the dead, even if the enemy had become a friend and the friend an enemy after the surrender, war was continuing in the shadows and Moll was a part of it.

He'd had a piece of the Fuchs case follow-up. He'd helped interrogate Abel. But after more than a decade of success, intelligence work began to go sour. It wasn't the long hours or repeated moves from field office to field office, the endless trips away from home. When he believed in what he was doing, he was very nearly oblivious of the damage it was wreaking upon his family. Over the years, though, he began to wonder whether espionage really served as substitute for the other, open, unthinkable kind of warfare or whether it had become an end in itself, a strange and ritualized game, an Olympics of deceit.

He no longer took seriously the blood feud between Mr. Hoover and the CIA. He got no satisfaction from pursuing the endless chain of deception and counter-deception to the vanishing point. What mattered were the arrays of missiles aimed at one another, and nothing a man could do would alter this balance of terror. The war had gone inside. The standoff depended upon the perfection of nightmares. The fields of battle had become men's most secret fears.

His change of attitude did not go unnoticed. He was taken off the cases that made a difference to the Bureau's standing in the intelligence community. He was put behind a desk. Eventually they shifted him over to the domestic side and transferred him to the inconsequential field office in New Haven where he remained, passed over, forgotten, until the tormenting business about his son pushed him out of intelligence work altogether.

The men's room was empty and silent as Moll stood before the mirror, his face sagging on a big, square skull. He went to the towel dispenser and pulled out a few coarse sheets. They were rough against his stubbled skin.

Why they wanted to bring him back now, he did not know. Maybe just because he understood the rules. Maybe they thought he no longer had the energy to fight them. They would want to control the operation out of Washington in a case like this with so many bureaucratic implications. So why not put old Moll against it? He's safe now. The boy hasn't been heard of lately, and Moll has been checking up on his pension benefits. Perfect guy for it. Reliable, just in case there's some little errand that needs to be run.

Moll wadded up the paper towels and threw them into the trash. He began to leave, then turned back. The heels of both his hands drove against the metal towel dispenser on the wall. It sprang open with a crash. Moll left it that way, hanging like an underslung jaw, gaping open.

He was still rubbing at the pain in his palms when he entered Raskin's cramped, cluttered office.

"Bingo," said Raskin.

"Think you've got something already?"

"Locals got it," said Raskin, with an unfortunate edge in his voice. It did not amuse Moll that the young man was already trying to set him in competition with the New Haven police.

"What might it be?"

"Parking ticket."

"Get the locals to fix it for you."

"Out behind the law school. A three-wheeler found a car parked in front of a fireplug. The cop was new, green as hell. He wrote the ticket even though the plates were diplomatic. When he got back to the station for the change of shifts, he asked the desk sergeant about it. The sergeant had the presence of mind to pass the license number along to the dicks working the bombing. They ran a quick check, and what do you know, the car is listed to the Soviet UN Mission."

"So they had somebody in the audience for the speech," said Moll. "You don't think they'd send a hit man out with official plates."

"We put them at the scene," said Raskin. "It's a start."

"If they were going to hit Shevtsov, they wouldn't have been anywhere around," said Moll, just to test how the young man would handle the infinite regress of deception.

"Unless," said Raskin, with a pause he must have picked up from TV. "Unless that's how they wanted us to see it."

Raskin had failed the test, and Moll knew he was in for an ordeal.

As soon as he hit the city room, yanking off his coat and stuffing it into a corner of the counter behind his desk, Majewski went into his sprint. He had fifty-four minutes before his copy deadline.

Ruffalino had sent a couple of younger reporters to relieve him at the scene. The rewrite men were handling the sidebars and passing him notes on the best stuff so he could work it into the main piece. The thing had broken just right. The TV news had gotten a little part of it for the last broadcast, but only enough to whet people's appetites.

At first he did not even sign onto the computer. He worked the phones, calling in old favors from every cop whose daughter's wedding announcement he had gotten into the paper, every homicide dick he had flattered in print. He wasn't picking up anything spectacular, just little details that nobody else would have: Shevtsov's itinerary in town, whom he had met, where he had come from, and how he had arrived. He got a little of the background on Arthur Kamen, the other victim. He even managed to finagle a copy of the speech Shevtsov would have delivered. The Russian had left an extra copy of it in his bags at Kamen's house, and the dicks had retrieved it.

"Joe!" he yelled.

The copyboy was across the room.

"Joe, get your ass over here. Quick!"

He hesitated, then came to Majewski's desk.

"Here are the keys to my car," said Majewski, dangling them before him. "It's the blue Chevy out front, the one with the bent-in right side. You can drive, can't you?"

"Sure."

"Take these."

"I got to stay on the floor," Joe said, backing away.

"There's no time to argue. I want you to go over to police headquarters. You know where that is?"

"I been there before. Plenty of times."

"I'm not interested in your record, Joe. I want you to find Detective Sergeant Jim Carlson. Third floor. Homicide, Sex, and Aggravated Assault. It says so right on the door. He'll give you some papers for me. I want them fast. Run."

The copyboy balked.

"This thing is big. Go get it."

Joe lighted up, the excitement of it.

"Hell of a murder," said Majewski.

The copyboy turned on his heel and raced toward the door.

"Attaboy," Majewski whispered.

He felt good. He always did when the deadline was tight and the story was raw. You didn't have a chance to worry the thing to death. You didn't even let yourself appreciate the facts you were picking up and putting down. You could write it full of emotion, words that would make the reader gasp or wipe the tears from his eyes, and you did not feel a thing.

When he first noticed this saving mechanism, it had frightened him. It was more than just being able to stand on the end of a pier and keep your eye on the boats dragging for the body, knowing that every time the crew hauled the grappling hook to the surface it might bring up a bloated, decomposed corpse. That, he understood, was simply the effect of repeated exposure, the way a boxer's belly is hardened by taking punches. This was something much deeper, and he had discovered its power the night of the Pacek murders.

He had been writing for the paper for less than a year when that story broke. Nine students at the Catholic girls' college had been slaughtered in their apartment. One other had escaped by hiding in a closet when she heard screams coming from downstairs. Majewski was all over the story. It was his first big break in the business, and everything had fallen perfectly. He had wheedled the survivor's quotes out of the detectives who had interviewed her. He had been at the scene early—before the apartment was sealed—the only reporter to get a firsthand look. He had gone to the morgue and watched the coroner at work on the mangled bodies. He had written the main lead and several sidebars, and even now they still talked about the grim poetry of his account. Yet it was not until the next morning when he picked up the paper and saw what he had done that the enormity of the thing became real to him. A chill went through him as he read his own words, a fist grabbed at his throat. And when Rose came down for breakfast, she found him weeping.

He had been concerned about this reaction back then, but later he realized that it was the only thing that allowed him to function. You had to be able to imagine such horrible things—the terror of the victims, the demented motives of the torturer, all the extremes of fear and madness to which the mind is prey. You had to be able to understand the reasons men did these things to one another and appreciate the sheer physical vulnerability of flesh. Yet at the same time you had to protect yourself in order to go on. And you did, you did. The truth was like one of the four forces of field theory a physicist at the university had explained to him earlier in the day when he was trying to get a fix on Shevtsov's past. It was powerful only in the middle distance. If you got close enough, it lost its capacity to move you.

By the time Joe returned, Majewski had finished his telephone work and was ready to write. There were twenty-three minutes left. He eased back into his chair.

"Anything good in the speech?" he asked when Joe slapped the papers into his palm.

"Damned if I know," said Joe. "I'll tell you this, though. Your engine's skipping real bad. Needs a tune-up."

"Didn't you read it?"

"I had a look."

"What do you think?"

"Seemed like a lot of bullshit to me."

"Here's your first practical lesson in the profession of journalism, Joe. It's almost never entirely bullshit when you've got it all alone."

"You ain't gonna lighten up on me, are you, Mr. Majors?"

"A good reporter is observant. He notices things. You're getting the hang of it."

They would print the text of the speech in full, but Majewski scanned it to lift out a quote or two for the main story. With nineteen minutes left to deadline, he signed onto his terminal, punched in the slug Ruffalino had assigned him, and began to compose. This time it came easily. The lead wrote itself. The words were hard-edged. It was difficult at times like this for Majewski to conceive of anyone putting the thing any other way. The second graph identified Shevtsov more fully, with a few passing words for the unfortunate Mr. Kamen. The third described the tangled wreck outside the law school, numbered the injured students, set up the quotes.

He took the piece backward and forward in time as easily as a man tugging a kite in the breeze. This was where pure craftsmanship took over. He knew how to build the thing, one part at a time. After the preliminaries, he wrote of Shevtsov's background, drawing on what Professor Steinman had told him. The carpet slippers. The theories. The daring escape.

The next paragraphs carried the bits and pieces of evidence, scraps that every other reporter on the story would steal once they read them in the morning *Herald*: The bomb-and-arson dick's description of the blast. The smoking tires. The best guess as to where the bomb had been placed, all the various possibilities of how it had been detonated. He had not been able to nail down which one was the most likely, and it galled him. Surely the cops had a pretty good idea by now. Moll must have been sitting on them real hard, because whenever Majewski had asked about it, he had gotten only a chilly dismissal. Majewski glanced at his watch. Sixteen minutes left. There wasn't time to make another call.

The rest of the story simply poured out. The scene inside the auditorium. The blast and panic. The rain of broken glass. At two minutes to deadline, he read over the last take and moved it to the copydesk where they had gotten everything else out of the way to handle it.

"I'm clear," he told Ruffalino, who had been looking over his shoulder.

"If the goddamn machine holds up for just a few more minutes," said Ruffalino, "we'll have us a newspaper."

Majewski followed him back to the city desk.

"Think we might sell a few tomorrow, Tony?" he said.

"One or two."

"I want to ask you something," said Majewski. "What do you think about Joe Stawarz?"

"The copyboy?"

"He's got some fire in him."

"Maybe."

"I think the kid has the stuff to make it."

"Make what?"

"A good reporter."

"Come on, Stan."

"I'd like to give him a chance. Do a little legwork for me."

"Who do you think you are, Jimmy Breslin? Next thing I know you're going to want a paneled office with a window and a secretary who calls you mister. Where am I going to get money to give you an assistant?"

"There was a time when you guys couldn't do enough for me."

"I guess you should have thought about it then. Now we know you better. You love this dump."

"How about this? You free Stawarz up a little bit when I've got something for him. I'll give him overtime out of my own pocket if I need to."

"Out of your expense account, you mean."

"Catch me at it, Tony. Figure out where I hide it."

"You've been around felons too long."

"All I'm asking you to do is to keep Joe on the floor so I can pull him away from time to time."

"I got shifts to fill, Stan."

"Hey, give me a green light on this one and I'll show you something for it. I'm on a roll, Tony. I can feel it."

"Whatever," said Ruffalino.

He turned away, grumbling, and Majewski returned to his desk to make a pass at straightening it up for the morning. He pitched a few of the piled-up papers into the big trash can. The older, yellowed ones stayed. If something had been there long enough, that was a good enough reason to keep it around some more. He sifted through the other junk, tossing out some reminders that had long since gone out of date, stacking up the books that he might someday read. When he was done, he had made some progress. The trash can was overflowing. There was a small open space on the desk. He leaned back and stared at it.

The city room was emptying out. The copy deadline had passed, and the paper was now in the strong hands of the people down in the composing room sweating the hot lead. Majewski stood up and pulled his coat from under the books he had piled on top of it. The stack collapsed, but he did not bother to put it right again. Ruffalino was shuffling out the door alone. Majewski made a move to join him. But then he stopped. He was not interested in recapitulating the day over drinks in the bar next door. He sat back down in his chair, coat bunched up under him, and lifted his feet to the clear spot on the desk.

It was too late to catch the news on TV, and he was too tired to read. What he needed tonight was someone who didn't give a damn about the story, someone to talk to about simpler things. He thought about calling Susan Cousins, but Danny would come as part of that bargain. Majewski did not want to face Danny.

Instead, he picked up the phone and dialed his son's number. The line crackled and fussed. Once, twice, three times it rang. He had been known to let the thing buzz for an hour, receiver lying before him as he busied himself with something else. But his son had learned that trick; he simply lifted the receiver an inch and dropped it back on its cradle when he was not in the mood to talk. This time, though, he wasn't picking up at all. There was no telling where he might be.

But it was all right. There was no pain tonight. Majewski had gotten in so close that even the most tender spots were numb.

THREE

Dies irae, dies illa,
solvet saeculum, in favilla . . .

Day of wrath and doom impending,
Heaven and earth in ashes ending . . .

Fog hid the foot of the cliffs at the north end of the city and shaded up the walls. It obscured the graffiti splashed across the old, red rockfaces, the geological evidence that these ancient stones were in their final decline. It covered the whole city, leaving only the heights, like ruins of a purifying, immemorial fire.

From the courthouse Moll could not see the shore. But he knew the way the sea smoldered on a day like this, the way you heard the sound of waves in every direction and lost track of where you were. He gazed out and waited, phone in hand, for the bell to summon her. But there was no answer. He hung up. Sally liked to walk when there was a fog.

She had still been sleeping when he rose. She slept deeply, and it had seemed important not to disturb her peace. He made coffee and left it warming on the stove. He put out her breakfast, as she had put out his dinner the night before. He left a little note. It did not say much.

He hated to have to leave her. Not that there was any more to tell about his conversation with Brother James. There had been no crisis, no trouble, no details to report. He and Sally had learned to live on things unsaid. But when she walked alone, she liked to have him there at her side.

"Haze beginning to lift?"

Moll turned from the window in the squad bay and saw Dan Odom, the Special Agent in Charge, standing in the door.

"Getting thicker," said Moll. "Weather and PRIBOMB both." PRIBOMB, the bombing of a Prizewinner, was the caption Moll had assigned the investigation. "I've been dickering with the locals over the spoils. They hauled the car away last night and wanted to keep it as collateral against their fair share of the glory."

"We ought to ship it to the lab," said Odom.

"Funny, that's just what I said."

"They buy it?"

"They did when I told them about the radioactivity."

"You didn't overstate it, I hope."

"We wouldn't have known anything about it," said Moll, "if I hadn't noticed some pieces of rag last night around the wreck. Lab says that they were soaked in a solution they use in hospitals."

"What about the danger, Hank? Do we have to put out the word?"

"Locals agree the car is too hot for them to hold. The lab will have the wreck later today. Then we'll know more."

"You're checking the hospitals," said Odom.

"I've got men fanned out all over the place."

"What do we know so far about this stuff?"

"Lab says that in this concentration it's virtually harmless. People swallow the shit, Dan. It's about as harmful as the dial of your watch."

"What have you gotten on the victims?"

"File check came back cold on the second guy, the professor. Somebody's gone over to the Library of Congress to give his books a read. Poor bastard had better like Pushkin."

"What about the Agency? You get anything there?"

"Langley bobbed and weaved at first. Seems Shevtsov got out of Russia on his own. The Agency learned about his escape at a press conference in Paris the same time everybody else did. They don't like to be surprised that way."

"Not a sparrow flies . . ." said Odom.

"It's a problem, Dan. Nobody knows very much about the network that got Shevtsov out. But since the Agency wasn't cut in, it has a reason to paint Shevtsov as a KGB plant. Langley's angle is that maybe he was killed by somebody on the right, maybe an émigré group, somebody who was onto him."

"I don't suppose they're committing themselves," said Odom.

"Don't have to. They just raise their eyebrows and blow smoke in our faces."

"Only an amateur would have played it the way Shevtsov did," said Odom. "The Soviets know that if they want to make a plant, they've got to get somebody on our side to sponsor him. The Agency or us. Somebody."

"That's how it's going to go down, Dan. Viktor Shevtsov on trial."

56

Odom sat in a chair across from Moll's desk and stretched his arms down between his legs like a basketball player on the bench.

"Raskin says he beat you in this morning."

"Did he?" said Moll.

"He seems to keep track of these things."

"He thinks that's what people mean when they accuse him of not knowing the score."

"He wanted you off the case last night," said Odom. "I jammed you down his throat. You deserve to know that, going in."

"I guess I'm supposed to thank you."

"You've got to know the lay of the land is all. Raskin's boss is afraid we're going to let this one slip away. Justice has been all over his case already. They're putting their money on the Russians."

"Always a safe bet," said Moll. "I don't play the odds myself."

He pushed aside the paperwork that had already accumulated, the 302 interview forms the agents had written up the night before, the lab report on the radioactive rags.

"Headquarters is going to want to go along with Justice in pushing the Soviet angle," said Odom.

"Raskin must have told them about the damned parking ticket."

"He's been burning up the wires," said Odom. "He's already had somebody in the Attorney General's office on the phone to give him a briefing. He's going around us, Hank."

"I don't think this one's going to unravel just because a cop on a motorcycle wrote a citation nobody can enforce," said Moll.

"You never know."

"My point exactly," said Moll. "Don't promise anything yet, OK?"

"The victim took a walk on them, didn't he? He knew their secrets. They had a beef, Hank."

"If the Russians come into it, we're going to have to wean Raskin off it and get somebody down from Justice, somebody who's been through the grinder before. This lad's idea of a tough investigation is when the guy before the grand jury takes the nickel."

"You mean the Russians don't depend on the Fifth Amendment?" said Odom. "Gosh, we're really in for it."

But Moll wasn't laughing.

"It's been a long time since I handled one of these, Dan," he said.

"You want to talk about it?"

"I thought maybe somebody was doing a number on me last night, once I saw what it was all about."

Odom went to the window and rested his knuckles on the ledge. They turned white as he bore down on them.

Moll leaned back in his swivel chair until it reached the balking point. They owed him an explanation. At least that.

"Why did you put me back on intelligence, Dan?"

Odom gazed out the window; it was not like him to avoid meeting your eyes.

"Look, Hank," he said, "the circumstances have changed. Headquarters is different since Mr. Hoover died. They're taking a lot of heat for what was done in the past. Maybe they're learning something about the unfairness of sons bearing the sins of the father, and maybe that has made them a little more sensitive about who should bear the sins of the sons."

"You've been pushing for this for a long time, haven't you?"

Odom turned to him but did not answer at first.

"You didn't wire together my rehabilitation overnight," said Moll. "You've been doing some heavy lobbying."

"I've kept Headquarters informed about Tom's progress," said Odom.

"You've been checking up on him?"

"Very low profile. I talked with a Brother James at the monastery."

"Lay off the boy, Dan. What happens if he finds out you're making calls about him? He's not all that steady on his pins, you know. He gets ideas. Look, I don't care what you do with me. I'm all played out. But stay away from Tom."

"Brother James seemed quite understanding."

"I didn't ask to be rehabilitated," said Moll.

"Look," said Odom. "At first I pushed this thing with Headquarters just because it was a matter of principle. That was before Tom got religion. They were treating you like they'd found out your uncle was a mobster. Guilt in the blood. I didn't like it. Show me something on Moll himself, I said. Show me a ten-cent fuckup on a voucher. Show me one time he went light on somebody he shouldn't have. But don't just tell me about the jerks his son's hanging around with. The boy's doped out; he doesn't know *who* the hell he is."

"Nice of you to say so," said Moll.

"Look, when the Shevtsov thing came up, it was just the leverage I needed to force a decision. They were ready to go along, and I put it to them this way: Who the hell else do I have who can do the job?"

"I appreciate the vote of confidence."

"I thought maybe you'd appreciate the challenge. You worked the original Bomb spy cases. You wrote the book. Well, here's the guy who was on the other end of the line, taking all that stolen information and turning it against us. You fought him, Hank. And now somebody's knocked him off. I thought you might want to be the one to close the file on Shevtsov."

Odom moved up next to Moll and wrapped his arm around Moll's shoulder.

"You're the best I've got," he said.

"Just stay away from Tom," said Moll.

"I always kind of liked the kid," said Odom as he turned and left Moll in the squad bay.

The room was deadly still except for the slow ticking of the radiators. All the other desks were neat down to the empty in-baskets. There were no coffee cups left out in the open, no ashes in the trays. But Moll's place was heaped with paper, great clots of it. He tried to systematize the mess—the 302 interview forms in one pile, the preliminary lab results in another. The old classified serials the Records Section had dug out on Shevtsov he locked away in the safe to catch up on later.

He was most interested in the business about the radioactive rags. His agents were on the street now getting a crash course in hospital administration and the handling of hazardous wastes. This lead intrigued him not only because it was something that might be traced but also because it seemed to be a clue to motive. Somebody had added the radioactive material to the bomb as a gesture. It had no other purpose, so far as Moll could gather. Whoever wanted to make the bomb scene hot to the Geiger counters had an idea in mind. And an idea was like a latent print. It could lead you to your man.

Moll was less enthusiastic about the car with diplomatic plates. For one thing, that was somebody else's problem. New York would have to try to trace who had been using the vehicle. And even if the driver turned out to be KGB, it wouldn't prove very much. They all were KGB as far as the Bureau was concerned.

For the time being, Moll figured he would concentrate on the political fringe groups. His contacts had withered, left and right, during his years of exile from intelligence work. But he knew how to revive them. You just had to get out on the street and spread the word. The city was a tangle of conspiracies, and it did not really matter where you began. Wherever you touched it, the web vibrated to its farthest moorings.

But first Moll had some internal business to attend to. John Sandquist, United States Attorney, was in Raskin's office when Moll got there. Sandquist stood with his arms folded across his chest as Raskin finished filling him in on the business about the parking ticket.

"Don't let me interrupt," said Moll.

"Sounds promising, Bob," said Sandquist, flipping a neatly styled shock of blond hair back into place with his fingers. Moll did not trust any man who felt he had to hide his ears.

"I got Agent Moll checking up on it last night," said Raskin.

"It takes time to get information out of the Soviets' UN Mission," said Moll. "It's been our experience that they do not respond well to subpoenas."

"I can understand that," said Sandquist.

"Right," said Raskin, and Moll could see that it galled him that his boss was blown by every breeze.

"I wanted to talk tactics for a minute," said Moll, "what we should release to the press. You'll want to hold a news conference soon, I trust."

"We hadn't discussed it," said Raskin. His eyes warned Moll away from the subject, but Moll went right on.

"The remarkable thing about this is that no one has claimed responsibility," he said. "I would have expected one of the groups to be on the phone to the newspapers or wire services by now. But not a peep."

"The Soviets don't advertise," said Raskin.

"No they don't," said Moll. "But it would be useful to try to draw out anybody who might have had a hand in this. That way if nobody does take the bait, it will strengthen the inference that the Russians were involved."

"What kind of bait?" Raskin demanded.

"I want to needle them a little," said Moll. "The way to get to terrorists is through their vanity. I've seen it done any number of ways. Usually the idea is to call them cowards, insult their manhood. But I'm not sure that works anymore."

"Well, I'm not going to go out there in front of the cameras and flatter them," said Sandquist, casting a look toward his subordinate, who would get the job if that was the way they decided it should be played.

"Nothing of the sort," Moll reassured him. "I want an announcement that the bombing was clearly the work of a madman. Somebody certifiably insane. There can be no other explanation. That sort of thing. I want you to make them hate the demented bastard."

"I can handle that," said Sandquist.

"I don't like it," said Raskin. "What if we do catch the guy and he pleads insanity? I'm going to have to prosecute this sonofabitch. And it won't be easy if we've already admitted that he's nuts."

"I thought you were sure it was the Soviets, Bob," said Sandquist, and Moll's estimation of the man rose a notch.

"I'm just saying," said Raskin.

"If you had to, you could put John here on the stand," said Moll. "Explain the circumstances, the strategy. The jury would eat it up. Spy stuff. You don't think John could handle being cross-examined on a thing like this?"

"Sure he could," said Raskin. "It's just a risk, that's all. I'd like to think about it first. Look into the law."

"What's to look into?" said Moll. "We'll draft a memo to the file right here. We can turn it over to the defense if it comes to that, scare them off. Write it so that it's clear we think we're dealing with a very rational criminal."

"Rational but crazy enough to stick his head up just because we insulted his emotional stability," said Raskin.

"He had his reasons for the killing. He wanted to make a political statement. We assumed this was his motive and so we put out the word that the murder was an act of madness. We made him see the whole point of the bombing slipping away from him. He had to step in. Just had to."

"It makes sense, Bob," said Sandquist. "It's worth a try."

"The press is going to push you," said Raskin. "They're going to want to know what you've got that makes you think the guy was nuts."

"They're only going to want to get the quote right," said Moll. "They aren't lawyers, John. You think these guys are going to stand there arguing that it's sane to blow up somebody's car in the middle of the university?"

"Moll's right," said Sandquist.

"Soon as possible," said Moll. "Let's get it all over the news."

"We can do it in an hour," said Sandquist. "The press is waiting downstairs already. We'll just need to set up the podium with the Justice Department seal."

"My guys will take care of it," said Moll. "Now maybe we should write that memo to file."

"Bob can work out the language," said Sandquist. "I don't see any reason to tie him up on the press conference, do you?"

"We're both pretty busy," said Moll.

"I can make time," said Raskin.

"I don't think that will be necessary," said Sandquist.

Jenkins bent slowly at the knees, leaning into the pain and then through it until his fingers touched the ground. The ache spread along the backs of his legs as he pried a few small stones from the sticky soil of the overgrown garden behind the flat. Damned joints. He had pushed himself too hard during the night.

He stayed on his haunches for a moment, took a breath, and heaved himself up in one great exertion. As the pain subsided, he rolled the mossy pebbles in his palm. Then he took aim and pitched them upward toward a shaded window.

"Get up there, you," he whispered.

Most fell short of the mark, clattering like rain on the scaly wooden frame and sill, but a few reached the target. They tapped sharply against the glass.

"Anybody still alive?" he shouted.

It was not exactly early. The traffic was busy on the street. He had gone shopping after getting off work. He had picked up the paper and read it over coffee at the deli, read every word about the bombing. He had tarried in his apartment to listen to the breathless news on the radio, then changed out of his uniform and waited a half hour so he could listen to it again. He had given his young friends plenty of time to sleep it off, whatever it was.

"Up and at 'em!" he yelled. The shade did not stir.

When he had arrived at work the night before, he was running on adrenaline. The Russian was dead, and he was as alive as he had ever been. The fog was dense, great choking pools of it. At the plant they thought he was nervous for the same reason they were, for fear the bomber would strike again. Never know what the crazies will try, they said. They told him to double the frequency of his rounds. The cops laid on extra patrols. A man at the station-house expected him to check in by phone every half hour. Anything at all and you just give a holler, Jenkins, they said.

He told them they did not need to worry about the bombing,

but they did not take him seriously. They laughed and said they admired his courage. Fools. Courage isn't in what a man says or feels. It only shows itself in what he is willing to *do*.

In fact, he had been afraid during the night, but not of another attack. It was the fog itself that frightened him. He could not see the dingy residences that ringed the perimeter, oblivious of the danger behind the plant's windowless walls. He could not see the lights in the apartments burning late except diffused to a pallid glow in the haze. Sounds, too, were shrouded. He could not locate them precisely: the slam of a car door, angry voices, the hiss of an engine. Headlamps swept the compound like beams of searchlights, and even though he was the guard, his instinct was to hide.

Once an hour he made his rounds and then returned to the little shack overlooking the main entrance to the building and placed his call. Inside, the space heater ticked and glowed. He pulled off his heavy gloves and opened his wool uniform coat. He kept the conversation short.

"This is Jenkins at Nufab. Nothing going on here."

"Looks OK from this end, too," the cop would say. "Dead dog in the alley. Somebody doesn't respect his wife the way he should. The kids are tucked snugly in bed, dreaming narcotic dreams. All is well."

Jenkins had walked his post dutifully all night, tiring himself on the long, lonely circuit, inserting a key in each watchbox and turning it right on time to deactivate the automatic alarm. He walked through the smoky fog, gazing up at the jagged wire, not only because this was his job but also because it was his curse to know that the only antidote to fear is motion and that even constant motion could not leave behind the memory of smoke in the nostrils, could not breach the coiling wire of the past.

"Come on, Sib!" he shouted up at the window above him.

As he walked the dark perimeter of the plant the night before, he had directed his mind away from the violence and concentrated on the young, his purpose, the proper aim of fear. Jenkins had moved through the suffocating smoke, counting off the watchboxes, each marked with a squat black figure on a yellow field. It was a shattered cross that no longer promised an unseen agent of mercy but instead warned of an invisible agent of harm. He had walked and walked and thought of courage.

"You've got me worried down here," he yelled. "I'm about to do something rash."

The flyblown shade rattled against the pane. Then it rose in angry fits and starts. Her worn, child's face appeared in the window. Sibyl looked down upon him without a sign of welcome. Then she motioned him around to the front.

"There's a good girl," he said and picked up his bag.

She had unlocked the front door by the time he shuffled up to it. He heard her barefoot steps retreating above him as he came inside. Leaning over before mounting the first flight, he picked up a wad of damp cardboard stuffed into a corner. A beer carton. It was surely not theirs. They only took wine, and then only because it gave the other chemicals a certain edge. Jenkins carried the piece of trash with him up the stairs. On the landing there was more garbage, but he left it. He did not want to impose his fastidiousness upon them; they would not entertain his visits if they thought he was judging them. They took him as a harmless old eccentric who simply liked to hang around them to slake his loneliness. Slightly nuts, full of strange talk, but funny sometimes, definitely *very* weird. *Much madness is divinest sense to the discerning eye.* It was the way he allowed himself to be seen, and it was the way he saw them, too. His strategies of approach arrayed against all their desperate strategies of avoidance. A mutuality of madness. A family.

"I'm not interrupting anything, am I?" he said as he stepped into their hallway.

"Funny," said Sibyl, her voice from another room, phlegmy and low. It was impossible to imagine interrupting them at anything come morning. "In here, Pops. You might as well join us."

The apartment was big enough. But it looked as if it hadn't been fixed up since the day it was built. Yellowed wallpaper with a quaint, faded pattern of flowers. Water stains from leaks long since patched and forgotten. Blackened brass light fixtures with dusty rose-glass shades. Cast-off furniture. Worn rugs scrounged from somebody's trash.

He moved through the hallway, past the room where they had their monstrous old bed, disheveled in the gray morning light, past the room where the boy did his tinkering when his hands were steady enough. He was glad they could not see him as he surveyed these things, for it was hard to restrain his eyes from revealing his feelings, and today there was so much he did not dare to show.

When he reached the kitchen, they were both seated silently at the beaten-up table, shades still down. They hid from the day.

"Hard night?" he asked, lifting his bag to the counter next to the stove.

"What's that you've got there, Pops?" Sibyl asked.

"Just some junk I picked up," he said, stuffing the cardboard into an overflowing wastebasket in the cabinet beneath the sink. A rotten odor like the stink of something dead in water reached up to him. He turned his head and closed the doors, but it stayed in his nostrils.

The boy barely raised his head from his trembling hands. The girl stood and stretched. Her long T-shirt rode up, revealing the panties that were all she wore on the bottom. When she dropped her arms, the shirt settled back over her breasts, and she pulled it down tight with both hands, stretching it until her nipples poked out—dark, broken buttons beneath the cotton.

"David really crashed last night," she said. "I mean crashed and burned. Pow! He came home wired. I mean really wired to blow. Then he came down hard."

"Aren't you rather cold in those flimsy things?" Jenkins asked. He was aware how different his language was from theirs. The King's English he had learned in school overlay the darker consonants of his mother tongue. As much as his age, this held him distant from them. They thought he came from a different world.

"You getting hot, Pops?" she said with her sweetest, most taunting smile as she stretched out her thin, child-woman's body before him again. He looked over at David, hoping that he would assert some claim over her. But David was off somewhere else, still falling, not ready to come up for air.

"I brought breakfast," Jenkins said, and he began to pull the makings from his bag. Eggs, fresh-baked bread, coffee, a small ring of sausage. He always left them food, plenty of it. And it vanished between visits. Despite appearances, they did seem to eat from time to time. He did not know whether it was when they were high or low that their appetite came. In the mornings when he visited, they rarely did more than pick at the meal. Their impulses were chemical, for gratification or punishment. And Jenkins's eggs and butter and wheat were not nearly strong enough to restore the balance.

"I'll need a pot," he said, "a fairly large one. For the *kiełbasa*." He held the sausage ring up to show them.

"What's that?" Sibyl asked.

Jenkins dug a deep, cast-iron pot out of the oven, then he pulled a can of cleanser from his bag and went to work at the sink.

"Ask David," he said. "It's a delicacy."

Jenkins scoured the pot clean and filled it up with tap water. The sink itself was a mess. He took a few passes at places where

65

clots of grease had hardened on the chipped porcelain. Sibyl moved next to David and shook his shoulder.

"Hey. Wake up, Mighty Mouse. Pops here says you know what this funny-looking circle of shit is supposed to be."

David looked up, his eyes so withdrawn into the dark hollows of his skull that you might have thought he had been beaten.

"Pops says it's a delicacy," Sibyl said.

"It's Polish," David managed to say. "It's OK."

"Maybe I'd better give him a little lift," the girl said to Jenkins, and for just an instant she seemed genuinely concerned. "I'm a regular watchamacallit, a regular wet nurse when he's like this. I've got just what the doctor ordered."

She found a cellophane bag of brightly colored pills in a drawer and fished out two of the same color. Then she went to the refrigerator and pulled out an open can of sweet soda. She set the can and the capsules in front of him.

"We'll start him out easy," she said. "I've already had mine. When I heard you throwing rocks against the window, Pops, it was like a message in some kind of Morse code or something telling me, honey, it's time to get stoned."

Jenkins turned away from them and dropped the sausage into the water boiling on the stove. The gas sputtered orange from all the grime.

"Mellow is all," she said. "Don't worry, Pops. We're just trying to mellow out a little bit here. From where we were last night, everyplace else seems high. Ain't that right, Mighty Mouse?"

"Lord, have mercy," said the boy.

Jenkins turned to see him lift the pills between his bridged fingers and bring them to his lips like a wafer.

"There you go, Mighty Mouse," said the girl. "The dawn of another day."

Jenkins watched her as she put her hand on David's shoulder with a proprietary smile that made it clear she knew that no matter how little she had to offer the boy, it was what he wanted. Jenkins caught her eye and acknowledged her power. It hurt him, but he did it. His only chance with David was at her sufferance. He did not blame her for what David had become. She had not brought him down; she had met him there. Her father had pushed her out of his house at sixteen, and she had lighted on David. He had taken her into his own mysterious suffering, and she had staked a territorial claim upon it.

When Jenkins had first met her, only days after she moved in, she had been afraid of him. She hid away in closed rooms out of sight as he and David talked. But over time she realized what Jenkins had known all along: that pain is specific, generation by generation; it sunders as powerfully as it binds. And because of this, she had more influence over David than Jenkins could ever hope to have. If there were any expelling to be done, it was she who could drive him away. So she had become bold, flaunting her body, bringing out into the open the drugs that were another form of degradation she shared with David to Jenkins's exclusion. What made it all the harder for Jenkins was the remarkable cunning of the girl. She knew that if ever David came out of his daze, they would separate. They had nothing in common save their sorrow.

"Now for the bread," said Jenkins. "It ought to be warmed."

"You feeling any better now, Mighty Mouse?"

"It's happening," David said.

Jenkins cleared the clutter from the oven and lighted the gas with a wooden match.

"There," he said.

Then he took the frying pan he had brought with him, cut a cube of butter, and held the pan high over the fire while it melted down.

"How many eggs will you have then?" he asked.

Sibyl sidled up to him and stood there, making sure her breast lay lightly against his arm where he could feel it moving with her breath.

"I have an appetite," she said.

"Two eggs for Sibyl," he said, moving away from her. "David?"

"Nothing."

"Try one," said Jenkins, "just to humor an old man."

When he finished counting out the portions, there were half a dozen eggs left in the carton. He put them away in the refrigerator, where he found an intolerable piece of moldy cheese. He removed it and discreetly deposited it in the trash. Then he went back to the refrigerator and surveyed the rest of its contents, making a mental note of what he should bring on the next trip and how he should structure the meal around those items so that David and Sibyl would not have grounds to claim he was patronizing them. The only natural sense they retained was pride. They refused to admit that they needed someone to care for them. But they were so addled that the connections in the brain which led a body to water and sustenance seemed to have corroded out. They had no sense of what was good for them and an unfailing instinct for what would cause them harm.

Was this why David was so fascinated by science? Jenkins had first caught up with him on a visit to the library. He followed David inside and sat across from him at one of the long wooden tables. David plunged into a technical journal, and Jenkins skimmed another. Their first conversation was about the abstract symmetry of quarks. David accepted Jenkins's interest as if the two of them were kin.

But their approaches to the subject were as different as their ages. Jenkins read science in order to understand and defeat it. He joined David in fiddling with the high-tech gear, even kept an electronics workbench in a corner of his own apartment, but only because he saw some instrumental value in the circuits he broke down and altered. David threw himself into the thing with a kind of painful mysticism, like a yogi testing himself against fire.

Jenkins beat the eggs with a fork in a plastic bowl, then blended in a touch of sweet cream. He poured the mixture into the frying pan. The sizzling butter gave off a warm smell that overcame the mustiness of the flat.

"There now," he said. "Take a whiff of that."

Bent over the stove, he began to sweat. He pulled off his flannel shirt and worked in the lighter cotton one he wore layered against chill. The sweet aroma of the bread rose up to him, the fleshy odor of the boiling sausage, and for a moment it was just as it once had been in his own home, many years ago, before the flames.

"Don't be fooled by his eyes, Pops," said the girl. "A doper's eyes are as big as the sky. But there's only one thing he's looking for. Ain't that right, Mighty Mouse?"

Jenkins felt cut off from their generation, and not because age had brought him wisdom. If anything, Jenkins's generation was the more innocent. At least it still had memories of boyhood, of the sweet certainty that life goes on. His own nightmares had been populated by ghouls and monsters, not the true images of film and photographs. And when he had awakened in the night, it was still possible for those in whom he believed to comfort him and tell him it was all in his imagination, it was not real.

For a time during the worst years after Korea, Jenkins had worked as a janitor in an elementary school in the suburbs of Detroit. He had seen the little boys and girls marching into the multipurpose room at the sound of the air-raid siren, lining up in long, squirming rows, bowing down, hands over heads. They drilled in the proper posture for dying. He had heard the teachers telling them in flat, unembarrassed voices that the first thing to remember when the bomb exploded was to turn away from the light. He had listened to the little children talking about it in the halls. Some of them cried, but most did not. You wept only for what you had lost, not for things you had never known.

Age and experience were all turned around. It was the young who had missed their youth, the old who still hung on to its nurturing memories. He sometimes tried to talk to David about these things. He wanted to persuade David that he must not surrender, that it was folly to think you could run away. But he always came up against a barrier of distrust. How could the young believe in those who offered so little solace? The failure was in the utter insufficiency of every saving lie.

"My father is very big on reality," David had said once. "He likes to think he is strong enough to carry anything. But it's just too much for me. Lead. Heavy metal. All the new elements we've made. Sometimes I feel like a lump of the stuff, spitting off energy, but too weak to move under all that mass."

This was the difference between the generations. In the years between them, all the sustaining images had been destroyed. The nice parables of virtue and reward had been replaced by the horrible question of whether the living would envy the dead. By the modern alchemy, even the golden rule had been transmogrified. Prepare to do unto others what you fear they may do unto you; mutually assured destruction. Gold into lead.

"I'm ready for you here if you want to bring some plates," Jenkins said.

Sibyl found a few on the counter, gave them an inadequate rinse, and wiped them with a dirty towel. David had finally hauled himself up to full height in his chair. Jenkins spooned him out a good portion and carried it to the table. David looked down at the steamy yellow fluff as if it were a sickness. He pushed the plate away.

"You've got to eat something," said Jenkins. Sibyl had already plunged noisily into hers.

"Nothing needs nothing," said David.

"I'm nobody. Who are you?" said Jenkins, hoping David would recognize the words. "Are you nobody, too?"

The young man rewarded him with the smallest, most furtive of glances. He picked a corner off the slice of bread and tried it warily in his mouth.

"How about some *kiełbasa*, David?" Jenkins asked.

The boy seemed to be coming up out of the hole. He sampled the sausage.

"I have milk or coffee," said Jenkins, building on this small victory. "Which will it be?"

"Maybe I could use a little coffee," said David, "with milk."

Jenkins poured and David held the cup. The color was returning to his face. He turned in his chair and raised the blind, then he squinted out into the fog.

"Did you hear all the commotion last night?" Jenkins asked. "Quite an uproar."

"We try not to hear nothing," said Sibyl.

"That's something of a challenge," said Jenkins. The young man looked at him curiously.

"Somebody blew up a car over at the university," he went on. "Killed a Russian scientist."

David was silent.

"Mighty Mouse isn't too quick on the uptake after a bad night," said Sibyl.

"Are you sure Shevtsov is dead?" said David. Jenkins was pleased that he remembered the name.

"That's what they're saying on the news," said Jenkins. "Shevtsov and another man. A professor at the university. He was driving the car."

"Who the hell is this guy anyway?" Sibyl asked, between bites of food.

"Ask him," said David. "He knows all about it."

"What's this shit about?" Sibyl demanded, her eyes darting between them.

"Take it easy, Sibyl," said Jenkins. He was sorry he had not waited to tell the news to David alone. "Shevtsov was the father of the Soviet Bomb. He defected to the United States, became a hero. He even won a prize for peace."

"And somebody just went and killed him?" she said.

Jenkins snapped his fingers. "Just like that," he said.

"Far out," said Sibyl. "Like that other guy, Martin Luther King."

"Nothing of the sort," Jenkins said. "The young have no memory. The Russians are liars."

"You hit a nerve, girl," said David.

"The man had everyone fooled," said Jenkins. "They're good at that. They act like they're going to save your world, then they stab you in the back."

"What's he talking about, David?"

"He has a thing about Shevtsov," said David. "We've been through it all before."

"I've had experience with Russians," said Jenkins. He was calmer now, more wary. "Take it from me. The father of the Russian Bomb meant us no good."

Jenkins watched them for any sense of recognition, but they were too numbed to respond.

"It was quite a scene last night," he said. "Crowds of people milling around the wreckage. Fire engines. Ambulances. I hadn't seen anything like it since the war."

"Were you actually there?" said David.

"I heard about it on the radio when I got up for work," Jenkins said. "I went right over. I kind of thought I might run into you."

"We never go nowhere," complained the girl.

"They have any idea who did it?" asked David.

"Who gives a shit?" said Sibyl.

"Sibyl is perfectly apolitical," said David. "Like she said, she doesn't like listening to nothing."

You never knew when David was going to pick up on what you were saying. You had to be careful. He could fool you; his blank expression and silence could make you push further than you wanted to go. Then he would turn around and give it back to you, point by point and all the implications.

"They don't seem to have any idea who the culprit is," Jenkins said.

"Culprit," said Sibyl. "What is this, anyway? Some old Roy Rogers movie? Culprit."

Jenkins forced himself to shrug.

David leaned back in his chair and clasped his hands behind his head.

"I remember once when I was in school," he said, "the teacher asked if anybody could tell a story with a moral. Little Ricky Grady raised his hand. The teacher looked around for somebody else because she knew what she could expect from him. But nobody else's hand was up. 'OK, Ricky,' she said. 'Tell us your story.' Ricky stood up at his desk. 'Roy Rogers was riding into town,' he said, 'when a bandit stopped him on the road and demanded all his money. Roy Rogers pulled out his six-gun and blew the guy's head off.' Then Ricky sat down. 'What kind of story is that?' the teacher said. 'There isn't any moral.' And Ricky said, 'Oh yes there is. Don't fuck with Roy Rogers.' "

Sibyl laughed convulsively and poked David in the shoulder.

"Outasight," she said. "The teacher must have just shit."

David smiled as Jenkins drew back from them.

"It's an old joke," David said. "I don't know what made me think of it."

"It's nothing to joke about," said Jenkins.

Sibyl stopped laughing and turned to him.

"If you don't like it, you can just leave, you know," she said.

"Don't be too hard on him," said David. "Maybe he has his reasons."

"Hard on *him*," she said. Her hands were at her hair, worrying it. "He talks about the guy who made the Bomb. But look where he works. It's a death house."

"Nufab does not make weapons," Jenkins said softly.

"Fucking poison," she said.

"It's all right, Sibyl," said David.

"No, it's not all right," she said. "Not. Not. Not." She was up on her feet now, pacing. Her hands were flat against her temples now, her face contorted.

"Don't, Sibyl," said David. "We were doing so well."

"Then he ruined it!" she screamed.

"Maybe I'd better go," said Jenkins.

David tried to take her hand. She wrenched it away.

"You say you're so hung up on it," she said. "You talk about how it killed your mother, how much you hate it. Then you let the poison right in the door."

She broke and ran into the hallway. David followed her. Jenkins heard their voices from the bedroom as he began cleaning up after the meal.

"You don't know *what* you hate!"

Sibyl's shrill voice came through the wall like the blade of an ax. Then she burst from the bedroom and fled, her steps pounding down the stairs. Jenkins washed the dishes and pans. He heard David moving in the hall.

Jenkins finished up, packed away the frying pan in his bag, and picked up his coat. He stepped softly into the hallway and stopped outside an open door. Inside, David was bent over an intricate array of electronic gear. Soldering irons, circuit boards, transistors, each tiny chip embalmed in gaudy wax. Wires of various lengths were organized by color.

"What's that you're working on?" Jenkins asked.

72

David was startled.

"I shouldn't have disturbed you," said Jenkins. "I was just about to leave."

"It's all right."

David reached up and switched on the elaborate radio Jenkins had helped him build. The lights behind the meters and switches came on. It was a receiver powerful enough to pull in signals from all over the globe. He could pick up airplanes in flight, the tick and jumble of encrypted messages, official lies in every tongue. But all that came from it now was the sound of a low, moaning guitar.

"I understood about Shevtsov," he said. "I understood it the first time you told me about him."

"I thought you would," said Jenkins softly.

"I was just trying not to get Sibyl upset. She doesn't know any better. She's like all the others. They fix on something they can see, smoking chimneys, nuclear power, the extinction of some rare kind of bird. The other danger is just too big, so they put it all on something else."

"But you are different."

"I'm afraid for everything," said David.

Jenkins moved up next to him and picked up a long strand of wire.

"You can do such fine work, David," he said.

"You have to work in close to what you hate," said David. "That's right, isn't it?" He turned to Jenkins, his eyes ablaze. "You closed the distance with it."

"I've been known to run away."

David was on his feet now, pacing the room. His hand fluttered up to his face, something flushed from the flames.

"You're glad that Shevtsov was killed," he said.

Jenkins went to the window. He looked out over the fog-obscured street. He did not want to lie to David. He needed to acknowledge certain things, even if others had to be hidden.

"Yes, David," he said. "I suppose I am."

David collapsed into his chair and drew a long breath.

"What's happening to us, Pops?" he said.

Jenkins took the young man's shoulder and held him. The old were the innocent; they could not comfort the young. David twisted away.

"You don't know, do you?" David demanded.

"I'm sorry."

David's body went slack, as if he had taken a physical blow.

Then the telephone broke the silence. It rang again and again, but the boy did not move. Finally, Jenkins went to the living room and found the phone under some blankets in a corner.

"Hello," he said.

A woman's voice came on the line.

"This is the *Herald*," she said. "Stan Majors calling."

"The man is so important he can't dial his own phone?"

"I put the calls," the woman said. "It's my job. Do I have the wrong number or what?"

"You have the right number," said Jenkins, and he put the phone on the floor.

David had not budged. He just sat there where Jenkins had left him, slumped in a chair.

"You'd better talk to him, David," he said. "It's your father."

Moll did not have a chance to get into the main Shevtsov file until after the press conference. Sandquist had been quite convincing when he described Shevtsov's murder as motiveless—the act of a madman. Just as Moll had predicted, none of the reporters had quibbled. But if they had thought about it, they would have known that even madness has its motive. And if you wanted to understand it, you had to begin with its object.

The early memoranda in the file only mentioned Shevtsov in passing. He was just one name among many, a faceless scientist the Americans knew was working on their crash program to build the Bomb. The main texts were devoted to the primary concern: how to stop them.

Moll had been a part of that effort, and it had been righteous. He remembered the way they had fooled themselves into thinking that the basic knowledge could somehow be guarded, that men could hide what nature had revealed, as if it were the identity of an operative behind enemy lines.

Once the Soviets exploded their device, this illusion vanished. Information about who had been instrumental in their success began to leak out, and attention zeroed in on Shevtsov. The Agency, and to a lesser extent the Bureau, had gathered quite a dossier on him.

He was born into the revolution, a member of the first generation that knew nothing of the old, reactionary ways. His parents had lived in Moscow, and as freethinkers, they had welcomed the end of the old order that had bound them to a life of obsequious clerkship. Though Shevtsov's father never rose very high in the Party, his enthusiastic obedience meant that important men took notice of him. And this cleared the way for his two sons' talents to be recognized and nurtured. Shevtsov's brother Yuri excelled in athletics; he was singled out as a leader, a fine example of Soviet youth. In the beginning young Viktor's genius showed itself in music. By the time he was five years old, he was already able to play the simpler classics. His parents must have been astounded by the way he could learn a piece overnight. They probably did not realize that for a mind such as his, it was not so much a feat of memory as an ability to recognize patterns that, once seen, were as unforgettable as the simplest children's rhyme.

As Shevtsov's mother worked with him on the piano, his father introduced him to the more abstract relationships of mathematics. The boy took to this discipline immediately, and his father enrolled him in the best technical school in Moscow. Meanwhile, Yuri prepared for the military officer corps.

There was not much information available about Shevtsov's student days. But it was easy for Moll to imagine what he was like: a driven, humorless young man caught up in the abstruse moments of higher math and physics. Moll had known people like that when he was in college. They were not the men on the GI Bill, but rather the young ones straight out of high school who had never known anything else. It was one of the curses of music and mathematics that the mind could be grasped by them early. They required none of the more mature forms of knowledge. And they could isolate a man, deform him, leaving him a kind of *idiot savant*, comfortable in the sphere of pure thought but oblivious of the world. The strongest antidote, of course, was war.

Shevtsov had not been required to fight, but nobody in western Russia was free of the consequences as the Germans pressed forward. He lost his parents to the cold. For more than two years he thought his brother had been killed in the terrible retreat. He went hungry as he fled the approaching guns. He saw the broken bodies of childhood friends who had been wounded at the front and felt the vulnerability of flesh and sovereignty. Even though he never fired a rifle, he must have learned the same lesson Moll had learned in battle—that as soon as you draw a line you must defend it, that integrity is just another way of defining a target.

Once the Red Army regained the initiative, the word came that Yuri was still alive. And Shevtsov was transferred from the laboratory where he had been working on radar and sent to a special unit outside Moscow. There, among the pine groves and potato fields, the deprivations of the war came to an end. This was Laboratory 2 of the Academy of Sciences, and it was dedicated to nuclear research. Shevtsov had followed all the developments before the war. He had read with interest the journals reporting strange new concepts of energy and mass. Compared with them, the old ways of thinking about the universe were as dull as a sentimental folk tune compared with the cold elegance of Schoenberg or Berg.

Laboratory 2 was run by Igor Kurchatov, whose skill was not so much scientific as bureaucratic. This was all the better for young men like Shevtsov, for it meant that their physical needs were taken care of and their intellectual endeavors given free rein. They lacked many of the resources they needed, but they did not want for bread and comfort. None of them, of course, knew for sure that the Americans were barreling toward the development of an atomic weapon. But as intelligence and captured scientists reached them from Germany, they concluded independently that such a thing was possible. So when the bombs were dropped on Hiroshima and Nagasaki, it was merely the confirmation of a hypothesis.

Curious the way that event defined the members of Moll's generation. The mushroom cloud was an inkblot that led men to reveal the deepest secrets of their hopes and fears. To some it marked the beginning of an American Century. To others it was a mark of Cain. Moll remembered vividly what he had been doing when he learned that the Bomb had exploded and brought the enemy to its knees. He had been on the docks on Saipan, where his unit was building back up to strength for the last big push. Huge freighters loaded ton after ton of supplies. And they were all bound for the mainland of Japan.

The soldiers, of course, knew nothing of the existence of the Bomb. An invasion seemed inevitable. Moll had been through enough already that he did not allow his imagination to play consciously upon the idea. He tried not to think about how bitter the fighting would be. He did not mix with the new replacements because he already saw them as dead men. He sank down into himself, and he spent his free time on the docks just gazing out to sea.

Then one day a GI raced up to him so excited that Moll was sure the man was drunk.

"It's over!" said the GI. "The fucker's over!"

"You're nuts," said Moll, pushing him away.

"It's true. It was on the radio. We have a secret weapon. Blew two Jap cities away."

Now, decades later, Moll still recalled the way the feeling welled up in him then; the pressure was almost sexual in his belly, a longing. It was not that he believed he was going to survive. That dawned on him slowly, long after the end of the war was official. No, it was more like waking up, opening your eyes for the first time, squinting against the light.

Moll did not know how many babies were sired the night the surrender was announced. But no matter where they were, men found women. And ever since that day, Moll shuddered whenever he heard anyone refer to the baby-boom children, conceived by soldiers saved by the Bomb, as a generation of peace.

In other places, minds were set upon different imperatives. At Laboratory 2 the news of the American bomb was met with an attitude of curiosity and respect. But in Moscow Stalin realized that the world had been fundamentally changed. While in Laboratory 2 the proof that theory could be translated into practical power was a vindication of the nationhood of science, in Moscow a narrower sovereignty was at stake.

Orders came down from Stalin that nothing should be spared in the effort to catch up with the Americans. This brought on a sense of panic. Resources and pressure were brought to bear. The gas-diffusion technique for separating U-235 was given priority despite its lack of intellectual appeal. Men were deployed against the problems of compression and yield the way soldiers are thrown against an enemy gun emplacement. They battered the wall with a sheer mass of computation. Fundamental questions were left unanswered, even unasked, as all emphasis was placed upon design and technique. The bureaucracy, which until then had served to free them, now made nonnegotiable demands.

Shevtsov thrived on the new urgency. While others let themselves be swept into the narrow, unrewarding business of endless calculation, Shevtsov managed to stay just far enough above this to see the whole. He had faith in the serendipity of discovery, in both his own insights and the fruits of the more unscientific investigations of the KGB.

During the long debriefings after his defection, Shevtsov made quite a point of minimizing the significance of the secrets stolen from the Americans. He said the Russian scientists had come up with solutions to most of the design difficulties on their own. Since the emphasis was on speed, the first Soviet device did use the American methods—but Shevtsov said it was only a matter of time.

This contention touched off a spirited interagency debate within the United States intelligence community. The Agency argued that Shevtsov was lying, that independent assessments had demonstrated that the bomb espionage had gained the Russians some of their basic insights in the development of the weapon. The Bureau questioned what motive Langley thought Shevtsov would have for duplicity on this point, even if he were a Soviet plant. It was ancient history. The individuals who had figured in the spy rings had long since been disposed of. All the technology was now available to any enterprising physics student. No Soviet agent would risk casting doubt upon himself over such a senseless point, the Bureau argued. At worst it was only the vanity of a scientist that his own achievements have been independent. But this did not satisfy Langley, which fired back a long memorandum reminding the Bureau of Hoover's many statements on the manifest dangers of Soviet espionage. If the idea that nothing was lost to Fuchs and the Rosenbergs gained currency, Langley concluded, this would tend to discredit the counterintelligence effort, with adverse budgetary impact.

Moll thought the whole controversy was beside the point. Common sense told him that if Shevtsov had a mission in the United States, it was more important than revisionist history. Whether abetted by the Soviets or not, the defection of a Prizewinner was a bold stroke. The cause it served had to be of explosive significance. Moll plunged on through the file.

When the first Soviet device was detonated in the Kazakhstan deserts in 1949, it had been like a great, collective sigh of relief for the Soviet state. Shevtsov was on hand to watch the test, and he described his feelings in later writings: "As the fireball rose in the sky, it was a bursting new dawn. A man could not look upon such a display of power and still believe in the continuity of human events. The earth trembled under our fists. The nature of things had been revealed, and in the revelation, changed."

Moll could not argue with Shevtsov about that. The weapons magnified every flaw in the human character, made decent people wonder whether their principles were worth the risk. Images of apocalypse corrupted the future, ate away at the young. The Bomb drew a line in history, and there was no going back.

Witnessing the A-bomb test may have begun Shevtsov's transformation, or his awakening may have been the most elaborate cover the Soviets had ever devised. But before he turned away from the abstract discipline of his youth, there was one more physical idea that burned in Shevtsov. He knew that once a fission device was perfected, man had within his reach the ultimate force. He could fuse matter, achieve the power of the sun.

By then he had already reached the top of the hierarchy of Soviet scientists. A relatively indifferent Party member, his perquisites still rivaled those of the most powerful Politburo member. He was known to have vanished for nearly two months after the successful test, and the explanation he gave upon his defection was rather vague. He said he had gone to visit his brother, but he could not recall exactly where. Yuri had risen to the rank of colonel and was assigned to work that required the utmost loyalty. Shevtsov often became restless under questioning about Yuri, and the Bureau attributed this to concern about what damage Shevtsov's flight had done to his brother. All that was known for sure about Yuri was that after the war he was involved in the administration of what has come to be called the Gulag Archipelago.

Once Shevtsov returned from his visit with Yuri, there was little time to enjoy the dacha, the car and driver, the grand office in Moscow. Shevtsov buried himself in the remote laboratory complex and cut himself off from everything but the single task at hand. And to the astonishment of everyone, he brought forth an H-bomb. In a few short years he had caught up with the Americans in what he later called the "race to extinction." He had reached the limits of abstract reasoning. Nature had yielded in a single, angry flash the only secrets that mattered to him, and he left the laboratory to contemplate the consequences of what he had done.

At first his mind naturally turned to technical matters, the dangers of radiation to plant and animal life. He was the author of that era's most compendious examination of the risk. Though the data were deeply flawed because of security constraints, Shevtsov mounted an effective argument both as to the statistical probability of injury from fallout and the mechanism by which radioactivity damaged the living cell by altering its fragile chemistry.

From here on out, it was possible to see every item in the file in two distinct ways. Shevtsov's progress from the architect of weaponry to the apostle of peace could have been either a genuine personal transformation or a triumph of disinformation. It all depended upon your angle of vision, what you feared the most.

But one thing was objectively certain: Though Shevtsov had attained a leading position in the Academy of Sciences, his material utility to the regime had played itself out. The practical imperatives were now in a field in which his skills had little bearing. The Soviets had the weapons, and it was time to perfect the means of delivering them. The obsession with the heavy mass of matter gave way to a fanatical interest in the weightlessness of space.

It was at this time that the first of Shevtsov's essays began to appear in the West. They were modest pieces, picked up from Russian publications, and they found their way into pretentious little journals in London, Paris, and New York. Later, when curiosity about the father of the Russian Bomb began to take hold, the newspapers and mass-circulation magazines hurried translations into print. Shevtsov's tone became increasingly strident as he argued that the new weapons had made the ancient idea of sovereignty an evil and dangerous anachronism. He was universal in his condemnation of dependence on this power. He became a common scold. In the West the novelty of the implied criticism he made of the Soviet state obscured the fact that his analysis applied equally to the free-world alliance, where words still had force.

Moll was not surprised that this was precisely the gloss put on Shevtsov's work by the analysts at Langley. They were deeply concerned about the growing public interest in Shevtsov and certain other Communist writers. What alarmed Langley most was the surface appeal of the humanistic arguments they made, the deceptive universality of their ideals. The poets and essayists might succeed where no Soviet army ever could, the Agency argued. They might penetrate our borders and subvert our hearts and minds with the notion that at bottom we were all really one, that the balance of terror was a balance of evil, equal on both sides, and that the differences in the way we described the world—those irreducible differences of ideology—were really no more significant than the case structure and conjugations of our native tongues.

It took almost a decade before Shevtsov's writing had advanced so far that the Soviet state was ready to act. The break came with the publication within the Soviet Union of an essay in which Shevtsov announced his theory that the strategy of mutually assured destruction was a fundamental violation of human rights.

It turned the population of the world into hostages to the designs of the great powers, he argued. It deprived men of freedom as surely as the work camps or the jailer's chains. His essay drew heavily upon his study of the physical consequences of nuclear war, and it predicted with scientific elegance the extinction of the species if such a war ever broke out. It was an uncompromising document, and it should have set off alarm bells in the minds of the Soviet censors. Yet there it was in the files, in the original Cyrillic version as published in the *Journal of the Academy of Sciences* and as translated by the literalists at Langley. The *Journal* was, of course, quickly recalled. But not before a number of copies had been spirited out of the Soviet Union. In fact, even before it was officially published, it had been obtained by the Agency's contingent in the American Embassy under circumstances that only added to Langley's speculation that the whole affair was orchestrated by the Soviets to promote Shevtsov's name in the West.

At this point the debate between the Agency and the State Department (with Bureau encouragement) became quite sharp. But by the time Shevtsov won the Prize and appeared in Paris with only the vaguest explanation of how he had gotten there, the temptation to believe in him had become overwhelming. Langley's doubts were pushed aside.

And even the Agency never disputed that a great change had come over Shevtsov's material circumstances in the Soviet Union before his flight. He was publicly stripped of his perquisites and honors. He moved into a tiny flat, was barred from any further scientific research. But he continued to write, and the works continued to appear in the West. This was during a time of relative calm in relations between the Soviet Union and the United States. Western journalists, who took advantage of the thaw to move freely in Soviet society, were the conduit by which these writings found their way into print. No one doubted that the government could have silenced Shevtsov if it had chosen to. But there was profound disagreement about why this was not done.

There had never been a satisfactory explanation of just how Shevtsov finally escaped. He dropped out of sight in Moscow the month before he showed up in Paris. The Western correspondents who had become accustomed to visiting him were told by intermediaries that he could not see them, and they took this as evidence that the authorities had cracked down. Despite pleas by Shevtsov's friends that it would only put him in peril if the correspondents wrote about him, they began to speculate in print that he had been taken into custody. Even if Shevtsov had initially managed to go into hiding unnoticed, the newspaper stories certainly would have raised the hue and cry. Still, he crossed the border with his dying wife and all his nontechnical papers, and nobody knew where or how.

Accustomed as Moll had become to dealing with the optical illusions of counterintelligence work, he could not get a fix on Shevtsov. If the Russian scientist was nothing other than what he appeared to be, then it was plausible to assume a Soviet role in his murder. But ever since Shevtsov had arrived in the United States, the man had been touring about, giving his dispiriting speeches about the consequences of a nuclear exchange. Though his talks were couched in the language of morality and human rights and did not spare the Soviet Union condemnation for its part in the terror, you could easily see them as a threat more effective than all the Soviet desk-pounding could ever be. And while the United States government did not exactly embrace Shevtsov as a member of its community of weapons scientists, he did have access to these men in circumstances in which the demands of secrecy might succumb to the desire to share the excitement of a common endeavor.

Yes, it was also plausible to assume that Shevtsov was a Soviet plant, a voice of warning to sap the Western will, a covert ear upon the deepest secrets of the sovereignty of arms. And if this were so, then the Soviets would have sent an observer to Shevtsov's speech at the law school only to reinforce his cover, knowing that we would expect them to keep track of anyone speaking against them. They would have had no reason to want him killed.

If Moll had doubts about the scientist's authenticity, then others, too, might have seen his talk of peace as a ruse. To them Shevtsov could have seemed the very embodiment of the terror whose instruments he had helped perfect. And if one man were unbalanced enough to feel the implications of the weapons Shevtsov created, he might have sought revenge. He would have to be insane, of course, to think that anything could be accomplished by such an act. The forces at work in the world were impersonal. The knowledge that set them into motion could only be eliminated by an apocalypse that leveled human civilization. And even then, if anyone lived, the knowledge would eventually return like a dormant virus that attacks the tissue of the brain. But it was possible to imagine that a man who had seen the terror plain might suddenly lash out. After all, the strategy of nuclear balance depended upon striking fear deep into the minds of men, and fear is not so easily channeled. It wells up. It overflows. In these times madness was simply the pursuit of war by other means.

The old television sat at one end of the conference room, colors out of whack, ghost-haunted. Majewski leaned toward it, flicking the dial from channel to channel. It was already past the first commercial on the evening news, and they still hadn't said a thing about the Soviet diplomatic car. The nightleads moving on the wires were no more threatening. AP went with reaction—shock and horror, the usual. UPI led with the word from *Pravda*, which condemned both Shevtsov and the West.

Richardson arrived and started tacking up photos on the corkboard wall for the doping session.

"They say anything about the weather yet?" he asked.

"Chance of showers," said Majewski. "You doping early tonight?"

"The usual hour. I'm just getting a little jump on them is all. You think they're right that the guy who did the bombing was crackers?"

"I'm getting it both ways, Pete."

Sid James was the next to join them. His turf—and let no man set foot on it—was administration. Budgets, policy, numbers.

"Hate to disturb your investigation, Stan," he said, nodding toward the television.

"When are you going to get that set fixed, Sid?" asked Majewski. "Look at that picture. Guy has three noses, for Chrissake."

"You're supposed to be out beating the bastards, not in here on your ass watching them."

"I guess Sid hasn't read the schedule," said Richardson.

"Did I say that I had?" said James. "Did I say that?"

"Stan's got an exclusive," said Richardson. "The networks aren't onto it yet, are they?"

"Don't seem to be," said Majewski, moving toward the door.

Majewski was not one to get nervous when he was all alone with a fact. He loved to be out there in front on his own, the others yapping at his heels, trying to bring him down. Just as long as his fact was solid. And the fact that a Soviet car had been spotted near the law school had come straight from Hank Moll.

Strangely enough, it had been Moll who had initiated the contact. He extracted from Majewski a promise of confidentiality, which was standard. But he also negotiated a pledge that Majewski would not go poking around the cop shop double-checking or trying to lever what he had into something even bigger.

"I'll give you everything you need," Moll had said. "Take it or leave it."

Majewski wanted a taste of the stuff before buying.

"A Soviet angle," said Moll. "But I'm not talking speculation here. Something hard you can put your hands on."

"Gimme," said Majewski.

"I don't want this out before the morning edition," said Moll.

"We don't print extras anymore."

"If the locals get even the slightest whiff that you're onto something, it'll be all over town before you can type your name at the top of the page."

"You aren't setting me up, are you, Hank?"

Majewski put it this way because it was a kind of ritual. You had to make sure the other guy knew that you were savvy to all the possibilities and that you knew he was one savvy fellow, too.

"Not me," said Moll. "I'm a regular altar boy. What I'm prepared to tell you is absolutely straight. If there's heat on the story, it'll all be on my side."

"Hell of a nice thing you're doing for me."

"Look," said Moll, "I'll sweeten it, OK? If it doesn't prove out to be a hundred percent gospel, I give you permission to burn me by name."

"It wouldn't be a pleasant thing to do, burning a friend."

"The information is that solid."

"I trust you," said Majewski, and they both had to laugh at the word.

Majewski had figured one of Moll's angles right away. Giving him the tip was Moll's way of covering his tracks. The out-of-towners were crawling all over this story. But the only man who had all the sources was Majewski. If the story broke with his by-line, it could have come from anybody.

But what Majewski couldn't figure was why Moll wanted the story out at all. It couldn't have been to put pressure on the Soviets. When the government wanted to do that, it booked space on the front page of *The New York Times*. And if Moll were trying to give the impression of movement on the case, he had picked a strange piece of news to make the point. The credit went to the locals. In Majewski's experience, when the Bureau got into the game, it was to grab all the glory, every last banner.

"How's it look, Stan?" asked Ruffalino as he swept past Majewski's desk on the way to the doping session.

"It's still our copyright."

"If it holds, I'll get you prizes for this."

"Kid me," said Majewski. "What do I need another plaque for?"

The dirty little secret of journalism was that most of the time it was pure tedium, keeping endless lists, fighting finicky machines, waiting for somebody to do something. Journalism was to the rush of events what the Quartermaster Corps is to war. But every once in a while you got onto something that changed the very nature of the enterprise. All the plodding, bureaucratic wrangling came to an end. The whole world was there under your fingertips as you punched out the lead. And when you were finished, you sat back and waited for the world to blink at what you had done.

The telephone rang. Majewski grabbed it.

"Yeah," he said.

"Stan, can I talk to you somewhere?" He recognized the voice, her soft, nervous trill.

"You've got my ear," he said, easing back in his chair.

"I don't trust the phone."

"Name the place."

"Remember where the four of us used to go on Sunday mornings after Mass?"

He was willing to play Twenty Questions with Susan Cousins. His deadline was past.

"Sure, I remember," he said.

"Can you meet me there right away?"

"Susan . . ."

"Don't say my name," she said. He could hear traffic in the background. She was calling from a booth. "If anything seems wrong when you get there, don't even stop."

"Are you all right?"

"I don't know, Stan. I just don't know."

Majewski held the line open after her for a few moments, then put the phone back in its cradle.

He and Rose had become like family to Susan Cousins during the early years of her marriage. Whenever Danny was a shit, she came to them for comfort and advice. Late at night, Majewski on the phone downstairs, Rose on the extension in the bedroom, they had listened to her troubles. It was just the way Cousins was, they had said. He wandered off, but he always came back. And after the tears had ended and Susan had rung off, they wondered why Danny had taken a wife so sweet and straight, so out of step with the creeps he was hustling. A nice Polish girl, Rose always said, what does she know about men?

The fog was coming in again as he drove the back streets to the highway. The pavement was slick. Big semitrailers roared past him, sending cascades of spray onto his windshield. At the exit he eased carefully down the tight, banked curve.

The road to the beach was built up with apartments and commercial strips. Diners, Laundromats, discount houses. Years ago, when he was courting Rose, they had come this way often, and it had been like a drive in the country. Now the only open space was the sea. Rose had loved the sea.

These were the times when he missed her the most, alone in the dark. It was not the silence that troubled him. They had always been satisfied with silence together. He felt her presence, a wordless truth that once had said, *I am here.* But now it said, *I am gone.* Lord, how he had loved her.

Rose Kielwicz had waited for him during his four years at the university, waited even when he became too busy to join her at the dances or Mass. She had faith that he would return to her, and he did, for she was as inevitable as his past. His mother adored her, but the rest of the family was quick to make class distinctions. He could have done better, they whispered, with his fancy degree and a job where you had to wear a Sunday suit five days a week. As they came to know her, their attitude changed. They saw her make a home for him, bear him a son. They learned that even though she had no interest in their get-rich schemes or gossip, they could count on her to be there when the kids had their first recital or something went terribly wrong. A saint, they said. Stash has married a regular saint. Too good to live in this world, they said, meaning too good to live like them. But they did not understand the woman she was in private, the way she made space for him in the silence, the way she took him inside of her laughing, the joy. That was for Majewski alone.

He saw the lights of Tommy's Restaurant up ahead against the black waters of the Sound. It was the last survivor of what had once been a dazzling amusement park. Little Coney Island, people used to call it, with roller coasters along the sand and big whirlygigs that spun you so fast you could not lift your arms. When he had first gone there as a child, it was a vision rising from the sea. He was still fresh from his flight across the ocean then, and he did not yet recognize the brightly colored names of all the perils. It was a perfect fantasy, a dazzling, wordless adventure, all the dangers mechanically simulated and tamed. He had taken Rose there a number of times during the summers before they were married. They enjoyed the sun and sand, their closeness as they hurtled down the chutes. But by the time David was old enough that they could take him to the park, it was beginning to go to ruin. The bright paint on the signs was fading, the rides closing one by one for lack of maintenance. They worried about those that were left, how safe they were. They declared most of them off limits. When David was old enough to mount the rickety machines, the danger had become real.

Majewski pulled into the lot, sand scraping under his tires, and came to a stop near the restaurant door. He saw Susan's car. There weren't many others out on a night like this. He closed the front of his coat against the mist and hurried across the pavement.

Inside, it was dark. Candles in red glasses on the rows of empty tables flickered like reflectors along a deserted road. The windows on three sides of the big, open room were still shuttered against the winter. Along the back, though, they were fitted with storms to give a view of the fogbound Sound.

A few people sat at the bar near the door. Above them, on a television, ten men ran back and forth across a polished wooden floor to the silent cheers of a crowd. In the dining room proper, couples sat at two or three tables, eating seafood from baskets lined with paper napkins, sipping wine. Susan was in a far corner, away from all of them.

"What will people think, our meeting like this?" he said when he reached her. She did not smile.

"Thank you for coming," she said.

She was a handsome woman in her thirties and looking much younger, as if lack of affection were, like lack of oxygen, a preservative. In a way, she was the opposite of Rose, blonde and fair, angled more than curved. She dressed in fashion, made herself up with obvious care. You might have taken her as a little too fancy, a little too concerned with herself, unless just once you had heard her say aloud what it was that she really wanted. Then you knew that this other was only a way of compensating for what she did not have.

"What're you drinking?" he asked, waving a waitress over.

"Tonic and lime," she said.

"Another for the lady," he said. "Rye and ginger for me."

He piled his stained old trench coat on the other chair.

"I'm scared," Susan said.

"What has that sonofabitch done to you now?"

She shook off the words, but it was not so much a gesture as a chill.

Majewski looked across the table at her. Something stirred in him, but he denied it, pushed it out of sight.

"I think Danny is really in trouble this time," she said.

"What kind of trouble?"

"I don't know," she said. "There was a man asking questions this morning. Then Danny packed up his things and left. I think something terrible is going to happen, Stan."

"Do you know where he went?"

The waitress brought the drinks, and Susan waited until they were alone again before answering.

"He asked me to see you," she said.

She put out her hand to be held, and he took it. The softness of her touch moved him. He wanted to give her comfort and protection, but all that passed between them was a piece of paper she had secreted in her palm.

"He wants to talk to you," she said. "But if you see anything, don't go."

"What would I see?"

"If you think somebody is following you."

"Susan, what's this all about?"

She looked down into her drink, the little piece of fruit floating there on the bubbles.

His hand was back on hers now; this time there was nothing to exchange. She drew away.

When she stood up, he helped her with her coat. Then she turned and embraced him. He gave her a chaste kiss in the air, but she held him. He felt the soft, sweet hair against his cheek, the woman's shape pressed tightly to his chest. He let her hold on to him.

"I'm sorry," she said. "I shouldn't do this to you."

"It's nothing," he said. "I understand."

He walked her to the door and watched her through the glass panel as she got into her car, switched on the lights, and pulled away. As soon as she was out of the lot, another car started up and turned into the street behind her. He took out his notebook and wrote down the make and license number.

When the cars were out of sight, he returned to the table to put some money down to cover the tab, then he went into the men's room. After checking the stalls, he pulled the paper from his pocket and unfolded it. The only message was the address of a place along the shore, written in Cousins's nervous hand. He wadded up the paper and flushed it down the toilet, then he washed his hands. As he left the restaurant, eight parts curiosity and two parts loyalty carried him along. That was the troubling thing about a situation like this, those last two parts.

Nobody followed him. In the fog the lights would have given away any tail car. Majewski kept his eye on the mirror. All he saw was the rose glow of his brake lights in the gray.

If he had not known the area so well, he might have missed the little wooden sign on the mailbox at the outlet of the private road. He swung into the gravel drive, turned out his lights, and waited. A battered pickup clattered past a good four minutes later, but that was all. He went the rest of the way with only his parking lights on. The amber cut through the fog and gave him a few feet of clear road in front as he inched up the driveway through the trees. Then the gravel widened out and the trees fell away. The house ahead of him was dark. He switched off the engine and went the last distance on foot.

The house wasn't much more than a glorified cabin, a place to get away from the conveniences of home. When he knocked on the door, the sound closed in behind him, like a noise under water. He heard movement inside.

"It's Majewski," he said. "I'm alone."

The door opened against a chain. He could not see the eyes in the darkness.

"Do you want to see my press credentials, Danny? Come on. It's OK. Nobody saw me coming."

The door closed, the chain rattled. Majewski let himself inside. He shut the door behind him, and he could feel the presence of the other man in the blackness.

"You hung over or something, you can't stand the light?"

"There are other houses near here," Cousins's voice whispered. "This place is supposed to be vacant. Belongs to friends of mine. Come on back this way. Watch out for the furniture."

Majewski groped forward, following the footsteps into another room. A match flared, and when his eyes recovered from the flash, he saw Cousins's face above the candle, all the lines deepened by shadows.

"I'm glad to see you," said Cousins.

"I'm glad to see anything," said Majewski.

The windows were draped with towels. There was a dining room table, a lowboy, and some chairs. Majewski left his coat on because there was no heat.

Cousins wore blue jeans cut for fashion and a fisherman's sweater, a shiny pendant on a chain drooling down his front. A few dirty dishes sat on the table, a half-filled whiskey bottle, a single glass.

"Can I get you a drink?" Cousins asked.

"Susan is scared to death, you know. You've really done a number on her this time."

"They aren't after her," Cousins said.

He found another glass in the cupboard and poured Majewski three fingers.

"Who isn't after her?"

"The heat," said Cousins. "The heat is really on, my friend."

He sat himself down across from Majewski, handed him the glass and took a pull from his own.

"That bombing you wrote about this morning," he said. "The Feds are all over my case."

"What the hell do you have to do with that? Jesus Mother of Mary, Danny, you've got no sense of prudence at all."

"Are we talking as friends here?"

"We're talking," said Majewski. "Just like we always do."

Cousins nodded. He knew the ground rules. No names to the quotes. That was firm, a commitment. Majewski would not go out of his way to screw him, but he did not want to hear anything that he could not write.

"It's that butcher Moll," Cousins said.

"Hank Moll?"

"He got to me this morning. In my own home, for Chrissake. He flashed his shield to Susan. The bastard."

"Butcher Moll," said Majewski. "Where did you get that?"

"My guys know him. Know him from way back when. They say he pushed a guy so hard once it killed him."

"How?"

"Overdose."

"Moll gave it to him?"

"The guy broke, Stan. He couldn't take it, and he went down."

"Junkies aren't exactly the steadiest guys around."

"This Moll is hard. Blames my guys for something that happened to his kid. Very hard."

"What exactly did he want from you?"

"He wants me to deliver somebody to take the fall. He's squeezing me, Stan."

"He thinks your guys had something to do with it?"

"How do I know what he thinks? I look like a shrink to you? I told him I never heard anything about the bombing. You ask me about folk singers or poets or actors with an ax to grind, and I'll tell you how to put together a gig, who to contact, how much dough it'll cost to sweeten their commitment to peace. But when you're talking Russian defectors, then you're in somebody else's league. That's what I told him, Stan, but he wanted more."

"Do you have anything more you could give him?"

"Look, my guys, you know, they get to talking some pretty nasty business sometimes. They get a little carried away. Sure I got something to give Moll, but where would that put me?"

"Why would they want to kill Shevtsov?"

"You keep asking me to get inside people's heads. And listen, you did not hear me say anything about the Russian here. Not a word."

Cousins took another drink of whiskey. His fingers tapped on the glass.

"Where does their money come from, Danny?"

"I don't ask."

"You've got to have some idea."

"Lots of rich people out there feeling bad about how they got that way."

"What else?" Majewski was beginning to see how Cousins was in a position to square the circle for Moll. The Feds might be thinking Cousins's guys were doing somebody's job for them, at a price.

"Hey, Stan, I asked you here because I thought you could tell me what the hell is going down, and you come on with the third degree."

"They think the Russians might have something to do with this, Danny," Majewski said. "They placed a Soviet agent at the scene of the killing."

"Oh, Jesus."

"Maybe he was there to check on what their investment bought them, how well the job was done."

"I don't know anything about Russian money. Man, that's all I need."

"You hear any talk?"

"Talk," said Cousins. "I hear all kinds of talk. But nobody's whispering about Russian money, I'll tell you that."

"Talk about Shevtsov in particular, I mean."

"They knew he was coming," said Cousins. "They read your newspaper."

"More, Danny."

"There isn't any more." Cousins's hand shook as he raised the glass to his lips to finish off the last of his drink. "If I had more, I'd give it to you."

"And to Moll."

"I think maybe these are bad guys we're talking about. I think if they find out I even let the man in the door, they're going to be all over me."

"You're in a jam. You don't have anything to give either way."

"Moll wants me to do his work for him. He wants me to come up with names."

"Maybe he thinks you know something already. It isn't like him to move on somebody just for the hell of it."

"That's not the way I hear it," Cousins said, leaning into the flickering light. "He used to have his claws into everybody. He followed my guys around. Their kids would come out the school door, and there he'd be, the candy man. How come you think you know him so well?"

"I know everybody, Danny."

"Well, I think I know this Moll guy better. I know him like he was a knife sticking in my side. Look, can you maybe talk to this guy for me. Get him off my ass?"

"I don't think so," said Majewski. He stood and took one step from the table.

"I thought you were a friend."

"Can I bring a message to Susan? She's awfully scared."

"What does she have to be scared of?" said Cousins. "She just cashes the checks."

FOUR

Voices of old despondency resigned,
Bowed by the shadow of the morrow, slept.

The story Moll had leaked to Stan Majewski about the Soviet car had come out exactly the way Moll wanted it. And when he arrived at the office early, the reporters were all over him for official comment, full of wounded innocence because they hadn't been given a piece of the impropriety. But Moll was the great stone face with them. We do not discuss pending investigations, he said.

When he was finished with the courthouse regulars, there was a message for him from Majewski. Whoever had taken the call had written down the reporter's pen name. But Moll always knew exactly whom he was dealing with; the reporter was right on schedule.

The night before, the surveillance team had reported making Majewski on his way into a restaurant to meet Susan Cousins. Moll had to give the man credit. He was very well-wired. Moll had told the team to let him go unmolested to the shack where Cousins was holed up. He was a great believer in the freedom of the press; if the creep had anything interesting to say, it would show up in the *Herald*. And he also had confidence enough in the reporter's powers of observation to think that Majewski would have noticed the tail on Cousins's wife. He certainly hoped he was right about that. He had put on the shadow primarily so that it would be seen. Moll dialed the phone.

"Real interesting story you had this morning, Stan," he said when the reporter answered.

"I've got something else I wanted to talk to you about," said Majewski. "Word on the street is that you've been sweating some of the radicals."

"You do what you can," said Moll.

"Somebody was following one of their ladies last night. I saw the car. Cops wouldn't trace the license for me. It had to be yours.

95

You chased her husband up a tree. I don't want to tell you how to do your business, Hank, but Danny Cousins doesn't have the stomach to blow off a firecracker on the Fourth of July."

Moll switched the phone to his other hand and leaned back in his chair.

"One time you told me that the trick of your trade was to find the angry man," he said, "the guy who didn't get the promotion or thinks he's been swindled. That's the guy, you said, who'll give you anything he's got. Well, there's a secret to my business, too. Angry or not, the guy I'm looking for is the snitch. Find the weasel. And Danny Cousins looks like that man to me. Most people who get involved in these causes, they stand for something. But not your buddy, Cousins. When he gets up in the morning and looks in the mirror, he doesn't see anything."

"Squeezing Cousins is one thing," said Majewski. "But going after his wife, Hank?"

"She didn't have to marry the bastard."

"You *are* a mean sonofabitch, aren't you?" said Majewski.

Moll thought he heard just the faintest trace of mutuality in it, if not respect.

"The local connection," Majewski went on. "I still don't figure it. You know these guys. They're all talk. It's their way of meeting girls."

"If you think I'm on a wild goose chase, you just write it that way. I can't stop you," said Moll. "But let me give you a little advice: Don't be too quick to dismiss anybody. These guys destroy people. I've seen it happen."

"They didn't take Tom away from you."

Moll closed his eyes. He had left himself wide open for that one. He had almost begged for it.

"They were just a center of gravity, Hank," said Majewski. "They drew Tom in. Take it from me, it isn't any better when your kid is living out there somewhere in free space."

"Play it however you have to, Stan. But I'll tell you this. I don't hold any grudges."

He hung up and let his hand drop to the stack of papers on his desk. He did not blame anyone for Tom's troubles but himself. He had only seized upon Cousins and his crowd because he wanted to get the pot boiling to see what came up off the bottom. He had long ago stopped believing that their faddish ideas had drawn away his son. The stronger force was repulsion, and the closer you were, the more powerfully it worked.

Moll did not like to remember just how close he once had been to his son, sitting for hours together fishing, wrestling on the floor. When he was little, Tom used to wait at the front window in the evening to catch sight of him coming home from work. Work. It was one of the first words Tom had learned to say; they always knew the words that touched you most deeply. He had pronounced it *gwerk,* and he had acted out the ritual of leaving and returning again and again at the closet door.

At first it was all imitation. Tom would follow his father around the house, banging at the nails Moll had driven, wiping down the walls Moll had washed. His very expressions had been Moll's own. The grin, the exaggerated grimace, the way he stood at the top of the stairs and bellowed for Sally to come up and find something he had put away and forgotten where. There had been so much time to shape him, and you thought that you could just be what you were and they would always follow. But imitation gave way to opposition. Tom had gone spinning off into the craziness, and by the time Moll realized what was happening, it was already too late.

The first sign of trouble had been his language. Moll had an ear for all the rhetoric, so when he heard it creeping into his own son's talk, he told Tom exactly what he thought about it. That did not help, of course. And soon the rebellion went way beyond words. Tom had been a wonderful catch for the opposition. The local underground paper had even run a story on him complete with a picture of Tom in his beard, workshirt, and jeans, carrying an obscene sign. Pig's son as prince of the revolution. That was the gist.

Tom had gone through all the classic phases: disorderly conduct, drug arrests, his name coming up in connection with the radical underground. He made his way to the West Coast, and Lord knew what he might have tried there. He flirted with the theatrical left, a drug-crazed hanger-on, and ended up in San Francisco, down and out. Then the overdose, the time in hospital, the trip back home.

He was a changed young man when he returned, as surely as if he had gone off to the islands. The angry rhetoric had given way to sheer, sullen distance. Though he lived in an apartment not five minutes from the courthouse where Moll worked, he might have been in a different universe.

Moll stood up at his desk and rubbed his stiffened neck. He hoped Majewski would not play this thing as Moll's personal vendetta. It wouldn't hurt him. It might even raise his standing in the Bureau if he got some bad press for his zeal. But it simply wasn't true that he was acting on a grudge. And it would only bring all the private troubles of his son into the open if the story came out that way. He wanted to spare Tom that much, at least. Tom was out of the battle now, safe.

Moll slipped through the squad bay where the other agents were getting themselves ready for the day. A few of them looked up as he passed, but he did not stop to talk. He rode the elevator to the prosecutor's floor, brushed past the receptionist, and flung open Raskin's door.

The young man was on the telephone when Moll burst in. It was clear that the conversation was one that Raskin did not want overheard. When he saw Moll, he turned his back and muttered a few guarded words. Then he hung up. Moll felt sure he was talking to a reporter.

"Don't let me interrupt," he said.

"Justice is hot as hell," Raskin said.

"I thought you'd be pleased," said Moll. "Nobody has claimed responsibility. Your boss called them nuts and they kept quiet. The dog that didn't bark. It strengthens your position that the Russians were behind it."

"Washington isn't hot over the press conference," said Raskin. "They're upset about this." He put his hand on the *Herald*, which was spread out before him on the desk, the leaked story about the Soviet car blaring all over the front page. "What do you know about it?"

"Funny," said Moll. "I came down to ask you the same thing."

"Makes it a lot tougher."

"Does it?"

"The Soviets have clammed up tight about the car."

"Damn," said Moll. "And I was hoping they might cooperate."

"New York is pissed."

"Wouldn't you be if you were them?" Moll said, smiling. "It puts the pressure on them to come up with a name."

"Sure took the edge off the boss's press conference," said Raskin. "Whatever else they might be, the Soviets are not nuts."

"No harm done. We had a ride with the madman story on the radio all day before this one came out. Nobody took the bait."

"You don't even seem concerned."

"Me?" said Moll. "I'm outraged. But you have to learn to look on the bright side. It does take some of the heat off us."

"Don't be so sure," said Raskin. "They're talking about sending somebody down from Washington to supervise. They're talking about a leak investigation. I mean, they take this counter-intelligence shit seriously."

"We're talking about a parking ticket here," said Moll.

"We're talking about a goddamned international incident."

"You ever been through a leak investigation? Let me tell you something about them. Funniest goddamn things in the world. Nine times out of ten the guy who starts the investigation is the very guy who did the leaking in the first place."

"You start this one?"

"I fired off a duly indignant memo this morning," said Moll.

"Come on, Hank. Everybody knows you're asshole buddies with Stan Majors."

"There you go, pointing fingers like a hundred-buck-a-week numbers runner in a jam," said Moll. "By tomorrow Justice will have something better to worry about."

"You know something I don't know?"

"The word is out on the street that I'm looking to pin this thing on one of the old reliables," Moll said. "One guy has already gone into hiding. We know where he is. We're watching him sweat and riding his lovely wife to make it clear we aren't just farting around."

"You're giving up on the Russian angle? I don't think that's very smart."

"Fact is, no matter how we go about it, we're just wandering around in the dark. We've only got one thing solid, and that's the detonating device. It was crude. But that doesn't rule the Soviets out. If I were them I wouldn't have left a calling card either."

"That's how I was thinking."

"I'm sure you were," said Moll. "But let me tip you off to something. There are certain things that are expected of us. We can't report to Washington that we are confidently waiting for a lucky break. We have to be moving, even if we don't have the foggiest idea where we're going."

"I get a bad feeling about the radical angle," said Raskin.

"So do I," said Moll. "I'm not sure Shevtsov wasn't on their side."

Raskin finally smiled.

"You aren't going to tell Headquarters that," he said. "That's the CIA's line."

"Maybe I have my own ideas. Maybe I think some things are more likely than others. But one thing is sure: We have to look like we know what we're doing."

"You did leak the story to the *Herald*, didn't you?" said Raskin.

"See? We do know what we're doing," said Moll, "both of us."

Majewski waited in the parking lot of the nursing home, the car radio tuned to an all-news station. His story dominated the air, but the credit was already lost. He switched on the ignition and pumped the gas pedal until the engine caught. As the temperature gauge moved up, he flicked on the heater. The fan blew hot wind into his face and riffled the pages of the paper on the passenger seat.

He listened to an interview with the driver of the three-wheeler who had written the ticket. The cop expatiated on the Soviet threat. Then came the police superintendent complimenting the quick thinking of his men. Next a reporter held an inane conversation with a State Department spokesman explaining the meaning of diplomatic immunity.

There was something about the way the all-news stations handled a story that annoyed Majewski. They groped breathlessly after it as it broke, flashing on every little piece that came their way. Significant or trivial, true or false, each detail became the most important thing in the world for sixty seconds, and then it passed. They presented the process of news rather than the simple fact of it. They left the truth half-completed, with all the wires and plumbing exposed.

When the air became stifling, he turned off the engine and checked his watch again. David was already a half hour late.

He could not really blame his son for avoiding the nursing

home. David hated the place. He said it reminded him of where his mother had died. When Rose was in the hospital, Majewski had taken David to visit her every evening. The boy had not resisted, but you could see that it was an ordeal.

Majewski had tried to penetrate his son's defenses with fact, showing him the huge machine that delivered radiation to kill the gnawing tumor in her belly. It was a space-age device in chrome and enameled steel, turned on its calibrated gears by silent engines. The doctors demonstrated how the beam was focused. David listened politely and never, never told them what, in tears, he told his father the night she died: that he had always blamed the machine and medicine for her suffering. Fact was not enough; he confused the cure and the cause.

David had only visited his Grandma Statia a few times since she entered the home, and Majewski knew how much it disturbed him, the wheelchairs, the nurses in their vain, unblemished white, the smell of tinctures, and the bite of oxygen pure from the cylinder. Eventually he had stopped visiting altogether. And now, whenever Majewski stepped into his mother's tidy little room at the home and took her knotted hand, her eyes always went right past him to the corridor, searching for her only grandchild.

They were the same expectant eyes that had scanned the train platform years ago on the day when they were reunited, mother and son. She had needed help getting off the car. A porter had held her hand. Her cheap lavender housedress and black shawl had hung about her shoulders like a shroud. He took a few steps, tentatively raised his hand. His uncles and aunts rushed forward to embrace her. But she looked past them all, and when those eyes finally lighted on him, grown strong into manhood now, her hard, drawn face collapsed in joy.

Seven years they had been apart. He had never given up hope that she would someday return. His spirit had soared and sunk during those years as he tried to imagine where she was and what she was doing. But even on the worst days, his mind was not strong or corrupted enough to touch the reality of the camps or the awful damage they had wrought upon her. He vowed that day when he saw her on the station platform that he would never again allow himself to be surprised by the truth. He vowed to seek it out, never to run away.

His father had been a professor of history, an author of texts on

Polish nationalism. Majewski read those books much later, when he was grown. They were not the work of a firebrand. They were slow and scholarly, capturing both the aspiration and the vanity. But still they marked him out as someone the invaders could not tolerate.

Majewski was only nine years old the day the Nazis came. Terrible explosions burst all around, bringing down whole buildings, setting vast, cackling fires, stomping up the streets like the footsteps of a giant. Then the soldiers arrived in columns. The family watched them from the upstairs window. His mother was horrified, but his father just padded off to the library every morning as if nothing had changed. In the small, isolated group of academicians of his circle, he was a rock and a consolation. And Majewski clung to the illusion his father had created, utterly unaware of what the man was secretly planning.

Then one evening his father brought home Karl Jankowski, the son of one of his faculty colleagues. He was a somber fellow, a graduate of the university himself and so full of learning that he was immune to Majewski's father's dry wit as they sat at the dinner table. Karl seemed put upon by the hospitality. He was distracted, perhaps even angry. In contrast, Majewski's father was more relaxed than he had been for months, as if some terribly difficult puzzle of the past had just yielded its solution. Then, after dinner, when the brandy came out and the fire was set in the parlor, his father invited both son and mother to join them, though this was never, never done.

"We are sending you abroad, son," his father said. "Karl here has agreed to accompany you."

"No," said Majewski, but it was not taken as impertinence. Everything was suddenly different; all the old rules had been swept away.

"It is important to your education that you travel," his father said. "A man of a certain age must leave and see the world so that he may be able to look back on his homeland with real affection."

"And pity," said Karl. The elder Majewski silenced him with a wave of his hand.

"You will be leaving tonight," his father said. "The way from Warsaw is better in the dark. You will be going to America. You must obey Karl. The trip will be difficult. Your mother and

I would join you if we could. But this is not possible. We will wait here until the time comes when we can all be safely together again."

"I won't go," said the boy, running to his father and wrapping his arms around him. It was only when Majewski had become a father himself that he understood just how strong this man had been to go through with it. His father embraced him, told him everything would be all right because in distance there was protection and the preservation of memory. Then he took the boy to his room, where his mother had packed clothes and food in a rucksack and laid it with his folded overcoat neatly on the little bed. His father helped him on with his coat. The boy was limp with fear and duty. The rucksack was heavy on his back.

"Good soldier," said his father as he led him back into the parlor where Karl was waiting. "We shall be very proud of you. You must carry on and always, always remember your family and your homeland. You bear the future. Be strong."

Majewski kissed his mother and father, but not as he should have, in gratitude or perfect sorrow. Instead, he felt a sense of desertion, and he could not overcome the idea that somehow they were sending him away for something he had done. Later, when he began to realize what he had escaped and tried to make sense of the abandonment, the very act of leaving seemed to be the source of both his transgression and his punishment.

Into the blind, foggy night they went. Karl held him viselike by the hand. The boy squirmed to be free of the grip, but without a word the man brought him into submission. Grim as the devil's own messenger, he led the way through the shrouded streets and cursed the smell of smoke in the air. They traveled the alleys, dashed across the main roads, eluded the Nazi patrols. "The smoke," Karl said. "Can you smell the burning?" But to Majewski it was still the smell of the hearth, of warmth and comfort, of what he was leaving behind. He choked on tears. Then, when they reached the outskirts of the city, he finally looked back. The fog diffused the light so that it seemed the whole metropolis was engulfed in the yellow, deathly aura. And for an instant the boy understood the man's vision. Through his tears it seemed that, even though the bombs had given way to the peace of surrender, Warsaw was on fire.

Karl did not prove to be the man the boy had first feared him

to be. He was, in fact, a warm and gentle fellow, a teller of
lovely fables that tamed the terrors of the night, his tight grip on
Majewski's hand a comfort in times of cold and danger. They
traveled together for more than a month. When Majewski grew ill,
Karl carried him on his back. When the boy was able, they walked
at night until their legs grew numb. At times they were caught out
in the open by the knifing probes of Nazi searchlights on the
frontier. They fell to their bellies and crawled like night creatures
trying to elude the traps.

Karl ministered to his sadness and fright. He explained that
their country had been divided between the Germans and the
Russians until by God's will the force of arms could deliver it. He
told of his own father and brothers, how much he hated to leave
them, how ashamed he was. The boy felt better, knowing that
someone shared his feelings.

The two of them stayed in barns and attics during the day,
hidden by men and women who feared less for their lives than for
their souls. And when it seemed to Majewski that he could go no
farther, that his will and strength had reached an end, they broke at
dawn onto a beautiful, rolling plain. It was the Swiss border, amber
in the morning light. Even before Karl told him, he knew that
across the broad field was freedom.

The crossing was safe only during the day. Karl made connection with a group of Swiss who had business on both sides of the
border and whose real trade was the smuggling of refugees. He paid
them from the gold he had brought with him. And on the frontier,
at noon, they discovered that even the death's-head legions would
aid survival, for a price.

On the other side, they were promptly separated and sent to
jail. The Swiss took no chances. They wanted to be sure both that
the émigrés were in fact who they claimed to be and that they
had no intention of settling. Majewski did not understand this.
The imprisonment, following the long, tormented escape, was the
culmination of a wrong.

There were a few other Polish boys in the barracks where
Majewski was assigned, but they were much older and knew all the
savage ways of confinement. They stole whatever they could and
bartered it for cigarettes with the guards. They talked a vulgar
language that horrified Majewski. *Idź na dupa śpiewać.* Go up my
ass and sing. They called his mother a terrible name. *Kurwa.* Filthy

whore. Majewski was too small to fight for his family's honor. He sank into a silent corner and wept.

Finally, the guards called him out. The louder boys taunted him, telling him that he was in trouble, that the punishment would be severe. Others had gone, they said ominously, *and never come back.* He was weeping as the guards led him across the yard.

When they arrived in a little building with lace drapes and candy-colored walls, he saw Karl waiting for him. He broke from his escorts and ran toward his old companion, who hitched him under the arms and swung him in a joyous circle. They embraced like brothers, like father and son.

"It's all right now, little man," Karl said. "The arrangements have all been made. We are going to America."

"America," said Majewski. Then Karl said it with a different accent, and Majewski repeated it the proper way. Together they practiced the magical word.

The Americans did not separate the two of them when their ship arrived. They went through the immigration lines together, and at the other end they changed the last of their gold for the strange, vegetable-green money of the new land.

Karl knew English well, and he had no trouble getting them to the right train station in New York. The boy was amazed by the crowds, the faces of different colors and shapes such as he had only seen in books. He listened to dozens of new languages, saw a carnival of strange costumes. When Karl asked directions of a man wearing a dark business suit and carrying a briefcase, the man showed no surprise at all at Karl's accented words. He answered quickly and easily, even led them to the right track, waved them on their way, citizen to citizen. Majewski fell in love with America, where a man could be anything he pleased.

When the train slowed to a stop at their destination, Majewski watched crowds of people stroll past the vestibule door. A porter carried their faded rucksacks, and Karl lifted the boy to his broad shoulders as soon as they stepped onto the platform. It was a strange vantage, so high, the unfamiliar faces turning up to him with smiling eyes that winked and passed. They had never seen the uncle they had traveled across Europe and over the ocean to meet. So they just stood there waiting on the concrete, the two of them a tall totem, as groups united and moved away. When the crowd thinned out, a man stepped up and introduced himself. He was dressed in a suit and tie, but his beefy body did not seem cut for such fashion, and when he held out his hand to be shaken, his fingernails were discolored and outlined in black.

It was Uncle Joseph; he wanted to be called just Joe. He was the brother of Majewski's father. He had left Poland as a banker, but he had changed his occupation here. Now he was a machinist in the local weapons company. It paid good money, turning out parts for all those arms.

Only when they had settled in with Uncle Joe, Majewski entering school and Karl taking a job as a night janitor in one of the plants, did they begin to hear about what was happening in Poland. The stories came from many sources: smuggled letters, the church, new refugees. There were tales of beatings in the street. Long trains of people transported away. Resistance fighters hanged from lampposts above the snowy streets like Christmas ornaments.

Majewski's curiosity about these things was boundless. He worried for his father and mother. He remembered the sounds in the night, and they became legions coming to hang him, too. He pressed Karl for more details, for an explanation of the Nazis' terrible designs. But with every new report, the man grew more remote from the boy.

Karl avoided the big family dinners where the travails of Poland became the subject of conversation and prayer. He retreated into the odd pattern of his work schedule, sleeping when Majewski got ready for school, going away before he returned home in the afternoon. Uncle Joe worried aloud about him. Did you smell the whiskey on his breath this morning? How could the man abuse his freedom so when others left behind were in such peril? Majewski took Karl's side, retelling the story of their dangerous trip, how they had foraged for radishes or a tossed-off scrap of fat. How Karl had pressed on when both of them were weakened by fever. But these things, though they were respected in the boy, did not seem enough to redeem the man. Karl sank lower and lower in the eyes of the family and, Majewski sensed, in Karl's own as well.

Then word came of Majewski's parents. The report was third-hand. It was brought by a group of refugees, one of whom had spoken with a friend of the family who claimed to have witnessed the event. The Nazis had entered the university intent upon eliminating all heresy. Majewski's father had been one of those arrested. He had been herded into the great square with all the others, made to stand there all day under the taunts of the guards and the students whose minds had been warped to the Nazis' will. Majewski's father had told the Nazi captain that he needed insulin for his diabetes. The captain had merely smiled and placed him among the Jews.

"He is dead, Stash," said Karl.

"When?" asked Majewski. "What day?"

"There are no days in the place where he was taken," said Karl. "Time ceases to exist. History ends. You must mourn him as if it happened today."

"But what about my mother?"

"She has been spared. Others have seen her. She lives with a group of widows. The Nazis are too busy to worry about these women. There are so many men and Jews already on their lists."

The news was crushing. He could not imagine why anyone would hate his father, who wanted nothing more than to provide for his family's future and to know the troubled past. Someone suggested one afternoon just within Majewski's hearing that he might have become suspect just because he had smuggled out his son. Uncle Joe had silenced that thought and told the garrulous woman to mind what such an idea might do to the boy. But it was only the articulation of something Majewski had been feeling anyway. In his nightmares he saw his father going through a diabetic episode, falling into the dust, dazed and pleading as the Nazi captain laughed and placed a large cloth Star of David on his chest. He imagined his father's dead, vacant eyes, his open, wordless mouth. He knew these things had happened. But where? When? Did they bury the dead with services? Did the Nazis mark the graves? Majewski had even gone to a priest to find out the penalty for dying without the last rites. God, the priest reassured him, understood the circumstances. But if God really understood, young Majewski pressed on, why did He not stop them? The priest touched the boy's shoulder and told him that this was a question God did not entertain.

As Majewski tormented himself in silence, Karl seemed to take fire. He talked crazy talk against America for letting this happen, wild talk against the Russians who had signed a pact with the devil. Karl became the scourge of the household. They tortured him with disregard, and when he was away at work they clicked their tongues.

Then one day he was gone. He made no announcement, and as Uncle Joe was at pains to remind anyone who would listen, he did not so much as thank them. Majewski was bereft. At the dinner table, the family told nasty stories about Karl's habits, his ingratitude. Some, who did not realize the true nature of his obsession, even sneered that it was the military draft that had driven him away. And no one raised a word to defend him against the charge, even though the plant where he and the others all worked had already been designated a vital defense installation so that no one employed there faced any risk.

The petty sniping only stopped when they finally received Karl's letter. He had gone to Canada to volunteer for service. He simply could not wait, he wrote, for America to decide where she stood.

The years of total war were like a void in which all knowledge of home was drawn. There were rumors of the camps, and Majewski studied the papers every day, looking in vain for confirmation, sure that such a thing could never be hidden. He had a map of Europe and North Africa on his wall, and little blue pins represented the Allied positions. Poland seemed so far from deliverance.

The Polish language dailies carried small advertisements asking for information about lost families and friends. This was the main network of intelligence from behind the lines. Majewski spent part of the money he had made on a paper route and mowing old people's lawns to place inquiries about his mother. Uncle Joe helped him with the text, for already English was displacing Majewski's native voice. Carefully worded, the queries went out, even as far as the papers in New York, but all he ever received in reply were short notes of condolence from kindly folk who had nothing more to offer, solicitations from relief organizations, and scores of anonymous Mass cards for the dead.

On the glorious day when the Russians advanced across the Polish frontier, Majewski knew little of the hammer and sickle except that it had finally been turned against the devil and that people said it would surely shatter the Germans' broken cross. Majewski waited eagerly for news of his mother, the precise circumstances of his father's death. He imagined liberation to be an instantaneous event: One day you were enslaved, the next day you were free. Just like that. But no news came. Instead, the papers carried reports of the devastation of Warsaw, the destruction of the ghetto, the valiant rising of the resistance that came too early, before the Soviets made their final move.

The word was that the Russians had encouraged the resistance to come out of hiding and attack as Soviet troops entered Warsaw. But instead of storming the city, the Russians waited and watched the Nazis cut the freedom fighters down; only when the spirit of liberation was crushed did the Soviet Army finally drive the Germans away. The family heard that Karl's brothers had all been killed in this final treachery, that they had been slaughtered in the street. Uncle Joe wrote a letter to Karl telling him what they had learned, and Majewski began to lose all hope that anyone remained alive.

Karl did not respond to this letter. Majewski's own notes to him went unanswered. Majewski nagged his uncle to contact the Canadians to see if Karl could be located. They wrote to Ottawa asking whether Karl Jankowski had been listed as a casualty. The answer came back, but it was ambiguous. The records did not show Karl among the dead or wounded, it said. But the letter did not say he was alive. Again the horrible sense of not knowing. Majewski felt he was losing everything to the great, sucking void of war.

The accident of his age spared Majewski from facing the void himself. Before he graduated, both Germany and Japan had been vanquished. America had dropped the Bomb. And the country was gearing down for a perfect, technological peace. It was during his junior year in high school that he finally received word that his mother was still alive in a displaced persons camp in Germany. Majewski wanted to go and rescue her, but Uncle Joe persuaded him that the matter would be handled more safely at a distance. Europe was awash in refugees, Uncle Joe had said. There was no telling where a nice Polish boy might land.

They filed papers to arrange for his mother's release and travel to America. They wrote her long letters, enclosing pictures of her son in sweater and chinos, a handsome young Yank. Occasionally somebody would write back on cheap camp stationery saying she had received the mail and was moved by it. One of the letters said that she had spent more than a year in Auschwitz. The letter referred to the place only in passing, as if it were the most common thing in the world.

By then the rumors about the death camps had all been confirmed, and Majewski thought he had steeled himself against the worst. But until she came down the hard, metal steps of the train from New York and he saw the way she had wasted, he'd had no idea how bad it could be. He went to her, embraced the frail old body gently, afraid that after all the suffering her bones might shatter now under the pressure of his love. And he was startled at how tightly she clung to him, how much strength was left in those withered arms. She said his name over and over again. He held her, a stranger now. And it was Majewski, not his mother, who finally wept.

The others moved off to give them room. He pointed and said, "They have waited for you, too." The old woman looked up, and a strange radiance came over her. She turned to him and whispered so that no one else could hear it, "*Cacy lala. Cacy lala.*" Dancing, smiling words from his past. And as he looked at them standing there in their Sunday suits and bright, pleated dresses, he could not help laughing with her. The phrase meant fancy, high-falutin'. Only another survivor could understand the truth of it, *cacy lala*, the utter vanity of those who had been spared.

During the first months they were together again at Uncle Joe's, she regained her strength. She seemed to grow younger in his presence, talking about the future, pressing him to go on with his schooling. She showed no signs of depression, and whenever anyone brought up the subject of her husband's death or the camps, she just pushed the matter aside.

Majewski took a job at the paper to put away some money for college. With help from Uncle Joe, they moved into their own apartment, visiting the rest of the family only on Sundays and special occasions. She picked up pieces of the new language quickly. He would have tried to speak Polish to her at home, but she wanted to practice her English. At first he thought that this was what made her so uncommunicative about the past, that she did not yet have the words to describe her ordeal.

But on other subjects she could express herself eloquently, if only through the fingers that touched his arm, the smile that came over her face when she met his eyes at the kitchen table as they ate. She gossiped about the family, who was engaged, who was going to have a baby. She spent her days cleaning other people's homes. It galled him to think of her doing this, she who had presided regally over a house staff of her own when he was a child. But whenever he mentioned it, she just said "*cacy lala*" and laughed.

He went out of his way to meet other survivors of the camps. He pressed them for information, and he was horrified at the stories they told. The Jews had suffered the worst of it, of course. Unless they had some special skill, they were dead straight off the trains. They were sent to the right at the prison gate and went directly to the showers. The others, Poles and Gypsies, Russians, political prisoners, they had a better chance. Unless they were sick or pregnant when they reached Auschwitz, Mengele would send them to the left, where death came more slowly.

Would diabetes be enough to send one to the right? he asked them.

If he needed insulin, they said, your father probably died in the boxcars. The ovens awaited his arrival. There were many the Germans did not need to kill.

They told him of shit and starvation, of the SS men and convict kapos who could murder at will. They spoke of the ditches full of corpses. And most of all they remembered the smoke. Clouds of it every day belching from the chimneys. We choked, they said, upon the souls of the dead.

One day Majewski met a woman who had actually known his mother in the camp. When he was introduced to her, she looked him up and down as if she were inspecting a piece of goods in a store. He invited the woman to visit their home. But to his surprise, the woman flatly refused to go anywhere near his mother. And then to his further surprise, she insisted on seeing him again.

"After all," she said, "you are the one we always heard about. Day after day."

He visited with her often. She was a small, wiry woman, and her face was as hard as her words. She told him of the tight, stinking barracks where they had lived, the consuming importance of simple things like food and warmth and sleep without dreams. The bowels, she said with an angry, mocking grin, the bowels were the moral center of the universe. All the inmates were plagued by diarrhea. The guards amused themselves by withholding the privilege of a trip to the foul latrine. The women soiled themselves and then were beaten for their incontinence.

They developed strategies for meeting their elemental needs. Some tried to go it alone in the F.K.L., the *Frauen Konzentrationlager*; they perished. Others who had kept their looks offered their favors to the staff. It was a proposition of exceeding risk, for when they were no longer pleasing, they would quickly find themselves consigned to the flame. Many inmates organized to steal and share food to supplement the starvation rations, a little extra fabric to stand between nakedness and the cold. They learned the shoplifter's arts of concealment. They came to accept complicity in the evil mission of the camp, stripping the bodies, sorting the lost possessions of the dead. And they also learned to kill—informers or those who were about to fly off into some mad form of resistance, for either could bring down on everyone a mortal retribution. They took care of one another, in a fashion. Those who got special work assignments capitalized upon them whenever possible. The women who were assigned to the hospital hid condemned inmates in the contagion wards the SS feared to enter. The fixers—handy with pipes or hammers or electrical wire—served as messengers as they made their rounds of repair. Those who worked in the administrative offices saved lives by expropriating for endangered inmates the names of the forgotten dead. Majewski's mother, the woman told him, worked in a warehouse they called Canada. There the Nazis kept all the personal effects taken from the prisoners as they entered the gate, and the workers pawed through them for valuables worth sending back to Germany or stealing for themselves. In Canada you could find real treasures: a tin of fish or jam, woolen underwear, tobacco, a kit with needle and thread. The guards tolerated some theft, so long as the stolen items were of no use to the Reich or themselves. The inmates pilfered what they could. "Even your mother did it," the woman said, "even your sainted mother."

There were three types of inmates, the woman told Majewski one day. The Beasts made a separate peace with the SS; these the others killed at the first opportunity. Then there were the Realists, who did whatever they needed to do in order to survive, who were willing to man the ovens in order to avoid the flame, who struck whatever bargains they could with necessity and accepted the terms without remorse, which was an emotion as useless in extremity as anger, and as deadly as doubt. And finally, she said, there were the Beatific Ones. Most of them died early, broken upon their own damned ideals. But some managed to drag themselves up out of the abyss of dreams and survive.

"The Beatific Ones," the woman said, "would not make the ultimate compromise, and so they were only useful in limited ways. They would steal, but they would not kill. They would never inform on someone else, but when it came time for action against an informer, they would balk. We protected them, but they were luxuries to us, young man. Do you understand? Useless luxuries in the shit."

Majewski nodded as the woman fell silent. Her knotted fingers, ten painful red crooks, tangled together around her coffee cup. Her eyes, which until then had always held him hard, were now cast down.

"Let me tell you about your mother," she said. "She worked in Canada. And she was not above bringing back spoils. Well, one day when she returned to the compound, she had something she said was really quite special. Those were her words. Quite special. I think I shall never forget it.

"She turned away from us and pulled from beneath her skirt a photograph and a bright, silver crucifix. She held them out to us like Christmas gifts. We could not believe what we saw. The cross was old, worn from the burnishing of a million vain prayers. The photograph showed a large family on the banks of a river. Boats floated behind them, sailing to the jagged edge where the picture had been torn away. The people sat on a blanket spread with baskets of food. One little boy proudly held a kite. She said he reminded her of you.

"We had no idea who these people were. And yet we passed the photograph and crucifix from hand to hand. We looked at your mother's treasures in silence until finally somebody spoke. 'What is this shit?' she said. 'You risked our lives for such things? Can we eat what you have brought? Can we sew with them? What will this worthless piece of metal bring in trade?'

"Your mother took the things back. We moved away from her, angry at the risk but also at what she had reminded us of. Later, after we had shared our day's take of moldy food and smoked the flakes of tobacco we had allotted ourselves, we finally came together to find a place to hide the photograph and cross. We never took them out again. But they were there with us. They were there. . . .

"So," said the woman, looking up at him. "Do you see why I cannot face her again? Your mother was useless, as useless as that cross. I have no time for such shit anymore."

It was only then that Majewski thought he began to understand his mother's silence. He wanted to know more. He gathered up all the information he could find. Books and clippings about the camps were strewn all over his room. His mother did not comment on his obsession, but he could tell that it troubled her. In the evening when he returned home from work, he would find the materials stacked neatly away on his shelves. Sometimes she laid the Bible on the table next to his bed, open to the solace of the Psalms. She took him to Mass, where they prayed different silent prayers—hers, he supposed, to the world that had been destroyed, his for acceptance of the world as it was. Finally, the silence became intolerable to him. It lay like a secret between them. The thing unspoken was corrupting; it held them apart. One night he went to her in the living room where she sat with needle and thread mending his clothes.

"I need to talk to you, Mother." He spoke in Polish, and it made his words seem all the more grave.

"You have troubles," she said. "It is something wrong at work?"

"It isn't that," he said. "I know you would rather not talk about it, and I think I understand the reason. But, you see, when you and Father sent me away, it was as if I was cut off from the most important thing in our lives. Whatever happened to you happened to me, too. I felt it, but I did not even know what it was. I need to know about Father, about you."

"Your father was killed," she said. There was no emotion in her voice. It was the same tone she had used when he was a child to warn him of the danger of sharp objects or the stove.

"How did he die?"

She looked at him curiously, as if she did not know the meaning of the words.

"It does not matter," she said. "All ways were the same."

"And you?"

"I wept, of course."

She turned away from him, and he could not tell whether it was to hide her grief or anger.

"It is over," she said, "and we are together again, you and I. The memory of your father is still alive in us. I suppose I could weep again if you want me to."

"I do not want to hurt you. But I need to know. We aren't what we used to be, none of us. The war changed us, changed everything."

114

"Please do not say that," she said. "It is the one thing I cannot bear to hear."

Her head was bowed, her shoulders bent. He could see her aging again before his eyes, the pallor spreading across her face.

"You bore so much," he said, "and the rest of us so little."

"I knew you were safe. So did your father. Word came to us that Karl had brought you through."

"Karl went back," he said. "He was ashamed to have run away."

"Ah, so that is it," she said. "Karl was a fine young man. He did not want to leave. But he was a dutiful son. He obeyed his father's wishes."

It was a form of rebuke, for what would his own father have said now of his stubborn insistence on touching the source of all her pain? It was one thing to want to know the past, another to force it upon someone who had suffered its tortures. But Majewski did not relent. Once upon a time he had retreated, and then he learned that truth and evil were not things a man could hope to flee.

"Karl may have died," he said. "He was trying to get back, to fight for you."

"He came from a brave family. They all died."

"And your courage," he said, because he needed to honor it, "your courage was to survive."

She leaned against the table, weaker now than on the day she had come off the train.

"Do not speak of my courage," she said slowly. "The word had no meaning there. We were all the same. Yes, the same. That was the horror. The people who degraded us were human beings just like ourselves. And the worst degradation was the way they made us imitate them.

"Lord, don't you see? I wanted to spare you. That's what kept me going. If both your father and I had perished in the dark, you would have been left with only the nightmare of it. But I am here for you. I lived so you could see that a person could live. I lived for you, and now you make that seem like folly."

She was weeping, and he went to her. He took her arm and led her to a chair. But he could not comfort her. She was somewhere else now, eyes blind, open wide to the horror. Suddenly he realized that she had only held back the truth for his sake. If she had been a Beatific One inside the camp, it was not for herself but so that

115

he would never hear of her otherwise, never know what she had learned of the collective human heart. Now it was as if she was reliving it all again without the hope that had sustained her. And the truth hung in the air like the ashes of the dead.

Majewski shivered behind the wheel of the car. The last heat had gone out of it, and David was nowhere to be seen. He buttoned up his coat against the wind and opened the door.

FIVE

Judex ergo cum sedebit
Quidquid latet, apparebit:
Nil inultum remanebit.

When the judge his seat attaineth,
and each hidden deed arraigneth,
nothing unavenged remaineth.

Moll directed the taxi to Tenth and Constitution and tried to calculate the fare from the zone map of the District hanging from the back of the driver's seat. The administrative stiffs at Headquarters liked nothing better than challenging an item on an expense voucher and making it seem as bad as if you had gone out and arrested the wrong man.

The air was clear and the wind coming through the open windows was warm. Moll pulled off his trench coat as they sailed up The Mall past the monument and the heavy, pillared buildings. It was a different season here, and men were still dressed for the heat. You hardly ever saw anybody in work clothes. Everyone wore coats and ties, and they washed their hands whenever they got dirty. It was another country.

The driver pulled to the curb and turned around in his seat. Rastafarian curls hung down to his shoulders. Moll paid him with a ten-dollar bill. He held it out flat on top of his identification case, hoping the man would catch a glimpse of the Bureau seal and mistake him for an immigration agent. The driver fished in a little cigar box for change. Moll took the bills and left the silver.

"They raise the fare?" he asked.

The driver looped his arm over the back of the seat and gave a nervous smile.

"Same as always, mon," he said.

Moll left the cab and entered the big building by the revolving door. He flipped open his ID for the guard and caught an elevator to the fifth floor. It let him out near the Attorney General's suite. He stopped in the corridor and admired the quaint old mural on the wall. A man in handcuffs. A cop with a whistle. A prison cell.

The whole child's garden of justice. Down the way hung portraits of former Attorneys General, and they said that recently the whiff of scandal in the department had gotten so heavy that some jokester had come in the night and hung a little sign under a figure in cuffs and prison uniform. The sign bore the incumbent's name.

Moll walked past the Attorney General's door. He had only been in that office once, during the great spy investigations twenty years ago. When he had entered the conference room, he had seen the grand mural above the far fireplace. It was an idyllic scene depicting women in flowing gowns, men playing musical instruments, laborers toiling under a bright sky. Presiding over all of it was the powerful figure of a judge in his black robes. Moll had not realized until he stood to leave that this was one of a pair of murals. But once the meeting was over, the business of law and national sovereignty transacted, he had seen above the exit doors the companion piece. Dark figures with whips and rifles oppressed a multitude in a shadowy landscape. The judge was not presiding. The sun did not shine. Moll had always wondered what the order of those two artworks was meant to portray. You entered the room facing a sunlit scene, and after the strategies of the law had all been discussed, you left under a vision of doom.

When Moll reached the Assistant Director's outer office, he glanced at his watch. He was right on time, but the secretary told him to have a seat and wait. He picked up the Washington paper from a low table and was relieved to find that the Shevtsov story had moved off the front page. There was only a modest item buried deep inside reporting the Soviet Union's claim of diplomatic privilege against discussing the details of its UN Mission car. The piece also quoted an unnamed source warning of the possibility that the bombing was an act of purely domestic terror. That would have come from New York, Moll figured, somebody huffing and puffing to blow a little of the heat back up north to the scene of the crime.

He leafed through the rest of the paper until the secretary took a call on the intercom and told him the Assistant Director was finally ready for him.

Moll found quite a crowd waiting for him around a confer-ence table, including three men from the New York field office. They had been discussing the case without him. He was the odd man out, and they looked up at him as though he were asking for parole.

"Hello, Henry," said the Assistant Director, rising from his chair. He was a wan, nervous man, new in the position and showing it. Moll had seen many men overestimate their power when they got a promotion. They got so used to looking up the ladder at all the looming forms above that when they advanced a few rungs themselves, they forgot that the appearance of great size was only a trick of perspective. It made the newly promoted especially dangerous.

"We got started without you," the Assistant Director said.

"Maybe I should have caught an earlier shuttle," said Moll.

"No harm done," said the Assistant Director, and Moll accepted his false forgiveness gracefully. "I think you know my staff. Don Paulson has come up from New York along with Sam Perry and Dick O'Neill."

Moll made the round of handshakes, leaning over the table to reach the hands that did not strain to meet him halfway.

"We were just puzzling over how quickly the word of the Russian car got out," said the Assistant Director.

"Press was all over this one," said Moll, preempting anyone who might have been tempted to start in on him. "You know how it is when the locals get into it."

"When I sat up in bed that morning, my nose hit a brick wall," said Paulson. "I heard about the Russian lead on my clock radio."

"I think I can explain that, Don," said the Assistant Director. "Somebody here at Headquarters dropped the ball. The message should have gone out to you immediately."

One of the section chiefs shifted in his chair and examined his manicure.

"I'm afraid it has complicated our side of it," said Paulson. "Put the Soviets' backs up."

"We all appreciate the difficulty this has caused you," said the Assistant Director.

Moll nodded his head. He appreciated it, all right. Appreciated it the way you appreciate a good cut of beef or a kind word, the way you appreciate a joke. But he did not smile.

"As I said before you arrived, Henry," said the Assistant Director, "in my opinion, this aspect is a dry hole."

Moll now understood that he had been excluded from the earlier part of the meeting to protect him on the question of the leak. Paulson was putting up the small residual fight simply to underline his own blamelessness and secure a little extra time to come up with something tangible in the case before fingers in Washington began drumming on the desk.

"I don't think we should be dividing our attentions at this point," said the Assistant Director.

"I agree, of course," said Moll. But he did not feel particularly relieved. The leak was the easy part. And even if he had been tempted to relax, the Assistant Director quickly yanked him back to attention.

"The locals seem to be the only ones getting anywhere," he said.

"Maybe we should review the bidding," said George Watling, who handled the Soviet side of the counterintelligence unit. "See just what in the hell we know."

"Yes," said the Assistant Director. "That might be helpful. Henry?"

Moll drew back slightly and put his hands flat on the table. He was prepared for this. It was hunch time, and in the Bureau a man was known by his instincts. The FBI liked to pretend that investigative work was a science: precise, meticulous, inductive. But like science, it was also highly intuitive. The facts, such as they were, only took you so far. As a case developed, endless scraps of data began to collect around you. And at some point no single mind could comprehend them all. If you tried to work that way, piecing the thousands of little misshapen items together like a jigsaw puzzle, you were doomed to fail. The picture in the puzzle was too obscure, the pieces badly cut. So you had to go at it a different way. You had to have an idea of what the thing might be and test that guess against the file. Out of the infinite possibilities and mass of detail, you made up a story. And what you made up depended on everything you had ever experienced—every observation of the way people and things behave when ignited, every ugly thing you had ever discovered about yourself.

"It is, of course, too early to narrow the thing," Moll began.

"Of course," said the Assistant Director, nodding. "That goes without saying." Everyone's first instinct was to hedge his bet.

"We have pretty well established the way the murder went

122

down," said Moll. "The explosive was dynamite. It was detonated by a remote-control device fashioned from a telephone beeper."

Watling's thumb tapped against a legal pad that sat before him on the table. The Bell System was not the network that interested him.

"The serial number was partially obliterated," Moll said, "but it was enough to lead us to a man who had reported his device stolen weeks before. The police had a file on it, but the victim had not told the phone company to stop service. Expected the locals to run down the thief immediately, I suppose. Hated the thought of losing a single call."

"You come up with any traces?" said Watling.

"Through phone company records, it was possible to determine exactly the time the call that detonated the device was made. Records show that in the preceding several days the beeper code was dialed a half dozen times. Unfortunately, they do not show where the calls came from."

"Somebody was testing it," said Tom McCullough, the domestic security section chief. He fingered the Phi Beta Kappa key on a chain across his vest. It was an affectation everyone tolerated because they knew that if he was an intellectual, his field was Bureau politics.

"That's a good bet, Tom," said Moll. "But it does not get us very far. There is another point worth reviewing: how and when the device was placed in the car. Now to begin with, I must say that this was not a technically perfect piece of work. The way the beeper itself was acquired suggests an amateur, though a clever one. And the placement of the charge was not the most efficient."

"Efficient enough," said Watling. There was no mistaking what kind of story *he* planned to tell. For him it was the wily Soviets tricking the thing up to look crude. This was congenial with the way the Bureau wanted it to come out; Watling was occupying the most comfortable square on the board.

"Yes," said Moll, "it was good enough. Even though the wiring was amateurish, the beeper worked nicely. And while the dynamite was poorly placed, the charge was sufficient to guarantee that the passenger would die. It could have been set by an expert who wanted to make it look like beginner's luck."

Watling nodded.

"The interesting part, though, is not the bomb itself but the other material," said Moll. "The lab has verified that the device was wrapped in rags soaked in a mildly radioactive solution. There was no functional reason for the chemical to be there."

"Odd business," said McCullough.

"Another piece of deception," said Watling.

"Maybe," said McCullough, fingering the chain again.

"If the radioactive material was of local origin," said Moll, "we think it could only have come from one of the hospitals or from a firm that handles disposal of the wastes. There are, of course, any number of people affiliated with the hospitals who have histories of political activism. And it turns out that the firm . . ." Moll consulted his notebook, ". . . Nufab is its name . . . the firm is not overly cautious with this material. Its records are not in good shape. There could have been slippage at any number of points."

"You spoke of political activists," said McCullough.

"There are people who have been connected with émigré groups," said Moll. The response around the table was as he had expected. Nobody was leaping on *that* possibility. It played right into the CIA's hand. "There are also plenty of young people—medical students, nurses—who were in the antiwar movement."

"Doesn't point anywhere in particular then," said the Assistant Director.

"No sir," said Moll. "And I'm afraid that other leads are not much more promising. The second victim in the car was its owner, and his habits made it an easy matter for anyone who wanted to tamper with the vehicle to find an opportunity. He parked in an alley behind his apartment every night. Unlighted. Very little traffic. A guy could slip in, plant the thing, slip out unnoticed."

"Are you going to get into the matter of who knew that this particular car was going to be used?" asked the Assistant Director.

"Unfortunately," said Moll, "we are dealing with a university here. The fact that Shevtsov was going to stay with Professor Kamen was widely known and resented. Shevtsov agreed to visit only if he did not have to make the usual round of teas and dinners. The invitation came from Professor Kamen personally. The only other person he wanted to see was a man named Steinman.

"The whole matter of Shevtsov's plans became quite a topic of conversation on campus. There was some debate about Professor Kamen's behavior in the matter, whether he had been out to monopolize the glory of the great man's presence. The story even got into the student paper in the weeks before Shevtsov arrived, names, photographs, every detail of his itinerary. Anyone who wanted to could have found out about it."

"Henry," said the Assistant Director, "you mentioned the man you traced the beeper device to. Maybe you ought to touch briefly on him."

Moll could see that he had almost no interest in the point. He only brought it up because Moll had left it dangling. The Assistant Director's sense of a meeting was as orderly as his polished old desk and credenza. You did not leave a torn-off piece of paper sitting there. You looked at it, and then you filed it away.

"His name is Roger Greenwood. Upright citizen. Middle manager. A little stiff, maybe. A little unsure of himself. But smart enough to know that he isn't supposed to show it. You know the kind I mean."

Moll looked around the room at the pinched smiles on his colleagues' faces. They knew the type, all right. They met him in the mirror every morning.

"Belonged to the JCs," Moll went on, "a churchgoer. Wife and three kids. Nice home out in the suburbs. He kept the access code taped to the beeper. I bet he has his name sewn into the collars of his shirts."

"And where does this all lead you?" asked the Assistant Director.

"Doesn't sound like jack shit to me," said Watling.

"Maybe not," said the Assistant Director. "But it is a very curious way for the Russians to do business. Radioactive vials. Stolen beeper devices."

"Sounds to me like a domestic group," Paulson hazarded.

"That would be consistent with the general pattern," said McCullough. He was a man who knew when to make his move, and how far to take it. "Most of the radicals have graduated and taken jobs in Daddy's company. The ones who are left are the cadre, the hard core."

"We're starting to put the squeeze on," said Moll, "but so far nothing has turned up."

"I don't know why you guys keep looking the wrong way on this," said Watling. "We've got the motive. The Russians hated this sonofabitch. We've got their man placed at the scene, probably to report back how the thing went down. I think we've got them by the short hairs."

"It's true that we don't have anything specific on local talent," said McCullough. "But stealing a beeper device from some poor mope on the street? It isn't the Russians' style."

"Look," said Watling, "they could have been using some free-lance talent. Maybe some of McCullough's hard core were in on it." Moll admired the man's ability to compromise, to let everybody have a little piece of the action. "They may be operating through six layers of cover, but you can bet your ass that the Soviets are there at the bottom."

The Assistant Director did not commit himself. He straightened up in his chair and lighted a cigarette. The others fell silent as he snapped his silver lighter closed and rubbed his thumb over the round brass Bureau seal that decorated it.

"I have heard nothing about a possible anti-Soviet motive," he said, raising the point to see whether anyone was fool enough to get on the record taking the Agency's hypothesis.

"Highly doubtful," said McCullough.

"I don't see it," said Paulson.

"No way," said Watling.

"Henry?" said the Assistant Director.

"It's my understanding that our position is that Shevtsov had broken all his Soviet ties," said Moll. Watling shook his head at this evasion.

"Everyone is agreed, I take it, that there is probable political involvement," said the Assistant Director, raising a big enough tent that everyone could get under it.

"Jumps right out at you," said Watling.

"We seem to have reached a consensus," said the Assistant Director.

"The Agency will be furious," said Paulson.

"The Agency is always in some state or another," said the Assistant Director.

"I don't think we can rule out the possibility of one man acting alone," said Moll.

"I see that your U.S. Attorney has gone out on that limb," said the Assistant Director.

"Only because I thought we might smoke out a statement of responsibility," said Moll.

126

"But you are going further than that now. How strongly do you feel about this?"

"Strongly enough to mention it," said Moll.

"Yes," said the Assistant Director. His cigarette was burning down toward his yellowed fingers, but he made no move to stub it out.

"I guess I'll just have to find the sonofabitch to be sure," said Moll.

They all had a good laugh at that, even Watling.

"You do that, Henry," said the Assistant Director.

Bishop Tadewski's Home stood on top of a hill surrounded by meadows and woodlands. The cleric whose name it memorialized had held the property back from development during all the boom years after the war. The poor immigrants in his flock did not scrimp at the collection plate even when special offerings were exacted. They loved him for the way he linked their past and their future, preaching to their small community in their native tongue the honor of their nationality and the glory of America. He was their only spokesman, before they mastered the ways of free politics, and they were glad to confer upon him the immortality of stone and mortar when the days of his administration of their own imperishable souls came to an end.

The Home was a functional monument, squarish and squat, a blockhouse of a structure faced with red quarry tile that always reminded Majewski of the inside of a kiln. It was staffed by Sisters of the Immaculate Conception in martial blue habits. The Sisters superintended the professional nurses and nurses' aides and a cadre of strong and lovely young girls straight from the old country who did the heavy lifting and filled the halls with the language and laughter the elderly men and women had known as children.

When Majewski came in out of the wind, he found the old folks queued up from the elevator to the chapel doors. This was the way they always moved, like soldiers or inmates. Wheelchairs butted up against one another at odd angles. Stiff and useless legs jutted outward on the metal braces; heads hung down as if in prayer.

A few people looked up as Majewski pulled off his coat and draped it over his arm. He nodded and forced a smile. Their faces, twisted by stroke, suggested either laughter or tears.

"Psst. Sonny."

He turned and saw a gray, regal lady crooking her finger in his direction.

"Good morning, Mrs. Cincowicz," he said, and moved up next to her. His mother had been her cleaning lady years ago in an enormous old frame house near the university. Mrs. Cincowicz reached up and took his hand, pulling him toward her.

"They are trying to rob me," she whispered. "Here. Take this. I want you to have it before the damned DPs make off with it."

She placed an imaginary object in his hand and then closed his fingers around it.

"What have you given me, Mrs. Cincowicz?"

"It is very special," she said, her words so perfectly articulate that it was hard to believe she was senile. "It is everything you ever wanted in the world."

He opened his hand slowly, looking down at the emptiness, the deep crevices of his flesh.

"Why yes it is, Mrs. Cincowicz," he said. "Yes it is."

"I knew you would be pleased."

A nurse had been watching this transaction as she passed out medication in little white paper cups.

"Have you been handing out imaginary diamonds again, Mrs. C?" she asked in a tone of gentle chiding, like a mother lecturing a child.

"I can give anybody anything I want."

"Mr. Majewski," said the nurse. "Please open your hand and show it to Mrs. Cincowicz."

He did so, with a certain reluctance, as if they were children caught at a nasty game.

"See?" said the nurse. "It's empty."

"Good boy," said Mrs. Cincowicz. "Keep it hidden from that she-devil in white."

Majewski winked at her and smiled. The nurse caught him doing it.

"Don't humor her," she said, and then she turned to the old woman. "Now if you want to give him a real gift, why don't I go get that piece of ceramic we worked on yesterday in crafts? That would be a nice present."

"Stay away from me."

"It's important to know what's really there and what isn't," said the nurse. "It's too easy to let go of what you don't have."

The old lady sank into a pout, and the nurse patted her hand. "She's been drifting off from us lately," the nurse said, "and we've been trying to get her back."

Reality therapy is what they called it. Addled by stroke, senility or Alzheimer's disease, the old folks slipped into fantasy as if it were a place to hide. This one held conversations on an imaginary telephone with friends long since dead. That one reified his quite reasonable fear of pain in the shape of thugs closing in to beat him up. The attendants were trained to intrude upon these moments. When they caught a patient slipping away, they would go up close to him, lips an inch away from his ear, and repeat again and again some simple facts. There is no telephone here, Mr. Polanski. The phone is down the hall. Would you like to go call your daughter? No one is coming to hurt you, Mr. Wallach. It's only the girls. They have to get you out of those wet pants.

"I think Mrs. Cincowicz's little game was harmless," Majewski said. "She likes to give me gifts because I knew her as a child." And now, he thought, I am a parent defending her. "My mother worked for her years ago, did her housecleaning."

"We are all equals here," said the nurse, with great authority. And Majewski could only smile in submission.

Just then Father Reba skimmed into the big parlor outside the chapel, his black surplice trailing along behind him like a wake. As he passed the line of patients, some of the ladies reached out for his hand and kissed it. He allowed them to, but then he knelt down next to them and shared a few quiet words. When he had made his transit, the attendants began to move the last of the patients into the chapel, and he went across the room to a long wooden cabinet. He slid open one of the doors. Behind it was an array of electronic equipment. He snapped a few switches. Two big reels of tape began to circle, and an organ sang softly from the speakers in the chapel. Majewski stepped up beside him.

"Welcome," said Father Reba.

"Hello, Father."

"Your mother is already inside. She always sits up front. A rare devotion. We could make room for you there. I have some folding chairs in the closet."

"Thank you, Father, but I'd just as soon not interrupt."

"It will be a short service, I promise you. The quality of mercy."

"Has she been doing all right, Father?"

"Splendidly. Splendidly. The infection has cleared up. She is making great progress."

"Holding her own."

"We measure progress oddly here, I suppose," said the priest. "But just yesterday she was out of her room. And last night she had a visitor."

"Who?"

"You needn't be so surprised," said the priest.

"It wasn't one of the family, was it?"

"That would not be such an enormous miracle, would it?" Father Reba said, smiling. "But no, I didn't recognize him. He was an older gentleman. He was speaking to her in Polish, and I would have sworn that she was talking, too."

Father Reba kept track of everything. Not one little sorrow fell from the lips of one of the patients that he failed to notice. He knew what kind of medication they were taking, who was having trouble with his bladder or his faith. He remembered who had sent them postcards, and he could state the name of each grandchild, niece, and nephew whose pictures were tacked up on the wall.

"You haven't seen my son around, have you?" asked Majewski.

"I'm sure I would have heard about that miracle."

"He was supposed to meet me here."

"Kids," said Father Reba. "No sense of time."

"I've been taking too much of yours," said Majewski. "You have work to do."

"It's always a pleasure to see you, Stan. Why don't you stop by after you've had your visit?"

"I'd like that," said Majewski.

The priest turned and went into the chapel. The ladies' heads turned to follow him up the aisle. Majewski could see his mother up in front, her face lighted by the promise of the Mass. Father Reba began to intone the immemorial words, make the ancient gestures. Her head bent downward, and he saw her lips moving, shaping responses she could no longer speak aloud.

He moved away from the chapel door. When Rose died, he had stopped going to Mass. And long before that, he had realized that for him the words of hope were hollow. He had continued to say them only so that Rose and his mother would hear them in his voice and be reassured. Now it was painful for him to watch the ritual motions. He was thrown back upon his memories, the truth, immune to solace.

His mother's room was bright and airy; a window stretching all the way across one wall looked out on the meadow. The bed was made up tightly, and the smell of disinfectant soap was piny and fresh. The silk flowers he had brought the last time were arranged in a dry vase on the chest of drawers built into one wall.

When the attendant wheeled his mother in after Mass, Majewski embraced her awkwardly, his arms taking in not only her shoulders but also the cold steel frame of the chair. She accepted his kiss impassively, looking past him into every corner of the room.

"David couldn't make it today," he said. "He wanted to, but something came up. Maybe the next time."

He reached into his breast pocket and pulled out a photograph.

"Alice's new little baby," he said. "They named her Morgan. Can you imagine? A nice Polish girl named Morgan."

His mother took the photo and held it out in front of her. Her fingers bent it, and Majewski resisted the impulse to stop her.

"Shall I put it on the board, Ma?" he asked. She shook her head an emphatic no and raised her hand toward the chest of drawers.

"Here. I'll lean it up against this vase," he said.

Only pictures of the immediate family went on the corkboard, and most of them centered on David. The big, touched-up graduation picture. The shots they had taken when he had been confirmed. There were pictures of him with Majewski, the two of them with ball and bat and glove, pictures of David and Rose; it was hard to look at them now. Then there was one with all four of them standing out in front of the house saying cheese. It had been Easter, and they were off to Uncle Joe's for the annual sharing of the blessed, unleavened bread. Rose was dressed in a sweet pink skirt that billowed at the knees when she twirled. David had on a new blue suit and a thin tie. Father and son had wrestled with that tie at the mirror, four hands working on the knot that seemed as important and difficult as the bond of love.

"Do you remember when we had the neighbors take this shot?" he asked his mother. "It was Easter. Nice and warm. A perfect day."

His mother nodded and then her head dropped down.

The attendant did not balk at the door when she came upon

them consoling one another. She just rolled in the meal cart and slid from it a tray. As Majewski took out his handkerchief and dried his mother's eyes, the attendant put the tray on the bed and swung the invalid table around in front of her, adjusting it to the proper height. Then she put the tray on top of it and took the plastic cover off the dish. Steam rose from the mush of meat and vegetables.

"I'll just go ahead and feed her myself," Majewski said. "Are you hungry, Ma?"

His mother slowly lifted her arms one at a time with utmost concentration, placing her hands on either side of the plate. Then she moved her right hand uncertainly toward the spoon. The fingers twitched open and then tried to close upon the metal shank. But they could not get a purchase on it.

"That's very good," he said. "You almost got it. You've been working on that, haven't you, Ma? Here, let me try."

He picked up the utensil and scooped up a dab of potatoes. She opened her mouth and took the food, a little of it smearing under her nose. She affected a look of great disappointment. Majewski smiled.

"Pretty bland, eh?" he said. "I wanted to bring you a good spicy *gołąbki* and a chili dog, but they wouldn't let me. That will just have to wait until we can get you home."

He did not know whether she really believed that this was still possible, and he was sure that she heard him pause on the words whenever he said them. He had never been comfortable telling her lies.

He fed her the pureed vegetables and meat, lifting the cup of tea from time to time to her lips to wash it down. Then he treated her to the ice cream, which was the part she loved. When she was finished, he wiped her face with a warm, wet cloth from the bathroom and swung the table away.

"We need a little music here, don't you think?"

The radio sat next to the vase with the silken flowers. He switched it on and the sound that came out was Muzak, a million strings playing "Eleanor Rigby." The attendants must have put it on. He turned the dial to the public broadcasting station, something classical. She seemed to brighten.

"They like their music as mushy as the food, don't they?" he said. "Here. I'll leave orders to keep your diet solid."

He pulled out his notebook and a pen and jotted down a courteous note saying what stations she liked. Then he poked his finger through the paper and affixed it to the knob.

"That should do it. Mama don't allow no accordion music around here," he said. "Say, I understand you had a visitor yesterday. Nobody could tell me who it was. An older gentleman, they said. It couldn't be that Uncle Joe finally stopped by, could it?"

She shook her head no.

"Some new beau then?"

She moved her lips to try to say something, but the word came out so pinched and muted that he could not begin to make out what it was.

"Well, I hope he keeps coming around, whoever he is. I believe that it would do you a world of good to have a few gentlemen callers. I have always believed that, as you know."

He used to like to tease her about this, suggesting good prospects from among her widower acquaintances. She would always become a bit flustered. But this time her reaction was altogether different.

"Do I know this fellow?" he asked, and she tried to say the word again. She labored at it, fighting the distortion of her lips, the unresponsiveness of her voice. He bent over to try to catch the sound, but it was only a nonsense syllable.

"David?" he said.

She shook her head again.

"Kah," she said. "Dah. Dah." She leaned still closer to his ear and whispered it, putting all her energy into shaping the sound.

"Father?" he said. "It was Father Reba who told me about him. He said the man spoke Polish with you."

She continued to shake her head. Then she paused, took a long, slow breath, and her fingers clamped on the arms of the chair.

"Dah," she said. "Kah. Dah."

"Did you think you saw Father?" he said. "Is that what you're trying to say? That my father came here?"

She slumped back into her chair, and he could not tell whether it was because he had gotten it right or because she had failed.

"Did you have a nice time with him? I hope it was a good visit, Ma. I truly do."

He took her hand, and he could feel her fingers holding tightly to his.

Father Reba's study was on the third floor above the chapel. It was as modest as the patients' rooms except that it had a table for writing and bookshelves on every open wall. Majewski looked at the titles as the priest poured tea. Some were ecclesiastical. Others were philosophical treatises and thin volumes of verse by people whose names he did not know.

"Did you have a good talk?" asked Father Reba as he cleared a place at the table, pushing aside papers and books and setting out a cup and saucer for Majewski.

"She seemed well."

"But not as well as you had hoped."

"When you come regularly I guess it's hard to see the improvement. Her color looked better."

"Progress is a subtle thing. You have to have an eye for it. Sugar?"

"No thanks."

The priest stirred a couple of packets of sweetener into his tea and then sat down across from Majewski.

"You mustn't get your hopes up too high," he said.

"I think it is accurate to say that I have none."

"Ah, the consolation of apostasy," said the priest. "I have always believed that we underestimate our competition in that respect. If a man is in the habit of preparing for the worst, he is rarely ready to accept the good news we offer."

"In my business good news is no news. I guess I've been thoroughly corrupted."

"By the truth, I suppose you would say."

"It all depends on what you've developed an eye for," Majewski said.

"Yes, I read your paper quite . . . I almost said religiously," said the priest. "But when I think of what some of the people in this home have gone through, it is an inspiration to see how well they have kept their faith."

"My mother seemed to believe even more deeply after she came out of the camps," Majewski said.

"Faith can be power against evil incarnate."

"Maybe the unseen evil is more destructive," said Majewski.

"Sometimes it seems that way, doesn't it? The thing that worries me most is the children."

"Maybe for them power *is* evil."

"They have seen so little to test their faith."

Majewski wished he knew what they had seen, what they felt. He sipped his tea.

"I have an indulgence to ask of you, Father," he said.

The priest obliged him with a little laugh.

"It isn't for me. It's for my mother."

"Name it," said the priest.

"That man who visited her yesterday. She thinks it was my father. He's been dead for more than thirty years, but somehow he has returned to her. And I think it makes her happy. I hope that no one tells her it is not so."

"I thought you were a great believer in truth," said the priest.

"I believe in fact," Majewski said. "I also believe in resignation to it."

"In giving up."

"I suppose neither of us is perfectly consistent."

"How do you mean?" said the priest.

"You insist that the people here renounce their fantasies and then offer them the Mass."

"It is not so odd as all that," said the priest. He stood up and placed his hand on a shelf next to a dark, framed Rouault print of the face of Christ. "The Church has always recognized the power of things a person can touch. Medals. Rosary beads. Votive candles. The icons at the Stations of the Cross. Some have ridiculed these things as primitive. But they are the very substance of our faith."

"I don't know who the man was who visited her, Father. But I hope he returns, and I hope she continues to believe in him."

"I'll try to find out who he is if you'd like," said the priest. "It's not uncommon here for people to lose track of who is who."

"Don't let them take him away from her," Majewski said.

"Some of the nurses may not like it. They think your mother is still strong enough to save from delusion."

"Maybe they don't understand the source of her strength any

better than I do," said Majewski. "But if she can reach out for something that gives her hope, that is good enough for me."

"I'll do what I can," said the priest.

When the day guard came to relieve Jenkins, the morning sun was a cold, tarnished coin in the clouds. In the old country they used to say that men should take a lesson from the sun, which shares its blessings equally with peasants and princes. Oh, last communion in the haze. That was before men had tricked out its secrets and turned them to sovereign purposes. Now the only equality was fear.

"Cold one last night, eh?" said the day guard as Jenkins let him in the gate. "Looks like rain."

"Pretty quiet," said Jenkins. "Police patrols are back to normal."

They walked briskly to the shack, where Jenkins was ready to transfer responsibility: keys, hourly log, pot of coffee, and night-delivery receipts.

"They're saying the Russians had something to do with the bombing," said the day guard. "Somebody spotted one of their cars."

"Where did you hear that?"

"It was on the tube this morning," said the day guard. "I didn't pay much attention. Old fart like me, it takes a while to get going anymore. Slowing down, good buddy. I could sure use some of that coffee right now."

Jenkins poured him a full cup and then just a little for himself.

"I brought some doughnuts if you want one," said the day guard as he opened a brightly colored paper bag.

"They're wrong about the Russians," said Jenkins.

"Here's a plain one."

"They don't do business that way."

"What do you know about it?" said the day guard, stuffing his mouth.

"Enough."

The day guard swallowed and washed it down with coffee.

"Don't let that fancy uniform go to your head," he said.

Jenkins pulled at the heavy coat as if it were infested.

"This fool thing? Tin soldiers. That's what we are."

"They say the Russians had a reason to want the guy dead.

136

They say he knew too much. You never know what the hell they're up to."

"They aren't serious, are they?" asked Jenkins.

"Sounds like they are. Since when did you become such an expert?"

"I've seen what they do and how they do it," said Jenkins.

"My wife hates them, too. She's got family behind the Wall."

Jenkins signed out at five minutes past the hour. The day guard let him through the gate, locking it after him. He walked past David's apartment on the way home but did not stop. He turned onto the main boulevard and passed the soul food joints and jazz clubs, the squat, ugly projects, the high school with its boarded-up windows decorated with obscenities: "FUCK TOMORROW. THERE IS ONLY ROCK AND ROLL." A few blocks farther, a huge old church rose up from the rubble like something left by war.

Some impulse drew him to it. He mounted the steps and pushed open the door quietly. A priest was at the altar. The pews over-flowed into the aisles at the rear. Some things had not changed at all over the years. Women wore babushkas, bright, gay colors against the stone. The men kept on their heavy leather coats, and the air was thick with incense and flesh.

The priest lifted his hands high and began to speak. The Mass was not in Latin anymore. It was in his mother tongue, and it seemed odd to hear it said that way. But Jenkins did not give back the responses. He did not kneel. It was all lost to him now.

Ever since he returned from the war, he had been haunted by the words his commanding officer had spoken once as they pre-pared to go into battle. "When you are close to your enemy," the officer had said, "you are close to God." The man thought it inspirational, and there was no denying the way you could be drawn to Him in fear. Perhaps this was what had brought him to this church today after so long. But when the fighting was over and he saw the consequences, the remark became bitter in his memory. He had gotten close to God, all right, and all His works.

Before that day, Jenkins had been spared by chance. His unit had been held in reserve. He had encountered Germans—stragglers, most of them just looking for an excuse to be captured—but he had never met them in force.

Then finally he faced his one great test. It did not come without warning. Intelligence predicted that the Germans would mount an offensive against his unit's share of the line. The men waited on a cold, empty field. They dug in and huddled together, each of them alone. The younger ones seemed almost eager, and they must have thought of Jenkins as a weary old veteran who had seen it all, for he had nothing to say to them. He just stared across the distance and prayed for the courage to hold on.

When the attack came, it began with artillery. The first shells clattered like switching trains over his head. Then the world exploded. The ground heaved up and shook. He tasted the wet soil as the sides of his hole collapsed around him. He was an insect madly burrowing to avoid a great, stamping foot. The very thought of courage had suddenly become absurd.

As the barrage lifted, he dug out from beneath the debris and gazed across the acres of pounded earth. He shouted left and right. No one was alive to answer him. Then he saw the German tanks, great, merciless Titans roaring toward him. When they stopped, their big guns turned and fired. Flames leaped from the cold, steel snouts. There was no way a man could stand against the total fury of such machines. Jenkins climbed out of his hole and ran.

He stumbled over corpses, headless, limbless, meaningless lumps of flesh. He threw himself down into craters when the explosions came near. One officer tried to stop him. But the man was gravely wounded. He barely had the voice to call Jenkins a coward before Jenkins bowled him over. They were the last men alive, and this officer spoke of bravery. The man was a fool.

Finally, Jenkins reached a forest. The sounds of the battle grew muffled as he ran. When he stopped to catch his breath, he condemned himself for the vanity that had led him to believe he could ever free his homeland. The only freedom in a world of instruments of such incredible violence was the freedom to flee. He opened a tin of rations and ate it, greedy for every last, sustaining morsel.

It was getting dark when he reached a farmhouse. He sneaked up to it on his belly, then lifted himself to peer through one of the shattered windows. The noise of shells had gone away, and the air was still. Nothing moved, outside or in. He tried the door. It came off its hinges and fell crashing to the floor. The roof had gaping holes in several places. But there was still a hearth undamaged and, incredibly, a carefully made bed. Jenkins built a small fire that night to stop the chills that ran through him, and he fell into a deep sleep without dreams.

It was days later before he began to realize the immensity of what he had done. Only then did he resolve to reach his homeland a different way, to get there by stealth. This was the only thing he could do.

The priest up in front of the church prayed for the sick and the dead. Jenkins's head bent down. It was up to man to redeem the works of God from evil. And yet we are prostrate before the horrible power, cowards in the face of the terror of the machines. No one dares to think of liberation. We dream only of survival, like burrowing worms. Let us pray. For fathers who cannot protect their sons and sons who cannot defend their fathers' failure. Lord, hear our prayer. For children who do not know what it is to be brave. Lord, hear our prayer. For those whom You have given the instruments of doom. Lord, forgive our vengeance. For impotence and defeat and fear. Lord, grant us peace.

Jenkins slipped back out the door, the litany a hushed singsong behind him. He breathed the cold air deeply and felt the indifferent sun on his face. After he had stood a few minutes on the steps, the shuddering stopped and he was ready again.

From here on, the neighborhood was more familiar—neat storefronts and well-kept flats. He stopped at a little grocery on the corner near his apartment. The big door tripped a little hanging bell as he stepped inside. He looked up into the round, distorting mirror high on the wall and saw the grocer's widow moving around by the meat counter.

"It's me," he announced.

"Hello, Mr. Jenkins," came the voice from the back.

"Don't trouble yourself," he said to the spherical figure in the rounded glass. "I can find what I need."

He went to the refrigerated case and picked up a quart of milk and a half dozen eggs. Then he felt the loaves of bread stacked up next to it and took the one that gave his fingers the most satisfactory resistance.

"This is all I have today," he said as he padded toward the counter. "And a paper, too, I guess."

She reached behind the counter and pulled out one with his name neatly printed in pencil at the top.

"I saved it for you," she said. "Everybody wants a newspaper today. You'd think it was the day the war ended. But you're too young to remember that."

"Oh, I am old enough to remember," he said. "I remember it vividly."

"Did you live here then, Mr. Jenkins? Did you go out on the street and dance? Maybe I danced with you that day. There were so many. And some, I have to admit, I may even have kissed."

"I'm afraid that I did not have the honor of your company," he said, smiling and formal. "You see, I was not here."

"It's a pity, Mr. Jenkins," she said, taking the bills he held out to her and ringing up his change on the old register. "You must have been a very handsome young man then."

She folded the *Herald* over on its big headline and put it in the brown bag before he could read it.

"Not so handsome," he said, "and not so young. By then I was very, very old."

"You are too modest," said the widow, touching his hand lightly as she handed him the package. "Come again."

He was weary as he left her and walked the last half-block to his apartment. He disengaged the three dead-bolt locks in turn. On the first floor, you had to wall yourself in like a prisoner, and even then sometimes you came awake in the daylight hearing strange voices that sought you out. He closed the bolts behind him and lifted off his heavy coat.

It was a small apartment: kitchen, living room, bed and bath. The living room was for work, a table set out for all the electronic parts he liked to fiddle with when sleep would not come, and next to it an ancient black typewriter on a stand. He went to the kitchen and poured himself a glass of milk.

He thought of David. The boy did not let anyone but Jenkins see what troubled him. Perhaps he did not really know it himself. *You have to work in close to what you hate*, David had said. But the young man did not yet fully understand what was right to hate and fear. He was all tangled up: his grandmother's tormented past, his mother's early death, the things he blamed.

Jenkins wanted to uncouple these matters one from the other, to relate them to the larger issue behind them all, the thing that corrupted, that burned. *You have to work in close to what you hate*. As if you could hope to get away. When you are close to the enemy, you are close to yourself.

He forced himself to eat a little breakfast, just toast and jam. He was afraid that he would again be unable to sleep. And so when he finished, he went beneath the sink and pulled out a bottle of vodka he kept for times of trouble. He did not like to drink to relax, and the bottle had lasted him many months. But now his need was great. He poured an inch of liquor into a glass and sipped it. The liquid burned in his throat.

Then he went into the living room and put some Chopin on the record player he had bought secondhand and repaired himself. The rich night music soothed him. He took a seat, put down his glass, and unfolded the paper.

PROBE SOVIET LINK TO BOMBING

It was an official diplomatic car from the Soviet UN Mission, of all things. Somebody was quoted saying that it was the first good break in the case. He shook his head and took another sip of liquor. It went down more easily, and he began to feel the deadness spreading across his windburned cheeks. Did they take the Russians for a bunch of idiots? The Russians did not capture nations by being fools.

His eye moved to the accompanying article, and it struck him like a blow.

PROSECUTOR CALLS KILLER A "MADMAN"

It had to be a trick. Such incredible quotes from the federal attorney, a man who should have known better: "We are obviously dealing here with the work of a madman, some deranged and deviate personality that finds satisfaction in the death of innocent people." Innocent! This man was supposed to be a lawyer, and yet he talked like an ignorant peasant. Jenkins did not expect them to countenance the act, but at least he was sure they would recognize its gravity. A madman.

He read every sentence about the bombing, the inconsistent speculation about radical groups, the chronology of domestic terrorist incidents, the whole obvious business. It was absurd. They cheapened the thing. Didn't they understand what Shevtsov had done?

"The thing that makes an investigation like this so difficult," the prosecutor was quoted as saying, "is that the person we are seeking is so clearly irrational that the question of motive is useless to pursue. We cannot hope to follow the demented twists and turns of such a troubled mind.''

Jenkins slapped the paper down and began to pace. Soviet assassins. Terrorists. Insanity. All the rage that was in him surged to the surface. He went to the telephone, looked up the *Herald* in the book, and dialed the number. But when the girl answered, he just eased the piece back into the cradle. This was the wrong way. He had to keep on a steady course. If he wanted to make his point, he would have to do it cleverly. He would have to plan, work in close to what he hated, to all the works of God. He took two deep breaths, went to his desk, and buried his face deeply in his scarred old hands.

SIX

Was it for this the clay grew tall?

When the music came on the clock radio in the darkness, Majewski did not know where he was. A cello cried out like a siren or a man in pain, and he sat up in his bed, sweating.

He had drunk too much whiskey the night before. Though it had failed to block the nightmares, he was paying a price anyway. His head throbbed and his eyes ached as he lowered himself back into the pillow. He had been dreaming of David again, of losing him.

After a few minutes, he could no longer tolerate the sound of the radio, so he rolled out of bed and slouched into the bathroom where he emptied his bladder, threw water onto his face, and shaved.

If he had not been drunk, he might have done better last night when Susan Cousins called. He might just have listened. He might have accepted her apology for bothering him when Danny went away, or he might have brushed the apology aside. But he would not have gone on and on about his own problem. He would not have been tempted by her consolation. And he certainly would not have accepted the offer to join her for dinner the next evening at her home. More than his headache, this was the measure of just how drunk he had been.

Majewski chose his newest suit, a dark one that did not show a stain of newsprint at the pockets, and put on a fresh white shirt and a gaily colored tie. Rose had always bought his ties for him; they were stylish and bold. He wore them with all the ease of a little boy in his first Sunday suit.

When he had finished dressing, he noticed a spot on his cheek that he had missed with the razor, just a few little pinfeathers. He took out the blade again and scraped at the dry skin. The metal pulled. Blood beaded up along the cut. He ripped a sheet of tissue from the roll next to the toilet and dabbed at it. The paper soaked up the blood but did not stop the oozing. Somewhere in the medicine cabinet he had some aftershave that would dry it up.

There were still women's things on the shelves: lotions, balms, and blushes. He had left them there after Rose died, just as he had left all her clothes in the drawers. The cosmetics sat in clusters, bottles whose caps had hardened shut, whose labels were faded and curled. Behind them he found the lime-scented stuff she had gotten him once for Christmas.

He put his index finger over the hole and tipped a drop of fluid onto it. When he touched the finger to the cut, he winced at the sting. The diluted blood smeared on his skin. He wiped it off with the tissue again and leaned toward the mirror. The smell was not unpleasant. What the hell. He poured some of the lotion onto his palm and slapped it all over his face. Then he tore off a little corner of paper and fixed it on the wound. Limed and patched, he moved from the bathroom to the bedroom, where he picked through the clutter on the bureau and filled the pockets of his suit jacket. Then he went downstairs.

In the kitchen he filled a saucepan with water and put it on the stove to boil. When he opened up a package of English muffins, crumbs scattered all over the shiny countertop. He tried the toaster, just in case it might somehow have healed itself, but the coils lay cold. So he lighted the broiler and put the muffin on it, crumbs igniting in bitter smoke under the flame. In minutes the bread had charred on top. And by the time he had peeled the foil back from the margarine stick, the water was in a frantic boil. He spooned crystals of coffee into a mug and spilled the hot water over them—some of it pouring onto the counter and dripping over the edge onto his shoes.

He ate quickly, the melted margarine somehow finding its way onto the cuff of his shirt. He wiped his shoes with a napkin and left it wadded on the counter. As he walked back into the living room, he made footprints in the puddles of water on the floor. The muffin wrapper lay crumpled in the sink. Crumbs trailed across the counter and the linoleum. The saucepan had boiled down to a calcified scum.

When he turned on the radio, somebody was interviewing somebody else about cats. He left it barely audible and sat down in his favorite old chair. David had always liked to sit on his lap in this chair. Something about the deep cushions, the way it seemed to engulf you, hold you safe from harm.

There had been so much promise in the boy. All his teachers

had agreed that he was bound for good things. Majewski remembered the way the boy had discovered language, like someone waking out of a deep sleep. Within a matter of weeks he had gone from nonsense syllables to complete sentences. It had been a joy for Majewski to come home at night, just to hear what his son had to say, the new connections he was making, the way he worked a word until it was as smooth and polished as a looking glass.

He had loved to teach his son. Together they had put out a little newspaper, with David's compositions on the morning trip to the grocery and Majewski's wry observations on the neighbors' quirks. But from the very beginning, David had been most interested in science: infinity, the periodic table, the whirl of atoms, and the unthinkable distances of the night sky.

There were other, harder lessons to learn. In Majewski's house they could not be avoided. Grandma Statia was a living example of the extremes to which human beings could be subjected. Majewski and his wife did not try to hide the facts. They told him about the war, what had happened to his grandparents. It was never clear just how much he picked up on. But Majewski tried to teach by example how a man could endure, as steady and encumbered as a beating heart.

"Why would anybody want to do those things?" David had asked him once.

"I don't know, son. They just did."

"They must have been monsters."

"It's harder than that. They were ordinary people, just like you and me."

It was harsh, and at times Majewski was tempted to soften it. David would have believed him if he had. But Majewski just did not have it in him to lie about this. The recognition of the monster in each of us was the only way he could make sense of the past.

For a long time, David did not show any ill effects. He was a little nervous, perhaps, full of the usual morbid fantasies. But in every outward manifestation he was just a normal little boy. And yet, Majewski could feel David beginning to slip away from him, as if the things the father taught repelled the son like an opposite pole.

Only when the going got very rough did David seek him out. This gave times of trouble a strange, sweet dissonance. During the missile crisis, David was at an especially vulnerable age. Like all the children of his generation, he had grown up on the images of destruction, the films of thermonuclear tests on Pacific atolls, great spheres of fire beyond imagination, even the imagination of a child. All along he had known the possibility that something might someday touch off this terrible thing, but until the crisis, it had never quite been real. Then came the picture of the missiles lying just off the southern shores, the President's grim warnings. The possibility was upon them. It was there.

They sat in David's room every morning, sometimes talking, sometimes silent, the dim light from the hallway throwing shadows that made them both seem older than their years. Majewski stayed until David's eyes grew heavy and he drifted off into a sleep which rarely lasted through the night.

Majewski did not know what to say to the boy, so he told him true stories of his own past, the Nazi columns marching beneath his window, the night he left home and looked back to see Warsaw aglow like fire. He told David how hopeless it had all seemed then, as if everything he had ever depended on had been swept away. And yet, even the Nazis had not been able to destroy the future. Evil had not triumphed. Good men and women had prevailed. This, he said, was simply fact.

"You won't send me away, will you?" the boy asked.

"No, son. Of course not."

And Majewski wondered in silence which was worse, the flight or the impossibility of it. He took hold of his son's hand in the darkness.

David pulled his fingers away slowly, held them to his eyes.

"I don't want to die," he said.

"You have a long, exciting life ahead of you."

"Everybody dies," said David.

"You're too young to be worrying about it now."

"No, I mean everybody dies at once. That's what makes it different. Everybody."

In the end, the crisis passed. Eyeball to eyeball, said the men in the White House, and the other guy blinked. Everybody was blinking in the aftermath, like men coming out of a dark hole.

Afterward, David did not call his father into his room at night anymore. He seemed almost embarrassed by the way he had behaved, as if he realized that they had both gained something through the danger and that it was wrong for anything good to come of such a thing.

New troubles came along, of course, the murder of the President, the growing war in the tropics, events that took your attention away. These things were palpable, immediate. The other sank down like regret. The testing had gone underground; no more pictures of the fire. The missiles were hidden in the wheat fields. You did not see the explosions anymore, only an occasional tremor, a camera wobbling, a wide, shallow hole opening in the desert, a sinking feeling whose origin you could not quite place. You did not need to dream about it, or at least you could forget that you had. The vapor trails in the sky diffused into long, soft clouds. The ululating sirens in the night were no longer a terror; somebody had simply gotten hurt, and help was on the way.

David did not do well in high school. This was a warning sign that Majewski might have noticed if he had not been so preoccupied with the news from Rose's doctors. David's homework went undone, and the lapses went unpunished. It was not that he had fallen into the wrong crowd. There was no crowd at all. David was a loner. He spent hours by himself in his room listening to that awful music and tinkering with his electronic equipment. Now and then he had other boys over, but they were sullen, too. Losers, Majewski thought; he is attracted to those who attract no one else. Looking back on that time, Majewski realized that he should have been alert to the lack of feeling, the way David walled people out of his world. There was no fire in the boy, no fire at all.

When the doctors discovered that Rose had cancer, she drew even closer to her son. As soon as they accepted it themselves, Majewski and Rose explained the situation to David, the treatments and the effect they would have on her, the odds. Rose worried about how he would take the news. But Majewski believed it was foolish to try to protect him from a truth he would soon be able to see. The boy did not flinch when they told him. He did not cry or demand to know why. Perhaps, like Majewski, he saved his tears for the bathroom, water running loudly, so that no one else would know. If you did not see the affection, you might even have thought that he did not care.

Except that he often protested that not enough was being done for her. It was natural, Majewski supposed, that he should expect the doctors to have an answer to everything. And David could see as well as anyone else the toll Rose's treatments were taking on her. David got an idea into his head that the medicine and radiation therapy she underwent were killing her. And it did little good when Majewski tried to explain to him that they were meant to kill the errant cells, that they were weapons in a mortal struggle inside her body.

David retreated further from his father and moved closer to his mother, as if when the question became life and death he felt he had to choose sides. They spent hours together, David reading to her when she did not have the energy to sit up with a book, or else just talking. Rose found excuses for his behavior, the deteriorating grades, the nights when they could hear him pacing past midnight, unable to sleep. When Majewski raised the question whether David might be experimenting with drugs, she simply refused to discuss it.

Rose hung on bravely for almost four years and somehow managed, as she drew David in, to hold Majewski tightly, too. In an odd way there was sweetness in those years, a deepening of all his affections. When Rose became too ill to keep up the pretense of cooking and doing the errands, Majewski's mother moved in with them to help carry the load. They were a real family, the three of them at least, with David hovering at a steady distance, held there by Rose's strong gravity, like a moon.

Majewski kept working at the paper, but he found himself shaving time from his duties, hurrying out before his copy cleared the desk, going into the office late in the morning. Rose chided him about this. She accused him of changing his habits for her sake, and she would not have it. But finally he persuaded her that this was not the case. He just wanted to spend time at home because, more than ever, he felt happy there. It was, he said, like falling in love again. And Rose, pale and drawn now, put her hand to her wasted cheek and blushed.

She lived to see David graduate from high school. Majewski did not know what magic she used on him, but she managed to persuade him to go on. He did not even try for admission at the university. His scores were high enough, but his grades had been so bad and his record so bare of other accomplishment that even with Majewski's connections he did not stand a chance. Instead, he entered the state school that crouched in ugly new blockhouse buildings on the other side of town.

The doctors never did give up hope for Rose. They were quite content to renew the struggle each time the remission came to an end. When one poison could no longer hold the disease in check, they moved on to something even stronger. But each episode was more painful than the one before, each new therapy more severe. Finally, she had had enough. It was time to surrender.

150

Majewski supported her decision. He knew that even though he wanted her to live on at all costs, this had become a form of selfishness. He had to let her go.

David refused to accept it.

"You want her dead," he said. "I don't know why, but you do."

"Nothing of the sort, son," said Majewski. "It is a question of suffering. It is very, very hard."

"Get different doctors. Take her to someone who knows what to do."

"They all say the same thing, David. You know, accepting something is not the same as wanting it. A man must accept many bitter things."

"You're good at that. Giving up."

Sometimes when he was especially tired or full of doubt, Majewski raised his voice against such wounding lies. But most of the time he simply listened David out and said that, of course, it was not true. Someday, he said, you will understand what can and cannot be done. It comes with age, with experience in sadness.

The final course of the illness took nearly a year. Once the poisons had washed out of her veins, her own inner strength seemed to rally. But it was not enough, and the final suffering was terrible to watch. The pain grew so intense that no drugs were powerful enough to touch it. It was as if she were shrinking away before his eyes, her voice so small toward the end that he had to lean his ear to her lips to hear it whisper.

There was little time during the period of her dying to concentrate on David. The dark thoughts only came in the empty hours of the night when Rose was drugged asleep and David was off somewhere beyond communication.

During the final months, Majewski's only narcotic was work, and he took it in large doses. The biggest story going was the radical movement. He threw himself into it. He already knew the cops, but he made new contacts among the student leaders, the older agitators, the hangers-on. He covered all the rallies and marches, suspended between the adversaries. He followed the byzantine struggles within the movement for ideological supremacy and personal power. He watched wave upon wave of young people enter the ranks as confused little children and emerge hard and bitter, lost. He attended the meetings, pumped his sources for information about what went on in the closed sessions where the tactics of taunts and trashings were discussed with all the seriousness of a council of war. Unlike his friends in the police, he did not so much fear what all this was going to do to community and country; he worried most about what it was doing to the kids.

Even more than before, he lost touch with David. Then by chance one night they found themselves together. Majewski had gone to cover an emergency rally against a new phase of the war. It was held in Woolsey Hall, which was festooned with obscene banners, crude effigies, and National Liberation Front flags. The crowd was excited, gay with rage.

But when the speeches began, there was an edge of violence in them. This time it would not be enough simply to obstruct the repressive processes of the university by a strike. Now it was time to contemplate destructive direct action. Majewski wrote down the phrase, noted the scattered cheers. There seemed to be a division in the crowd, even among the speakers themselves, between those who thought the revolution was at hand, right there under the grand rococo ceiling of the hall, and those who for whatever reasons of up-bringing, temperament, fatalism, or fear preferred the gesture to the act. The atmosphere turned solemn. Faced with a decision with consequences, the majority retreated into the secure comfort of collective guilt. The speakers, an impressive array of national figures who had not yet gone underground, tried very hard to whip up a frenzy, but it did not work. The voices of self-interest prevailed. The strike was on, but the revolution would have to wait for another day.

As the young people filed out of the hall, Majewski saw David alone in the lobby, leaning against a high marble wall that commemorated the university men who had died in battle. There were hundreds of names chiseled into the white stone, only a few of them from Vietnam. Above David, carved into the arch, were the words "We who must live salute you who have found the strength to die."

"David!" Majewski shouted.

His son saw him, turned away.

"You need a lift somewhere?"

"There are a few things I have to do," said David.

Majewski looked at his watch.

"I have plenty of time before edition," he said.

"I'll just hitch."

"Back home?"

David just looked at him.

152

"Your mother seemed a little better today," Majewski said. "She might still be awake if you want to talk to her."

"I'll be pretty late. Don't wait up."

The crowd was streaming past them, and Majewski moved closer to his son to get out of the way.

"Which side were you on in there, David?" he asked.

David took his father's measure for a moment, glanced around to see whether anybody else might be listening.

"You want it straight?" he said.

"The truth."

"I'm supposed to be angry," said David. "But most of the time I don't feel anything at all. It's like being dead."

His eyes were frightened.

"I don't want you to get involved in violence," said Majewski. "That won't help."

"What will?"

"I don't know."

"You can't do a fucking thing about it. That's what you would say, isn't it? Just sit back and take whatever anybody dishes out."

"Life goes on."

"Does it?"

Majewski took it as a challenge. And yet he was powerless to save a single soul.

"Nobody's giving any guarantees," he said. "I wish I could, but I can't."

That was as close as they ever came anymore. The boy wanted something beyond Majewski's capacity to provide. And so it surprised him when David came to him with his problem about the draft.

David began by announcing that he was dropping out of school because of bad grades. That left him without a deferment, all exposed. He was afraid, and Majewski was, too. The war was getting bigger. The casualties were in the hundreds every week.

"Why don't I talk to the dean," he said. "Maybe he'll give you another chance." This way was best. It was clean. But David wasn't having any of it.

"Don't get on me about that again," he said. "It's over."

"You're bright enough. I've seen your scores."

"It isn't working."

"What about enlisting in the navy or the air force? That would keep you out of the worst."

"I don't want to fight their war."

"I don't blame you, son," said Majewski. "How about conscientious objection then? If that's the way you really feel."

"They don't believe you unless you're Quaker or something."

"We could write the papers together. We could go over all the arguments. I know lawyers who could give us a hand."

"Forget it, Dad," said David. "Just forget I even asked."

He did not want to let David down on this. He watched David's face, the trouble there, the need, and he decided to do something that defied everything he had ever believed in. He remembered his own father, the terrible decision he had had to make. There was no other way.

"Give me a couple of days," he said. "I'll work something out."

"How?"

"Leave it to me."

"I'll go to Canada."

"I don't want to send you away."

"Everything's all turned around."

"Yes it is, David," Majewski said. "Yes it is."

One week later David went to see the doctor Majewski had spoken to. It was all arranged, and the fee was high. A diagnosis was written, an X ray procured. David failed his physical with flying colors, and he never spoke of it to his father again.

Majewski stood up from his living room chair and pulled the tissue off the cut on his cheek. You had to try to protect them, even if it meant a lie. But at least he had never lied to David. That much was absolute. You had to be honest with your son.

This was the part you were supposed to enjoy. When you were onto something and you had a man on the spot, you could spill out all your anger and make believe it was virtue. The young reporters lived for such moments.

There may have been a time when Majewski did, too. Even today, knowing how small and pitiful the truth could be once it was exposed, he was a man to do his duty. And maybe a little more. When the thing was so secret that the voice on the telephone dropped down to a whisper and pleaded with him to let it lie, the forbidden thing drew him on like the pull of a black, collapsed star.

As soon as Majewski had read Devine's new letter, he had known somehow that this time the crazy old man had something to say.

Dear Stash,

Like I said, the only good Russian is a dead one. Didn't I tell you that man's visit would lead to no good? These are the days when the birds come back, a very few, a bird or two, to take a backward look. Ah, sweet Emily. If she were here, she would have a verse to mark his passing. Chickens coming home to roost.

But don't look for that kind of understanding in the *Herald*. I searched in vain for any reference to the fact that the Federal Bureau of Indignation is trying to find out why the blown-up car was hot. And I don't mean stolen, Stash. I mean hot. Radioactive. The Brownshirts want to know where the nuclear material came from. They're all over town asking about it. Don't you hear anything but your own stomach growling, Stash? I thought you were supposed to have sources.

Now maybe you'll understand why I think you've been missing the boat on this thing from the beginning. It's big, Stash, very big. And you can't let them get away with kissing it off as the work of a madman. In these times, everybody's mad. Power is only pain, stranded, through discipline, till weights will hang.

Check it out.

Sincerely,
John Devine

The first thing Majewski did was to shag Joe Stawarz out to the police auto pound to get whatever details he could. Then he set to work on the phones.

Nobody in the city room knew what angle Majewski was pursuing, but they all sensed he was onto something. They looked his way as he hunched over the telephone making his first tentative moves. They came by his desk and rubbernecked his notes. He did not look up. As he got nearer and nearer to the center of the secret, he became lost to everything. His work closed behind him, a perfect sphere.

By the time he put through a call to Bob Raskin, he was sure that John Devine had been right. Majewski's sources in the police department would not confirm, let alone elaborate, but they sent him signals in the silence that told him it was true. And so when Raskin came on the line, he put the question bluntly.

"I'm not asking you to give it to me," he said, and his fingers tightened on the telephone's curving throat. "The lead's already written. And it doesn't look good. You knew about the danger, and you covered it up."

This was the way it had to be done. You could not simply show the fact. You had to turn it against the man who could improve it, make him feel the point against his skin.

"That's not how it was," said Raskin.

"I imagine even your buddies from *The New York Times* will see it my way once they read my piece."

"Hey, I had to be on the square with those guys," said Raskin. "No favorites. Not even you, Mr. Majors. I am the U.S. government here."

"You're nothing of the sort."

Certain parts of the ritual were always repeated: The raised chalice of innocence. The reading of the creeds—your pure duty and mine. The confession that finally poured out behind the anonymous screen.

"I've got a problem talking to you about this," said Raskin.

"You've got troubles. I've got troubles. All God's children."

"You're playing Russian roulette here."

"Now is when you tell me about my responsibilities and I tell you about your vulnerable ass," Majewski said. It was all so predictable, the defenses and the way they shattered. "I want to know about that car, Bob."

"Look, I haven't actually seen the lab report. Moll's holding it close."

"But you know what I'm talking about," said Majewski. "Don't give me a line of bullshit. If you do, it'll only make it worse when the Bureau hauls out the memos showing that you were fully briefed."

"I heard something about it," said Raskin. "Look, are we off the record here?"

"No names, if that's the way you want it."

"Hey, I don't mind seeing my name," said Raskin, trying to be funny about it, the way small men did when it was the most important thing in the world. "It's very weird, Stan. The shit was some kind of medical product. I mean, we're not talking here about a thermonuclear device. The radioactivity wouldn't hurt you. It wasn't strong enough to do any harm."

"What do they call it? Does the stuff have a name?"

"I hope you aren't going to blow this thing out of proportion. You know, people get scared when they hear about radioactivity."

Shouting fire in a crowded theater when there was no fire, Majewski thought. Maybe it was wrong even when the fire was real. But this got him into questions he could not afford to consider just now. When there was a conflagration, he only allowed himself to ask about the extent of the damage and the way the dead spelled their names.

"I'll tell you what would help," he said. "Some details. Just exactly what the nuclear material was, where it came from, what it's used for. In my experience, the best antidote to fear is fact." Except, he thought, the fears that are justified, the fears that fact inflames.

Majewski held the telephone cradled against his ear, and he signed onto his computer terminal in a few silent strokes so he could take his notes directly onto the screen.

"There isn't much more I can tell you," said Raskin. "Like I said, I never got a look at the lab report. The Bureau is working the leads. Somebody said the name of the stuff, but I don't remember it. It was something they use in hospitals."

"Did you consider notifying the people who might have been exposed?"

"I raised the point as soon as I heard about it. Hey, I was out at the scene, too. I got a dose of it myself."

"But nobody was told."

"The level of radioactivity was very low. Nothing to worry about."

"Shit, Raskin. You don't even know what the stuff is called. This isn't adding up to a whole lot of comfort, my friend."

"Just say that we received assurances that there was no danger. Let's put it that way. Sources said the U.S. Attorney's office received assurances that the dosage was trivial."

"Assurances from whom?"

"From Hank Moll."

"You don't mind his name being used?"

"Pin him," said Raskin.

Majewski punched the keys, and the name lighted up on the screen.

"When was this thing discovered?" he asked. "Right there at the scene?"

"Not to my knowledge," said Raskin. "I only heard about it after the locals had dragged the wreck away."

"Somebody must have been onto something."

"Way I hear it, Moll noticed some scraps of rag around the wreck and had samples flown to Washington."

"Smart man," said Majewski.

"It was a lucky hunch. He's a plodder, Stan. You have to keep after him all the time."

"What I don't understand," said Majewski, "is why anybody would go to all the trouble of putting this stuff into the bomb if it wasn't going to do any damage."

"Maybe he didn't know any better. Maybe he thought it was potent."

"But he exposed himself to it, too. Had to in order to make the device."

"It doesn't make any sense," said Raskin.

"Where can I get hold of Moll?"

"He's paying a little visit to Washington. Headquarters has him on the hot seat."

"You have a number for him?"

"Forget about Moll," said Raskin. "Stick with me, Stan. I'm in a position to do you a lot of good."

"This isn't holy matrimony, Raskin. I don't sign a contract. I deal with whoever comes by."

"Round heels."

"Call it whatever you want."

"I can't help you with a phone number. I haven't talked to Moll since he left."

"Well, if you do hear from him, just tell him I need to have a little chat."

"No way," said Raskin, with a pathetic little laugh.

Majewski was first off the line. Even though he had the story nailed, he was still uneasy about it. You had to be careful when you were dealing with radioactivity. People were afraid of it, and much as he respected Henry Moll's judgment, the assurances of an FBI pavement pounder were not going to allay anybody's fears. He remembered what had happened when the new power plant had gone on-line out by the river. There were a few hitches, nothing unusual, just the normal mechanical bugs that show up in any sophisticated piece of work. The papers reported these and ran sidebars with fancy graphics showing precisely how the process worked. Nobody had even been exposed. The core of the reactor simply had to be shut down to make repairs. But from the way people responded, you would have thought somebody had dropped the Bomb.

Majewski wanted to answer as many questions as he could in the very first piece, to lay the thing out plain so that at least no one could claim that he had played it on the cheap. He put a call through to Bureau Headquarters and left word that he needed to talk to Moll. Nobody there was too encouraging about finding him. So Majewski worked the thing another way. Raskin had said that the mystery substance had something to do with nuclear medicine, and this was a break. If there was one place a reporter developed sources over the years, it was at the hospitals.

The university medical center sprawled along a spur of the Interstate. It had grown haphazardly, matching need to endowment with little thought to appearance. Here an old red brick wing named after the great Depression benefactor rose stately and grand. Next to it, connected at the hip, was a concrete and glass addition put up after the war. On the inside, you could tell where one structure ended and another began by the awkward breaks in the corridors. The wings were not only different in style but also in scale, so the long halls were fractured by stairs and wheelchair ramps where the older vision had given way to the newer, the proportions scaled down.

He did not need to ask directions. He knew his way through the maze, past the closed doors of the labs, the waiting rooms where nervous men and women held their vigils. The sweet smells of alcohol and unstarched linen were a memory, the nurses' impersonal smiles.

He walked through the wing where Rose had so often stayed, and he remembered the mornings when he would wait there as she underwent treatment. At the time, there were several cases of cancer touching the *Herald* staff. He would pick up the paper and leaf through it, and almost always he would find some story on a new form of therapy, a promising line of research, a miracle remission. The newspapermen passed messages to one another on its pages, sad little notes that said maybe it could still turn out all right. And when it didn't, they simply found other stories to fill the void.

"May I help you?" asked the secretary in the administrator's office. She did not recognize him. She was new.

"I'm Stan Majors from the *Herald*."

"Was Mr. Tompka expecting you?"

"He never expects me, but he's never surprised when he finds me poking around."

"Can I ask the nature of your business?"

Sure, he thought, it's in the nature of a shouter of fire. But he did not say it.

"Are you Polish?" he asked.

"Pardon?"

"I was just wondering if you were a Polish girl. You kind of look like you might be, but I haven't seen you before. I thought maybe you were somebody's daughter."

"Can I tell Mr. Tompka why you need to see him? He's very busy."

"He'll know."

She was not persuaded.

"It's OK," he said. "I give you my word."

"Well," she said, "I'll page him then. But I don't know."

He turned away from her and took a chair on the opposite side of the room. He flipped through a magazine on health and hygiene.

"Can I offer you some coffee?" the secretary asked.

"Says here I drink too much of the stuff already. I'll take it black."

He had barely taken a sip of it when Tompka came through the door.

"What's up, Stan? Are we in for it again?"

"No emergency," Majewski said.

"It isn't a social call, I don't suppose."

"Not that either. I'm here about that incident the other night over at the law school."

Bud Tompka did not hesitate, not even for an instant.

"They were both DOA in the emergency room," he said. "As I understand it, the coroner took possession of the bodies and did the posts himself."

"Could we go into your office?"

"Judy, hold the calls for a few minutes."

"She looks out for you," Majewski said at the inner door so she would be sure to hear it.

"Keeps the sharks at bay," said Tompka. "Most of them."

His office was modest. There were filing cabinets out in the

160

open and prints from the drug companies on the wall. Tompka pulled out a drawer of his beige desk and braced his foot against it.

"Cigar?" he said, taking a package from the pocket of his shirt.

"Never touch the things. Doctor's orders."

"Doctors give a lot of orders," he said, inspecting the wrapper and ring before lighting up.

"What I came here about might be trouble, Bud. I don't want to kid you about that."

Tompka shrugged.

"Why is it I'm not surprised?" he said.

"I want to know what the FBI's been asking about the nuclear material you use here. And what you've been telling them."

"What took you so long, Stan?" Tompka said, and he took a long, leisurely pull on the cigar, turning it gently between his big fingers to get the burn to roll evenly at the tip.

"I want to be right on the technical parts, Bud. And I don't want to stick it to the wrong people."

"It's going to send everyone right up the wall," said Tompka.

"Not least the people at the university."

"Rest assured," Tompka said. He pulled off his glasses and tugged at the ridge between his eyes.

"You've already informed them," said Majewski.

"They aren't the kind of people who like to be surprised."

"So the material did come from the hospital."

Tompka slipped his glasses back on and took his foot off the drawer. He put his cigar down in the tray and looked at it as if it had turned into something foul between his lips.

"Maybe I'd better walk you through this from the beginning," he said. He punched the intercom button and leaned toward the speaker. "Judy, bring in that file on special materials, will you?"

She was quick with it; the file must have been one they were keeping ready to hand.

"We handle a variety of radioactive substances here, as you know," Tompka said, taking the manila folder from her. "Some are used for therapy, some for diagnostic purposes. Then there are the research materials we use on laboratory animals. By and large the nonresearch materials are not particularly dangerous. They are not toxic and the radioactivity is very low-level. We expose patients to them, Stan."

"Can you guarantee that exposure at the bomb site was harmless?"

"Oh my, yes," said Tompka. "There is perfect agreement about that. We've been over that ground thoroughly—our people, the doctors, the physics department, the public health experts. We estimate that the largest dose anyone could have gotten is still no more than twenty percent of the government safety limits. Even the occupants of the car had nothing to fear from their exposure."

Majewski wrote the grim quote in his notebook.

"The material itself probably was part of a batch of a therapeutic cancer preparation that was recalled," Tompka said. "The total amount involved can only be estimated, but you have to realize that the bomb spread it over a half acre of stone and concrete. The concentrations at any given spot would have been minimal. As I understand it, the liquid had been soaked into rags. So when the fire department hosed the area down, we assume that most of it washed harmlessly away."

"Is the bomb site still hot?"

"We have checked it, of course. There is some faint suggestion of a residue, but nothing to worry about."

"You seem to be taking this thing pretty lightly," said Majewski.

"I'm not saying that the drug is something you'd want to take every morning with your vitamins. But it isn't the end of the world either. Let me put it this way, Stan, the preparation is similar to one the doctors used on your wife."

Majewski did not write that one down. You had to keep the story at arm's length. That was the rule.

"What do they call it?" he asked.

"Oncyllium," said Tompka, and then he spelled it. "The manufacturer had sent out a bad lot. Ordinarily, we would only have to dispose of the bottles and syringes that had contained the drug. But in this case we had a fair quantity on hand when the manufacturer wired us to destroy it."

"How can you be sure the stuff in the bomb came from the bad lot?"

"All the rest is accounted for within the hospital," said Tompka. "We keep the material in a secure vault. When a doctor draws some out, he must sign for it and record its disposition. Here, this is an example of the paperwork."

He flipped through the papers until he found the one he was looking for, then he handed Majewski the file. The page was busy with notations—initials, dates, times—in barely legible doctors' scrawls.

"I assume there are no discrepancies here," Majewski said.

"That's why we aren't worried," said Tompka. "If the Oncyllium used in the bomb was ever on the premises of this hospital, it did not get away from us here. We have our ducks all in a line."

"So you're saying the stuff wasn't yours."

"Not exactly. I'm just saying it didn't go astray while we had custody. It could have been part of the recalled shipment. But that was all accounted for when it left the hospital."

"To go where exactly?"

"We contract with an outside firm that routinely handles radioactive materials. Nufab is the name."

"Reputable outfit?"

"We've always been satisfied with the service."

"Of course it's always possible that somebody here was corrupted," Majewski said. "I mean, your system isn't exactly fail-safe."

"Show me something, Stan," said Tompka. "That's what I told the FBI. I said, sure anything is possible. But you have to have more to tie the can to me."

Majewski's next step was to do the piece and talk it into the paper. The writing was easy. He had it banged down so tight that every fact was fastened to a name.

But when he made a printout and showed it to Ruffalino, the city editor balked. Pointing fingers at the Russians was one thing, but going after local concerns like Nufab and the hospitals was something else again. So Ruffalino shuffled off to consult with the editor. It didn't worry Majewski too much at first. At the *Herald* you had to get everyone into the boat before you took off down the rapids. But when Ruffalino returned, he was shaking his head.

"Samuels is having an anxiety attack," he said.

"Show me where I libeled somebody, Tony," said Majewski. "Show me where I'm out on a limb."

"It isn't the lawyers, Stan. Samuels read it to them. They're happy."

"You'd be happy, too, if you were pulling in that kind of money. . . . Don't tell me. Let me guess. Samuels has a tennis game with somebody from Nufab coming up and he doesn't want the guy calling foot faults."

"The man's got responsibilities to think of," Ruffalino said.

"Tell me about it. Two kids in college. A third who wants to be a doctor. The man likes his job."

"I gave him a pep talk," said Ruffalino. "I hauled up the flag. It's true, I said. One hundred percent. Stan doesn't take chances, I said."

"I imagine that impressed him."

"He didn't salute, Stan. He didn't sing the 'Battle Hymn of the Republic.'"

"Maybe I should have words with him," said Majewski.

"Sid James is in there now."

"Terrific. Just terrific. What's he got to do with a thing like this?"

"Samuels listens to him."

"It must be like listening to his own stomach growling."

Majewski took a step toward the editor's office. Ruffalino stopped him.

"Let it percolate for a while," he said.

"I've got a better idea," said Majewski. "I'm going to turn up the heat."

Samuels's door was closed, but the secretary wasn't at her desk keeping guard, so Majewski just knocked once and let himself in.

"The man of the hour," said Sid James.

"I wanted to make the pitch, Dave," Majewski said to the editor. "I wanted to urge you to go ahead with this."

"Somehow I just assumed you'd take that position," said Samuels.

He sat behind a big wooden desk that didn't have anything on it except a telephone, an ashtray full of pipes, and a newspaper that did not look as though it had been read.

"Can I talk to you alone?" asked Majewski. James did not move.

"Sid and I were just talking about your story," said Samuels. "I don't see any reason to rush."

"It won't be any easier to go with it tomorrow than it is today," said James, and Majewski was not sure whether this was an argument for or against.

"I've got some problem with scaring the bejesus out of everybody before we even know what we're dealing with," said Samuels.

164

"We've got it all, Dave," said Majewski. "This is it. There ain't no more."

"Who leaked, Stan?" asked James.

"Nobody handed it to me gift-wrapped," said Majewski. "I got an anonymous tip and worked it."

"I'd feel more comfortable," said Samuels, "if you had gotten it first from somebody we knew."

"Sorry," said Majewski. "I'm afraid I went out and did my job."

Samuels rested his elbows on his desk and pulled the cuffs of his shirt out of his suit jacket.

"What's the urgency?" said the editor.

"We've got it all by ourselves for now," said Majewski. "I thought that was what we were in business for. To get things first."

"You know, you guys piss me off," said Samuels, "the way you'll sit on your ass for weeks and then expect everybody to jump when you decide it's time."

"Stan's been on top of this from the start," said James. Majewski could not believe James was on his side. He wondered what kind of carom shot the man was lining up.

"Let's get some more details," said Samuels. "We'll look at it again tomorrow."

"What more do you want?" said Majewski. "I've got it cold."

"There aren't many holes," said James, but he was too smart a man not to give Samuels something to hold on to when the waters were rough. "Maybe we could get some experts to explain the risks, some doctors, to put it into perspective."

Majewski was not in a mood to negotiate.

"It's going to get out," he said, "one way or another."

"I don't think that's your decision to make," said Samuels.

Majewski was ready to make the threat precise. There were reporters from the national press who would be glad to get a line on a story like this. And Majewski was inclined to give it to them, and maybe even say why he was doing it. But James got in before him.

"Stan means it isn't going to hold," he said. "If we got it today, somebody else is going to pick it up tomorrow. Maybe sooner."

"You're trying to put me in a box, Sid," said Samuels.

"We're in it already," said James. "If the story breaks somewhere else, we're going to have to write it anyway. And maybe somebody else isn't going to be as careful as we would be."

"Civic duty," Samuels said.

"Limiting the damage," said James. "If we break it off ourselves, we can control it. That's all I'm saying. Anybody gets a burr up his ass about it, we can say we wanted to make it responsible. Ask them which is better, a cautious piece in the *Herald* or getting fucked by some bastard on the six o'clock news."

"I want you to get some doctors into the story, Stan," said Samuels. "I don't want to blow this thing out of proportion."

"I quote people from the university hospital already," said Majewski.

"More, Stan. More," said James. "Make them think the shit is good for them."

"I'll put the calls," said Majewski in the doorway, going out. James followed him.

"Thanks, Sid," Majewski said when they were beyond the editor's hearing.

"You owe me one," said James.

The second time the agents interviewed Jenkins, they came in daylight. A knock on the door awakened him from the shallows of sleep. He did not know who it was, so he yelled from his bed to go away. But then they identified themselves, and he pulled himself up. After wrapping a stained and frayed old robe around him, he opened the door against the chains and demanded to see the proof of their authority. The hall light flashed against the glossy color photos and official, laminated seals. Jenkins grunted and let loose the locks.

"Can't be too careful anymore," he said as they came inside.

"Sorry to bother you, Mr. Jenkins."

"I'm afraid you caught me asleep. Night work gets you all turned around."

"I'm Special Agent Richard Hollings. This is Phil Masselli."

"There were two others before."

"Yes, sir."

Hollings was thin and balding. His partner had a great shock of jet-black hair. They took off their overcoats, and he could see the bulge of their pistols under their well-tailored suit jackets. Neither of them wore a hat. Jenkins thought all secret policemen wore hats, if only to hide any softness in their eyes.

"They had a lot of questions," he said, moving back toward the kitchen. They did not follow him. "I answered as well as I could."

"Of course," said Hollings. "Would you like to get dressed?"

Jenkins tried to hide the way his breath caught in his chest.

"Are you taking me somewhere?" he asked.

"No, sir. Nothing like that," said Hollings. "You just might be a little more comfortable, that's all."

"Of course," Jenkins said, and he felt like a transparent old fool.

He pulled the bedroom door partway shut behind him and sat down on the bed where they could not see him struggling with the buttons of his shirt and buckle of his pants. He heard the agents moving around the apartment, looking for something.

"Can I offer you some coffee or tea?" he asked when he joined them again. They were at opposite corners of the room.

"No, thank you," said Hollings.

Jenkins cleared the newspapers off the chairs and stacked them on the floor, making sure that the headlines about the bombing were not on top.

"This is quite a setup you have here," said Masselli, gazing at the table spread with splayed radios, transistors, and wires.

"I guess you would say I am a tinkerer," said Jenkins. "I like to fix old things. Just to show that they can still work."

"I tried to make a crystal set for my little girl once," said Masselli. "Never did get the thing right. You could hear voices in the static, but you couldn't really tell what they were trying to say."

"It's tricky," said Jenkins, straining to hear what this man was saying beneath his words. "It takes practise."

"They say the kits are so easy a child could do them."

"Sometimes the children do better," said Jenkins, but he was not taken in. Even if these men were polite and did not wear hats to shade their eyes, it was only because they had no weakness to hide.

"We don't want to take up too much of your time, Mr. Jenkins," said Hollings. "But there are a few points we want to go over with you."

Jenkins sat down and steadied his hands on the arms of the chair. He had already shown them that he was ready to be taken away. This was the secret policemen's advantage. You did not know their secrets, and you could not tell how much they already knew of yours.

"I'm afraid I don't have much more to tell you," Jenkins said.

"We've examined the records of deliveries of medical wastes to Nufab," said Hollings, consulting a notebook the way a gambler consults his cards. "They show that you have signed for a number of shipments in the past year."

"Anytime they come in on my shift I sign for them. It's all in the logs."

"Yes, sir."

"It was usually the high point of my night."

"How's that?"

"Somebody to talk to. Something to do."

"Can you tell us the procedures you follow?"

"There are rules," said Jenkins. "Nufab has rules for everything, right down to the color of your shoes."

Both of them wore plain black ones, like a soldier's, spit-shined at the toes.

"In your own words," said Hollings, as if there were any others available to him. Jenkins picked up a pencil from the end table beside him and tapped the eraser against his knee.

"The van shows up at the gate," he said. "Usually I know the man who is driving. But I ask for identification anyway, just as I did a moment ago with you. When I have seen the proof, I open the gate and let him drive in. He pulls up to the guard shack, which is next to the main building, maybe fifty yards from the gate. You have been there, I assume. I don't need to draw you a map."

"Don't make any assumptions, Mr. Jenkins," said Hollings.

"No, of course not," said Jenkins. "That would not be smart."

"It's all right if you repeat yourself."

The better to catch me up in a contradiction, Jenkins thought. But this was easy. This was all true.

"Together we unload the drums and roll them into the shack," he said. "There is a place we keep open on the floor for this purpose. You never know when a delivery is going to be made."

"You aren't notified in advance?" asked Masselli.

"We're there around the clock. There is no particular need."

"Why are the deliveries made at night?" asked Hollings.

"Perhaps to please an old man," said Jenkins, humiliating himself before them, just as any experienced victim might. "To brighten a dark and lonely night . . . I don't know really. I am not consulted on such grave and important policies."

"Are the containers sealed when they arrive?"

"They are, and together with the driver, I open the outer drums to check the contents against the receipt that I sign. This also is policy."

"So you are sure that you receive everything on the list."

"The irradiated corpses of laboratory monkeys and rats. Broken flasks and beakers. Hospital masks and gowns that have been exposed. I check what is written on each container and mark it on the list. I do not actually look inside the individual containers. These are sealed, for safety. Yes, I am dutiful about recording the precise nature of the offal."

"Someone somewhere was not so diligent," said Hollings. "A batch of this stuff got away from you."

"From me?" said Jenkins. He stiffened. "I cannot see how."

"Not necessarily you," said Hollings. "The record-keeping inside the plant is a mess. This is what we are trying to pin down, you see, just where the chain of custody might have been broken."

Jenkins slowly allowed himself to relax.

"I am surprised," he said. "They are so particular about everything."

"They don't take the medical wastes seriously," said Hollings. "That much is clear."

"I suppose it is easy to become too familiar with danger," he said, but he did not believe it. You never got used to that peril. Never.

And yet at times it could be absolutely exhilarating. When the delivery man had shown him the receipt that night listing a shipment of Oncyllium, he realized immediately what he must do. He knew what that drug was used for; he had read about it in the science magazines. Together with the van driver, he counted the packages, each heavy, shielded cylinder holding a single vial. He replaced the top of the drum and placed the clipboard on it as he signed his initials on the line. And when the delivery man had left, he went back into the drum and withdrew one cylinder. It was heavy in his hand. He had slipped the container into the pocket of his coat where it hung on a hook. When his relief arrived, he heaved the coat onto his shoulders. The container pressed against his side. He had left the gate and made his way home, and for a time the danger seemed localized; he could feel its weight, touching him through the cloth.

"About the chain of custody, Mr. Jenkins," said Hollings. "Do the drums ever leave your possession once you have brought them inside the shack?"

"I have to make the circle of the plant," he said, pushing the memory back under the fear again, measuring his words. "But there is no one else on the premises. The plant is empty at night. The gates are barred."

"But it is not utterly impossible that someone could get in," said Masselli.

"Very unlikely."

"Over the wire," said Masselli. "A well-trained team could easily accomplish it."

"To steal a bottle of Oncyllium?" said Jenkins. "That would be going to a lot of trouble, I would say."

"We don't know who we're dealing with here," said Hollings.

"Wait a minute," said Masselli. "I want to ask Mr. Jenkins how he knows the name."

Jenkins was surprised by this, but it did not threaten him.

"Wasn't I supposed to know?" he said. "I am sorry. At the plant they talk about your questions. I could not help but hear. I must learn to close my ears to such things. They are not my business, and an old man is too likely to say things he should not."

"It would be best if you did not speak to anyone about this matter," said Hollings. "It is a serious affair, as you no doubt understand."

"You can see that I do," said Jenkins. "You can see that I am not at ease."

"You are doing just fine, Mr. Jenkins," said Hollings, and it only put him more on his guard. "Now tell us about making your rounds."

"Yes," he said, leaning forward against the stiffness of his knees. "I am out of the shack for a few minutes every hour as I move to the far side of the plant."

"How much time?"

"Ten minutes. Maybe a little more."

"On a regular schedule?"

"Perfectly regular. There are keyboxes I must deactivate at certain times each night or else they will send an alarm."

"Can you recall any time recently when you felt there might have been someone inside the wire with you?"

"Some nights I have been afraid," Jenkins said. But he did not say why. He did not tell them about fog and smoke, the memories they touched off.

"Afraid of anything in particular?"

Fearful only of what he knew, what he remembered, what he hid.

"At night, alone," he said, "it is easy to let yourself see things that are not there. But there has never been evidence of a security breach. If there had been, I would have reported it. These are just an old man's fantasies, nothing more."

"Do you routinely make a second inventory of the drums, Mr. Jenkins?"

"I don't understand."

"When you turn over custody at the end of your shift, do you recheck the contents?"

"This is not required. I assume my count is checked by others."

"Do you?"

"Assume it? I suppose so, yes. It is not really my place to worry about such things. All I know is what is required of me."

"Wouldn't it be just as good an assumption to believe that the material is transshipped without any further inventory?"

"I suppose it might be," said Jenkins. In fact, he had guessed that this was the practise. He had seen how carelessly the drums were handled, stacked about in a storeroom inside the plant, neglected. This was what had first emboldened him.

"So you might have felt free to take some of the material yourself," said Hollings.

He supposed they expected a denial. But he would not give it to them. When it came to what a man might think to do, a secret policeman would know that anything was possible.

"I might have felt that way," he said, "if I had some reason to want the chemical. But what would I do with it?"

"Thank you for your cooperation," Hollings said abruptly. "We'll be back in touch."

After he had shown them out to the street and given a polite little wave good-bye, he returned to his apartment and went to the window. Hands shaking, he parted the drapes a fraction of an inch. They were still sitting in the car talking. He went to the cabinet in the kitchen and poured himself a double measure of vodka. He swallowed the fiery liquid and closed his eyes. He had to talk to David. David was the only one who knew that Jenkins had taken the vial of hateful poison. David, David, David.

As the vodka warmed him and settled his troubled hands, Jenkins went to the table where the wires and capacitors were spread. Next to them, an old typewriter sat under its plastic cover. He picked up the electronic components and turned them in his hand. It was no wonder that men resorted to such things. Matter's behavior was predictable. It was only men who failed.

For a woman alone, Susan Cousins certainly put out a lot of light. Every window in the big old house was aglow, warm yellow lanterns in the night.

The curb in front was free, but Majewski pulled up a few houses down the street. The only other car in sight was a block down, moving away. Its blinker flashed like a warning sign. He took the wine bottle from the seat next to him and slid out from behind the wheel.

The streetlights were old and dim; it was easy to avoid being seen under them. The lawn muffled his footsteps, and the only sound was from the bare branches above him, squeaking in the wind.

He climbed the steps of her big house, his fingers choking the bottle, and was about to ring the bell when he heard something behind him. He turned. It was only an old man walking a dog.

Susan opened the door before he had a chance to ring.

"How long have you been waiting?"

"I thought maybe I'd forgotten to turn off my headlights," he said. "I was about to go back and check."

She took a step outside.

"They're not on," she said. "I can see from here."

"The only time you remember you might have forgotten is when you have remembered in the first place. That's Majewski's First Law. Would you like to hear the others?"

"Oh, Stan, come on inside, for heaven's sake."

He brushed past her, excusing himself for the touch. She laughed and took the initiative with a quick kiss on the cheek.

"Here. Let me take your coat."

Her blouse was white and high-collared, like something from long ago. Her hair was brushed back from her face and held in place by a clasp of shell. Majewski handed her the wine and his sloppy trench coat, then his fingers felt for his tie and pulled the errant knot up a half inch to the top.

"You didn't need to bring anything," she said.

"I hope the brand is all right," he said. "I'm not very good at this sort of thing."

When she disappeared, Majewski fumbled with his collar button until it popped off into his palm. There was a mirror in the hallway, and he looked at himself. His shirt was wrinkled and his suit jacket showed the day's negligence. He should have shaved again.

"Did you come straight from work?" she asked from another room.

"Something came up," he said.

He had been plotting out the next move on the story. It was clear that they had to find John Devine. Joe Stawarz had gotten a description from the guard in the lobby who had accepted his latest letter. The guard remembered the man's full head of white hair and his hefty paunch, not much more.

Joe had volunteered to hang around the office late just in case the fat man decided to drop off another piece of mail. Majewski did not hold out much hope of it, but he gave Joe Susan's phone number and told him not to hesitate to call.

"I hope I'm not too late," he said in the direction of the kitchen.

"Not even fashionably."

But that was her world, not his. When he was late, it was only because his car wouldn't start or somebody tied him up on the phone. Fashion was a different part of the paper.

"Have you heard any more from Danny?" he asked when she reappeared.

"Funny," she said. "I was going to ask you the same question."

"He might be coming home soon."

"You've talked to him?"

"Not since the other night when I saw you," he said. "But there's been a break in the case. It may mean he won't have to worry anymore."

"He always seems to do all right for himself," she said.

She had gone to a glass-topped table that held the bottles and tumblers. Her back was to him, and since he could not see her expression, he could not be sure whether she really meant to sound so indifferent.

"Would you like a drink?" she asked.

"Scotch and soda, I guess."

She dropped the ice into a glass and poured him a long pull of whiskey.

"Do I seem that anxious?" he asked.

She filled the glass with soda and handed it to him.

"It is really very sweet that you are," she said and took for herself a small measure of wine.

She was pale and proud, like old porcelain, not at all the little girl he remembered from years ago. Only her smile remained the same, the odd expression he used to go to the greatest lengths to provoke, teasing her like a big brother. The corners of her mouth would turn downward as her eyes lighted up. Her smile was inverted, as gay and troubled as the past.

It was the long-ago past that he saw in her now, the dignity of the women, their strong, quiet unwillingness to show any pain. Even the look of her place touched off memories—the polite sitting room in Warsaw his mother had decorated with heavy drapes and fragile figurines, the smell of flowers and old wax. He remembered the way they had entertained his father's colleagues from the university. The conversation then was too polite to linger for more than a moment upon the war. And now he felt again as awkward as a boy among adults, trying to be so very wise and yet showing his discomfort with every movement of his hands. Watching Susan's grace, he was struck by the way everything changed and then came around again. It had been Majewski who had tried in vain to hold on, but it was Susan, letting go of everything, who had found the way back home.

"You seem so distant," she said, sitting down across from him.

"I was just thinking about the house I grew up in. Something here reminded me of it."

"The one on Pearl Street?"

"I can't even recall the name of the street. It was near the university in Warsaw."

"My parents never talked about how it was in Poland," she said. "I had the idea that it was painful for them to remember."

"They would have been proud to see how you've done. Re-creating it."

"I don't know what you're talking about," she said.

"The style."

"You mean this furniture, the house?"

He leaned back and hooked his arm on the cushion of the couch.

"Something deeper," he said. "The way you are."

"Now you're just being foolish," she said. "You know how they raised me. I think they would have been horrified by the way I live."

"There's a difference between what happens to you and what you are," he said.

"I remember when I was a little girl, they asked you to a tap-dance recital. I was afraid that you would come and even more afraid that you wouldn't. Then that night I saw you in the first row. It must have been terribly boring for you, all those fat little girls pounding away on the wooden floor. You were just out of college, and Rose came with you. I remember how nice you looked, the two of you.

"Then my turn came, and I got up there and went into my routine. Halfway through I tripped and fell. I was mortified. I didn't want to look at you, but you caught my eye. There you were, winking at me and nodding your head that I should go on. So I did, my pudgy little knee bleeding, tears running down my cheeks. And when I was finished you stood up and applauded. I didn't know whether to be proud or just to curl up and die."

"You had a lot of guts," he said, laughing. "You always did."

"How can you see me now and not think of the round little girl in sequins falling on her face?"

"I only remember that you finished. You picked yourself up and went on with it."

Try as he might, he could not bring back the little girl he had been so protective of long ago. The memories were all confused, some lost, some regained. And he was seeing her now in a new and unsettling way.

"Last night you seemed awfully upset about David," she said.

"I had too much to drink," he said. "I should know better at my age. He let me down."

It was inevitable, he supposed, that she would get to this. He had invited it when he unburdened himself on the telephone the night before.

"Maybe you expect too much of him," she said.

"I've learned to scale down my hopes," he said.

"We all have."

"I'm afraid for him, Susan."

"Rose's death must have been hard," she said, "hard on both of you."

"At least I had my work."

"It's different when you're older. You're more ready."

"We've all grown up some, haven't we?"

"I have," she said. "But you were there already. I can remember how much I looked up to you. You were going to the university. So smart and successful. Everyone admired you."

"Except the family. They thought I was getting fancy. Even after I married Rose, they said so."

"*Cacy lala,*" she said.

He burst out laughing.

"Where did you pick that up?" he asked.

"You don't like my native tongue?"

"*Cacy lala.* It's an expression my mother used to use."

"About Rose?"

"About the family. I suppose she found other reasons to worry about Rose and me."

"You take after her, Stan. You worry too much. The times have been hard on kids. They have a lot more to deal with than we ever did. For us the big question was whether to kiss on the first date."

"That one never bothered me," he said. "But it wasn't a matter of ethics. I was agonizingly shy."

"David will straighten out."

"It's amazing how naïve we were, even during the war. We didn't think anything could touch us."

"Maybe you would rather not talk about him," she said.

"There's nothing to talk about," he said. "He's on his own." Then he stopped himself. "That sounds awfully cold, doesn't it?"

"Ice is a way to dull the pain."

"I wish it worked."

"You would be close to him if he let you," she said. "You can't blame yourself for all the things that get in the way."

"They all seem so hell-bent on hurting themselves."

"It's what you stand for, Stan. That's what he wants to get away from now."

"There's a comfort," he said.

"You stand for the truth," she said, "accepting it, no matter how hard it is. No wonder he's afraid."

"It's just my job," he said, "what I see."

"But you never look away."

"He can't run from everything."

"Maybe he's just trying to dull the pain, too."

Scientists said that gravity was the weakest force, but he did not believe it. His failure with David, the way she explained it, the attraction he felt, drawing him toward her; it was very strong.

"I think I hear the timer ringing," she said. "We can start dinner now if you'd like."

"That would be fine."

They did not talk much as they ate. He managed to compliment the food she laid out before him, and she managed to demur. He caught her watching him and began to say something. She shook her head. There was no need.

He felt in a strange way safe with her, the way he had as a boy when he went to church and poured out his worst to the faceless priest on the other side of the screen. He did his penance and then just stayed there kneeling, the candles flickering against the wall, knowing that the moment was sanctified and that outside the big wooden doors a world waited to drive him again into error and remorse.

"I should help you clean up," he said and began to pile up plates and bowls in a precarious stack.

"It's all right," she said. "I'll take care of that later."

They moved into the other room, and when he took his place on the couch she sat beside him.

"The dinner was wonderful," he said. "You know, Danny has been after me for a long time to come over. I didn't know what I was missing. I'll not make that mistake again."

Something came over her, and it was all out of line.

"When this thing is finished," she said, "when the trouble has passed . . ."

"Don't even ask me to come over again if you don't want me to take you up on it," he said. But she was not listening. "Is something wrong?"

"When this business is over and he comes home again," she said, "I'm going to leave Danny."

"Susan, no."

"It's something I finally decided. I thought I ought to tell you."

"Are you sure it's what you want?"

"Do you really have to ask?"

"Separation?"

"Divorce," she said. "We've been separated for years. I don't need to go into the lurid details, do I? Most of them you already know."

"You loved him once."

"Don't defend him," she said, "or me. It was a terrible mistake from the beginning. You tried to tell me so. But you were a friend. You held back."

"I didn't want to poison it. You seemed so sure."

"You know what kind of friend he was? He laughed at you, Stan. He said you were a fool. He thought of you as an instrument to get the things he wanted, a dumb, unfeeling tool. That's the way he sees everyone."

"Maybe you need to get away and think about it," he said.

"I knew you would try to talk me out of it. Maybe that's why I asked you over tonight."

"Because you weren't sure?"

"Because I needed to be certain that I really was."

"There's something to be said for hanging on," he said.

"That's what you've told me all along. Rose did, too. Bear with it. Keep going. Don't mind the pain and the tears. These are unavoidable. And, of course, you were right.

"I managed. I held together. I knew what he was doing, and after a while I stopped confronting him with it. We had a standoff, Danny and I. There were things I thought I needed in order to keep up the proper front, and he gave them to me. In return, I was never, never to ask for what he would not give. I can't let myself grow old this way, Stan. I don't care about the things. They were always just in place of something you've always had."

He did not want to see her tears.

"Have you told him?"

"He would have to be a stone not to feel it coming," she said.

"Is there a man?" His voice was so quiet it broke upon the words. She stood and turned from him. He did not know how he wanted her to answer. All the established ground was slipping from beneath him; the forces that held him in check were letting go. It was wrong that he felt this way. It was right. He could not deny what he was feeling, but he hated himself for it.

"I wish it were that easy," she said, and he heard her giving in to the tears now. "There isn't anybody else."

Her hands were at her face, hidden from him, and he did not know whether he dared to let himself comfort her.

"I wanted so little," she cried.

Majewski stood and went to her, a brother again. That was all.

178

"It's all right, Susan. It's all right to cry."

He put his hand softly on her shoulder, and she turned to him and held on as if he were the only steadiness in the world.

"Don't be afraid," he said.

She lifted her face and made a small, decisive movement that brought their lips together. And when hers opened to him, he closed his eyes in agony. It had been so long that he did not know what to do with the feelings she stirred in him. He was lost.

"Susan," he said, drawing back.

But she held on to him, brought his hand to her breast.

"Please," she said.

He could have stopped it then. He could have pulled away from her and stood there in a flush of embarrassment. And it would have been nothing at all.

"I'm sorry," he said. But then she arched against his touch, and he was not willing to resist the force that tugged at him. He held her close and cradled her head in his palm.

"It's all right," she said. "Lord, it is all right."

And when they kissed again, he did not hold back. She led him up the stairs, and they came out of their clothes somehow. Her breasts against his skin were soft and miraculous.

The sheets on the bed whispered as they moved. He touched her legs, the length of them, working slowly upward. And when he reached the place, she opened to him and made a foreign sound.

It was as if he did not know the way. He kneeled over her and she guided him. Deep beneath him, she held him in a curved, closed space where everything else was excluded. He moved slowly inside her, the rhythm as sure as his breath. And when it came to an end, she let out a cry that could have been his own voice.

The other world came back to him slowly, the smell of the linen, the cramp in his arm, the tick of the clock. She was breathing apart from him again, retreating.

"What have we done?" he said.

"Don't you know?" she said.

He only realized that he had fallen asleep when an angry sound startled him awake. He could not place himself at first: The warm presence touching him, a dream. The unfamiliar proportions of the bed. Then the telephone rang again, and Susan reached for it.

"Hello. . . . Why yes, just a moment," she said, putting her hand over the mouthpiece. "Stan, it's somebody from your office. What time is it?"

He found his watch on the floor and picked it up by the band. "Eleven-thirty," he said. "We must have slept."

"Like infants," she said and handed him the receiver. He looked, but he did not see the regret he expected in her. He wondered if she could see it in him.

"Majewski," he said into the phone.

"Hope I didn't bust up anything."

It was Joe Stawarz, and he was laughing.

"Don't worry about it."

"Hey," said Joe, "I'm not the lady's husband."

"Did you find the fat man? Is that why you called?"

"Never did show, Mr. Majors. I'm getting ready to go."

"You don't need my permission, Joe."

"It's just that I came up to the city room to get my jacket and saw there was a message for you. I wouldn't have called, but I thought maybe it was important."

"Hank Moll finally get back to me?"

"Not that. It was a guy named Reba. A preacher or something. From that nursing home."

"Oh, Christ, no." He drew in a sharp breath against the dizziness.

"I thought you'd maybe want to know."

"Was there a message?"

"Just to call him right away. And the number."

Majewski sat up and swung his legs over the edge of the bed. The sheet lay across his lap, but it was not nearly enough to cover him.

"I have the number."

"Hope everything's OK, Mr. Majors."

He hung up and then began pulling on his clothes. They resisted him, tangles and catches. He cursed.

"Business?" Susan asked.

"Is there another phone?"

"You can use this one," she said.

"The nursing home was calling me," he said. "I've got to talk to the priest."

He left the room without looking back at her. He found a phone in the kitchen and dialed it. A nurse answered and, he thought,

180

turned grave when he told her who he was. In the minutes before Father Reba came on the line, Majewski confessed it all, every failure, wrapped up in the last. And when the priest's voice finally sounded, the word was a rebuke. It was his name.

"Stan? Are you still there?"

"Yes."

"I tried to get you at home a number of times."

Lord, if you must punish me, please don't do it through her.

"Has something happened to my mother?"

There was a short silence, the sound of breath. It scourged him.

"I should have realized that was what you might think," said Father Reba. "There's nothing wrong, Stan. She is fine. I should have left that much of a message. I hope you'll forgive me."

Majewski collapsed into a chair.

"It was just that old fellow we talked about the other day," said Father Reba. "He showed up again. I called you as soon as I heard he was here. But when I couldn't reach you, I went down to talk to him."

"Thank you, Father."

"I've managed to scare you terribly, haven't I?"

"I let my imagination run away."

"A funny thing, though," said the priest. "When I went into the room to introduce myself, he bolted. Got clean away. I'm afraid I didn't find out much to compensate for the fright I gave you. I'm sorry."

Susan appeared in the doorway in a long, wheat-colored robe. She stepped up to him and put her hand on his shoulder.

"How did my mother react?"

"She was rather cute, in fact," said the priest, "as if I had caught her in a tryst. She was as embarrassed as a schoolgirl. I don't think it did her any harm."

"So she's all right then," Majewski said for Susan's benefit. She closed her eyes in relief, and it moved him how deeply she had shared his mistake.

"She's asleep now. There's no need to worry."

"I'll see you in a day or two," said Majewski.

"Maybe the next time we'll catch him."

"So long, Father."

When he hung up, he did not dare look at her. He was humbled and ashamed. And yet, despite everything, she embraced him as he stood.

181

"I was so worried for you," she said.

He did not return the embrace this time. His arms hung awkwardly at his sides. She stepped back.

"Would you like to talk?"

"I think I'd better go."

"I'd like you to stay."

"I don't think that would be a very good idea."

"Please don't be sorry, Stan."

"I don't know what I am."

He found his coat and pulled it on. She put herself in front of him and kissed him once more. And it was like a vain promise you make to yourself at the edge of sleep when everything seems possible, all reality yields. She did not try to stop him as he left, but when he reached his car, he looked back and saw her watching, small in one of the big, bright windows, a shadow, all alone.

The turnoff was marked by a humble wooden plank nailed up on a tree. Moll turned into the narrow stone road that cut through the forest. The sun was going down, and it set the needles and bark ablaze.

He was coming unannounced, and he did not even know whether the people at St. John's would allow him to see his son. There had been plenty of chances to phone ahead, but he did not want to risk being turned down. In person, he hoped, their charity would respond to need, their mercy to an object of pity.

The road wound for miles through the trees before it opened out onto rolling fields, auburn in the dusk. Up ahead, the monastery tower rose to the sky. The sun was hidden now behind a hill, and it lighted the tower as it lighted the moon, its flame reflected by cold, dead stone.

There was nobody about in the courtyard as he pulled to a stop. He parked and stepped into the biting air. Before him the main buildings were built on tall, beautiful arches. The entryways, the top of the tower, the warm, lighted windows all repeated the same curve, which rose and fell with such perfect grace that you had to believe that somewhere it would rise again.

He went to the heavy front door and looked for a bell. There

182

was none. He did not know whether this meant that visitors were not welcome or invited them to enter unbidden. But he was not a man to be deterred by closed doors. He seized the iron handle and turned it. The door swung free.

Inside, he stood at the end of a long, arched corridor illuminated by simple fixtures hanging from the apex. The floor was tiled in brown and white, polished to a deep glow. Moll moved forward, his footsteps tapping like a blind man's cane.

A door opened on his right, and a young man stepped out next to him. Moll stopped. The man was dressed in a plain white surplice bundled at the waist by a braided cord. His hair was close-cropped, revealing all the bumps and ridges of his skull. Moll nodded to him and waited for guidance. He did not know the etiquette. This was, after all, a place of silence. Blind and dumb, he was completely cut off.

"Can I help you?" the young man asked at last.

"Yes," said Moll, and his voice cracked in his throat. He coughed into his fist. "I was hoping to see Brother James Toolan. But it looks like I've come at a bad time."

The man eyed him curiously, from his well-polished shoes to his neatly trimmed hair. Moll did not move.

"No sweat," said the young man. "You a cop?"

"Pardon?" said Moll. He doubted all his senses now.

"I just thought you kind of looked like a cop," said the young man. "Did I get it right?"

"You did," said Moll.

"Here about the thefts?"

"I'm here to see Brother Toolan."

"Somebody's been ripping off things from the outbuildings at night. Feed sacks, a harness or two. Nothing much yet. You ask me, it's probably just some kids from the farms. We've caught them on the grounds loving up their girlfriends. It really shakes 'em when they see us."

"I bet it does."

"I figure they've been raiding the barn just to hassle us back, you know? You hate to put locks on things, but what are you gonna do? I heard that Brother James called the cops about it."

"Is he here now?"

"Come on," said the young man. "I'll show you through the maze."

The young man's robes hung nearly to the floor, hiding his feet, and this gave him the appearance of gliding inches above the floor, a gull in flight.

"This is the chapel, if you want to have a look," he said, opening a door. "Most visitors do. I don't know why. It isn't much."

Moll stepped inside the large, drafty room. The straight-backed pews were arrayed like ranks of soldiers, the Stations of the Cross nothing more than roughhewn tablets set into the walls. Votive candles flickered on a rack, as dim as men's intentions.

"So there you are," said the young man.

"Simplicity," said Moll. "That's what people are looking for."

"Yeah," said the young man. "To get away."

Brother James's quarters were across from the chapel. The young man knocked twice and entered.

"There's a man here to see you. Says he's a cop."

"Show him in, Richard."

The young man stepped back against the door, and Moll moved past him. Brother James was nothing like Moll had expected. His voice on the phone had seemed so young, but he was in fact older than Moll himself. Small and gray and weathered, the man stood up at his writing table. His face was deeply lined, as if purity of spirit had scored the flesh.

"Welcome," he said. "What can we do for you?"

Moll glanced back and saw that the young man still stood attentively in the doorway.

"I hope you'll excuse me, but I'd rather talk in private."

The young man cleared his throat, and Moll caught a glimpse of him rolling his eyes at Brother James in what was surely meant to be a secret communion.

"As you wish," said Brother James.

"My guide tells me you have been having a problem with your neighbors," said Moll.

"Why don't you go on about your business, Richard," said Brother James. "It seems that you have adequately introduced our visitor to the mysteries."

The young man obeyed, slamming the door with what, in these hushed and ethereal confines, was a loud, corporeal report.

"He likes to be in on everything," said Brother James. "We call him the gatekeeper. It is only because of the placement of his room on the center corridor. He knows who comes and goes."

"I wasn't sure whether I was even supposed to speak to him," Moll confessed. "I wasn't sure of the rules."

"A concern that reflects well on a good law-enforcement officer, Mr. Moll."

It startled him to hear his name.

"I recognized your voice, Henry," said Brother James. "And I must admit that I have been expecting a visit."

"I hadn't known I was quite so predictable."

"One attains over the years certain experience in dealing with fathers and sons. Please sit down."

"I hope it isn't too inconvenient that I came today. I've been so wrapped up in a case that I didn't know when I would get another chance."

"That was a nasty business you had in your city," said Brother James.

"You've heard about it?"

"We restrict what comes in, newspapers and the like. There are no televisions here, and I have the only radio. But we cannot afford to cut ourselves off completely. The world's dangers intrude, I'm afraid."

"Not this one," said Moll. "You don't have to worry about terrorists."

"One never knows," said Brother James. "In the Middle Ages the monasteries were a particularly inviting target for the radical millenarians."

"That some kind of political group?"

"I suppose in a sense it was. During the plagues there were whole sects of zealots roaming the countryside, wreaking violence. I have often thought that we are in a similar period now. Obsessed with eschatology. Haunted by universal destruction. Perhaps it is a form of God's judgment to expose us to these unspeakable nightmares and see how we respond. Many fail." He stood up behind his simple wooden desk. "But you are not here to talk about the obscure moments in the history of the faith. You want to know about Thomas."

"I was hoping you might think he was ready to see me."

"As it happens," said Brother James, "I've had a number of conversations with the men who work most closely with him. I was concerned that perhaps I had been a bit peremptory with you on the telephone. We are a very protective family here, and it is easy to forget the needs of others."

"I understand."

"After discussing it, we have concluded that he has come along well enough to see you if he wants to. It will be his choice, of course."

"He's an adult. I can't force myself on him."

"He may prefer not to," said Brother James. "You must not take this as a sign that he does not love you. You see, he knows how deeply he has disappointed you."

"That's behind us now."

"He may not think so. He may still feel inadequate before you."

"I don't mean to judge him," Moll said.

"You don't need to, Henry. In your presence he will judge himself. This cannot be avoided. He is a deeply conflicted young man. He is not persuaded of his own worth. And yet he wants very much for you to be proud of him."

"It would be good to think he wanted that again."

"So many come here now with a burden of self-hatred. And I have found that it is not simply a matter of finding absolution for what they have done. It is deeper. The devil is very much with them, Henry. They have seen his most repugnant works. They have been immersed in this element all their lives, and they know nothing else. It is easier for men our age to accept the possibility of goodness."

"He would have every right to blame me," said Moll. "I let him down somewhere along the line."

Brother James paced slowly in the cell.

"These things show themselves in such peculiar ways," he said. "We have men who do not even feel worthy to pray for forgiveness and others who think of prayer as an anodyne. No matter how much we strip away the complications of the world, it is a life's work to untangle the riddles of a single soul."

He stood before Moll now, and Moll looked up for any sign of hope.

"I don't want you to expect too much of him, Henry," he said. "Many people have idealized notions of what men become in the brotherhood. They think we are a breed apart, and I suppose in the literal sense we are. But this does not necessarily bring any special wisdom.

"The men who live here are not quite as different as people want them to be. They may, like Brother Richard, be curious and pesky. They do not speak in pentameter or chasten their words with biblical quotations. They may be transformed in their outward habits, but the inner changes are slow and unsteady. Now if you will excuse me for a moment, I will talk to your son."

With that, he left the room.

Moll went to the small windows that opened onto the night. They were high on the wall, and he stretched to see out into the deepening darkness where the lights of a distant city glowed above the trees.

He moved about the cell, touching the simple things that furnished it, the cot, the desk, the walls of stone. He lifted the Bible and read a psalm. And he remembered the way the rhythms had soothed him as a child, when the valley of the shadow of death was only a gentle cadence, when it was not real.

He heard footsteps in the hall and quickly closed the book. Brother James stepped back into the room.

"Thomas is willing to see you if you think you are ready," he said.

"I'm not expecting a miracle."

"Good. But don't expect too little of him, either. He is coming along very well. Here, follow me. I'll take you to him."

They moved through the empty corridors past the chapel where Moll could see a few men kneeling now at the pews. From other rooms he heard the sounds of voices, telling tales, even laughing. It reminded him of the barracks, the boredom and the camaraderie, the way men bolstered their illusions of themselves, when war was still very far away.

Tom was waiting at his door, and Moll did not know whether to embrace him or bow his head.

"Hello, Dad."

They stood there at arm's length, afraid to touch. Brother James turned to leave.

"Stop by when you are finished if you want," he said. "I would like to hear more about that case you are working on. We do not leave all our earthly curiosity behind, you know."

"Thank you for everything," said Moll.

"Just remember that Thomas rises before dawn. Don't keep him up too long talking."

When he was gone, they stood in silence. Finally, Tom suggested that they go inside his cell.

"You're looking well," said Moll. And it was true. Once he got beyond the strange costume and the shaved head, Moll was pleased at how healthy Tom seemed. The pallor had given way to a good, hard color from the sun and wind. They had put some meat on him. It showed in his face. And his eyes, which Moll remembered as vacant and heavy-lidded, were sharp now and alert.

"Your mother sends her love," he said. "Maybe you could call her someday. It would mean a lot to her to hear your voice."

"Someday," said Tom.

The room was bare: a bed, two chairs, a washbasin, a cross on the wall. Moll looked around for something that connected this place to the son he had known. Maybe a book or a photograph of all of them together. But there was nothing.

"We've missed you, son," he said.

"Come off it, Dad. I was a pain in the ass."

"We worry about you. That's only natural."

"I gave you plenty of reasons."

"When you're a parent, you don't need reasons."

It was all right that they were being careful with one another. That was better than the competition of rebuke they had engaged in so often before. And yet their caution held them apart. They were circling around the danger, which was the only ground they shared.

"Is everything all right for you here?" Moll asked. "Do you need anything we could send?"

"What they don't give us we can't have. It's that simple."

"It must be a little strange at first," said Moll, "the discipline."

"You do your work. You pray. There are vows. You memorize them. It's OK. Do you want to sit down or something?"

Tom pulled the two chairs into the center of the room facing one another. Moll put his coat on the bed. The chair was hard. It was sternly built and did not make any compromise with his shape. Tom settled his robes around him and kept his feet flat on the floor. His hands rested on his knees.

"What exactly do you do?" Moll asked.

"It's pretty routine. Nothing to write home about."

"I wasn't complaining about that. I understand."

"My work is with the animals. Sheep, pigs. I feed them. Clean up their mess."

"You always liked pets."

"This is different. You don't get involved with them. You just take care of their needs. . . . You know, I could have told Brother James that I didn't want to see you."

"I'm glad you let me."

"You didn't give me any warning."

"Maybe I was afraid that if you had time to think about it you would have refused."

Tom shifted in his chair.

"You're pretty good at getting to people," he said.

It was almost a relief, the edge he gave the words.

"I suppose I am," said Moll.

"I came here to get away," said Tom. "But I guess I was glad to hear that you had come."

"Things can be pretty confusing."

"I still don't know what happened to me," said Tom, but he did not risk meeting his father's eyes. "I mean before. I really screwed up, and I don't know why."

"It was easy," said Moll, "the way things were."

"That's what bothers me. How easy it was."

"It could happen to anyone, son."

"That only makes it worse. I look around and I see what people do to each other. And it disgusts me. But you know what? I say to myself, 'I could do that. I could do worse.' That's the trouble. I could do anything."

"You came here on your own," said Moll, "looking for a better way."

"A place to hide."

"Everybody's looking for some kind of shelter."

Tom leaned forward in his chair, and his face betrayed him. For the first time in many years, they were talking to one another with their weapons down, father and son.

"God forgives," said Moll.

"It's the other way around," said Tom. "That's what bothers me."

"Forgiving Him," said Moll.

"You escape here to find Him, but then you realize that He's responsible for what you're trying to escape."

"It isn't easy to forgive a father," said Moll.

"They say you can't begin to find His love until you first learn to love yourself," Tom said. "But it's hard. It's hard to love the thing He made of you."

Tom's head was bowed, confessional.

"It's all right to feel that way, son."

Tom stood up and went to the bed. He picked up the coat, and

Moll started to rise to go. But Tom just hung it on a hook, then smoothed out the covers and tightened them down.

"What was Brother James talking about before?" he asked. "Something about a case you're working on."

Moll sat back in his chair.

"It's just part of the job," he said. "One thing after another. You know how it is."

"Must be pretty big if Brother James has heard about it."

"I guess."

"We don't get much news here. You almost forget that time goes by."

"That can be a blessing, I guess."

"What kind of case is it?"

"A murder," Moll said, and it felt odd to speak of it within these walls. "A car bomb. It went off in the middle of the university."

"Who got killed?"

"A professor," Moll said, then he hesitated. He did not want to bring on the old conflict again, but there were no odds in lying. Even here, the truth might reach his son. "The other victim was a Soviet defector."

Tom turned back to him, and Moll could not read his expression.

"I didn't think they let you handle those cases anymore," Tom said.

"They changed their minds."

"Do they know about me?"

"Yes," said Moll. "They found out."

"You told them?"

"It was none of their business. They found out on their own."

"I'm glad that's all over with," said Tom, and it was as if this point of contention had never been the real thing between them at all, it was so easily forgiven. Tom took him by the shoulders. Moll stood up and embraced his son.

"It's getting kind of late," Tom said.

Moll did not want to go, but he did not want to push the fragile connection too hard either. For once he was glad simply to let Tom go only as far as he was willing, not to test it.

"Maybe I'd better start heading home. Your mother will be worried, and I've got a long drive ahead."

"Will you come back again?"

"As soon as I can."

"I'll be all right, Dad," said Tom. "I'll be here."

SEVEN

Then Abram bound the youth with belts and straps,
And builded parapets and trenches there,
And stretched forth the knife to slay his son
When lo! an angel called him out of heav'n,
Saying, Lay not thy hand upon the lad,
Neither do anything to him. Behold,
A ram, caught in a thicket by his horns;
Offer the Ram of Pride instead of him.
But the old man would not so, but slew his son—
And half the seed of Europe, one by one . . .

The newsroom was crowded. All the paper's bosses hovered around giving unwanted advice about how the stories should be arrayed. The editorial writers wandered out of their isolation asking sage, unanswerable questions and receiving polite dismissals.

The antinuclear groups were out on the street, picketing Nufab and the federal building, threatening to bring construction on a new power plant to a halt. There had been mass arrests, charges of police brutality. The Left, which had been hibernating since the bombing, had come out of hiding and bared its claws. All the helpful experts from the university had begun to lose the confidence of their earlier, private assessments of the risk and were tugging at their chins and confessing to a proper scholarly uncertainty. There was talk of cover-up, and a neighborhood group from a residential area near the law school was demanding an investigation. Shouting women waved death's-head placards.

Majewski had decided to stay away from the breaking story. His instincts told him to stick with the one lead nobody else had, the mysterious fat man, John Devine, even though Ruffalino had wanted him to go a different way.

"Nufab is the ticket," the city editor had said in the morning when Majewski dragged himself in. "See who's involved in it. What kind of connections they have. Where the money goes."

"Could be something there," Majewski acknowledged.

"Bet your ass there could."

"Somebody's brother-in-law," Majewski said. "Funny payments to the mayor's campaign."

"Something," said Ruffalino. "Find it."

"I'm working another angle."

193

"The story's going to get away from you."

"You've got to pick your best shots."

"Come on, Stan. A letter to the editor?"

"I've made mistakes before," said Majewski.

He couldn't blame Ruffalino for wanting him to do the document search. He knew his way around the files better than anyone else at the paper. But when he had declined the assignment, Ruffalino tried to take Joe Stawarz away from him, and that made Majewski angry. The bastard wanted to put Joe on the streets with the demonstrators.

"Don't stand in his way, Stan," the city editor had said. "Let him run."

"Maybe I can run him even faster."

"You look a little tired."

It galled Majewski all the more when Ruffalino took the proposition to Joe himself. And after the sweet-talking was finished, Joe came to Majewski at his desk. His voice was racing. He was high on the by-line Majewski had shared with him under the banner headline. He wanted more.

"Gonna be a big story," Joe said.

Majewski locked his fingers behind his head and stretched his neck where it was tight.

"Ruffalino tell you that?"

"Hell yes."

"He tell you the nature of your assignment?"

"Could be page one again. That's what the boss said."

"He wants you to count the crowd. Pick up quotes from the protestors' signs. Listen to guys shouting on bullhorns."

"I can do it."

"Of course you can, Joe. But it's nothing. A one-day wonder. You've got to take risks if you want to break new ground."

"You want me to keep chasing the fat man."

"That's up to you."

"I don't know, Mr. Majors."

"Call me Stan. We're in this together now."

"OK, Stan," Joe said, trying it out.

"When we find the fat man, we may just break this goddamn story open, Joe. Let Ruffalino get somebody else to do cleanup on what we did yesterday. We're way out ahead of them now."

Joe stood there a full minute thinking about it, then he pulled up a chair, took out his notebook, and turned to the page where he had all the phone-book listings for J. Devines printed in careful, schoolboy letters.

"What's the plan?" he said.

It wasn't complicated. To began with, they needed something more than the crude description Joe had gotten from the security man in the lobby. Majewski had already talked to one of the artists, a good man with faces, and sent him out to the guard's house to put together a composite sketch so they would know their man when they saw him.

"He isn't going to want publicity," Majewski told Joe. "He's got a compulsion to write me letters, but if he wanted to be found, he would have given a return address. He may not be happy when we catch up to him."

Majewski rummaged on his desk until he found his notes and the heavyweight sheet torn from the artist's sketchpad, tattered by the spiral binding at the top.

"Here are a few more names," he said, handing them over to Joe to copy out. "Their numbers were unlisted."

"How the hell did you get them then?"

"Secrets of the trade."

"Hey, come on. You're supposed to be learning me the business."

"You find a friend in the police department," said Majewski. "That part of it is up to you."

"What do you give them to do you a favor like that?"

"A kind word now and then, printed a hundred thousand times."

"You put their names in the paper."

"Coin of the realm," said Majewski. "Now where did I stick that drawing. Here. He look anything like what you expected?"

The face on the page had the strange, expressionless look you always got on composites. The hair was white, pulled back from a preternaturally high forehead. It must have been the feature that had caught in the security man's memory; the drawings always exaggerated the things a man recalled, the twist of the lip, the long bite of a scar, the heaviness of eyebrow or weakness of chin. What you ended up with was an image in a distorting mirror.

And yet there was something about this particular face. Majewski could not say that he knew the fat man. Maybe it was

195

just the immigrant look he had, something you saw coming and going on the street every day. But still, there were certain things in the drawing, things he could not precisely name, like snatches of a song that comes back to you and won't go away.

It was strange the way identity revealed and hid itself. The heavy jaw and tightly set lips on the sketchpad did not suggest what rage had shaped them. The eyes, deep-set and dark, did not reveal their intelligence or madness. It was different from a caricature, which carries the figure's personality in every line. It was flat and elusive, as if from a dream. The face in the distorting mirror was a cipher; it might even have been your own.

"If you find him, don't scare him off," said Majewski. "Tell him that you work for me and that I'll be coming along as soon as you can get word to me. See if he'll let you use his phone. The city desk will get me on the car radio. In the meantime, soak it all in. Don't take notes. That will only put him on his guard. Just talk to him. Talk to the man."

Majewski split up the names evenly between them and organized his list so it would take him on an orderly circuit around the city and suburbs. He began close in with an address not more than a mile from the university. It was a plain, frame house behind a broken picket fence. A woman answered the door. She was young and pregnant, and she wore a sloppy housedress. Yes, she knew John Devine. She had married the bum. But he wasn't at home. He was at the track with a bunch of the others from their high school class who had never grown up.

In the course of the day Majewski turned up Devines who were dead and buried, Devines who did not like solicitors, Devines who kept nasty dogs. There were tall, skinny Devines and others who were elfin and bald. There were Devines who were black and who thought Majewski was some kind of fool. Two others weren't named John at all. They were single women who listed themselves in the book only by their initials. One was quite friendly, but Majewski declined her hospitality.

By dusk he had finished the whole route and come up empty. The radio had been busy all day with orders to reporters and photographers as Ruffalino deployed his troops like a battlefield commander. But there had been no word from Joe.

When Majewski returned to the city room, he slipped in unnoticed. Two messages waited for him on his desk, one from Moll and the other from Susan Cousins. He was in no hurry to return either call.

Ruffalino was leaning over the shoulder of a rewriteman, watching the story scroll out on the screen. The managing editor was conferring with a group of his assistants in his glass-walled office, waving his arms like a symphony conductor. Even the copyboys seemed to have been energized. The kewpie moved briskly past Majewski, her hands full of printouts.

"Boy," he said. "Come back here when you have a minute. I need to get a little food in me."

"Sorry," said the kewpie. "You'll have to talk to Mr. Ruffalino. We have orders not to leave the room."

He dismissed the kewpie with a grunt and dialed Moll's number on the phone. The agent picked up on the second ring.

"We've had a little trouble connecting the past few days," Majewski said.

"Yeah, well, you really stepped in it this time, Stan."

"I made the effort. I had messages out all over the place for you to call."

"Hey," said Moll, "that was real kind of you."

"I'm just saying that I didn't go out of my way to screw you. That's all I'm saying."

"It isn't saying much. You've got the whole town going nuts here."

"Read my copy, Hank. I played it straight. I didn't hype the danger."

"Have you been watching the tube lately? They've got film of guys in gas masks and rubber suits. They've got jokers on there talking about cancer. I mean, they've even got me a little worried about this shit."

"I covered your ass, didn't I?" said Majewski.

"Did I forget to thank you, Stan? Jesus, it must have slipped my mind, what with the mayor trying to skin me alive and the congressional delegation paying a little visit to the Director to chat about the way I've handled this thing. I was probably thinking about what the police chief said about how I was playing with people's lives. So if I forgot to express my gratitude, Stan, I'm sure you'll understand."

"You want to blow off steam at me, it's OK," said Majewski.

Then he heard Moll's hand scratch over the mouthpiece of

the phone, and he closed off his other ear to see if he could pick up the words. All he got was a muffled grumble, then Moll was back at him.

"I want you to know how badly this story of yours set us back," Moll said, softly now.

"You know what I think, Hank? I think you've got somebody sitting there with you, and you're giving this little speech for him to hear it. Am I right?"

"Here's the way it is," said Moll. "I'm going to want some cooperation from now on. This thing is breaking all over the place, and there's no telling where something will turn up next. If you find out anything, I want to hear about it first. Do you understand? I don't want any more surprises."

"You know me better than that," Majewski said. "I play my stories in the paper. I write first. Then maybe I deal."

"Good," said Moll, for the benefit of whomever he was trying to impress. Then there was a pause, and Moll said, "No, I do not have any official comment, goddamn it!" And with that, the line went dead.

Joe was nowhere to be seen. Majewski moved things from one place to another on his desk for a while. Finally, he gave up the charade and headed for the vending machines.

He took the long way to the backstairs, cutting through the art department and photo suite to avoid awkward conversations. The color studio was idle at this hour, and the big, empty room was like a vacant TV sound stage, all the lenses and lights, the bright backdrops half a millimeter deep.

When he opened the door into the back end of the city room, he found Sid James waiting for him. Majewski tried to disregard him, but it didn't work. James stood barring the way to the stairs.

"I didn't hear your name come up in the doping," James said. "You take the day off?"

"I'm onto a good one, Sid. We're not discussing it yet. We're holding it very close."

"That's not the way I hear it."

"Maybe you don't hear everything."

"I hear you're slowing down. Legs giving out. Hey, don't worry. I've got a chair at the copydesk just waiting for you when you have to pack it in."

"Don't write my obit yet."

"I also hear you've got Joe Stawarz doing some work for you."

"Good kid," said Majewski.

"Did you ever ask me about it?"

"I cleared it with Ruffalino."

"The copy clerks are on my budget, Stan. Don't tell me you didn't know that."

"Frankly, I didn't give it a thought."

"Hey, I'd appreciate it if you cut your deals with me when you want one of my people."

"He's doing well. He's ready."

"He's mine," said James. "Remember that."

Majewski was in no position to negotiate turf with him now. The day had been wasted. Joe had come up with nothing.

"We'll talk about it, Sid," said Majewski.

"Don't try to do an end run around me," said James.

And then, as if to show how the thing was supposed to play, he stepped away from the door he had been blocking, made a grand, grating gesture, and let Majewski pass.

One floor down they were starting to make up the pages in the composing room. Majewski nodded to the foreman and stepped up to the stone where the front page was taking shape. It was still in pieces, like an unfinished jigsaw puzzle left for the night. A page dummy lay on the stone next to the form, and Majewski picked it up. The line story would be on the protests with a second lead from Hansen, the medical writer, on the controversy over the risk.

"Don't you trust us to get it right either, Stan?" said the foreman.

"No problem, George. I was just looking."

"Everybody's looking tonight. I got editors coming out the ass. No offense."

"I was just on my way to the machines. Can I get you something?"

"Thanks, Stan, but I value my health."

Majewski moved back to the stairs and down them. The vending machines stretched across a dirty wall like an arcade. He bought the usual poison and sat down at one of the rickety tables to eat. He had no reason to hurry.

The crowd in the newsroom had begun to thin out some by the time he returned. The copy editors were still busy at their screens, but most of the dayside hangers-on had gone home. Ruffalino looked up at him as he passed. Majewski was ready to give him a fill on what had happened during the day. But it wasn't necessary. Ruffalino looked away.

Joe was waiting at Majewski's desk in the corner, his feet up on the papers, his jaunty hat pulled down over his eyes. Majewski tapped a pencil against the soles of his shoes. Joe lifted the hat.

"We didn't do so good, did we?" Joe said.

He let his feet drop to the floor and then hauled himself up out of the chair to let Majewski sit down.

"You want me to wait downstairs again like last night?"

"Go on home, Joe. The fat man is hiding. We'll figure a way to smoke him out tomorrow."

"Mr. James said there ain't gonna be a tomorrow."

"He's a sweet guy."

"He was pissed. I don't know what I did to make the mother-fucker so angry."

"The motherfucker," said Majewski, "does not like to see a man get ahead."

"When you're hot, you're hot. When you're not, you're not."

"There you go," said Majewski.

After Joe left him, there was only one thing unfinished. But still he put off calling her. All day his thoughts had been coming back to Susan in the dead time as he drove from place to place. The night before was like a stone you pick up at the beach and put in your pocket. He took it out again and again, worrying it with his fingers, feeling every ridge and hollow. It was an ugly piece of creation, cast up by the waves. Adultery. That was what it was. And even if you had lapsed from the faith, this was still a sin. But in the course of the day he had rubbed all the rough spots smooth. The stone was as bright and polished as a gem.

When he finally called her, he began with apology, testing it to see if this was the way.

"I'm sorry I took so long getting back to you," he said.

"I was worried," she said. "You were there when the bomb exploded, weren't you? Do you think you should see a doctor?"

"There's no danger," he said.

"That's not what Danny thinks."

"You've heard from him?" Suddenly he wished that it could all remain in a state of suspension until he could work out his feelings,

200

decide whether it was right to want her, and whether it was really Susan he wanted or only a past that was gone beyond retrieval.

"He called me this afternoon," she said. "He's coming back."

"Now?"

"Not right away. He said there were some things he had to attend to. He'll be back next week. I don't know who she is this time."

"Maybe it's business. His friends are getting a lot of play out of the scare."

"As soon as he comes home I'm going to tell him," she said.

"Are you sure?"

"I wasn't. I really wasn't. Last night I said it to you because I wanted to hear my voice actually saying the words. When I did, they made sense. Everything did."

"I've been looking for the words to warn you away," he said.

"They don't exist," she said. "I know. I've looked for them, too."

"Maybe we were wrong last night," he said. "Maybe we were just convenient."

"Is that the way you feel?"

"I don't trust what I feel."

"Don't talk that way, Stan. I feel it, too."

"I wish we had some time."

"Will you come over tonight?"

"Maybe we'd better not," he said. But he had no idea what was better and what was worse.

"Leaving Danny isn't because of you," she said. "They are two separate things. And I know both of them are right."

"I envy you that," he said, "the knowing."

"Will you come then?"

"There's a lot I have to do here," he said, raking his hand through the worthless papers, the photocopies of the composite sketch, the dead-end addresses, and the pointless notes.

"If you can," she said.

"I don't want to disappoint you, Susan."

He let her get off the line first. And as soon as he hung up the phone, it rang again. He let it ring three times before answering, afraid that she was calling him back. He lifted the receiver but said nothing.

"Hello?" It was a man's voice.

"This is Majors."

"Oh, good. You're still there. This is the guard at the door. Your package is here."

"Package?"

"The one you had the copyboy waiting for last night."

"The fat man?"

"Yessir."

"He's there now?"

"I have it waiting for you, sir, if you want to come and pick it up."

"Hang on to him," said Majewski. "Don't let him go."

He grabbed a notebook and his coat and raced for the elevators. When he reached them, the door of one was just closing. He lunged but wasn't fast enough to get his hand in. When the next car finally came, he jumped inside. Slowly, the door slid shut and the elevator began moving. But not far. It came to a stop on three where several printers got on, talking about the Patriots' big win. It stalled again on two, taking on a couple of men from the mailroom and a telephone operator still wearing her headset.

When it finally reached the first floor, Majewski pushed out between them and ran into the corridor.

"Hey, buddy," said one of the men, "where's the fire?"

As he turned into the main lobby, he slowed down to a walk. His eye swept every empty corner.

"Where did he go?"

"Couldn't keep him," said the guard. "He caught on. He had an envelope for you, but I pretended to be too busy to take it. I guess he could tell that I was stalling. You're only a minute or two behind him."

Majewski raced out the revolving door and saw the fat man's shadow slipping around the corner of the building. The parking lot was the other direction. Majewski was in luck. The fat man seemed to be on foot.

When Majewski reached the intersection, he paused and moved up to the wall. Then he leaned out cautiously to see where his quarry had gone. The fat man was only about a block ahead of him, moving out at a brisk pace past the dark storefronts.

Instead of trying to catch up with him, Majewski decided it was better to keep the interval and see where he was going. Unless he was careful, he could scare him away for good.

Majewski stayed in the shadows of the buildings and ducked into doorways whenever the fat man slowed down. The storefronts gave way to a residential neighborhood, and Majewski crossed over to the opposite side of the street just to be safe. A police cruiser rolled up from behind and moved slowly past. Majewski did not allow himself to look at it.

At Whitney Avenue the fat man turned onto the bright thoroughfare. Majewski gave him even more room, stopping to look into the window of a furniture store, counting off the seconds. There were more people out and around here, kids from the university going for a late pizza and a beer, night-shift workers heading home. A woman in an old cloth coat was ahead of him as he started off again, a plastic babushka tied around her head, a wad of Kleenex sticking out of her pocket. As he passed her, she pulled it out and carefully peeled off one sheet, like a dollar from a bankroll, then wiped her nose.

Majewski walked steadily, trying to keep the space between himself and the fat man precise. He moved past the sandwich shops and bars, warmed by the exertion and the smell of malt and meat. A bum stepped out of an alley and asked him for change. Majewski swept past.

At the next corner, the fat man turned into the university grounds. Small groups of students passed him, their arms full of papers and books. He stopped at an entryway to one of the quadrangles, then slipped into the shadows. Majewski hurried forward. When he reached the arch, he saw the figure crossing the grass toward the opposite gate. Suddenly the fat man stopped and spun around.

Majewski darted into a door that led to the student rooms. He waited at the bottom of a stairway. There were footsteps above him, but they were moving away. He backed into a corner next to the door, head against the stone. He counted the time, hoping desperately that he had not been seen. Then the door started to swing open, and he got ready to confront the fat man right there. His hands were up, his leg poised to block the way. The door opened wide and through it came two young men. They were laughing, until they saw him.

"You looking for somebody?" one of them asked. Majewski pushed past them into the yard.

The fat man was nowhere to be seen. Majewski cursed himself

as he ran toward the high, iron gate. He had lost him. The sonofa-bitch had gotten away. But when he reached the street, he saw him on the other side, walking across the wide city green. There was someone with him now. They were talking.

Majewski crossed at the light and watched them move to the far side of the green, where they stopped at a park bench and sat down. He looked for a place where he could see them without being seen. A crowd of people had just come out of a movie theater and were moving up the sidewalk, so it was easy to make his way inconspi-cuously to the little stone chapel that stood near where the pair had come to rest. He turned off the sidewalk, losing sight of them as he came around the rear of the church. But it was all right. They could not easily get away from him now. They had yards of open park to cross, and he had the angle on them.

He made his way carefully, slipping around the far end of the chapel into the shadows, his fingers touching the weathered stone of the wall. When he reached the corner, he finally got a good look at them. But it was not the fat man he locked on. It was the other face that took Majewski's breath away. Sitting there impassively was someone Majewski knew intimately and did not know at all. It was David.

Moll could not concentrate on the important things because Head-quarters was hassling him every hour on the hour for reports. Who was organizing the antinuclear demonstrations? Were any basic Marxist-Leninist groups involved? Was there evidence of a Soviet presence? They were not shy about letting you know what they wanted to hear.

Every time Headquarters called, someone reminded Moll that the decision to hold back information about the radioactive risk had been purely local. The ass-coverers were never content just to make a record. They made it again and again, memoranda to file filling up the folders until you felt like one of the ten Most Wanted Men.

But Moll had little patience with them this time. Somebody had tipped off the press that the bomb was hot, and he wanted to know who it had been.

In the afternoon he got Majewski on the phone and was just beginning to work around to the sensitive subject of sources when one of the pests from Headquarters sat down next to him, and Moll had to put on a show. The conversation went nowhere, so Moll had to take a different approach. He checked with people he assumed the reporter had contacted as he worked the story.

Nobody was eager to admit that he had provided Majewski. Moll assured everyone that he had no desire to come down on the leaker, but it did not get him very far. There were certain assumptions about the way things work that Moll was powerless to overcome. He was in trouble for what he had failed to disclose, and no matter what he said, everyone figured that he was looking to pin a tail on the guy who had disclosed too much.

He finally caught up with Raskin in his office late in the day, following hours of friendly evasion.

"There are leaks, and there are leaks," Moll said.

"The pressure getting to you, Hank?" said Raskin, spinning a bent paper clip in his fingers in front of his eyes like a hypnotist's charm.

"I want to know what you told him, Bob."

"Hey, look," said Raskin, "Majors had it all before he called me. I mean, what the hell did I stand to gain?"

"I didn't see your name in his story."

"Yours either," said Raskin, staring at the whirl.

"No, Bob. But whoever talked to him made sure the Bureau took the fall."

"I talked to Majors, sure." Raskin came out from behind his talisman, sat upright in his chair. "He called me yesterday morning. He came at me with the disposition of the wreck, the lab report, the whole goddamned thing. He had it wired."

"That's what's got me interested," said Moll.

"Look, I don't give a shit if you believe me or not, OK? It's no skin off my ass if you want to bring charges. What's the worst that can happen? I look like a whistle-blower. I'll be a fucking hero."

"What I'm trying to figure out is where Stan got the tip in the first place," said Moll. "He was trying to get hold of me all day. He reached you early. Then later he was going around town saying he had the story from the Feds. If he had everything you say he did when he came to you, then somebody who knew something had already given him the tip."

"Could have been anyone. One of your guys. One of the people they questioned. Anybody."

"I've been checking around," said Moll. "He did drag a lot out of the hospital people. And there was some new kid from the *Herald* poking around at the auto pound. But they knew what they were looking for. You see what I mean? It could have come from the guy we're after."

"Come on, Hank. You're grabbing at steam. How many people at the university alone knew what we were onto? I don't know why you guys thought you could hold this thing tight. Half the fucking town knew about it, when you think about it."

"Don't you want to solve this case?"

"Hey, right now I wish I were back busting auto thieves."

"I told you it would get messy," said Moll.

"I thought you were just telling war stories."

"Next time you want to talk to a reporter, let me know."

"Majors is the least of our problems," said Raskin.

"See, that's where we differ," said Moll. "I think he's the key to them."

When the sun went down, the excitement began to wane. Most of the demonstrators went home. The press retreated to their typewriters and tape to bring the day's events to a shrill summation. The locals ran a mass arrest court to wash out all the illegal pinches they had made to break up the crowds. And Moll's own men drifted back into the squad bay to do their paperwork.

Moll had a report to write, too, so he called Sally to tell her he would be late again. Headquarters was demanding a full explanation of the decision not to release the findings of the crime lab. They wanted it ASAP, and it could have been to use either as a shield against criticism or as a talking paper for the inevitable round of in-house second-guessing. Moll did not intend to lay off the ultimate responsibility on anyone. It had been his draw, and he was prepared to defend it. But he wanted to make it very clear that there had been complete disclosure to the U.S. Attorney's office and up the ladder within the Bureau itself. Silence was concurrence. This was the rule.

The other agents finished their reports long before he did. One by one, they cleaned off the tops of their desks and stopped by to give him a word of encouragement before going home. Soon he was alone in the squad bay. The phones were silent. The only voices were those of the cleaning ladies working in the hall, jabbering away in a strange tongue.

Moll tortured every sentence to see how much weight it would bear. He wrote and rewrote, stood up, looked out the window into the deserted street. When the guard at the front desk called him and said there was somebody in the lobby insisting on seeing him right away, it came as a relief, even before Moll found out who it was.

When it dawned on Jenkins that the man in the *Herald* lobby was stalling, there was nothing he could do but run. By the time he reached the corner, he was dizzy with exertion. He stopped and looked back. It was all right. He had eluded them again.

But he had not retreated. You had to make distinctions. One thing was caution, another was shame. No, he was not a coward this time. His purpose was firm.

Distinctions. All dangers were not the same. You had to understand each one, *know* it, look it in the face. This was the mistake everyone made. They put their fears on the wrong things. They spent their time chasing a tired old man when all he wanted to do was to point the way. Dense as lead, they shielded themselves from reality. He had to break through.

But he had to be careful, too, for these were devious men. The secret police were surely looking into his past now, following it back through the years, job to job, room after lonely room. If they thought he was crazy, they would check up on his medical records. But they wouldn't find anything against him there. Even during the worst time, he had never shown them his secret. And now he was just an old man who'd had a scare. The heart episode had not been severe. The doctors had told him it was a warning. And he had acted on it. He had quit his job and come back east to settle his accounts before it was too late.

They would surely discover his old identity now. There was only so much he had been able to do to obscure it. But what did it matter who he had been? All the important connections were hidden in the chaos of war. And there was nothing illegal in this great, free land about changing your name and starting over afresh.

He had simply run away from his past. And no one knew the crime. They only knew its punishment.

He set off toward his rendezvous with David at a steady pace to save his breath. It would have been easier if they had been able to have this talk earlier in the day when Jenkins stopped by the apartment. But Sibyl had laid down the law.

"Mighty Mouse and me, we have a deal," she had said. "He wants to let you keep coming by. I'm not so hot for that. But I said OK, as long as there are some rules."

"Which are?" Jenkins asked. She stood in the doorway, legs apart, barring entry.

"I don't want the talk to get heavy," she said. "You know what I mean. It brings us down."

As the three of them sat in the kitchen, she had policed the rules with a vengeance. It wasn't until David announced that she had gotten a job that Jenkins saw the way around her. She had hired on as a waitress in a neighborhood hash house, night shift, four to midnight.

After about an hour, she finally left the kitchen and padded off to the bathroom. Jenkins was drying the dishes, and David was sitting at the table.

"I have to talk with you," Jenkins whispered.

"So go ahead."

"Alone. It's extremely important."

David turned his head away.

"Meet me tonight," Jenkins said. "On the green. Ten o'clock."

"What is this shit?"

"Trouble," he said as Sibyl rejoined them.

Jenkins busied himself loading the dishes back into the cabinets. She moved up behind him, a stalking cat. Then suddenly she was up next to him, her body pressed against his side. It was not meant to be erotic this time. She was closing in on his secrets, too. The plates were uncertain in his hands.

"Don't fuck around with me, Pops," she said.

"I don't know what you mean."

"You're a bummer." she said. "You leave David alone."

She was dangerous, all right. She hated Jenkins, and he was sure she would do whatever she could against him. He had to give her credit for that. She made distinctions; she knew what to fear.

Jenkins did not wait for the light at the intersection. The way was clear except for a bus picking up fares, so he crossed the street, fighting with every step the sense that somebody was behind him, following. It was Sibyl he thought of now, Sibyl he imagined in the shadows. Absurd. She was at work. Jenkins did not even permit himself to turn his head.

He moved on, the envelope he'd intended to deliver to Majewski rustling in his pocket. Old John Devine had just one more thing to say: *For what they have done to the children and what they have failed to do, the fathers will be punished. The children are in peril.* It was not enough just to kill the liar Shevtsov, the great man of peace. It was not enough to bathe him in radioactive poisons. A man's death had to stand for something. A man's sacrifice had to be a warning.

Jenkins looked back over his shoulder and the darkness was as empty as flight. This was something he knew, how to evade them. And it was not a coward's way to be aware of what is behind you. If you are to be daring, you must be cunning, too.

He had made his way back across Europe this way, moving among the great, dislocated masses at the end of the war. He had found clothes in the first farmhouse where he made his bed, and he had rid himself of all his soldier's gear except for the pistol, which he caressed in the pocket of the tattered coat he found in the ruins.

He spoke all the languages, had traveled widely before the war. And so he knew how to blend in with the homeless, hopeless castoffs. But the face of the land had been changed. The ancient places that a decade before had stood as reminders of the greatness that endures now had fallen. The polite conventions he had learned as a boy were useless to him. He stole food and demeaned himself to get a piece of change.

Always, always he assumed that secret eyes were looking for him, to punish him for his desertion. He hid in bombed-out buildings, spoke deceptive words to those around him, and when he slept, his hand was on his sidearm.

It was weeks before he actually set foot back on Polish soil. And since it was a Russian zone, he had new reasons to be afraid. He moved at night, eluding Red Army patrols as once he had avoided the Germans. He was taken in by partisans who had known of his family, bands of men who did not believe in peace until the last Russian soldier was expelled.

They warned him to expect the worst If ever he did reach

Warsaw. They told him of the uprising and the slaughter. No one knew who had lived and who had died. But he thought that he had already steeled himself against anything that might face him. He had seen the great machines of war breathing fire as they advanced against soft, human flesh. He had seen the displaced persons camps where the survivors—gaunt, diseased—stared out at him through the wire. He knew their faces, countrymen. One in particular burned in his memory at night in the forests when he could not sleep. It was a woman's face, old and wasted to the bone. He had known her in his youth, and the war had made them kin. He thought he heard her call his name, but he did not dare reply, for he was a wanted man, displaced from even the small honor a survivor could claim. Oh, *pani*. We are all dead now, those who remained and those returning.

The safest route, the partisans told him, was to the south. They showed him the way. When he came upon Auschwitz, it was not by accident. The partisans told him that he must see it if he wanted to know what had been done to his land, what men were capable of doing again. He was afraid as he approached it, but not because of what it had been. There was simply too much activity in the area, military vehicles busy on the roads, some of them bearing men who wore the uniform he had dishonored.

He went with a group of men, and he tried to keep himself hidden among them. They carried farm implements, as if they were returning from the fields. Nobody challenged them. The partisans said the soldiers would not bother with anyone who appeared to have somewhere to go. But still it frightened Jenkins to be out in the open after so many weeks of hiding. He cursed himself silently for agreeing to make this pilgrimage.

But when he finally reached the place, he gasped. It was so large and desolate, a great, dark scar on the plain. They pointed to the buildings they said were graves to millions. It was a place where the earth split open and revealed the hell beneath its skin. And as he stood there on his native ground, he felt an overwhelming shame for what others had done and what he had failed to do.

When Jenkins reached the university, he slowed down his pace. He had been moving too fast for his heart. Young students walked past him, but they paid him no mind. Still, he felt eyes at his back, and when he reached the middle of the courtyard, he turned around to confront the fear. In the darkness he saw nothing but a figure stepping into a doorway. It was not Sibyl. It was no one at all.

He passed through the iron gate and crossed over to the green. In the middle distance he saw someone pacing there. To his enormous relief it was David, his hands stuffed into the pockets of his blue jeans.

"I thought you might not show," David said when Jenkins reached him. They fell into step, moving along the walk that angled across the grass.

"Have you been waiting long?"

"No sweat," said David. "I didn't have anywhere else to go."

They stopped at a bench on the green. Jenkins glanced around them. There were people on the far walkway, but they all seemed to be heading somewhere.

"What's the big mystery?" David asked.

"Does Sibyl know you're here?"

"She's at work."

"You didn't tell her?"

"I didn't want to get her all keyed up. She's got a thing about you."

"She thinks I'm going to take you away, David."

"That's crazy."

"You must not say anything to her about what I'm going to tell you now. Do you understand that?"

"A deep, dark secret," David said. He refused to take it seriously. This was one of his ways, to mock everything, beginning with himself. Jenkins could understand the feeling. At some point you had to face the simple, irreversible fact that you are what you have done, the sum of every retreat. But despite all the totals, you also had to realize that you could still stand up. It was always possible. The sum was counted day by day.

"I need to have your word, David."

"What good will that do you? It's only air."

"I believe in you."

"That's your problem."

"Yes it is, David. Yes it is."

David laughed.

"Did you read the papers today?" Jenkins asked.

"Never do."

"Listen to the radio?"

"I was playing records."

"They've discovered that the bomb that killed the Russian was radioactive," said Jenkins. "It was all over the news."

Jenkins watched David's expression for any sign of recognition.

"So what?" David said.

"The radioactive material was Oncyllium."

"They know that?"

"They appear to."

"That doesn't prove anything."

"Maybe it does."

David turned toward him.

"You said they were all fools," said David. "You said they didn't understand anything at all."

"I'm not talking about their sense of history, David. I'm not talking about whether they appreciate the true nature of the human situation. They know what the material was, and they have records showing that I had access to it."

David moved away from him, just as he did the day Jenkins had shown him the vial of liquid and told him what it was. They had been in Jenkins's flat working together rewiring a radio receiver. Jenkins had gotten the bottle from the closet and held it out so David could see the warning label. "It's the stuff that killed her," David had cried. And for the first time Jenkins had seen precisely how all the filaments were connected, her death, the way he linked this to the greater danger, his sense of utter defeat. "It did no such thing, David. It is harmless. Here, I hold it in my hand." The glass had been cold and inert as he lifted it out of the canister. He had almost expected it to be warm to the touch, the energy captured there. David had cowered. "This is not the thing you fear," Jenkins had said. "This is a surrogate, a trick of the mind." And he had felt like a sorcerer, holding high the magic potion that would transmute the young man's secret dread. He had explained to David the science of the thing, how the therapy worked. The tumor, he had said, was there long before the chemical was administered. The drug attacked it. In the war for her life, this weapon was not arrayed against you; it was on your side. The young man had listened. He had not fled. "It is the other evil that terrifies you," Jenkins had said, "the weapons." At first David had resisted. "I don't know what you're talking about," he had said. But Jenkins knew better. "It is right to hate and fear them," Jenkins had said. "But you have to make distinctions. You have to know what it is that threatens you. You must not run away." And then he had moved toward David with the vial and held it out close to the young man's hand. "Take it, David. Hold it." And the young man had finally made a communion with the fearful element, which was transsubstantiated in the act.

But now there was no ritual that would deliver David, no magic spell in which to clad him. This danger was real.

"Do they think we killed those men?"

"I have told them nothing about you," said Jenkins.

"They might already know." David stood up from the bench and took in the full, empty circle of the green.

"I don't think so, David. It hasn't reached that point yet. But soon they will begin following me."

David looked behind him again.

"It's all right," said Jenkins. "I was careful not to be seen."

"We threw the shit away," said David. "Don't you remember?"

"I don't think that matters."

"But it's true."

"Yes."

"We threw it in a big old garbage can in an alley."

"Do you intend to take them there?"

"We put it back in the package and you said that it was so harmless that you could pitch it into the trash like old coffee grounds."

This had been a part of the demonstration, the way Jenkins had chosen to bring his point to a dramatic conclusion. They had wrapped the canister in paper and carried it around carelessly, talking as they went. And then they had simply tossed it aside, a worn-out obsession, a thing without consequence.

"Anybody might have retrieved it," said Jenkins.

"You do remember though, don't you?"

"Of course I do, David."

"I only touched it that once. You made me do it."

"Naturally, I wish now that I hadn't brought you into it."

"We just threw it away," David whispered.

"I don't think the secret police would be satisfied with such a story," said Jenkins.

"What the hell are we going to do?"

"We must stay away from one another for a time, David," said Jenkins. "We must not be seen."

The boy was too confused to trust with a lie. If the secret police made the connection, they would get it all out of him. It would be easy for them. Truth was a family curse; David carried it in his marrow like a disease of the blood.

"The problem will be Sibyl," Jenkins went on. "She is the only one who knows of our friendship. You must control her."

David waved this aside.

"She doesn't pay any attention to anything," he said.

"Sibyl may be cleverer than you think."

"I don't want you to go away," said David. He moved forward and took Jenkins by the arm. "I don't care what you did."

Jenkins nodded, and he was touched by the young man's closeness. He forced himself to say the words.

"I will be here," he said. "I will keep my distance, but remember that even though you might not see me, I will not have run away. I will be watching."

When the fat man and David parted, Majewski watched them move off a fair distance in opposite directions before he put his hand on the cold stone and pushed himself stiffly to his feet. In every chilled, aching muscle he wanted to pursue his son. But he did not know who the other man was, or what David had to do with him. He was not ready. He let David go.

The fat man moved more slowly now, and Majewski waited until he had reached the edge of the green, then started after him. Majewski crossed the grass, the ground soft and damp beneath his feet. He slipped, caught his balance, moved on. It was if he'd had too much to drink; everything around him stood at one remove. When he reached the university grounds, the shadows of the leafless trees were crooked fingers pointing at him; the gargoyles leered down, laughing.

The man led him onto the street where the bomb had gone off. The sound of the blast, the sirens, the screams echoed in Majewski's memory. He saw the twisted wreck again, small and fragile on the pavement. They had put up plywood in the blown-out windows at the law school, a castle sacked by Huns.

Majewski followed the man out of the university and onto a broad street that led to the neighborhoods. The projects, with their sad, blank faces, gave way to the older section where the original buildings had not been razed. The fat man turned abruptly into a side street, stopping briefly to look up at the lights in the rooms above a market on the corner. Majewski got to the intersection just in time to see him entering an apartment halfway down the block. He moved forward warily in case the man was lying in wait. But then he heard a door shut, a lock latch. In seconds a light went on in a ground-floor window.

Inside the front door, he found a row of mailboxes. He wrote down each name, but there was only one apartment on the first floor. Carl Jenkins. Majewski marked the name in his notes with a cross, then he moved away.

Back on the main street, he found a taxi and rode it to the office. The newsroom was almost empty now. The lights in all but the center section had been turned off. At the copydesks a few men still worked at their screens, shaping up late reports of catastrophes from the other side of the planet, where the sun still shone. At the newsdesk, the overnight editor was working a crossword puzzle. He looked up as Majewski passed.

"Don't tell me you've got something," he said, for it was his job to hold things together until the end of the press run.

"Don't worry," said Majewski. "I came up dry."

He moved out of the lighted section and sat down at his desk in the shadows. After a few minutes, he picked up the phone, then put it down again. He could not call Susan. He did not trust his reasons.

A pile of papers slipped off his desk as he pulled a copy of the composite sketch of the fat man from under it. He left them where they landed and gazed at the face. Now the eyes seemed haunted. There was an intimacy about this stranger, the return of someone dead. Majewski dug through his desk until he found all the old letters. He read them one by one. Devine's obsessions, once so amusing, turned dark and menacing. The insults and little references to Majewski's private life were like mortal threats.

When he was finished, he put the letters back in the drawer and stuffed the drawing into his coat pocket. Then he slipped out of the newsroom and went to his car.

The night nurse at Bishop Tadewski's was surprised to see him when he appeared before her.

"She's in bed," the nurse said.

"I want to see her."

"Father Reba told me he had put quite a scare into you. He thought you might show up last night to satisfy yourself everything was OK. Really, there's nothing to be concerned about."

"It isn't that."

"I don't know," said the nurse. "Last night Father Reba said it would be all right. But she's asleep now. We weren't expecting you tonight."

"My mother dozes on and off," he said. "It won't do her any harm."

"Well, she *is* alone," said the nurse. "We had to move Mrs. Slovik to a room with oxygen."

"Then it will be fine," said Majewski, and he turned into the silent corridor before she had time to make up her mind.

His mother's eyes were closed as she lay propped up on the bulky pillows. Her hair was spread about her head, and her hand held the bed cover clutched tightly beneath her chin.

Majewski did not touch her or even say her name. He just sat down next to her in the chair and stared at the strong, broken face.

"Tell me how to protect him, Mama," he whispered.

She opened her eyes to the dim light that came through the hallway door. If she was surprised to see him there, she did not show it. What crossed her lips appeared to be a smile.

"Mama, I've got trouble."

She turned her head on the pillows, and the smile went away. She lifted her chin in a small gesture that urged him not to spare her.

"It's too complicated to explain. But David might be in danger, and I don't know what to do."

She made a noise in her throat, a soft moan that did not need to be translated. She was afraid for David, too. Her hand dropped down from under her chin to the side of the bed. He took it.

"I'm worried that if I try to get help, I'll only make it worse for him. I don't know what he's into or how far he's into it. He'll think I've turned on him."

He looked away from her to the photographs on the wall.

"When you sent me away from Poland, you knew that it was the only way," he said. "But I don't even know what I'm dealing with here. It isn't real somehow." Then he stopped himself because he realized how much his parents must have doubted, too, how they must have scourged themselves when he had gone.

"You probably think I'm behaving like a fool," he said.

He took a long breath and tightened his hold on her hand. She looked into his eyes and nodded. There was a voice again, caught deep in her throat, inarticulate words of solace and support. And then something glistened on her cheek.

"I'm sorry, Mama," he said softly. "I shouldn't have done this to you. I just didn't know where else to go."

"You could have come to me," said a deep voice behind him. Majewski turned and saw Father Reba standing just inside the door.

"How long have you been listening?" Majewski demanded.

"You don't need to apologize to her, you know," said the priest. "She understands."

Majewski let go of her hand and stood up. The tear had slipped to the pillow, and he kissed the salty trail it left on her skin. Then he put his lips to her ear. It seemed that all his privacy had been violated, but he needed to say this one thing to her alone.

"I will try to do as well as you did, Mama," he said. "I will try."

When he stood up, her eyes were closing again. He went into the corridor, and the priest followed him.

"Do you want to talk about it, Stan?"

"I don't think so."

Father, I have sinned most grievously. My son wanted something to believe in, and I gave him nothing but the truth. I would gladly humble myself and ask your forgiveness, Father, but it is the sons who have been wronged, who must forgive.

Televisions were still on in a few rooms along the corridor, late-night talk and empty laughter. The nurses were busy at the desk. Majewski followed Father Reba into the elevator, and the priest pushed the button for the second floor.

"At least come sit with me for a minute," he said. "You look like you could use a glass of wine. It won't be a sacrament, but it settles the nerves."

Majewski said nothing as he let himself be carried slowly upward. In the priest's room there was sweet, sacred music coming from hidden speakers. Father Reba poured two glasses from a decanter.

"I hope you are not a connoisseur," he said. "This is very modest."

Majewski tasted it, and the liquid was tannic on his tongue.

"It's fine," he said.

"There is really nothing else you could do for her, you know," said the priest. "There comes a time when we are powerless to put things right. Then we are thrown back on God's mercy. May His will, not ours, be done."

"I have no complaints about the way you care for her," Majewski said.

"I deserved that, I suppose," said the priest, turning the glass slowly between his forefinger and his thumb. "I guess I was giving you my occasional text for grief and guilt. But so many of those who have family here, they blame themselves. And I often find that having put a person in the home is not really at the bottom of those feelings. They date back much earlier, a kindness they failed to offer, or even a resentment they feel is unworthy of them. At one time they may have wanted to punish the parent, and they cannot get beyond the guilty thought that they have finally carried it out."

"She's been punished enough," said Majewski. "When I told her I was sorry, it was only because she deserves better than what I bring."

"The worst thing for a parent is not to be asked to share," said the priest. Majewski put down his glass and rubbed his eyes.

"She probably doesn't even understand the words I say anymore."

"But she knows you have come to her. That is enough."

Majewski had kept the conversation away from David, but the effect was like one of those optical tricks in which you can only see the true image when you focus your eyes somewhere else. It was clear to him now what he had to do. The first thing was to warn his son.

"I suppose I ought to be getting on home, Father," he said. "Tomorrow promises to be another busy day."

And then it dawned on him that Father Reba just might be able to help him. The priest knew everyone in town. He might have a fix on the fat man, something beyond the name.

"I think I may be onto something," he said. "I've come up with a lead on the bombing."

"It was a terrible, terrible thing."

"Can I trust you to hold this in confidence?"

218

"The priest-penitent relationship is sacred," said Father Reba.

"I haven't been to confession in a long, long while."

The priest gave a conspiratorial little laugh and leaned forward across the table.

"Your secret is safe with me," he said.

Majewski fumbled with his coat, pulling out his notebook and a handful of papers. He unfolded the composite drawing, smoothed it out on the hard, wooden tabletop, and then handed it across.

The priest shuddered when he saw it. The paper rattled between his fingers.

"What's wrong?"

"It couldn't be anyone else."

"You know this man?"

"I don't know his name," said the priest. "I don't know who he is."

"I have to ask you to keep this quiet," said Majewski. "I'm not ready to break this thing yet. Please don't do anything that would compromise me."

"I don't know what to say." The priest put down the paper and stared at it.

"Don't worry about it. I've got a line on him."

"Stan," said the priest. "This is the man who visits your mother."

Majewski's chest tightened. He saw Father Reba as if he were miles away.

"Last night I got a good look at him," said the priest. "The likeness is uncanny. There must be some mistake."

"Don't let him in again, Father," said Majewski. "I don't want him to get near her."

"We'll have to call the police."

Majewski took back the paper and pulled on his coat.

"I'll get in touch with the authorities," he said. "You just make sure you head him off here."

"Is he the murderer?"

"He sure as hell is something, Father."

Majewski hurried out of Bishop Tadewski's and drove downtown. The street outside the courthouse was empty. He brought his car to a lurching stop in the No PARKING space in front of the door. The guard took his name and warned him that all the agents had surely gone home by now. He got on the phone, turned his back, whispered something.

"You're in luck, mister," he said after he hung up. "He's coming right down."

Majewski paced the marble floor, his footsteps lost in the high, grand emptiness of the lobby. He would have to be clever with Henry Moll. He would have to reveal part of the secret and withhold the rest. He had to keep his son out of it until he knew exactly what part David played.

"Don't you sonsofbitches ever go to bed?"

Moll had sneaked up on him, and Majewski turned toward the voice.

"I need to talk to you," he said.

"The morning isn't soon enough?"

"It's urgent."

"Well, you might as well go ahead," said Moll. "I was just cleaning up the last mess you made."

"This is different," said Majewski.

"You wet all over my shoes," said Moll.

"Is there somewhere we could go?"

Moll turned to the guard.

"Courtroom Two open, Billy?" he asked.

"Just be sure to turn off them lights when you're through."

"Come on," said Moll. "Hey, don't be so nervous, Stan. I'm not going to put you under oath."

He led Majewski into the darkened courtroom and hit the switch by the door. It turned on the lights over the bench, leaving the rest of the space in a dim, amber dusk, like a nave.

"I want to let you in on something," Majewski said. "I don't want to be responsible for what may happen before I can break it off in the paper."

"I can't tell you how refreshing it is to hear you talk about responsibility."

Majewski pushed ahead.

"Do you want what I have or not?" he said.

"What if I say no?" said Moll. "What if I played your kind of game? No deals. You go down your trails and I'll go down mine. Don't get me mixed up in your problems because they are none of my concern."

"This one is."

220

"What are you after from me?"

"I want you to cut me in on how the thing develops. Even if I can't print it, I want to know."

He had to get on the inside of the investigation, to see if it was leading David's way.

"You're horse-trading, Stan. I think maybe you're the one who's got nowhere to go."

"I'm not asking you to open up your files. I only want a break on anything that comes of what I give you."

"I don't like it, Stan."

Moll was playing upon the crumbling weakness of Majewski's position. It had been a mistake to offer Moll everything up front. Even though he was not in this one for the news, he should have made it appear that he was. Now he was in a hole, and he had to bluff.

"If that's the way you feel about it," Majewski said, "then that's the way it is. I gave it my best shot. Just don't say I was unwilling to cooperate."

Moll shrugged and took a step toward the door. Then he came back.

"Tell you what," he said. "Suppose you give me a little piece of it and see if it stimulates my appetite."

"I don't think you're in any position to demand free samples."

"You want to talk about position?" said Moll. "Here's how I read it. You come to see me in the middle of the night, and right away you start pushing a deal on me. We'll go hand in hand, you say. You and me. Cooperation. It isn't your style. Unless maybe you're scared of something."

"I'm onto a guy who knows about the bombing. He's the one who tipped me about the radioactivity."

"You going to burn a source? It's not like you, Stan."

"I don't have any relationship with the guy. Until tonight I didn't even know who the hell he was."

"Who is he?" asked Moll.

"Then it's a deal?"

"Anything you say. Now kid me a little bit. Talk to me."

Majewski took out the sketch and handed it to him.

"Carl Jenkins. He lives at 2205 Keystone. Ground floor."

Moll showed a little something when he heard the name, but Majewski could not tell whether it was real.

"I got a line on him because I'd been receiving a lot of oddball letters at the *Herald*, signed with the name John Devine. He seemed to be a crank. Then he predicted that something was going to happen to Shevtsov, but I didn't really think about it until I got the letter tipping me about the radioactivity."

"You're telling me you got that story from a crackpot letter?"

"Something clicked," said Majewski. "I decided to check it out. You know the rest."

Moll shook his head.

"You guys are unbelievable. What you'll do."

"It turned out accurate, didn't it? The guy was smack on the money."

"You said the writer was named Devine. Who's this other guy, Jenkins?"

"They're the same man," said Majewski. "Tonight he tried to deliver another letter and I caught him at it."

"So he knows you're onto him."

"No," said Majewski. "I followed him but he never saw me."

Moll handed him back the composite sketch.

"Keep it," said Majewski. "I've got the original."

"That's OK. I'll have a couple agents find this guy and have a talk with him tomorrow. See if it leads anywhere."

"I can give you copies of the letters if you want."

"When you have a chance," said Moll.

"I can get them right now."

"It doesn't sound like much," said Moll. "Word about the radioactivity was all over town."

"Don't blow this one on me, Hank."

"We'll check it out."

EIGHT

After the blast of lightning from the East,
The flourish of loud clouds, the Chariot Throne;
After the drums of Time have rolled and ceased,
And by the bronze west long retreat is blown,
Shall life renew these bodies? . . .

To Moll's surprise, he laid his hands on the right piece of paper quickly. It confirmed his memory. Carl Jenkins was an employee of Nufab, and he had access to deliveries of medical wastes. In fact, his initials had been found on the receipt for the shipment of recalled Oncyllium that was the most probable source of material for the bomb. Moll had earlier skimmed the 302 forms reporting the interviews with Jenkins, but he had taken no particular interest in them. Until moments ago, he had been betting that the diversion had been done by someone clever enough not to sign his name.

> *Captioned subject is a 59-year-old male Caucasian. He has worked at the Nufab firm for more than a year. A routine security check at time of employment showed a work record in a variety of maintenance and semiskilled jobs. No criminal history. No previous record in central files. Subject speaks with a slight accent of undetermined origin.*

Moll smiled. If it had been from Brooklyn or the Bronx, Masselli could have told you which block.

Moll worked his way through the tedious details of the interview, the description of the way the material was handled, the paperwork, the Nufab rules. Then he found what he had been looking for. It was recorded dully, without comment or evaluation.

> *Subject resides in a three-room flat. Agents observed numerous books and newspapers and a variety of science magazines, none politically sensitive. Agents also observed an electronics workbench in one corner of the living room.*

From the first day at Quantico, they taught you to be catholic in your observations. Don't filter them, gentlemen. Write it all down.

If there's a grease stain in the kitchen sink, make a note of it. If the subject stutters or has a lisp, put it in the file. If a little bird perches on your shoulder and whispers something in your ear, get it on paper. Everything, gentlemen. We want it all.

Moll got on the phone and pulled in Hollings and Masselli from home. They were the last to interview Jenkins, and that made him their property. He told them both it was still a long shot. They might have to stay on this man's tail for quite a while. But he also told them what he had gotten from Majewski, and they both agreed that it sounded damned promising.

When he finished mustering them into the dark, Moll set to work redoing his report on the leak. It was easier now that he had something specific to report. He did not feel obliged to acknowledge that Majewski had just walked in with the dope. What was important was that the debacle had been turned into an opportunity. And tomorrow, when the smug punks in the Justice Department began wagging their fingers about the marches and disruptions, the Assistant Director could just sit there and listen. The punks would wonder how this man could be so complacent. They would push harder and harder, trying to shake him. And then finally the Assistant Director would bring out his heavy weapon. Yes, he would say, the turmoil was indeed unfortunate. Any leak of this nature is a serious matter, especially when it breaks the case. The Justice lawyers would look at one another, confused, then look back to the Assistant Director. We know who passed the information, gentlemen, he would say slowly, and there is some reason to believe that he may be connected to the bombing itself.

When Moll was finished, he read over the report, then gave it to the night communications man. Next, he plotted out a series of inquiries into Jenkins's past. The Nufab security check had gone back only so far. Ten years, by the look of it. Moll wanted agents at every one of those previous employers come morning. Find old neighbors. Places where the man used to drink. People he knew. Anybody with a grudge. If there was a possible motive for the bombing hidden somewhere in the man's origins, Moll needed to find it. And if the thing was simply madness, he wanted every early symptom.

He was like a soldier closing with the enemy. The lead felt right. But at the same time he knew he had to be cautious about making a move too quickly. He was a long way from asking for an indictment.

After all, Jenkins was in a position to learn about the radioactivity of the car bomb without having had anything to do with setting it. In the tight community of risk that deals with nuclear material, the word had been out for several days.

The unexplained element was that Jenkins had felt compelled to reveal all this to Majewski, and that took you into the abnormal psychology of the snitch. Some did it for advantage or a feeling of power. Others simply liked the trouble it caused, little boys writing dirty words on a wall. Majewski had said that Jenkins had sent him a number of letters before the bombing, and this put the whole matter in an interesting light. There was an element of planning here. Moll made a note to get hold of those letters first thing tomorrow. But he could not allow himself to appear too eager. He had to keep the reporter at bay.

Now that was another interesting puzzle. Why did Majewski come to him with the information before he was ready to print it? Moll assumed that Majewski trusted him, but still the reporter was taking a mighty big chance. They both knew how quickly such a thing could go public, once the agents hit the street pursuing it. Majewski had to have a reason he was not disclosing. Whatever his angle, Moll knew that if he closed Majewski out, the man might race into print and bollix up everything. But if he let the reporter in on too much, that could bring on disclosure, too.

He made some effort to straighten up the things on his desk before checking out for the night. The classified files he put in the secure room, then set the alarm. The other material he either locked in his drawers or stacked up in piles. When everything was in order—troops deployed, morning orders transmitted, battle plans all plotted out—he left to go home and get some rest.

Outside, it was raining. In the distance lightning flashed, and Moll counted the seconds until he heard the thunder. The expressway was deserted except for the juggernauts that nearly blew him off the road when they passed his little car. His windshield wipers barely kept up with the pelting waves of water.

By the time he reached his turnoff, the storm was breaking right on top of him. The flash and thunder came as one, and it was all he could do to keep himself moving through the wind and driving rain. His breath caught in his throat. He could not see. His hands tightened and sweat rolled into his eyes. His grip was so tight that the wheel bit his flesh like the hot steel of a rifle.

He was transported back to the shell-wracked mud of the islands now, and mortars pounded around him, bracketing in. Lightning cracked nearby, and he swerved. The explosion drove straight into his spine.

Then, almost as suddenly as it had come, the storm swept past, moving inland, behind the hills. The rain let up, and he was cold with sweat under his coat. He slowed the car to a crawl and caught his breath.

It had been a long time since he had felt the war so near. Maybe it was just his fatigue or the danger of the lightning. Or maybe it was the fact that he was closing with the enemy again, getting him in his sights. But whatever the reason, when the storm broke and the thunder came, it had thrown him back into the terrible community of the dead.

When the rain first began to fall, it was no more than a thickening in the air. It gave form to the light that shone down upon the gate and sparkled on the wire. Jenkins did not even bother with his slicker when it was time to make his rounds. The murmur of thunder was still far away. And there was no time to waste. He had further preparations to make. He had decided after his conversation with David on the green that he could not delay any longer. The young man was too unpredictable. There was no telling what he might do if the pressure started to mount. Jenkins did not dare take the chance that his plan would be aborted. He had to strike again.

He counted his paces as he moved to the first alarm box. Fifty-six. Fifty-seven. Fifty-eight. The years of his life. It did no good. You could not walk away the past, the way it added up. You could only control the time that was left, sacrificing it. Fifty-nine. Sixty. There was so little time. He had resolved himself too late. This was his greatest shame. Before, when the time came to make a stand, he had run away.

Jenkins took the key from his pocket and opened the box. The metal was cold and slippery as he briskly inserted the key and turned it at the proper moment to keep the silent alarm from going off.

Oh, yes. He was very precise in the small things. It came from his classical education, the idea of discipline and rigor, the hope of justice in this world. Foolish old thoughts, rendered obsolete by the fire.

Twenty. Twenty-one. It was odd how in the end you found yourself depending on a boy. But Jenkins should have known. It was the old who were innocent; the young have fallen.

The rain grew heavier. Jenkins felt the individual drops striking his coat and tapping on the brim of his hat. He disarmed the next box and moved off behind the plant. His steps picked up speed. Twenty-four. Twenty-five. Twenty-six. It would have been better if he had never fled the first time, if he had been killed defending the old, classical ways. No, he could not have saved them, even if he had not run away. But survival was an illusion; only the shame was real.

He looked right and left. The windowless walls of the plant rose up before him, and water splashed down the gutters from the roof. He had been a coward. His world had been destroyed. He had abandoned everything, even his name. Until now, he had not been worthy of it. It was a name for heroes, for martyrs.

His hands and face were cold and wet as he rounded the back of the plant and caught sight of the lighted shack and gate. The overcoat grew heavy on his back. Sixty-six. Sixty-seven. Sixty-eight. The rain came down in long, sweeping waves.

When he reached the door of the guard shack, he saw a car pull up and park a half-block down the street. It was a beige vehicle of undistinguished make, not one of the crude, customized beasts the neighborhood people drove. He stood in the shadows under the tar-papered eaves and watched to see who emerged. No one. Five minutes. Six minutes. Seven minutes. No one. Foolish old man. They were probably only waiting for a break in the rain.

Then the lightning struck close and Jenkins turned away. The thunder exploded, and he hid his face in his hands. The next flash came through the flesh of his fingers and reached his eyes blood-red.

Nights on the run. The numbing rain. The crack of rifles and the flare of lights seeking them out in the forest. Heavy boots crashing through the underbush. And all you could do was hold your breath and stifle every instinct to cry out. The thunder crashed again, and Jenkins huddled against the frail beams of the shack.

He had arrived on the outskirts of Warsaw in the dark and groped his way through the shell-scarred alleys until he found a deserted place where he could make a place to sleep among the rats. He did not know where to begin looking for his father and his brothers. They were heroes; he was a deserter. And yet perhaps here in his homeland he could find a way to redeem himself. Perhaps they could show him the way to be brave. He fell asleep, and the prayer on his lips was addressed to them.

When he awakened and went outside the next morning, he was horrified by what he saw. Warsaw was not simply devastated. It was gone. There were no landmarks. All the way to the horizon, nothing remained but rubble fallen on the square-cornered outlines of stone foundations like ruins dug out of an ancient desert.

He ate the last scraps he had gotten from a farmer who had put him up two nights before. Then he tied the few things he carried into a cloth and put them in one pocket of his ragged coat. From the other he withdrew the pistol. It shone in the light. Ordinarily he carried it with one chamber empty under the hammer for safety, but today he loaded it full of cartridges.

The first thing to do was to get closer to what had been the center of the city. Jenkins could only tell where he was by where he saw the sun rising. He moved eastward through the barren streets. To his surprise, he saw other people were out, too. Some were scavenging. Others seemed dazed, as if they had also just returned from far away. He did not dare ask them what they knew. He was not sure who was a friend.

But he knew the enemy. Groups of soldiers in heavy overcoats and red-starred hats were everywhere. The first time he saw them, he stepped behind a wall to hide. But then he recognized that it would only draw their suspicion if he ran from them. The way to blend in was to wander, like a person dispossessed.

So from then on, he braved their glances. He did not nod or greet them, for this surely would be a sign. He did not meet their eyes. He moved past them without hesitation or undue haste. And the well-fed soldiers, grown lazy and content upon the stinking spoils, did not show the slightest interest.

All morning he walked, growing bolder as he heard the voices of his boyhood whispering around him, the rich, pulsing accents of everything he had lost. But lost, lost. He could not find any solid thing to hold on to. He did not know where he was.

Finally, he gathered up his courage and stopped a pair of young men who moved as though they had a destination.

"Yo, brothers," he said. "I am turned around. I am looking for Drieski Street. Do you know the way?"

The men stopped and looked at one another as if he had asked them the shortest route to paradise.

"My family," he said. "I am trying to find them."

The taller of the two, whose face was darkened by soot and whiskers, stepped up to him and squared off. Jenkins backed away slightly. He did not have anything to give them if these men were thieves. He felt the pistol through the fabric, then took his hand away.

"It is gone," said the bigger man. "Flattened. There is nothing left."

"I have been away," said Jenkins. "I thought perhaps someone there would remember my family and know where they went."

"Remember!" The man laughed. He turned to his companion. "That someone remembered. Do you hear him? He has been away."

"No offense, brother," said Jenkins. "I meant nothing by it. I am only confused."

"Perhaps the Russians can straighten him out then," said the man. Then he spat upon the ground as if to clear his mouth of the bitter words.

"I am afraid of them, too, brother," said Jenkins.

The man seized him by his coat and pulled him forward. Jenkins did not resist.

"Perhaps you are one of them," the man said. "Perhaps you have made your peace."

"You know that I am not," said Jenkins. "Look at me. Is this one who has found a way to prosper?"

The man let him go and all three began to laugh. The sound rang out across the stones and rubble. The smaller man put his arm around Jenkins and drew him aside.

"I knew some who lived on Drieski Street," he said. "What was the name?"

Jenkins hesitated before telling him, and when he spoke the name, he realized how much he was risking. The name was resistance itself. It was subversion and honor. The smaller man stiffened.

"They are your kin?" he said.

"You know of them then?" Jenkins asked. "What has become of them? I have been gone for many years."

He hated himself for giving such an excuse for his shame.

"They rose against the Germans in the last days," said the smaller man. "They all were killed."

"Are you certain?"

"As sure as the Red Army that betrayed us," said the big man. "I knew your family. They were very brave and foolish."

Jenkins did not want to believe them, but he knew that it was true. The men stood very close to him now, but it was no longer threatening. They made a single rank on the street, shoulder to shoulder. The big man touched his arm.

"We will take you to Drieski Street if you want," he said. "But you will find nothing there. No one dares to remember. You will be wise, too, to forget who you are."

"Thank you, brother."

They knew the way, and when they came near Russian soldiers, it was as if his companions drew together to protect him. The undeserved honor of his name was a shield.

After about a half hour they came to a corner where a Soviet truck had turned over on the street.

"What's this?" said the big man. He looked inside the cab. A soldier was pinned dead behind the wheel.

"Merciful God," said the big man, and he crossed himself with an ugly smile.

The intersection was deserted. Jenkins began to move away, but the big man hailed him back.

"God's bounty, man," he said. "Let's see what he was carrying."

"The soldiers may come," said Jenkins.

"Food," said the man, throwing back the canvas flap of the truck. He climbed inside.

It was beginning to rain. The skies rumbled and flashed. Jenkins stood back away from the wreck. The thunder announced itself loudly. He did not even hear the shot.

He simply saw the smaller man clutch his breast and fall. Blood pumped out between his fingers. Jenkins ran to him, pulling out his pistol as he went.

The big man poked his head out from behind the canvas.

"Shit," he said. "Let's go." He jumped down, but his legs failed him. He fell and clutched his knee in pain.

His pockets were stuffed with tins of food. Green vegetables poked from his jacket. He cried out. Two soldiers were upon them in an instant.

"Halt!"

Jenkins stood up and held his pistol at his side. One of the soldiers had a rifle. He raised it, and Jenkins pointed his pistol at him.

"Halt!"

For a moment the three of them stood motionless in the street.

"Kill him, brother," said the big man. "Kill them both."

The man with the rifle was young and very scared as he looked out over the barrel of his weapon at the pistol aiming at his heart. The other soldier showed no emotion. He moved toward where Jenkins's companion lay on the ground.

"Kill him," said the fallen man.

But it was hopeless. Jenkins and the young soldier held each other in the sights of their weapons in a paralyzed standoff. The other soldier just laughed. Then he raised the club and brought it down upon the fallen man's skull. Again and again he beat him. There was nothing Jenkins could do. He began to tremble. His companions both were dead, and then the soldier with the club moved up to him. Jenkins dropped the pistol and raised his hands above his head.

"I am not Polish," he said in Russian. "I beg you. I am not Polish."

When the storm passed and the rain stopped, Jenkins stepped out from under the eaves of the guard shack. He had stood his ground this time. He had not run away. The car down the street sat there dark in the shadows. Jenkins slipped into the shack and took off his rain-soaked overcoat. He had expected that they would be watching him. If he did the thing he planned, there would be no escape.

He stood before the electric heater, but the warmth did not reach him. One. Two. Three. Four. He counted again as he waited, the days of his youth. But those innocent years meant nothing anymore. Nothing at all.

These streets had never seemed so abandoned. Empty lots strewn with rubble surrounded burned-out ruins, the homes of wasted men with nothing left to lose. Here and there you could still recognize a building, succumbing to gravity and rot, and remember how it once had been: the families who had lived there, the way they had held court on a summer evening, sitting on the front steps all up and down the block, their laughter and hopes.

Up ahead, the old parish cemetery rose upon a hill. It used to be a park for boys like Majewski to play in, a greensward among the crowded tenements and concrete. And it had been all right to run among the graves. They do not mind, the elders said. They listen to your laughter in their tombs. He remembered how on a certain night each fall the survivors had placed a candle before every stone, how the rolling hills had come alive with ghosts and flame.

Majewski turned into David's street and searched the dark buildings for a number. It was very close to the neighborhood where he had grown up, but this turf had belonged to the Italians then. A good Polish boy did not dare stray into it.

When he found the apartment he was looking for, he pulled over and stopped the car. It was beginning to drizzle. He hurried up the walk to the door, not allowing himself to pause and rehearse. The buzzer gave a rude squawk. The dingy stairwell lighted up, and Majewski stepped back into the dark corner of the entryway near the mailboxes so his son would not see who it was until he opened the door.

"Sibyl? Don't play games with me. It isn't funny."

The door swung wide and Majewski moved out into view.

"What are you doing here?" said David.

"I needed to see you."

"It's pretty late for that, isn't it?"

"Can I come in?"

David blocked the entrance, and Majewski moved his foot to hold a purchase on the door.

"It's important," he said.

"I thought it was somebody else when I heard the buzzer."

"I would have called. But you never answer."

"Nobody has anything to say."

"You don't know if you don't give them a chance."

David looked blankly at his father, as if Majewski were selling something useless, something cheap.

"I wouldn't bother you if I didn't have to," said Majewski.

"Is it about Grandma?"

"In a way."

234

"Nothing's happened, has it?"

"She's all right."

David stepped back just enough to give Majewski room, and he took it. The door slammed behind him, and the noise echoed up the stairs.

"I've been wanting to come by for a long time," Majewski said, "just to see how you are making out."

"Yeah, well, it isn't much, is it?"

"Do you remember when your mother and I used to bring you back here to the old neighborhood, before everyone moved away?"

"Not really."

"It was a long time ago."

"You want to come up or something?"

They climbed the creaking stairs, David in the lead. Majewski noticed the papers littering the landing, the old light fixtures hanging from a single screw. He thought about fire. Rose had always told him he worried too much. But it was just that Majewski knew harm's way.

"This is it," said David, showing him into the flat.

"It's nice and big," said Majewski as he took in the sight of the beaten-up furniture, the musty smell, the sound of godforsaken music coming from another room.

"Go ahead," said David. "Sit down if you want."

Majewski unbuttoned his coat but left it on. He took one end of the couch, and David went to the floor where there were some pillows and an ashtray. He was pale in the dim light, and he seemed to have aged without growing up, like one of those cases you read about, a child turning old before your eyes, a flower in a time-lapse film, dying.

"The lady is late."

"The one you were calling to? Sibyl?"

"She said she'd be home at midnight."

"I'd like to meet her."

"Yeah, well, it's not exactly like we're going to get married or something."

"Don't do anything you'll regret later, son," said Majewski.

David forced a laugh.

"I guess I'll just have to roll right up and die," he said. "Sorry is the name of the game. I thought you knew that."

"I didn't mean to lecture you."

"Where the hell is she, anyway?" said David. "I'm getting a little worried here."

"Maybe she's just waiting out the rain. It looked a little threatening when I was driving over."

David stood and started for the window. The room lighted up and shook with the thunder. He froze. A terrible look snapped into his face and then snapped off again.

"It's only a storm, David."

David turned away.

"You were always afraid of thunder," said Majewski. "When you were a boy, sometimes you would come into our room in the middle of the night and ask if we were awake. You didn't want to admit that you were scared. We would talk then, man to man."

The next one came so close that Majewski flinched.

"Maybe you'd better unplug your radio," he said. "That was a sharp one."

David moved slowly to the window and looked out into the darkness.

"It isn't a good idea to do that, David. Lightning is nothing to fool with."

"I'm not afraid."

"You don't need to prove anything to me."

"It was never the thunder that scared me. But when I was asleep, it would get into my dreams. It turned into something else there. That's why I'd want to stay awake. So the dreams wouldn't come back again."

"It was a funny time to be growing up," said Majewski. "There was a lot to dream about."

Majewski stared at his son's back as the lightning struck again. It cast an aura around David, a charged corona of fire.

"I need to talk to you about something," Majewski said.

"I can't stop you."

"Do you know a man named Carl Jenkins?"

David kept his face to the window, and Majewski could not tell whether the expression reflected there was recognition or only the distortion of the old glass.

"He's an elderly fellow," Majewski went on, "heavyset. Full head of white hair." He reached into his pocket for the composite. "I've got a drawing of him here. That may help."

236

"I know who you mean," David said.

"I have reason to think this man is dangerous," Majewski said.

"What the hell do you know?"

"It's very complicated," said Majewski. "I'll try to explain it all later sometime. But this is trouble, David."

"He's a harmless old man. He comes around. We talk. That's all."

David had regained control of himself now. Majewski met his eyes and yielded, not looking away, just showing his own vulnerability, as if this might be the only place they could meet to negotiate their losses.

"He isn't what you think he is."

"He's interested in me. He treats me like a son."

The wound was quick and clean. Majewski tried not to show that he felt it.

"I believe he had something to do with the murder of the Russian scientist at the university," Majewski said. "I believe he may be violent."

"Far fucking out, man," David said, and then he drifted off for a moment into a place where Majewski could not follow.

"He's been in touch with me," Majewski said. "And he knows certain details about the killing that make me think he may have been in on it."

"In touch with *you*?"

"Letters, David. The man has been sending me crazy letters."

"Did he tell you about me?"

"Not a word. That's what frightens me. He knew."

David appeared relieved, and Majewski was not sure why.

"He's been to the nursing home, too," Majewski went on. "He has gone to see your grandmother. More than once. I discovered that tonight. That's why I came here, David. This man has moved in very close. And I don't know what to expect next."

"We talked about you sometimes," David said. "He always had good things to say, you know? He was disappointed when I would promise to go visit her and then back out. He told me I was being too hard on you."

This was no comfort to Majewski, hearing that the fat man had defended him.

"In his letters," Majewski said, "he predicted that the Russian was going to die. Then he wrote me that the bomb

237

had been radioactive. Don't you see? He knows all about the killing."

David fell silent. Majewski dropped back into the couch.

"It's not true," David said finally. "He didn't tell you anything."

"Why would I make up such a thing, son?"

"To confuse me. I don't know."

"I've never lied to you. Even when maybe I should have, I never did."

David stood up again and went back to the window.

"The police know about Jenkins, too," Majewski said. "I don't want you to get caught up in this. I thought maybe we could go away somewhere for a while, just you and I. We could go where he can't find us. Tonight."

"Sometimes," said David, then he hesitated, "sometimes you don't feel anything at all. It's like Novocain. You don't have pain, but you can't taste sweetness either. It's like you're dead. But then it wears off and you don't know whether it's really better to be alive, all the hurt you feel and cause."

"I don't want to hurt you, David."

"The old man understood. He really did."

"Maybe he just wanted to lead you on."

"He made me realize how scared I am."

"I think you were right to be afraid."

"Not scared of him. Scared in a vacuum, all the air sucked out of it, taking your breath away. So scared you don't even let yourself feel it, let alone say what it is. I started having nightmares again. The kind I used to have as a kid. I'd see a flash in the night and go to the window. And there on the horizon I'd see a flaming cloud rising up. Then another. And I'd just stand there praying for the one that would come and blow me away."

Majewski went to him. He took his son's shoulders, held him, the way he used to when David woke up crying in the night.

"It must have been terrifying," he said.

David allowed himself to be embraced, but Majewski still felt the separation, a barrier as hard as steel.

"That's the strange part," David said. "They weren't so bad. It was kind of a relief to have them again. See, they'd never really gone away. They were always in there somewhere, down deep, and

238

you might as well be able to see them. At least then you know who you are."

A cold shudder ran through Majewski. David must have felt it, too; he pulled back. They were standing there in a naked silence when the door slammed open.

Majewski thought for an instant it was the fat man. He wasn't ready. His first impulse was to find somewhere to hide.

"Mighty Mouse! Hey, give me a little comfort here. This weather is the pits."

The girl burst in, and when Majewski saw her she seemed much smaller than her voice.

"Well, what do we have here?" she said. "It's a regular surprise party, coming home to this dump. You were just going, I hope."

"Sibyl, it's my father."

Majewski moved to shake her hand.

"I'm glad to finally have a chance to meet you," he said.

She let him have her hand for a moment. Then she stripped off her coat and threw it on the couch. She was wearing a skimpy skirt that showed a lot of thigh and a blouse that was open too low.

"David was worried about you," said Majewski, for he felt he had somehow to win her, too.

"Is that right, Mighty Mouse? Were you afraid someone would come in and sweep me away?"

"You were late," said David. "I didn't know where you were."

"Hey, I'm beat," she said. "You mind if we end the visiting hours?"

"I guess maybe you'd better go," said David.

"I was hoping we could talk some more," said Majewski, "about what I told you about before. Getting away."

"Maybe later," said David.

"Getting away from what?" asked Sibyl.

"I had an idea," said Majewski, trying to put himself where he could see them both at once, measuring words that he thought might just straddle them. "I thought maybe I could persuade you two to take a little vacation with me. We've got a lot of catching up to do."

"Is this guy for real?"

"We can talk about it later," David said.

"Hey, pal. I just got a job, remember? I put out the money for this clown suit. I suppose he's going to make up the difference?"

"Don't worry about the money," said Majewski. "We can work that out."

"Maybe we'd better forget about it for tonight," said David.

"I was thinking maybe you two could come stay at my place," said Majewski. "Then tomorrow we could find a nice cottage on the shore."

"Don't I get some say in this shit?" said Sibyl.

"I didn't ask him to come here," said David, edging over against him. "He just showed up."

"You think about it, David," Majewski said. "Sibyl, you too."

He did not want to leave them alone, even for the remainder of this single night. But he did not want to lose what he had gained either. He moved toward the door.

"Stay away from Jenkins," he whispered to his son just before he left them.

"I know what to do."

Outside, the pavement was wet, but the rain had stopped. Off in the distance, lightning still blinked in the sky. But it held no special terror for Majewski. At least the thunder announced itself. It did not ambush you like an assailant in the night.

NINE

But they who love the greater love
Lay down their life; they do not hate.

The pavement was still dark and puddled from the rain as Moll drove to Nufab. Steam billowed from the sewers in thick, gray clouds. He took the long way around so that he could come up behind the agents' position and roll through the setup once before deciding the best way to link up with them. As it turned out, it was an easy field problem. He saw their car parked a little more than a block from the gate. He could stop on one of the cross streets well out of sight and reach it on foot. A high hedge would give him cover nearly the whole distance.

The plant grounds were empty and desolate as he passed. A shack crouched beside the concrete block building, but he could not see inside it. The gate appeared to be locked. Floodlights on high poles illuminated the strange pockets of fog that had collected here and there, giving the gravel yard the look of a moor. He turned at the corner and glanced down the alley. The only thing moving was a midnight dog rooting around in a garbage can that had been overturned by the wind.

He passed the alley by—too conspicuous to go that way—then drove two more blocks before circling back. When he reached the spot he had picked out, he stopped the car and waded into the darkness, staying on the sidewalk until he reached the corner house. Then he boosted himself over a fence and cut through the backyard.

Moll had to pick his way slowly through the obstacles in the dark. He could not see well enough to avoid the puddles. Dampness crept into his shoes. He was too old for this kind of thing, the gymnastics, the choking night air, the mud. He climbed the rear fence, hands soft against the cold, wet metal. Then he was over it, and he followed the hedges until he got within ten yards of the stakeout car.

Hollings and Masselli gave no indication that they had seen

him, so Moll squatted down on his haunches and ran his fingers over the wet earth until they came upon something hard, a stone. He picked it up and lobbed it gently toward the car. It struck the fender with a thunk, and when Hollings turned, Moll stepped a pace away from the hedges and gave a thumbs-up.

Hollings swung the rear door open a crack in perfect darkness. Moll made his move at a crouch. He was exposed no more than a few seconds before he got inside.

"Made good time," said Masselli.

"Damned weather," said Moll. "I'm soaked."

"They're both still inside," said Hollings. "I was worried at first that the old guy might have made us. During the thunderstorm, he stayed outside. He was eyeballing us pretty good. But he can't really see us from inside the shack. Here, have a look at the layout."

He handed Moll a pair of field glasses. Moll focused them and saw the door of the shack and the lettering on a sign hanging there. "AUTHORIZED PERSONNEL ONLY. KEEP OUT." He scanned the yard. It was lighted up like a playing field. If you had to sit on a place at night, this was the way you wanted it to be.

"Who's the other one?" he asked.

"Unknown male Caucasian," said Masselli.

"Covers a lot of territory," said Moll.

"Phil's a little uptight," said Hollings.

"Hey," said Masselli, "I'd just feel a whole lot better if I knew who it was."

"You get a good look at him going in?" asked Moll.

"Good enough to pick him out of the books later," said Hollings. "I make him to be in his early twenties. About five eleven, maybe a hundred and forty-five pounds. Thin. Like maybe he isn't eating right. He had on one of those army field jackets all the kids are wearing who beefed about the draft."

"We'll want to follow him when he leaves," said Moll.

"He seems to be on foot," said Hollings. "I planned to take him while Phil sat on things here."

"He's been in there for quite a while," said Masselli, shifting in his seat. "What the hell are they up to?"

"This guy couldn't be making some kind of delivery, could he?" Moll asked.

"You don't think we'd haul you out of bed for that," said Hollings.

244

"I'm just asking."

"The only shipments they get at night are the medical wastes," said Masselli. "And that guy always comes in a van. Drives it inside."

"I had my eye on the old guy when the kid showed up at the gate," said Hollings. "He was plenty surprised. The kid was pounding on the fence, yelling. The old guy came out of the shack lickety-split. He tried to chase the kid away, but the kid wasn't having any of it. They had words. I don't read lips, but I know this much: They were both pretty nervous."

"The guard's not supposed to let anybody in," said Moll. "No wonder he was jumpy."

"Well, he let this one in all right. Hurried him straight to the shack. All the time he was looking this way over his shoulder. I don't know. Maybe he made us after all."

"How could he?" said Masselli. "We haven't moved. He have X-ray eyes, this guy? He didn't make us."

"I'm just saying that he did a lot of looking in this direction, that's all."

"You have any ideas?" Moll asked.

"I'm full of them," said Hollings. "I got an idea how to make a car heater you don't have to leave the engine on to keep it ticking. I got an idea how nice it would be to be in bed right now. And you should hear my ideas about what the Bureau should do for people stuck out all night in the cold."

"I thought you enjoyed this kind of thing," said Moll.

"We've been trying to put it all together," said Masselli. "This business tonight. What you heard about Jenkins. You know, it could be a lot of nothing."

"But you don't really think so," said Moll.

"We called you in on it, didn't we?" said Hollings. "It wasn't just for companionship."

"Maybe it's a dead end," said Moll. "You never know."

"What about the visitor, though?" said Masselli.

"Maybe the old guy ordered dinner from a joint that delivers," said Moll.

"You want to take off again, that's your call," said Masselli.

"Hey," said Moll, "lighten up a little, OK? I'm not going anywhere. I want this guy."

Once this was established, they could all settle down to

wait. They passed the field glasses from man to man. They sniffed and coughed. They tried to get right with the uncomfortable seats.

It was Moll's watch with the field glasses when Jenkins finally emerged from the shack. Moll saw his face and was surprised at how old he was. He did not have the obsessive look of a terrorist. He could have been a scholar, a player of chamber music. High forehead. Thick, continental jowls. If there was madness in his eye, Moll could not see it from a distance.

"Look at the way he's watching the car," said Hollings. "He knows."

"It's time for his rounds," said Masselli, checking his watch. "Right on schedule. This guy doesn't miss a beat."

Moll stared at the doorway, hoping to get a look at the other man, but it was no use. The angle gave him no more than a small part of the inside wall. There was a calendar hanging there with the days crossed off, a clipboard holding some flimsy papers.

"He's going back inside," said Moll.

"Maybe he's going to report a suspicious vehicle to the locals," said Masselli. "That's all we'd fucking need right now."

"Anybody clear the surveillance with them?" asked Moll.

"Not if you didn't," said Hollings.

"Shit," said Masselli.

"You want me to get on the horn and warn them off?" asked Hollings. He switched on the radio under the dash. The little light glowed like the tip of a burning cigarette in the dark.

"Not yet," said Moll.

"He knows we're here," said Hollings. "I'm sure of it."

"Game of guts," said Moll "Let's see how tough this guy is."

"If they send around a squad to check us out, it'll blow our cover for sure," said Masselli.

"If he is who we think he is, he's not going to call," said Moll. "Nobody has guts like that. He's not going to want to bring in more heat. He's got as much as he can handle right now. . . . Wait a second."

He turned the screw on the glasses a touch to bring the image into a hard focus. The other man was outside the shack now. He was holding something, but Moll could not make out what it was.

"What the hell's going on there?" said Masselli. "Can you see?"

246

The young man was looking toward the car, staring straight into Moll's eyes.

"Sonofabitch," Moll said.

"What is it?"

He watched the young man, and suddenly many things began to clarify.

"Come on, Hank," said Masselli. "Let us in on it."

"They've spotted us, all right," said Moll.

Jenkins was behind the young man now, leading him by the elbow back into the shack. The door stayed open as they moved out of sight.

"What happens if Jenkins doesn't do his rounds?" asked Moll.

"There are keyboxes he's supposed to disarm," said Hollings. "If he doesn't, they put out an alarm."

"Where does it ring?"

"Police headquarters."

"Well, get ready for some company then," said Moll.

"You sure we can control it if the locals come screaming in?"

"Let it play out," said Moll. "See where it goes from here. It's his move."

"We don't even know who the other guy is yet."

"Don't worry about it," said Moll. "I have him cold."

"How's that?" said Hollings.

"I know his father."

The traffic lights blinked yellow and red. Majewski paused at every one, using the time. At some point in a big, complex story you always found yourself mired in details. The more information you got, the more confused you became. You could not get beyond the parts to the whole. Sometimes, if you were under pressure from the desk to produce or if you thought somebody else was onto the story, too, you forced yourself to write what you had. You skipped over the lead because you still didn't know what the damned thing was all about. Instead, you backed into it, putting together one true sentence and then another until they began forming themselves into paragaphs. Then you shifted the graphs around until they lined up like magnets, pole to opposite pole. And when you had enough of them in a row, you could go back and read it over to see what the thing was trying to say.

But more often the facts did not line up so neatly. Pieces were missing. The connecting points repelled one another. The chain did not hold. And somehow you had to discover why. Maybe some bum information had slipped through your defenses. Maybe you were being manipulated, and you thought that if you could just concentrate hard enough, you might be able to feel where the strings were tugging at your limbs.

It wasn't only a matter of digging for facts. It was a whole way of seeing. And this was when distance became crucial. You can't get a fresh angle on something when your nose is pressed flat up against it. That was Majewski's trouble now. The fat man had gotten too close.

And so Majewski drove the back streets, block by block, trying to break away from him for just a moment, to get a clear look. It didn't work. The circuit led him right back to where he lived.

His house was in a quiet part of town. He rolled slowly past the darkened Cape Cod, peering at the doors and windows. They all seemed to be secure. The cars on the street were familiar, the neighbors' Plymouths and Fords. But still he did not dare stop. It was as if his place had been invaded, taken away from him. The fat man had gotten inside.

He turned left, back toward the center of town. He drove quickly now because he knew where he wanted to go. When he reached the small building squatting between two factories, he could hear the heavy machines pounding away. The rhythms were as muffled and steady as a thudding pulse.

Majewski had come to this tavern often when he was younger. It was a place where the conversation was crude and easy, where men slapped you on the back and gripped your hand in a test of iron. The Pilsner sign in the window was off, a silhouette against the dim yellow light inside. He tried the door and found it open. It was always open as long as men were working and the pulse beat in the air. A few people at the bar turned his way as he entered. The bartender gave him a doubting eye. They did not issue all-night liquor licenses in this town. But they were realistic about what men needed. If nobody made a stink, they usually let places like this alone.

"How ya doin', chief?" said the bartender.

"Not bad," said Majewski. "Shot and a beer."

"Too late," said the bartender. "Bar is closed. Look at your watch."

Majewski glanced at the nearly full mugs of beer sitting in front of the other men.

"They been nursing those since closing time?" he asked.

"I never rush a man."

"The door was open. I came in."

"I'll sell you a burger or a bratwurst. Nothing illegal about that, is there, chief?"

"How about giving me a wink?"

"Now there's the way to get yourself in trouble, pal. Doing favors for strangers."

"I'm not the heat," said Majewski. "It's been a hard day."

"They all are."

"I remember when you used to be able to come into this joint anytime, day or night, and get what you needed."

"Must've been a long time ago."

"Don't be fooled by my suit. My name's Majewski. You probably know some of my kin."

"Guy who goes by the name of Majors in the paper, that you?"

"You got it."

"They may have mentioned you once or twice," said the bartender.

"Tell you what," said Majewski. "Let's put the shot and beer off the record, OK?"

The bartender smiled.

"Your word as good as your name?" he asked.

"Make it a double," said Majewski. "The good stuff."

"It's all good," said the bartender, "for the purpose."

Majewski took the shot in two swallows, then he pulled some of the beer through the foam. The bartender moved to the grill and busied himself stacking up patties and buns.

"How about another one?" Majewski said. The bartender came back and poured with a steady hand. "You ever been followed?"

"Kid playing bumper tag," said the bartender. "Gumshoe my ex-wife hired."

"Kind of gives you a funny feeling."

"Pay her what she wants. That's my advice. Get her off your back."

Majewski put the second drink down in one gulp and coughed. The bartender moved away.

There had to be a reason why the fat man was making this play. It couldn't be money. Majewski didn't have enough to make it worth the effort. Maybe it was somebody with an old grudge, somebody he had hurt along the way. If only he could place the fat man's face.

"You all right?"

Majewski looked up and saw the bartender leaning close.

"Huh? Oh sure. I guess I was just nodding off a little. How about one more of these to keep me going?"

"Maybe you've had enough."

Majewski stood up and fumbled with the bills and silver, got bollixed up trying to figure the tip. He was not exactly drunk, but the whiskey had worked into his fatigue and found a home there.

When he left the bar, he drove straight to David's flat. The lights were off, and when he tried the front door, it was safely locked. Good, David, good. Close yourself in.

He followed the sidewalk to the rear. The ground-floor windows were high. A fat man would not be able to reach them. Dim light came from a basement window, flush to the ground. He went to it. There were bars protecting the pane, and Majewski tried them with his foot. They were not exactly rock solid, but they held. The cellar door, too, was good and strong. He lowered himself down onto the steps, winded. When his breath came back, he began to weep. And he was not sure why.

He did not sit there long. Wit's end. It was a sovereign boundary, a line you stepped across and then maybe back again. You had to keep things straight. You had to know what was true and what was a ghost. The fat man was waiting. He was there.

Majewski moved slowly back up the walk, his hand against the damp boards of the wall to guide and steady him. He tripped on a crack in the concrete, stopped, balanced himself, breathed in the dark air. There was no one on the street. He reached his car, but then went back one more time to test the front door. It was still holding steady. He sat in the car outside the apartment for a long time, just watching, before he finally pulled away.

No conscious intention took him to Susan's neighborhood on

the way home. The car just seemed to drift that way on its own. Her lights were still on, one upstairs, one down. He drove by slowly and stared at the windows as if for a signal that would beckon him or warn him away.

It was not until the front wheel hit the curb that he realized something was wrong. He saw the car gliding toward a tree in the parkway. He hit the brake and spun the wheel. There was plenty of time. Slow motion. There was no time at all.

The collision wasn't loud, just a dull thud and the sound of glass. But it threw him forward against something hard, and for a moment he thought he might lose consciousness. He lay against the wheel, his vision as narrow as the beam of the one good headlight, glowing across the grass. It was the pain that finally opened the world back up to him. He pushed himself away from the dash.

When he put his hand to his forehead, his fingers came away smeared with blood. He took the car out of drive, and it rolled backward off the tree. The engine raced. His foot found the brake, and he threw the shift into reverse, easing back onto the road. Even this small exertion made him dizzy. He was not seeing right. The tires bounced over the curb and then back into it again. He jerked the car to a stop and turned off the key.

He took out his handkerchief and dabbed the wound. Blood was in his eyes. There was no way he could try to drive away. He hauled himself out of the car and made his way unsteadily toward her lights. He reached the steps and held on to the railing for balance. His hand felt for the buzzer.

She came to the door quickly.

"Stan. What happened?"

He held the handkerchief to his forehead as if that would hide the wound.

"I was driving past. Must have fallen asleep."

"Come in and let me look at that cut. Are you all right?"

He caught sight of himself in her mirror, and the blood was smeared all over the side of his face. It gave him a kind of satisfaction that it looked as bad as it did.

"Hit a tree," he said.

She sat him down on a chair and then disappeared. When she returned, she had a washcloth and a towel. She wiped off his face and then his forehead.

"Do you think you ought to go to a hospital?"

"Had a couple of drinks," he said. "Shouldn't have. Trying to stay away from you. Trying to work up the courage to come."

"It isn't such a bad cut, really," she said. "Here, let me just . . ."

"Should have called you."

"There's going to be a bruise. That hurts, doesn't it? Let me put a Band-Aid on to stop the bleeding."

He felt her hands touching him lightly, the pull of the tape as it tightened on his skin.

"If I can just call a cab," he said. "Pick up the car tomorrow. Before Danny gets home."

"Are you feeling woozy? You have to be careful about bumps on the head."

"Damned fool thing to do," he said. "Got me all turned around. Don't know what I'm doing anymore."

He started to stand, but she would not let him.

"You wait just a minute now," she said. "Don't be in such a hurry. I'm not going to make things difficult for you."

"Maybe just a little while. To get myself together."

She took away the washcloth and he heard her rinsing it out in the kitchen. He closed his eyes and rested his head against the cushions.

When he opened them again, she was standing above him.

"I don't know whether I should tell you this," she said, "but that young man called here for you again."

"What man? David?"

"The one from the office. The one who called here before."

"Joe Stawarz?" he said.

"That was it. He said he had been looking all over for you."

"What did he want?"

"Something about a problem at that place where the radio-active material came from."

"Nufab," he said.

"He seemed to be very excited. He said the police were already there."

"When did he call?"

Majewski was on his feet.

"Just a few minutes before you got here," she said. "He said he was on his way over to see what was going on. Your office had called him looking for you. They just won't leave you alone."

"I have to get there," he said.

252

"I don't think you should."

He got his coat and struggled it onto his back. He took a tentative step toward the door.

"You're not going to drive in that condition," she said.

"I'll make it. I'm fine."

"There are other people who can take care of it, Stan."

He had reached the hallway and was fumbling through his pockets for the keys.

"I think it's crazy," she said. "But if you just wait a minute, I'll take you there."

Jenkins had almost completed his final preparations when he heard David's voice. At first he thought it was only his imagination, an old man's nerves. Then the voice came again, and he put his work down on the table and went to the window. David was standing at the gate, arms spread wide, like a prisoner shaking the wire. He had pleaded with Jenkins not to go away, and now he had come back despite Jenkins's warning. The vain, fool love in it moved Jenkins. Everything had gotten turned around; now it was the young who sought to save the old.

Jenkins went to the door of the shack, but he hesitated. The surveillance car was still out there, waiting. He returned to his table and hurriedly made the final connections, then put the device in his canvas bag and placed it on the floor in the corner. It was not his finest piece of work. He had been distracted. His hands had not been steady as he poured the last of the radioactive liquid onto rags and stuffed them between the sticks of dynamite. Even though the blast would rip open the door of the plant and Geiger counters would not be able to detect the meaning of these scraps in the larger levels from inside, it was important to him that the device itself have a nuclear component, that it be hot with the energy he despised.

He folded the top of the bag carefully over the mechanism. The thing was crude and unstable, not nearly as well-made as the first bomb. If his plan had not been so simple, he would never have been satisfied with it. In its present condition, it would not be safe to carry far. The wires were too loosely fastened. The circuits were too fragile. But it was good enough to do the job.

Jenkins settled the bag around the device and then left the shack. He went to the perimeter, measuring his steps so he would not show the secret police any panic. He had to send David away quickly. It had to appear routine, just somebody at the wrong place at the wrong time.

"Get out of here!" he said. "Go on!"

"You've got to let me in."

He came up close to David and lowered his voice.

"It isn't safe," he said. "They're watching, David. Go."

He turned away, but David shook the gate.

"I won't leave until you open up! I swear it. You'll have to call the cops."

Fog crept in around their ankles, but it hid nothing. The secret police were waiting to make their move. David had climbed up on the gate and was shaking it with all his weight. It rattled like a rifle in the dark. There was no way to protect David's identity now. The only chance was to let him in and listen to what he had to say, then send him away. Tomorrow David would have to face them. But then everything would be different. It would finally be over.

"Get into the shack," he said. "Hurry."

David climbed down and came into the yard. Jenkins locked the gate again and waved David toward the guard shack.

"Stupid. Stupid," he said, pushing David into the door and closing it behind them. "Why didn't you listen to what I said?"

David took the insults without flinching, as hard and oblivious as a child.

"I had to come," he said.

"You've given away your identity now," said Jenkins. "We have to think."

But David could not seem to stand still. Jenkins cursed the chemicals. They were spices in David's veins.

"Guess who showed up at my door tonight, Pops?"

"The police?"

"My old man," said David.

"Is that what you came here to tell me?"

"He asked me about you," said David, his hands at his face. "He's afraid."

"Everyone is afraid."

Suddenly David's expression changed. The nervous movement

254

subsided, but it was not replaced by calm. Jenkins was frightened by the intensity he saw.

"Don't you understand, Pops? My father knows the truth. He says you wrote him letters. He knows about the stuff you stole. He knows you put it in the bomb. We have to get away."

Jenkins sat down in a chair and pointed David into another. The heater ticked in the silence.

"The secret police are here," Jenkins said. "I have seen them."

"Here?"

"On the street. It was stupid of you to come. Now they will surely ask you about me."

David's fingers tapped on the arm of the chair, passing the seconds, aging them both, boy and man.

"You must go now," said Jenkins. "In the morning you must tell them everything you know."

"No way," said David.

"By then it will not matter."

David looked at him strangely, as if he understood exactly what Jenkins planned to do.

"I will have thought of something by then," Jenkins said. "I will be able to explain."

"Who are you trying to kid, Pops? If I tell them about the stuff you stole, it'll be all over for you."

"I'm an old man," said Jenkins. "I don't have so much to lose."

David stood up and went to the door.

"If you leave now, they will follow," said Jenkins. "Tonight you must tell them nothing. Tell them that I had asked you to come here to play cards, to pass the time. Tomorrow will be soon enough for the truth."

David turned back to him.

"We have to get away together," he said.

"It is too late."

"Go where they would never find us. Up to Canada or something. I know lots of guys who went there."

"I've been there, David. It is not a place to hide."

"For a while, I thought I might go to get away from the draft." David's hands were cupped together, as if they held a precious liquid, then his fingers parted. "My father found a doctor instead."

"No lies this time, David," said Jenkins. "I was wrong to ask you to lie."

David went to the window.

"It rained tonight," he said. "Did you hear the storm?"

"Yes."

"It reminded me of a dream from a long time ago. Now the dream keeps coming back. Everybody's dead in it."

"David," said Jenkins, for it was the only word he knew.

The young man went to the corner of the shack and poked at the canvas bag with his foot.

"What's this?" he asked.

"Nothing, David. Something I've been puttering with."

David kneeled down. The fabric of the bag was old and soiled. It did not stand up under its own weight.

"Leave it alone," said Jenkins.

David opened the top of the bag and looked inside.

"You were going to do it again, weren't you?" he said.

"Be careful, David. Put it down."

David lifted the device from the bottom. The thing was ugly in the light, the tentacles of wire, the red cylinders, the tape.

"Why, Pops?"

He held it out in front of him like something dead, something he might once have loved.

"It is what I have to do," said Jenkins.

David put the bomb on the table between them beyond Jenkins's reach. Jenkins looked away from it. You had to protect the young, but they had to understand the reasons. They had to realize why you did these things in their name.

"The Russians destroyed my past," Jenkins said softly.

"Shevtsov?"

"When the Germans invaded Poland, the Russians took a part of my country. Whenever East and West come together, Poland is enslaved."

"The scientist didn't have anything to do with that," said David.

"He made their Bomb! Half of Europe is in bondage, and his Bomb has made us cowards."

"Shevtsov was speaking out against the weapons."

"What did he offer? Did he show us how to eliminate these instruments of evil? No. He wanted us to negotiate, to make a pact with the devil to save our lives. This is the price of what he called peace, David. Don't you see? If Hitler had possessed these

256

weapons, no one would have dared to move against him. There is no evil so vile that the Bomb cannot defend it."

"But there's nothing anybody can do."

"Look what has happened, David. Look at yourself. The drugs you take, the way you close yourself off. It is fear that does this to you, but it is also shame. Shame at powerlessness. Shame that no one has the courage to act."

"It's crazy to think you can change things."

"I understand cowardice," Jenkins said. He stood up and began to pace. "The first time I ran away. I left my family to die. I fled to carry the name, but I dishonored it."

He looked at David, and the pity he felt was overwhelming.

"I knew another boy once," Jenkins said. "He depended on me, too. Then I deserted him. He was like my own son, and I abandoned him. I thought I was going back to fight, to regain my name. But when the time came, I fled in fear."

He was shaking now, for he had never said the thing out loud before.

"Don't you see? I finally realized that you cannot compromise with the devil." Jenkins sat down in the chair again, and he felt the full weakness of his years.

"You were going to abandon me, too," said David.

"No!"

"If you do this thing," said David, his fingers touching the cylinders of explosive, "you will have to leave me."

"I would die," said Jenkins. "That is different. That is sacrifice. I would set it here and die. I have left a letter explaining everything. They could not fail to see the meaning this time. It is all written, just as I have told you. The last time I was not willing to face my own death. This was the mistake. I will not make that error again."

David's hand tightened on the bomb. He slid it a few inches closer to him.

"I can't let you do this, Pops," he said.

Jenkins stood and David stiffened. He slid the device into his lap, cradling it there. His eyes were wild. Once you touched the thing you feared, it changed you. You could not go back.

"They will not leave us in peace, David," said Jenkins. "You have to understand that."

He went to the door and stepped into the yard. The surveillance car was still there on the street. He came back inside.

"They've been there watching all night," he said.

It was past the hour for him to make his rounds. If he did not turn the keyboxes, the alarm would ring and the squad cars would come.

"There's a way," said David. "There's still a way."

He looked down at the mechanism in his lap then picked it up with both hands and went to the door himself.

"Stay out of sight, David."

But David was already outside. Jenkins stepped up behind him. The bomb was still out of his reach.

"Do you see them there?" he said. "The beige car. Come inside."

Jenkins touched the young man's elbow. David flinched. Jenkins let him steady the bomb and then led him back inside.

"Leave it here with me," Jenkins said. "You go. I promise that I will not desert you. I will not explode the bomb. I can take it out later. They will never know."

"I don't believe you, Pops," said David. "You mean to do this thing, and I can't let you." He started to sit down, and the bomb banged against the table. Jenkins lunged.

But David was too quick for him. His fist caught Jenkins solidly on the jaw, sending him tripping to the floor. He heard a sickening crack, something hard in him giving way.

"It was for the children, David," he whispered. "It was for you."

David bolted into the yard. Jenkins tried to pick himself up, but one leg would not move. The pain came late. And when it did, it was a hammer. He blacked out.

When he came to, he reached out to the table legs and pulled himself forward. He did not know how long he had been unconscious. Sirens cried out in the distance. He inched his way to the door, fighting past the pain that shot through him.

Finally, he reached a place where he could see into the yard. David stood there motionless, the low fog clutching at his legs. On the street the dome lights of the squads slashed red wounds in the air. Spotlights converged on the lonely figure, making him seem very small.

"David," Jenkins said. But his voice was weak. He could not be heard.

"I'll blow this thing up if you don't go away! I swear it!"

Then from a distance came the steel shout of a bullhorn. Jenkins tried to see, but the lights blinded him, the pain.

258

"We just want to talk," said the bullhorn. "Talk to us. Tell us what you want."

Jenkins summoned all his strength to drag himself farther across the wooden floor. Finally, on the edge of fainting again, he reached the doorway and, with one last effort, pulled himself outside.

"You there! Jenkins!" said the bullhorn. "This is Henry Moll. I'm with the FBI. Agent Hollings is right here with me. He wants to say something to you."

The lights spun dizzily in his eyes. He could not get them in focus. A word came into his throat.

"David."

David made a half turn and looked down at him on the ground. The bomb shone in the lights.

"Stay back, Pops."

Then the bullhorn squawked and tapped again.

"Mr. Jenkins. I want you to listen," it said. "I am Richard Hollings. We have spoken before. I want you to know that there is a way out of this now. If you surrender, I guarantee you fair treatment. You will not be harmed."

"All we want is to be left alone," David shouted. "We don't want to hurt anybody. Just leave us be."

"Mr. Jenkins. Listen to me. We want to come inside the gate and talk to you."

"Don't!" David shouted.

"We will not be armed."

Jenkins raised his hand to hold them back.

The bullhorn fell silent. Jenkins saw motion in the shadows behind the spinning lights. There were voices in the distance, the sounds of radios, passing urgent messages in the dark. David stood halfway across the yard. He looked at the lights, then at the doorway.

"Come to me, David," Jenkins whispered. "Please come to me now."

David's hands shook under the weight of the bomb. He moved a step, and Jenkins heard rifle bolts slamming home. David lifted the bomb to the level of his chest and held it tight against himself. He was weeping.

"David Majewski," the bullhorn said. "Can you hear me?"

"Stay away!"

"I have someone here. He wants to say something to you, David. It's your father."

David began to shudder.

"Tell him to go away," he said, so softly that only Jenkins could hear him. "Please."

"David," said his father's voice on the bullhorn. "I don't know what this is all about. But I will see you through it. I promise. Just get rid of the bomb and everything will be all right."

"Don't say that, Dad. Don't lie to me."

He looked back at Jenkins and then again at his father, as if he had to choose between them. Jenkins whispered: "Choose him, David. Do as he says." And for a moment he thought that David was going to put down the bomb. It shifted in his arms. But then it began to slide away from him. He struggled to get a grip on it. He grabbed for the cylinders, the ends of the tape. His hands fumbled. The bomb began to fall.

When it hit the ground, David was engulfed in a blinding ball of fire. The light came to Jenkins an instant before the blast. The explosion whelmed over him where he lay, a searing wave of pain. And then at last the darkness.

260

EPILOGUE

And of my weeping something had been left,
Which must die now. I mean the truth untold,
The pity of war, and the pity war distilled.

Requiescant in pace. Amen.

They were talking to him as if to coax him back to life. They called a name. He stirred against the immobilizing pain, testing it, reassuring himself that it left no way of escape. The shapes around him shimmered, like something very deep in water. But he knew that the light was only a trick of death. The sky above the yard was empty. It was night, and there was a fog. And so the wavering, luminous shapes before him had to be angels, the last figments of his mortality. Soon the darkness would triumph.

Then the voice began to resolve itself. It was not the metal rasp of the bullhorn. It was deep and full, chanting the words. They were calling him back, but it was no use. He was beyond retrieval, sinking into an oblivion where there was nothing left to save or lose. He heard his name, but it was not the one he had corrupted. Then he recognized the other words. Extreme unction. He gagged. They were praying over his corpse.

The idea caught him back from the depths, as sharp as a grappling hook. Why had they called a priest? He wore no crucifix. He had discarded it with all the other shards of faith and identity. The prayer was a cold metal point holding him. He wanted them to stop. He wanted to take his sins into the blackness. Whatever bitter God had made the world had not created it for cowards.

There were words on his own lips now, but he did not understand them. The other voice chanted on. Slowly the shapes came together. He was rising from the depths, pulled up against his will.

The words of the prayer started to take form. He listened, trying to get their meaning, the better to deny it. But then he realized what they were.

"... may be used against you in a court of law. You have a right to an attorney. If you cannot afford an attorney, the court will appoint one to represent you. Do you understand, Mr. Jenkins? You have the right to remain silent . . ."

"The boy."

Jenkins heard himself saying it. His voice came unbidden from whatever part of him still clung to the hard steel.

"I'm afraid we can discuss nothing, Mr. Jenkins, until you acknowledge your rights."

"Yes," Jenkins said.

"There are witnesses here. Do you attest that you understand your rights and speak willingly?"

One of the women in white moved close to him. She slipped a straw between his lips. He sipped the cold liquid, and it burned his throat.

He remembered the other hospital, where they had built back his strength and tended to the consequences of his torture. They had many questions for him then, too. The doctors probed for any hint of instability. Who could blame him if he had grown troubled? But Jenkins had fooled them. He hid the tumult he felt. He showed them no signs.

Yes, he told them of how he had been led away from Warsaw and interrogated. He told of his years in the Soviet camp, the torment and hunger, the beatings, all the death he had seen.

But he did not confess that he had fled in battle. He made up a tale of being overrun by the Germans. How, caught behind the lines, he had hidden until he could link up with partisans. They listened to his story, and it soon became clear to him that they did not know he had deserted. Army intelligence officers debriefed him about his confinement. They gave him photographs to see if he could identify other inmates. They copied down the names he remembered. They pinned a medal on his chest.

But there was one fact he did not give them, one story he did not tell. It haunted him so much that he was sure that to speak it aloud would open up a madness he did not dare to reveal. He did not tell them of the last night his captors had hauled him out into the cold.

The guards had awakened him from a tormented sleep and taken him from the foul barracks and across the frozen yard. The lights on the guard towers were blinding in the clear, frigid air. He had seen many others who had gone this way before. He had heard the executioners' shots at dawn.

They led him to the headquarters building and into the commanding officer's quarters. The colonel did not rise from the desk when the prisoner entered. Before him were two glasses and a bottle of brandy. Behind him stood another man. He wore civilian clothes, and his skin showed none of the hard pallor that comes of arctic exposure. But even though he was from another world, Jenkins knew he was still a man to fear. He did not have the colonel's commanding look or the powerful arms that could inflict a beating on the spot, and yet there was a deeper resemblance, something obsessive in the eyes. When power was absolute, the distinctions vanished. All devils were the same.

The man did not look at Jenkins. In fact, he seemed put upon by the presence of one so filthy and doomed. He stood by the fireplace, gazing off through the dark window into the empty depths of snow.

Was this person to be his jury? Did they submit the grim decisions of military authority to Party review before the execution? Jenkins did not know the devil's formalities, but he could not believe that they were meant to save such a man as he.

"So," said the colonel, "you have told us the truth?"

But it was not like the other interrogations. This question was put rhetorically. No answer was required.

Jenkins spoke anyway, if only to give himself strength.

"I am ready to die," he said.

"Well," said the colonel, "this is surely a good quality in a man, isn't it, brother?"

The other man did not feel obliged to reply. He remained silent in his disdain.

"To be ready to die is to know life in its fullness," said the colonel. "But I am afraid this prisoner will have to continue his preparations. You see, his government has attested to his identity, and we have verified it through our own means. Prisoner, please sit down."

Jenkins remained standing.

"I see you do not believe me," said the colonel. "You think it is a trick."

"I know what you do."

"Yes," said the colonel, lighting a cigarette and offering another to Jenkins. He took it, and the smoke made him dizzy. "I do not expect you to forgive. Nor do I care. I only want you to understand the imperatives. Our precautions. It is difficult to sort out the wastage of a war."

Jenkins breathed deeply and allowed himself the tiniest corner of hope. It trembled under his weight.

"In a week or less you will be transported from here and turned over to your government on neutral ground," said the colonel. "Until then you will be living in the visitors' quarters next door. You are done with the prisoners' barracks. We must put some fat on you. It would not do for you to go home this way."

"Why are you saying these things?" said Jenkins. "Kill me, but do not make me beg for it."

"We have not treated you more harshly than the others," said the colonel. "I am sorry if you think we are unjust. Even after all you have seen, you still retain your sentimentality. It goes very deep in the grain among your people, who like to pretend they are free."

"I have not been confused about that here," said Jenkins.

The man in civilian clothes turned and gazed upon him. There was no warmth or sympathy in his look. It was as if he were inspecting an alien form of life.

"You see," said the colonel, "we could not afford to believe the claims of all those who asserted their affiliation with our wartime allies. So many conspire to escape our dominion. But through good fortune, all has been sorted out. You fought for Canada. You are a friend."

"A friend," spat Jenkins.

"Yes," said the colonel. "A soldier of the West, which now must respect us, for we are strong. We are at peace. And so we may be magnanimous. You will be returned."

"Don't mock me."

"You shall understand better when you return to your homeland," said the colonel. "You see, my brother here has built a weapon that has changed the world. It has a power beyond the telling. Is that not so, Viktor?"

The other man looked at him sternly and shook his head.

"You should not speak of this, Yuri," he said.

"It is no secret what I tell him," said the colonel. "He will learn of our successful test soon enough. And then he will know that it was his rare honor to meet the hero of the revolution who made it possible."

266

"Send him away," said the other man. "If you say too much, it will be impossible to set him free."

"Ah, but it would be unfair to send him back into the world unprepared for what he will find. He has said that he is a man who is ready to die."

The colonel laughed. The other man went back to the window and stared out into the cold. Jenkins was sure now that they were toying with him, having their pleasure before sending him off to his execution. He looked down at the floor. There was a fine carpet beneath his feet. They would not spill his blood here. He was safe until they took him outside.

"Life will be different now," said the colonel. "My brother's success shall buy us a thousand years of peace." He seemed suddenly very weary. "The world has known so much suffering. My people died by the millions. It is true that now the earth is divided, but no one will disturb the balance. Our children shall not have to face the torments of war as we did. They shall have peace and power."

"In slavery," said Jenkins.

"Call it what you will," said the colonel. "But only a fool would deny the truth of it."

"I have been worse than a fool," said Jenkins.

Two weeks later, to his astonishment, the colonel made good on his word. Jenkins was repatriated and sent to a hospital in Germany. The doctors and intelligence officers asked many questions, but he did not reveal what had happened during the last encounter. He was afraid that they would think it was a hallucination, a manifestation of madness· He did not know until he was released from the hospital that what the colonel had said about the new weapon was true. And even then it seemed to be a nightmare: a thousand years of peace, a devil mocking him, a victorious devil who said that nothing would ever change. The rage sank down in Jenkins as he went about his cowardly life, changing his name, moving far from anyone who might have known him before. And it was only the heart attack and the fear of death that made him return to the place where he had lived before the war. He had come back to make amends, but then one day he picked up a student newspaper and saw his face again, the man who had brought the devil's peace, Viktor Shevtsov.

"Have you understood your right to an attorney?" said a voice.

And for a moment, Jenkins had no sense of time and place. "Your right to remain silent?"

"Yes," Jenkins said. "But David . . ."

"He is dead, Mr. Jenkins."

His eyes shut again, and he sought out the opening to the long passage downward. But it had closed itself off like a wound.

"Were there others involved in this with you, Mr. Jenkins? Or was it just you and David?"

He did not recognize the big man asking the questions. The man stood off to the side of the room where Jenkins could not see him clearly, only the dark shape, the size. The other two were at the foot of the bed, leaning against the white wall, silent. They did not wear hats to hide their empty eyes.

"This is all we need to know right now, Mr. Jenkins. Were there others?"

Jenkins did not reply. There had never been anyone else.

"You are hurt, Mr. Jenkins," said the big man. "There are broken bones. There are burns. But you are going to recover. There will be time to talk about this fully. For now, all I want are the names."

"David," said Jenkins.

"The others."

The big man moved out of sight for a moment. Jenkins tried to turn his head to follow, but the pain cut him off. He strained against it, but it was too strong. It was a weight. It held him down.

"We know all about you, Mr. Jenkins."

But that was absurd. They knew nothing, not even the name he had defiled. They did not know why he had sought David out or the meaning of what he had done. They did not know why he had returned to this place of shame after so many years, or how he had gone to see David's grandmother in the home. Sad, lost old woman. She had mistaken him for her dead husband. But he was nobody's father. Nobody's son.

"Mr. Jenkins, can you hear me?"

He opened his eyes, and the nurse wiped away the tears.

"Stanley Majewski," he said.

This was the only way. He had to see him and confess. He had to do it now, before he found the strength to make the last, ignominious retreat.

"He was there," said the big man. "He saw it all."

268

"I must talk to him."

The man looked at his colleagues.

"That would not be a good idea," he said.

"I will tell him everything," said Jenkins. "Nobody else."

"His son is dead, Mr. Jenkins."

"David."

"He is grieving," said the big man. "It would be wrong."

"I will speak only to him," said Jenkins.

The three of them began to whisper. Jenkins heard certain phrases: Move quickly before the others get away. Up to Majewski himself, after all. Don't push him. Make up his own mind. Very unusual, though. A fair amount of risk.

Lawyer's points. The big man brushed them aside and left the room.

"Are you comfortable?" asked a nurse. "Do you want some more water?"

Jenkins did not answer, and when the plastic straw touched his lips, he shut his jaws tight. He did not dare make any concessions. He had one word and one word only. And then, if the corridor opened down into emptiness, he would be free to fall.

When the big man returned, Majewski followed him. So many years had passed. This was not the boy Jenkins had known. He had his father's bulk, bent by the past. And yet the eyes, the eyes were the same. The curiosity and the danger they explored, the truth. It was there.

"Mr. Jenkins has something to say to you, Stan," said the big man.

Jenkins watched him for any sign of recognition, but there was none. So many years. They both had changed. Sons trying to become fathers. Fathers powerless to save their sons.

"We are waiting, Mr. Jenkins," said the big man.

"Who is he, Hank?" said Majewski. "Who the hell is this man?"

Jenkins took a breath and said his name, and all the shame drained into it, the cowardice and dishonor, the evil men died for, the things he had fled. The word explained why he had returned to the place he had left, the duty he felt, the hatred and the love.

"Jankowski," he said. The honored name on his lips was a condemnation.

Majewski's hands tightened into fists. Jenkins closed his eyes against the blow. He was ready to accept it. He wanted it. The darkness and the pain.

But the blow did not come. When he looked up again, a child's eyes gazed back at him.

"Karl," said Majewski. "It was you."

Moll gave the reporters something at the door, enough to hold them until the morning. They wanted further details, but he did not speak Jankowski's name. Tomorrow was soon enough for that part of it, after the agents had a chance to check the details.

The case was not over yet. Headquarters would not be satisfied until every aspect had been run to ground. And even then the Bureau would hunger for more. It was not enough that one man broke. A sense of proportion, if nothing else, demanded that there be something deeper: malign conspiracies, a tangle of secret relationships that could be charted on paper, a web.

But Moll believed that in the end this would be the whole of it: One man had vibrated to the madness of war that the rest chose not to feel. And when he finally succumbed to the insanity that told him it could be otherwise, he chose violence, and it destroyed the very thing he meant to protect.

Moll did not speculate in front of the reporters, of course. He simply gave them names, ages, addresses. He told them the way it had gone down on the Nufab yard. The stakeout. The confrontation. The blast. First this and then that. The bomb had gone off. Did young Majewski detonate it? The bomb had gone off.

He could have told the reporters what he really believed. He could have said that war seeds itself, stealing back upon you like a disguised old man in the night. He could have said that when you send a person to the islands, it transforms him. There are consequences. The islands now were everywhere, and the war went on and on. Children had been born to it. They had died of it as surely as if they had been buried in mud beneath exploding shells. War had been maternity bed and nursery to whole generations; the trolls under their cribs were real.

David Majewski had become a casualty, a lost number on the order of battle. First this and then that. Consequences. And the war went on. Sometimes it seemed to fall silent, and lonely men called out to one another across the lines. But they did not deceive themselves. They knew that it would always come back, because it was a state of siege and the battleground was in the mind of man. And there was no way anyone could stop it, no hole deep enough to hide in, no idea more powerful than the idea of death.

But he did not say these things to the reporters; he would not file them in his reports. Long ago, on the islands, he had realized that the end of war was impossible except in the silent, secret reflections of a soldier as he counted up the losses.

After he left Karl, Majewski walked the hospital corridors alone. The bump on his forehead throbbed, and he breathed tears he had been unwilling to shed in the company of men. He mounted the stairs and followed the corridors to a place he knew.

The coroner had claimed temporary custody of David's remains in the name of the state. There was no reason for Majewski to stay at the hospital anymore, but still something held him.

He did not understand all that Jankowski had struggled to tell him, the insane logic of the bombing, the reason he had returned, the need he had felt to make something up to Majewski through his son. But one thing was clear. David had no part in the killings. He had gone to Karl to warn him. He had taken the bomb away to prevent Karl from blowing up the Nufab plant. He had been trying to find a way out.

And now who was Majewski supposed to blame? The man who had led him to safety when the Germans came to Warsaw? His lost, innocent son? Time had circled back upon itself, and it did not end where it had begun. A man could not make his way through the forests anymore, leading a boy to sanctuary. There was no marked border separating past and future, evil and good.

Majewski looked out the window at the top of the stairs and saw the film crews waiting at the door for an explanation. He knew a way to evade them when the time came. He had only one thing to say, and it would not be satisfactory to them: David was my son.

The room where he had so often waited as Rose underwent her treatments was dark and empty now. He sat on a chair and shut his eyes against the throbbing. Instead of anger, a feeling of resolution came over him. It was as if she were present with him, giving comfort. If the dead could see, they would not despair. The truth was theirs.

He grew up in a bad time, Rose. The lies that might have sustained him were alien on our lips. He did not have a chance to be a child. But in the end there was something steady in him, a whirling gyroscope that held him tighter the more wildly that it spun. He never meant to hurt a living thing.

Majewski was weeping now, and it was right to weep when you could not hate. He wiped his eyes with his handkerchief. Something drew him upright and moved him toward the room where last she had lain. He crossed the carpet and pushed open the wooden door. There on the bed lay a tiny child, her breath controlled by a respirator, fluids dripping into fragile veins.

He closed the door again without a sound and walked to where Susan and young Joe Stawarz waited for him. He remembered what his mother had told him once long ago when he had tried to get her to talk about the war. You are a survivor, he had said; you have learned something nobody else can know. She had turned to him, her eyes deep and warm. I am not a survivor, she had said. A survivor is one who has lost everything.